Fishing for Islands

Traditional boats and seafarers of the Pacific

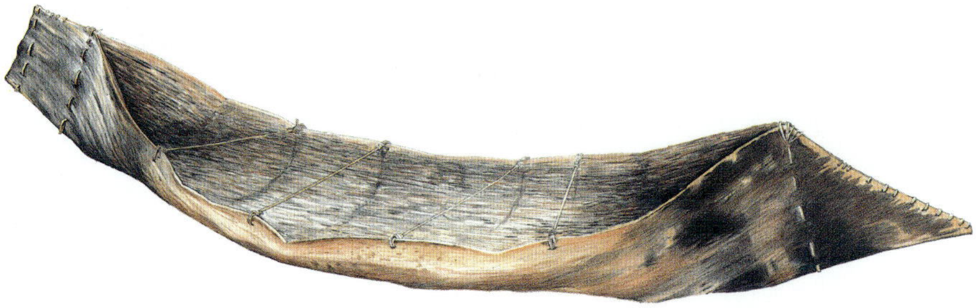

WRITTEN AND ILLUSTRATED BY JOHN NICHOLSON

ALLEN & UNWIN

First published in 1999 by
Allen & Unwin Pty Ltd
9 Atchison St
St Leonards, NSW 1590
Australia
Phone: (61 2) 8425 0100
Fax (61 2) 9906 2218
E-mail: frontdesk@allen-unwin.com.au
Web: http://www.allen-unwin.com.au

10 9 8 7 6 5 4 3 2 1

National Library of Australia
cataloguing-in-publication entry:

Nicholson, John, 1950- .
Fishing for islands: traditional boats and seafarers of the Pacific.

Includes index.

ISBN 1 86448 590 6.
ISBN 1 86448 587 6 (pbk.).

1. Boats and boating - Oceania - History. 2. Boats and boating - Asia, Southeastern - History. 3. Explorers - Oceania. 4. Emigration and immigration - History. 5. Oceania - Discovery and exploration. I. Title.

623.820995

Designed and typeset by Mark Carter and John Nicholson
Printed in Hong Kong by South China Printing Co.

Acknowledgements

Thanks to the following individuals and organisations for their help: Paul Clark of the Museum and Art Gallery of the Northern Territory, Auckland Museum, Colin Rose, Hugh O'Neill, Sarah Brenan, Mark Carter.

I am grateful for the information found in many books and publications. In particular, I want to acknowledge E. Dodd, *Polynesian Seafaring*; Haddon and Hornell, *Canoes of Oceania*; Clifford Hawkins, *Praus of Indonesia*; Tommy Holmes, *The Hawaiian Canoe*; R. Feinberg, *Polynesian Seafaring and Navigation*; Anne Nelson, *Nga Waka Maori*; Robert Pule, *Bina Bina, the Making of a Gela War Canoe*; Paul Johnstone, *Seacraft of Pre-history*.

Teaching notes for *Fishing for Islands* are available on the Allen & Unwin Web site (address at left)

CONTENTS

INTRODUCTION

THIS BOOK is the story of island peoples who built their own boats and sailed them to the far reaches of the vast Pacific Ocean. It's a story of courage, craftsmanship and vision.

These early seafarers knew about winds, currents, tides and the movements of the stars; they found out which kinds of bark and wood and which designs made the best boats for coastal or ocean travel; and they were expert sailors. The Polynesians, in particular, were able to voyage hundreds of kilometres to reach tiny island targets with pinpoint accuracy. They built boats that could withstand the giant waves of the world's biggest ocean. And they did all this at least 1000 years before sailors from anywhere else.

Comparison of early ocean-going ships

YEARS AGO	PEOPLE	BOAT	LENGTH (metres)	CREW	SEA
4000–2000	Polynesians	Double-hulled voyaging canoes	20	50–60	Pacific Ocean
3000–2000	Phoenecians Greeks Romans	Galleys (warships)	20–30	50–200	Mediterranean Sea
2000	Romans	Cargo ships	70	30–40	Mediterranean Sea
900	Vikings	'Gokstad' open boat	25	80	Atlantic Ocean
500	Spanish	Columbus's *Santa Maria*	27	40	Atlantic Ocean

South-east Asia had been gradually occupied by successive small groups of people from the west and north. Perhaps they were driven out of their homes by warlike neighbours or by volcanic eruptions – the whole region is peppered with active volcanoes. Or perhaps rising sea levels robbed them of their coastal land.

At other times sea levels fell, providing new land and allowing people to travel to areas that were once cut off by the sea. We know that at least five times in the last 100 000 years the ocean was so low that there was solid land almost all the way from mainland Asia to New Guinea and Australia. It was possible to sail or paddle across the narrow channel that still separated the two shorelines without losing sight of land.

The area immediately to the north of Australia became a 'highway' used by many groups of people moving east in search of new lands. The first to use it

The first Li-Lo
Floats made from inflated animal skins, stomachs or bladders were once used in many parts of the world to cross rivers, lakes or narrow passages of ocean. This one is a bullock skin from China

were the ancestors of the Australian Aborigines. At least 50 000 years ago they 'island-hopped' from Indonesia and Malaysia to New Guinea and Australia.

About 30 000 years ago, the Melanesians passed through New Guinea. They were the first people in the world who were confident enough, brave enough, or perhaps desperate enough, to sail over the horizon, out of sight of land. They discovered and settled in the Solomon Islands. One of their sleek black plank canoes with dazzling mother-of-pearl inlays is shown in Chapter 1, together with some Australian and New Guinean boats.

Later still, another group, sometimes called the Lapita people, swept through the area and out into the Pacific Ocean, sailing fast and sophisticated vessels with extraordinary skill and daring. They explored and occupied all the islands of the Pacific Ocean – from Hawaii in the north to New Zealand in the south – in just a few centuries. They became known as the Polynesians, and we'll look at their prodigious achievements in Chapter 2.

In Chapter 3 we'll return to Indonesia – the cradle of all this blue-water boating – to see what had been going on there in the meantime.

The map shows different coastlines over the last 100 000 years. When sea levels were low and more land was above water, you could walk almost all the way from mainland Asia to Australia and New Guinea

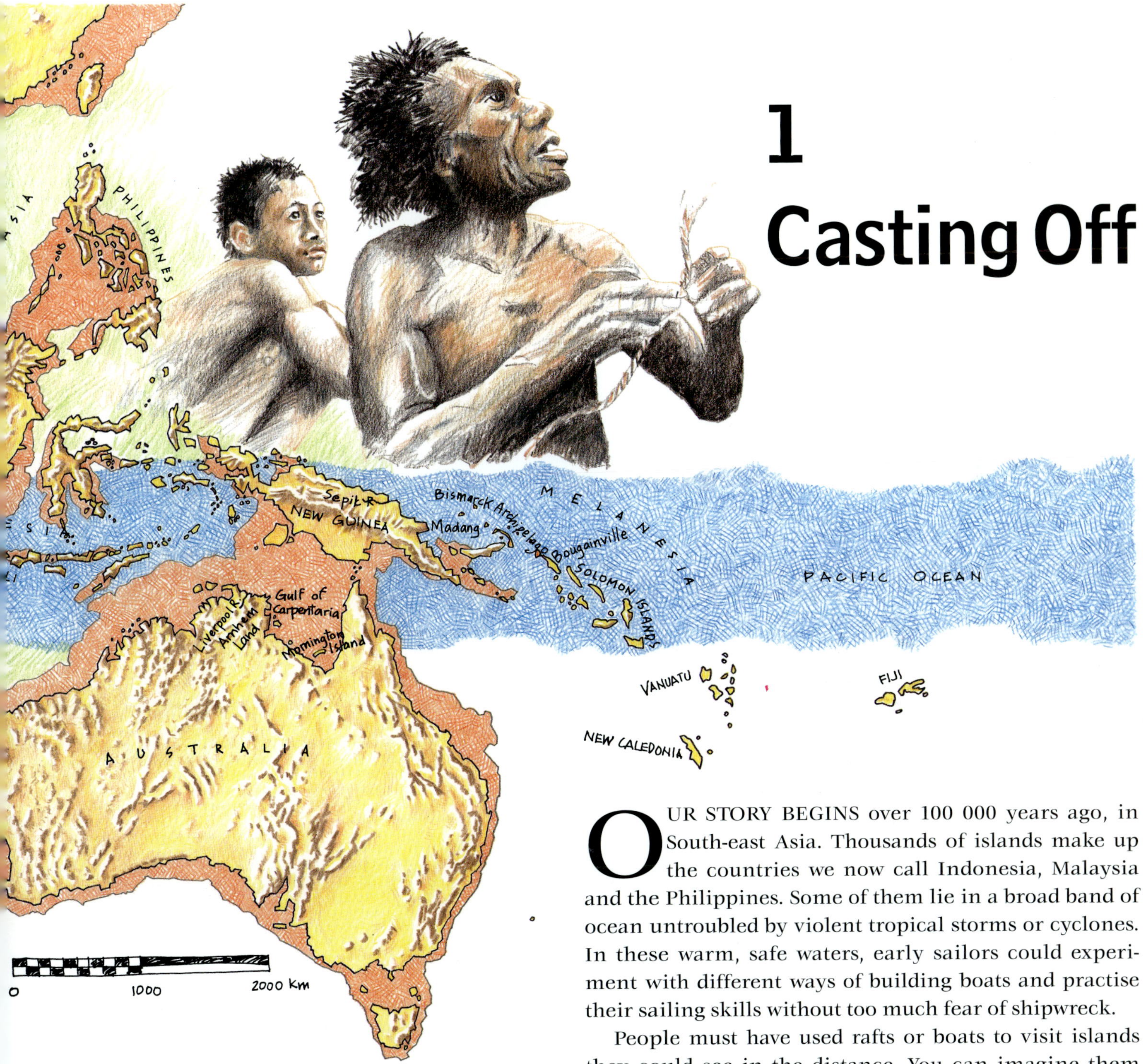

1 Casting Off

OUR STORY BEGINS over 100 000 years ago, in South-east Asia. Thousands of islands make up the countries we now call Indonesia, Malaysia and the Philippines. Some of them lie in a broad band of ocean untroubled by violent tropical storms or cyclones. In these warm, safe waters, early sailors could experiment with different ways of building boats and practise their sailing skills without too much fear of shipwreck.

People must have used rafts or boats to visit islands they could see in the distance. You can imagine them experimenting, pushing further out; some of the most adventurous would head over the horizon, encouraged by bird migrations, floating leaves and driftwood, or columns of smoke rising from distant forest fires.

As they moved on to new lands, these adventurers learnt how to use new types of wood, bark and other materials, and how to build faster, more stable boats capable of making long ocean voyages. The next step was to brave the unknown, and sail out into the mighty Pacific Ocean.

From Raft to Outrigger

Bamboo's hollow, watertight compartments make it light and buoyant – the ideal raft-building material. You can also strip long thin pieces off the bamboo and use them as string to tie the whole thing together

The very first 'boats' must have been tree trunks, or coconuts or bits of driftwood – anything that floated well enough to carry someone across a river. Soon people realised that lashing (tying) together two or three branches or logs made a more stable vessel – a raft.

People in South-east Asia were also lucky enough to have a ready supply of the ultimate raft-building material – bamboo. Wherever bamboo grew – Africa, Asia, the Pacific – people used it to make simple boats. They still do.

Other materials were used too – mainly wood, bark and reeds.

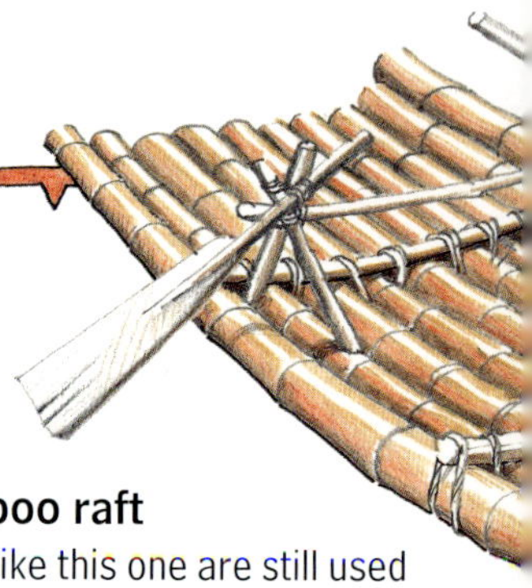

Bamboo raft
Rafts like this one are still used along rivers and coastlines throughout Asia and the Pacific Ocean

A simple raft made by Aborigines on Mornington Island, Gulf of Carpentaria, from mangrove wood and hibiscus bark

Bark canoes

People used bark canoes in areas where bamboo was not available. At first they were made by bending just a single sheet of bark into a sort of trough, but people gradually found ways to improve them:

- The ends were bunched or folded together, and tied or stitched up, then caulked (i.e. the gaps were filled) with mud or a paste made of vegetable pulp.
- The bark was heated over a fire so it could be more easily bent into the right shape.
- Spreaders or 'thwarts' were added – sticks going across the boat to stop the sides either folding in or spreading out flat.
- Ribs were added along the sides to stiffen the bark.
- Extra sheets of bark were stitched over the top to stop water splashing in (especially at the ends).
- The sides were raised by stitching on extra strips.

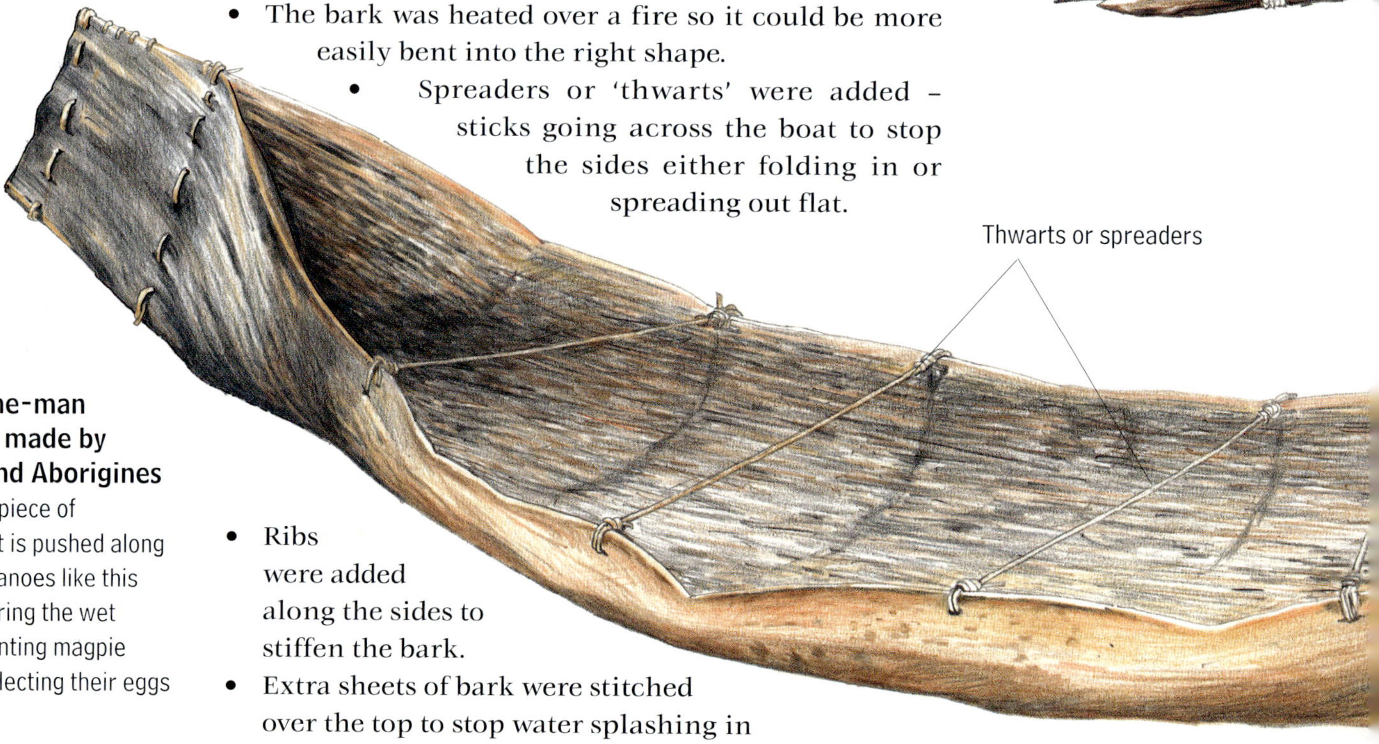

A simple one-man bark canoe made by Arnhem Land Aborigines from a single piece of stringybark. It is pushed along with a pole. Canoes like this were used during the wet season for hunting magpie geese and collecting their eggs

The earliest, simplest boats

Floating log or branch

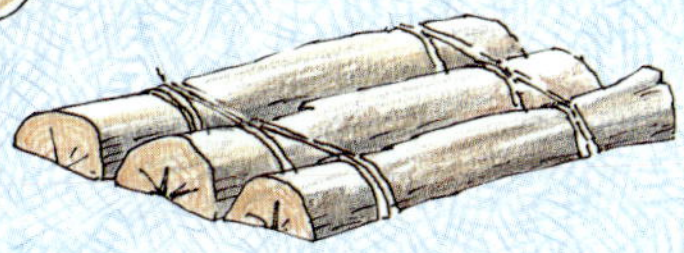

Raft (two or three logs or branches tied together)
More stable – it doesn't tip over – and can carry things, but is heavy and difficult to manoeuvre (steer and handle). Most useful for short crossings and when you can go with the current

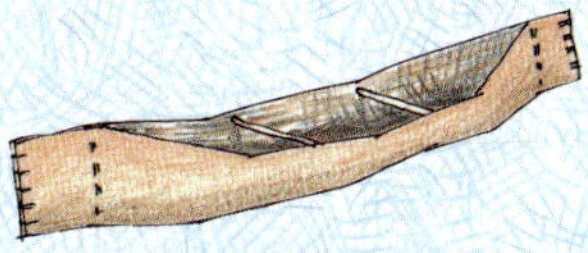

Bark canoe
A lighter craft, more manoeuvrable, but too flimsy for heavy loads or ocean travel

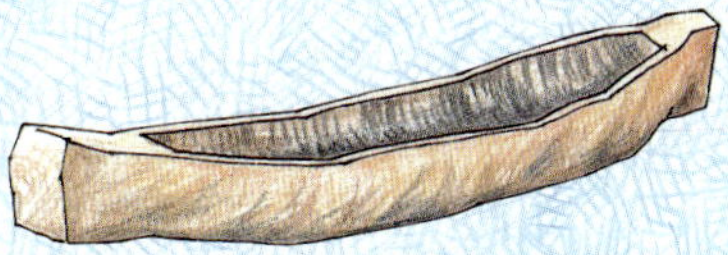

Dugout canoe
Fast, good carrying capacity, manoeuvrable and rugged, but a lot of work to build, and still a bit unstable

Double outrigger canoe (right)
The outriggers stop it from rolling over, but can snap off in high seas

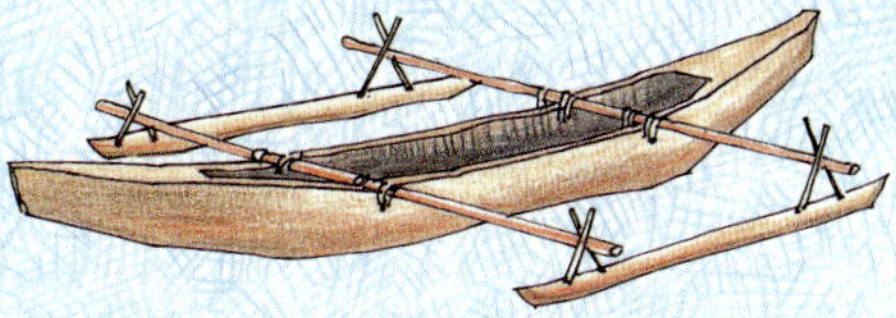

Canoes could also be made from other materials. People in many different parts of the world bundled up great bunches of reeds to make bulky but buoyant boats. They look a bit like today's inflatable 'zodiacs'. In time the reeds became waterlogged, so these canoes didn't last long. There's a spectacular version of the reed boat on page 30.

Facts and figures

Length: 2.1 metres
Width: 0.5 metres
Depth: 0.4 metres
Crew: 1

Sharp front end (bow) for cutting through weeds

Stitched bow and stern

Dugout canoes – a revolution in boat design

The dugout canoe was a technological breakthrough that was to have a huge effect on Pacific exploration. The breakthrough probably happened after bark canoes and rafts had been around for a while. Dugouts were as easy to manoeuvre as a bark canoe, and as strong and seaworthy as a raft, and added their own special quality – speed. They evolved in areas where there were plenty of big thick trees, like the south coast of New Guinea. The Asmat people, for example, have been using 20-metre long dugouts around the swampy delta region at the mouth of the Baliem River for centuries. Stone adzes were probably invented for the purpose of hollowing out logs, and later were used for other building jobs.

The main problems with dugouts were their instability – they could easily roll over – and the time it took to build them. A large dugout could take a year or two. The first task after choosing the tree was often to plant a large vegetable garden, to feed the canoe-builders.

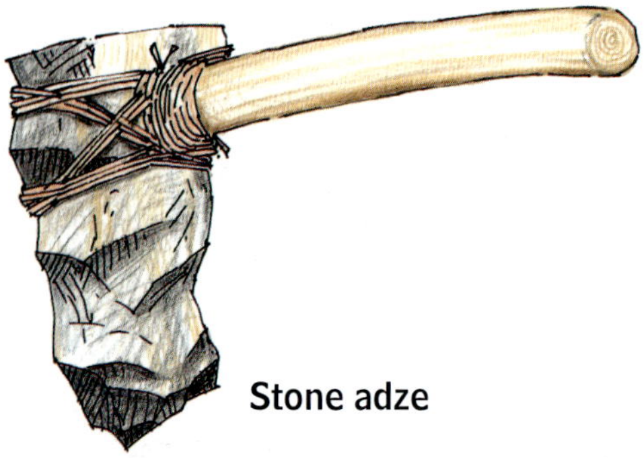

Stone adze

Facts and figures

Length: 2.8 metres
Width: 0.7 metres
Depth: 0.6 metres
Crew: 2-4

A solid workboat from Arnhem Land

Aboriginal people from the Liverpool River area of central Arnhem Land have a long tradition of dugout canoes. This one could be used for river or ocean transport or fishing. The sail must have made it very unstable in all but the lightest winds. It has no keel or outriggers to keep it upright. This type of sail is called a 'sprit' sail

Double outrigger canoe from Bali

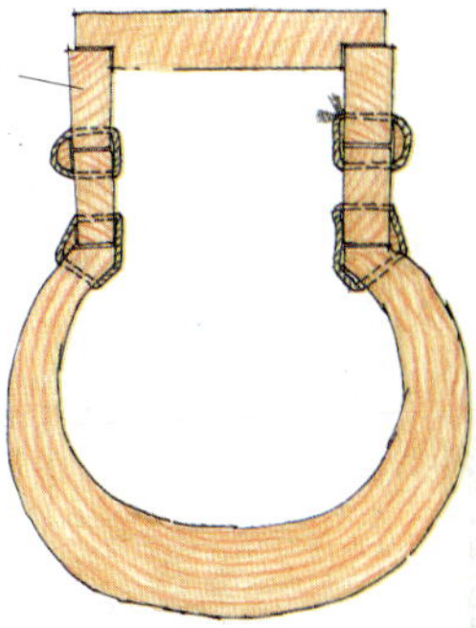

Outriggers

Dugout canoes are just as unstable as a floating log. (After all, a dugout is just that – a floating log, hollowed out.) One more invention was needed to create the fast, seaworthy vessels that would, in time, conquer a third of the earth's surface or half of its oceans. That invention was the outrigger – a device that not only stopped the boat from rolling over, it also made boats so stable that they could carry sails, and therefore go much faster. Even better, you could have sails without having the heavy keel and deep hull of the kind that later created such problems for European sailing ships in shallow coastal or reef waters.

Double outriggers – one outrigger each side of the boat – probably originated on the rivers of South-east Asia or among the Indonesian islands. This arrangement works well in calm water, but is a recipe for disaster in rough seas. If you're unlucky enough to get both your outriggers perched on top of waves, and your canoe suspended over the trough, then something is very likely to snap off.

Having only one outrigger avoids this problem, but a single outrigger has its own difficulties. You always have to keep your outrigger upwind of the canoe, otherwise it tends to dig into the water, slow the boat down, and eventually cause it to flip over.

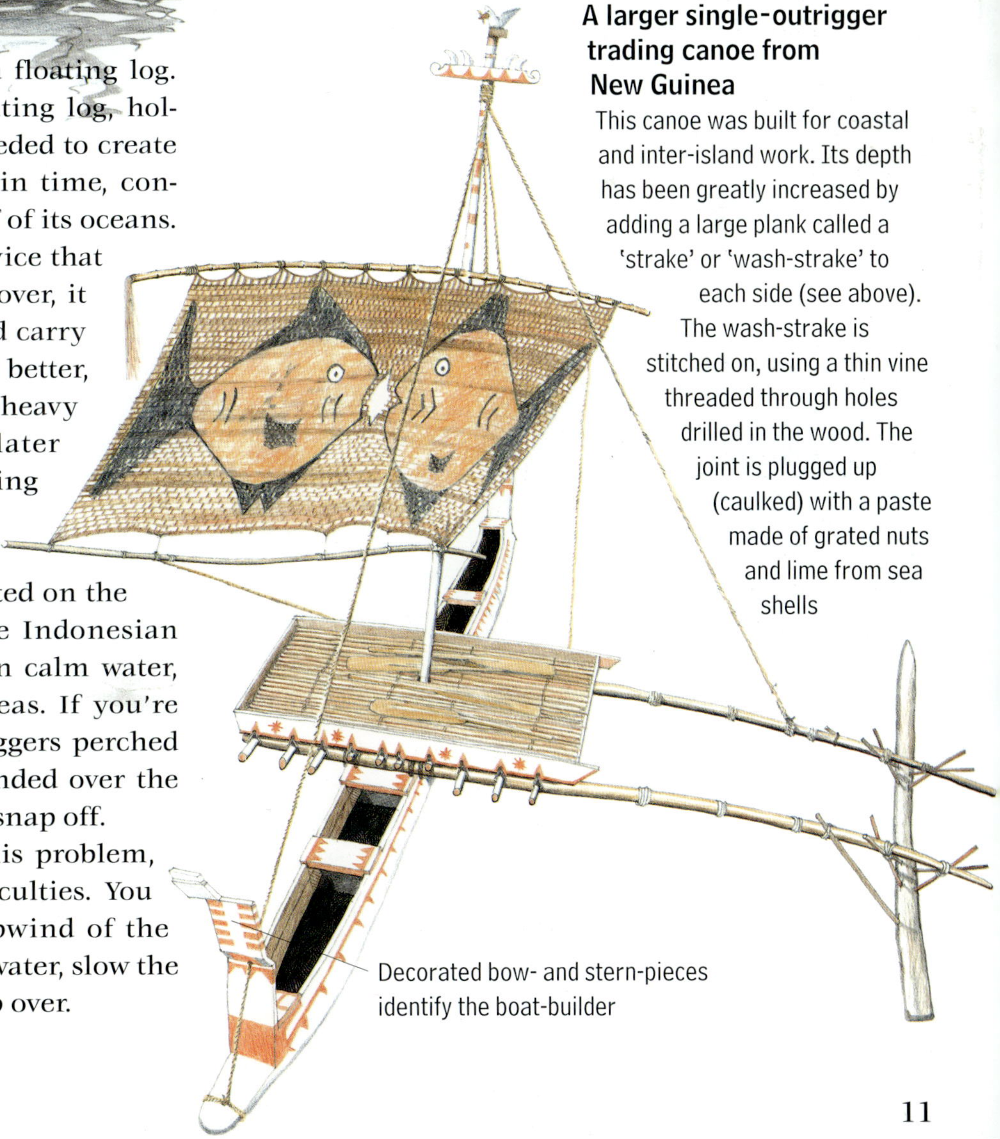

A larger single-outrigger trading canoe from New Guinea

This canoe was built for coastal and inter-island work. Its depth has been greatly increased by adding a large plank called a 'strake' or 'wash-strake' to each side (see above). The wash-strake is stitched on, using a thin vine threaded through holes drilled in the wood. The joint is plugged up (caulked) with a paste made of grated nuts and lime from sea shells

A War Canoe from the Solomon Islands

On PAGE 6 we said the Melanesians moved through New Guinea about 30 000 years ago. They sailed south-east from the Bismarck Archipelago, over the horizon, and kept going for at least another 40 km without knowing what lay ahead before they saw land again. They were the first people in the world with enough confidence in their own sailing skills to sail away from shore and into the unknown.

They settled first in the Solomon Islands, later travelling much further to reach other islands.

In the Solomon Islands they encountered a new problem – there were no trees big enough to construct the large dugout canoes they were used to. So they started to extend small dugouts: adding planks to the sides, joining bits to the front and back, and eventually abandoning the dugout idea altogether and simply building the whole thing out of planks.

They discovered immediately that there were advantages in this form of construction. The new style of boat was much lighter and faster, and they were able to experiment with the shape to improve the boat's speed and handling even more.

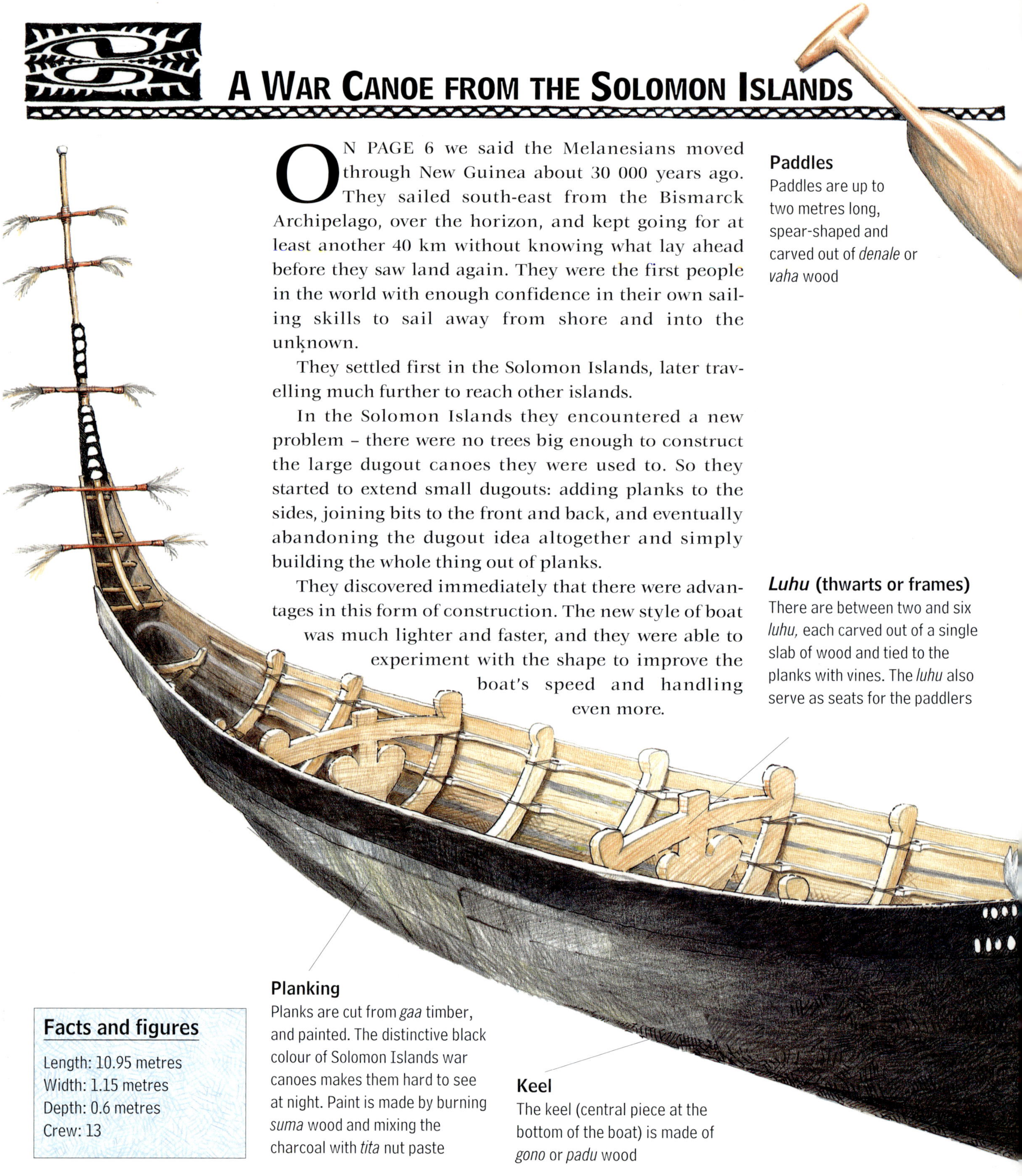

Paddles
Paddles are up to two metres long, spear-shaped and carved out of *denale* or *vaha* wood

Luhu **(thwarts or frames)**
There are between two and six *luhu,* each carved out of a single slab of wood and tied to the planks with vines. The *luhu* also serve as seats for the paddlers

Planking
Planks are cut from *gaa* timber, and painted. The distinctive black colour of Solomon Islands war canoes makes them hard to see at night. Paint is made by burning *suma* wood and mixing the charcoal with *tita* nut paste

Keel
The keel (central piece at the bottom of the boat) is made of *gono* or *padu* wood

Facts and figures

Length: 10.95 metres
Width: 1.15 metres
Depth: 0.6 metres
Crew: 13

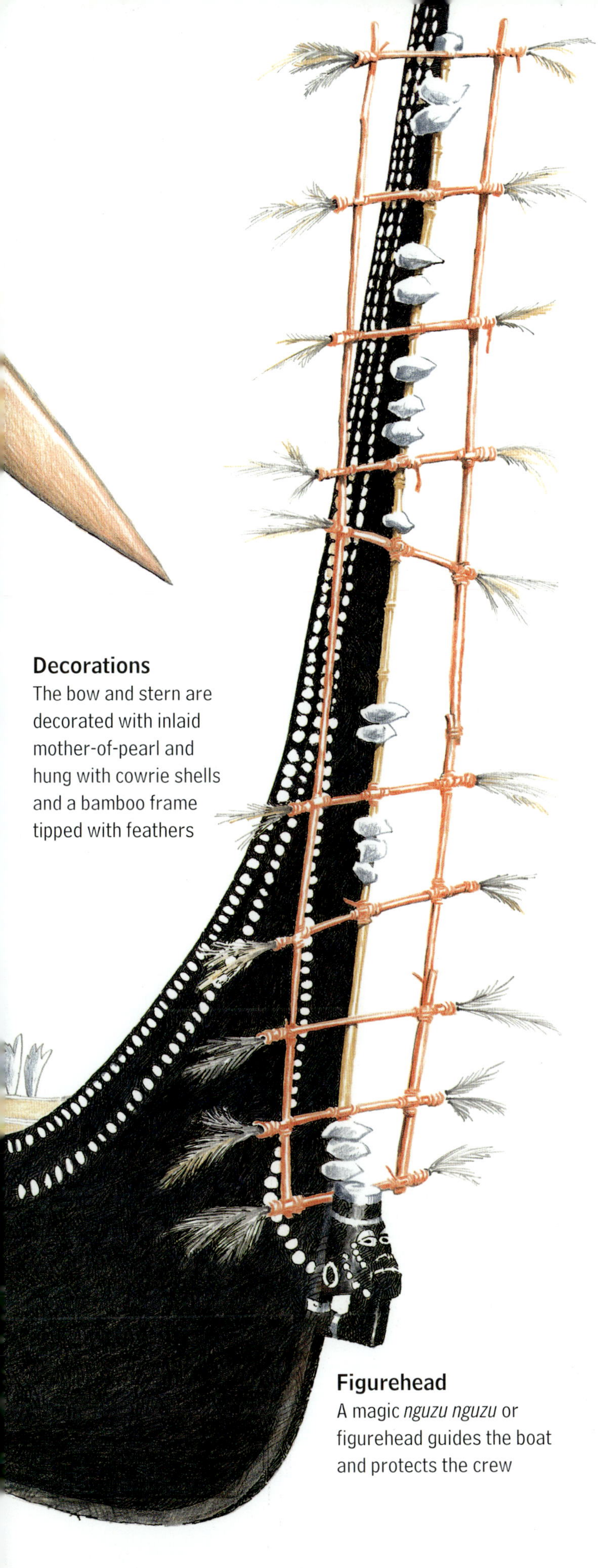

Decorations
The bow and stern are decorated with inlaid mother-of-pearl and hung with cowrie shells and a bamboo frame tipped with feathers

Figurehead
A magic *nguzu nguzu* or figurehead guides the boat and protects the crew

Building a war canoe

1 Three or four trees are selected and chopped down. They are split into thick planks, which are roughly shaped and left to dry for two or three months.

2 The boat-builders then carefully shape the planks using adzes. This job takes about nine months. They leave bits of wood called *puhis* sticking out from the planks, inside the boat. These are used later for fixing the planks to the thwarts or frames of the boat.

3 Now for the vital business of fitting the planks together. The edges are made flat and smooth, the corners are trimmed off and then holes are drilled ready for tying the planks together with *lape* vines every 50 mm. After tying, the V-joints are caulked (filled) with a waterproof paste made from crushed *tita* nuts. At this stage temporary spreaders are tied to the *puhis* to stop the boat collapsing inwards.

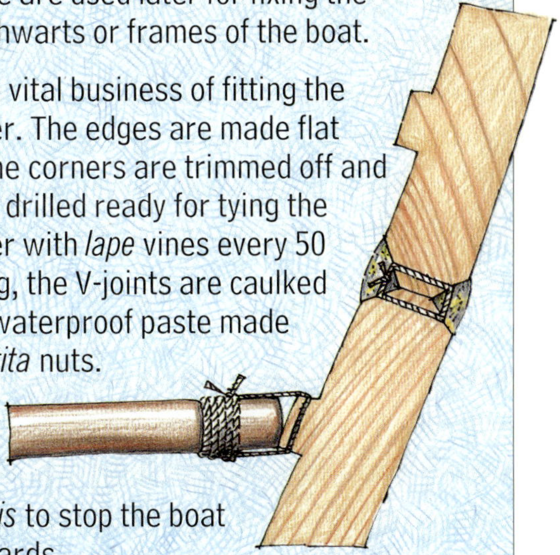

4 Next the tall decorated bow (front) and stern (back) pieces are added, and the outside of the boat is painted black.

5 Finally the spreaders are taken out and the *luhu* (permanent thwarts or cross-frames) are lashed to the *puhis* with *rova* vines.

Boats are People Too

I WROTE this book because I love boats. There's just something immensely pleasing and satisfying about them, isn't there? I like their sleek, graceful shape, their gentle curves and rakish angles. I admire their simple, straightforward, purpose-built look, and I'm always impressed by the painstaking, loving way that their builders have added little touches of colour and decoration.

Many people think of boats as living things. Europeans often talk about a boat as 'she', as if it were female – strong, protective and comforting, glamorous and beautiful. People from Anuta in the Solomon Islands hold a funeral when a boat is lost or sunk,

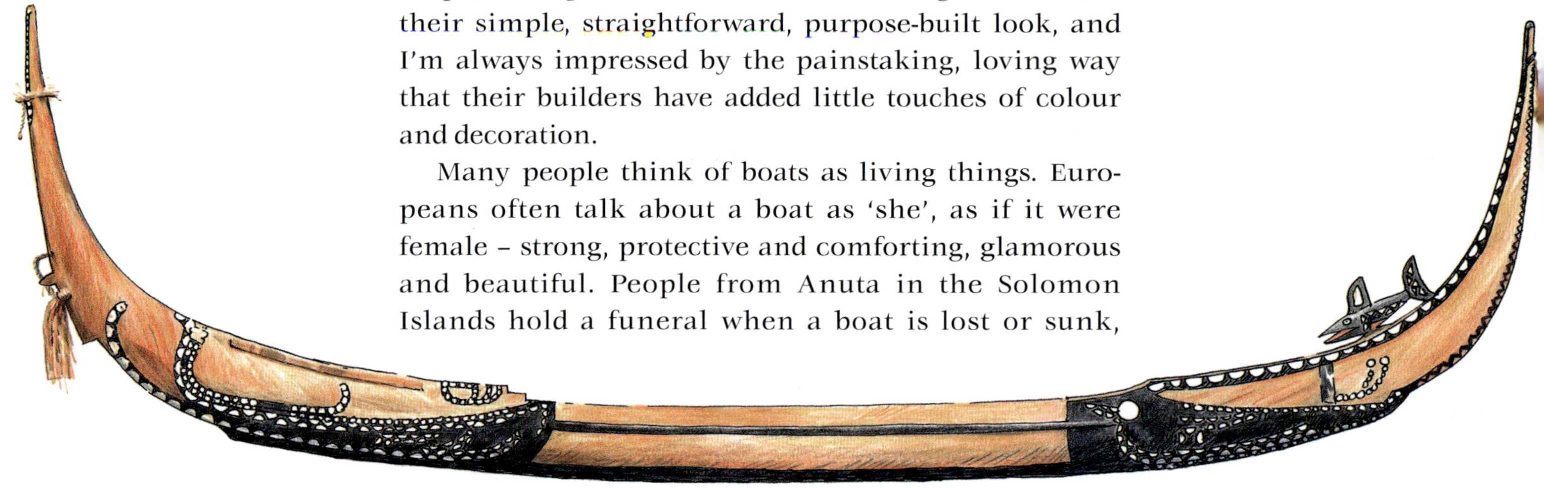

weeping and mourning as if they had lost a relative or close friend. Boat-builders often carve little gods or guardian angels on their boats to protect the boat and its users when they are out on the perilous seas.

Throughout this book you'll see that people have gone to enormous trouble – greatly increasing the work

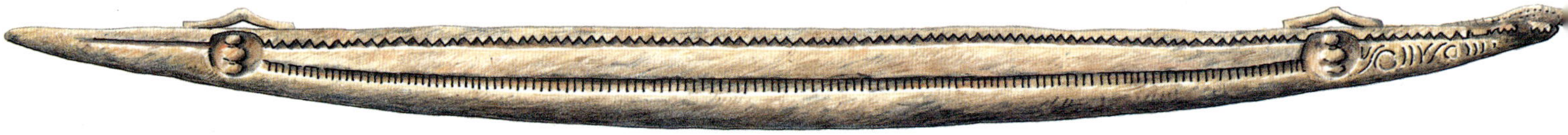

of building a boat – to make it look good, to make it more like a living creature, to provide some kind of supernatural protection, or just to identify the builder or the community that owns it.

Above and below

A dugout canoe from the Sepik River (New Guinea)

The bow is decorated with an ever-present source of danger (and food) for the people of the estuaries – a crocodile

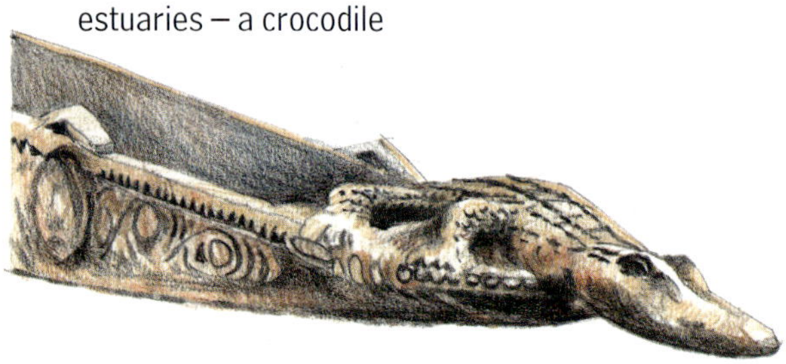

Top and right

Another planked canoe from the Solomons

This canoe is used to fish for bonito – an important source of food for the Solomon Islanders, and one that is part of their ritual and mythology. The miniature carved bonito fish on the stern of the boat is for good luck, and good fishing

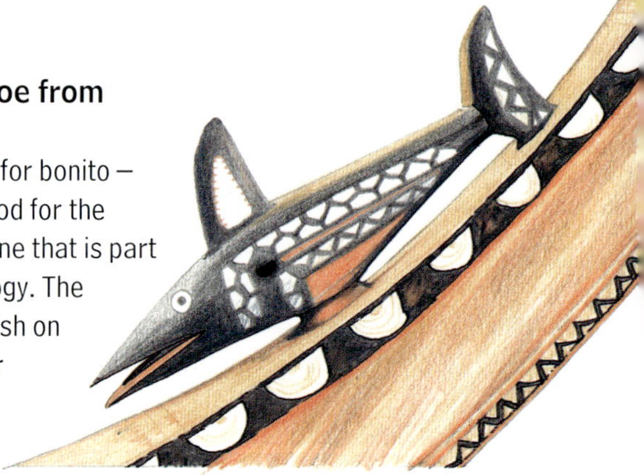

2 Conquering the Pacific

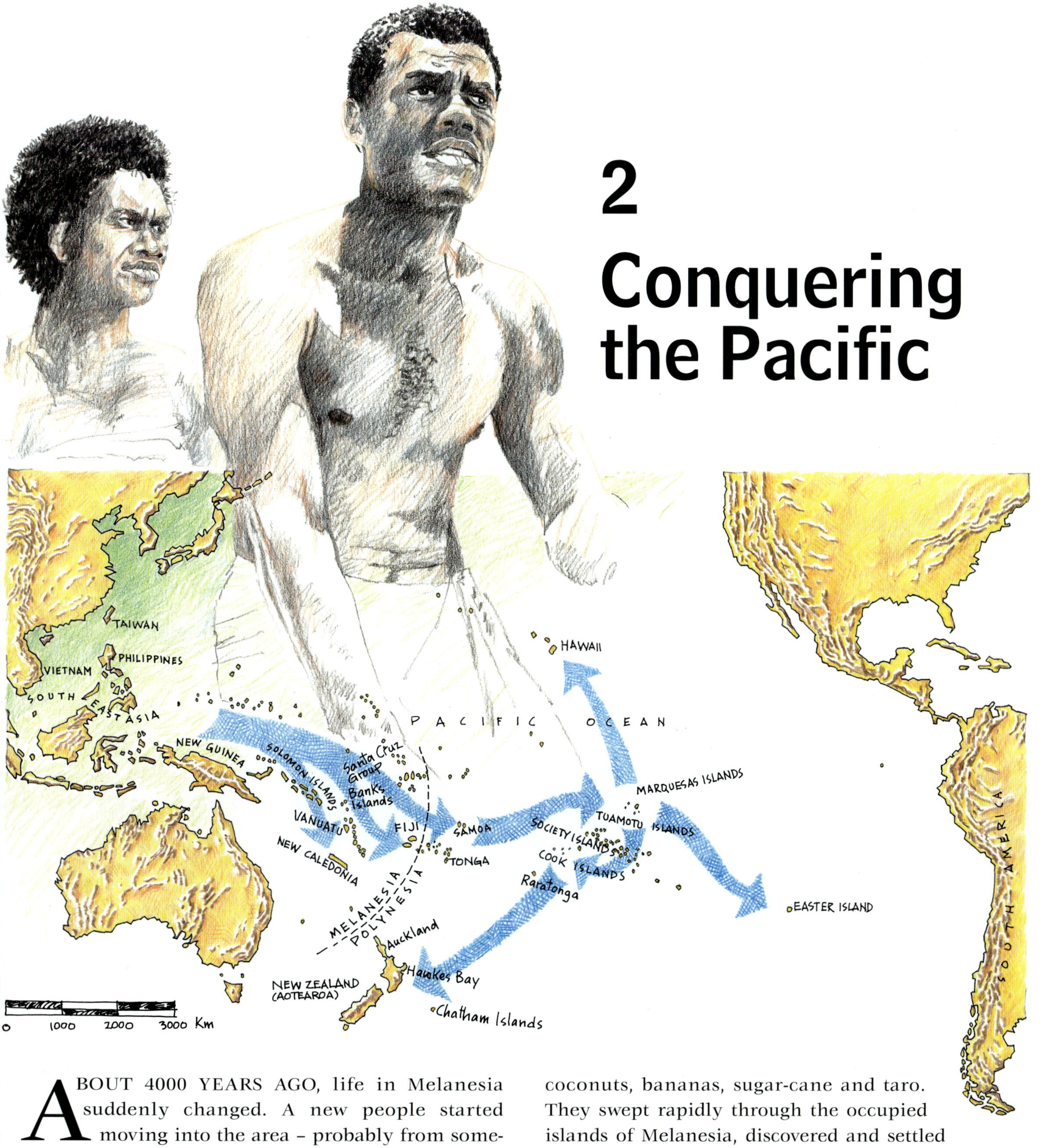

ABOUT 4000 YEARS AGO, life in Melanesia suddenly changed. A new people started moving into the area – probably from somewhere in South-east Asia (Vietnam, the Philippines or Taiwan perhaps). They brought with them a distinctive reddish-coloured pottery called 'Lapita' pottery. They also brought dogs, pigs and chickens, breadfruit, coconuts, bananas, sugar-cane and taro. They swept rapidly through the occupied islands of Melanesia, discovered and settled some new ones (New Caledonia, Vanuatu and Fiji) and explored further to the east, settling in Tonga and Samoa around 3000 years ago.

Voyaging Canoes

IF THE Melanesians were the world's first great coastal sailors, these new 'Lapita' people were the first blue-water mariners. They were masters of the ocean. They sailed in very large vessels and seemed at home in all conditions. They were also accomplished farmers. They brought their favourite fruit and vegetables and planted them wherever they went. Soon these daring maritime explorers had left the Melanesians far behind.

We now call them the Polynesians.

We know very little about the boats used for their mighty voyages of discovery and settlement. None has survived. They must have been big – big enough to carry large numbers of people and supplies, big enough for rats and other stowaways to get a free ride from Asia to the Pacific Islands. Legends suggest that they consisted of two large dugout canoes, placed side by side, one or two metres apart, with a platform between them – like a modern catamaran. Stories from the Marquesas Islands tell us of large double-hulled canoes called *kaahua,* used in ancient times to search for other islands. They were so big they had several huts built on them, and bailers working inside the hulls had to climb up the side to pour out the water!

The double-hulled canoe is an improvement on the single outrigger. It can be sailed no matter which way the wind is blowing, and it doesn't flip over as an outrigger can (see page 11). It is a fast, stable vessel with heaps of space for passengers and cargo.

Polynesian voyaging canoes could slice through the waves at up to 20 km an hour, covering 160 km in an average day, much faster than the European sailing ships still in use just 200 years ago.

'I do believe they sail the best of any boats in the world,' said the English explorer William Dampier in 1691. He had probably seen more of the world than anyone else alive, so he was in a good position to judge.

Fishing or exploring?

Some people have suggested that most Polynesian discoveries were accidental – a by-product of fishing trips. Polynesian legends support this. Huku, a fisherman from Raratonga, is said to have stumbled on Rakahonga Island. Another legendary fisherman, Maui, is supposed to have caught a number of islands – Tonga, the Cook

Sails
Two oceanic lateen or 'crabclaw' sails of finely plaited pandanus leaf strips had rope hemmed into the long edges, which were fixed to bamboo masts and booms

Platform
Large beams or bamboo poles were lashed across the two canoes, probably extending a short distance out each side. Bamboo decking was lashed across the beams, forming a large platform on which a thatched, woven bamboo deckhouse was built

Islands and Aotearoa (New Zealand) – on his fishing line and pulled them out of the ocean depths.

Others say that Polynesian voyages of discovery were deliberate expeditions, with the aim of finding new lands to settle. This seems more likely because these voyages were usually made against the prevailing wind, suggesting that the explorers wanted the wind at their backs for the run home.

Accidental or deliberate, the fact is that Polynesians explored almost the entire Pacific Ocean – 176 000 000 square km of it – long before European sailors sailed away from their native shores.

About 2000 years ago, they were on the move again, venturing out another 3000 km to discover the Marquesas, Tuamotus and Society Islands. From here they sailed north to Hawaii 1500 years ago, south-east to Easter Island 1100 years ago, and finally south to New Zealand 900 years ago, following annual bird migrations. At some stage they also visited South America, and brought back the sweet potato.

Staple foods
Taro, breadfruit and pandanus fruit could all be grated, pounded or mashed and then dried and packed in neat pandanus leaf bundles, to be used as a basic food, in the way we would use flour or rice

Sugar cane: sugar came ready-packed by nature and lasted indefinitely

Fermented breadfruit was used as a preservative (like vinegar) to make other foods keep longer

Strakes (*rauawa*)
Lashed to the top of the dugout to increase the canoe's depth
Cover strip (*taka*)
Covering the joint where the strake is added
Lashings (*aukaha*)
Stitching the strake to the dugout. The lashings pass over cover strips on the inside and outside

Maori War Canoe (Waka Taua)

POLYNESIAN explorers discovered New Zealand 900 years ago. They arrived in seven double-hulled canoes similar to the one shown on page 16. The people in each canoe or *waka* settled in a different part of the country, beginning the seven major Maori tribes of New Zealand.

Two things changed the way these people built their boats.

- They found two new trees, *kauri* and *totara*, that were very tall, straight and strong, but soft and easy to cut. They were also very thick and so Maori could build extra-wide dugout canoes, wide enough to no longer need outriggers or double hulls to stop them tipping over.
- They also found that New Zealand is a country of large lakes and rivers. On these calm waters, outriggers were not usually needed.

Most Maori travel and trade was carried out in canoes. Canoes were the biggest, most valuable, most elaborately constructed things they owned. More work went into the building of a large canoe than a large community building like a meeting house. So Maori culture became a canoe-centred culture. The power and wealth of a Maori tribe were measured in the number and size of their *waka*.

The biggest of the Maori canoes were the *waka taua* or war canoes.

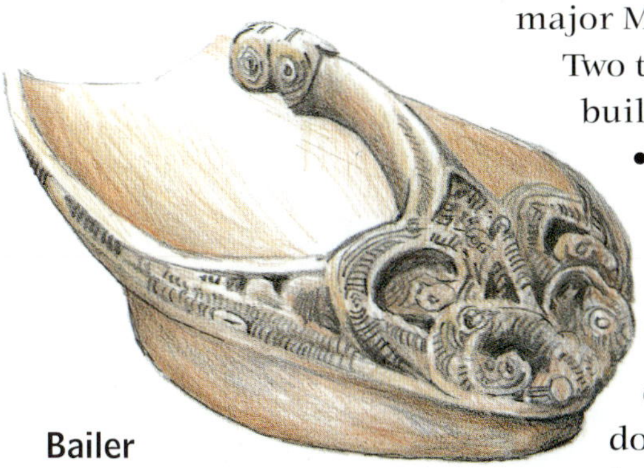

Bailer

Bailers (*tata*) were vital equipment for an open boat in rough seas. Depressions were left in the floor so that water could be scooped out of the bottom of the boat using these intricately carved implements

Facts and figures

Length: 25 metres
Width: 1.8 metres
Depth: about 1 metre
Crew: about 100. (Two-thirds of these could paddle at one time – the others sat in the middle, resting).
Time to build: 1-2 years

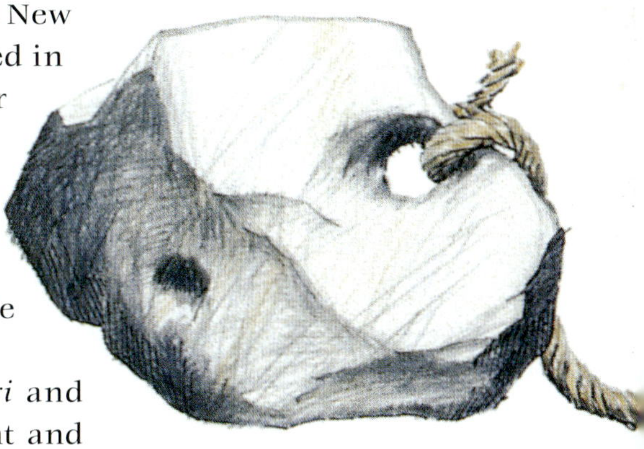

Anchor (*punga*)

A large heavy stone with a hole or kneck suitable for tying a rope onto

Below

A *waka taua* called *Te Toki a Tapiri* or 'The Adze of Tapiri'

This war canoe was built in 1836 near Wairoa (Hawkes Bay). It was used for tribal warfare. Several times it was captured or changed hands as a result of peace deals between tribes. Later it was taken to Auckland and sold to the Ngati Teata people. In 1863 British soldiers captured it and then left it to rot on a beach nearby. During this period a British sailor tried unsuccessfully to blow it up. It was repaired in 1868 and rests now in the Auckland Museum

Tauihi

Carved bow, usually representing creation

Coconut

Yam

Taro

What Did They Eat?
Provisions for a Long Voyage

Polynesian explorers faced return trips of two or three months, with no guarantee of finding food or water along the way. They had no refrigerators, so they ate fresh food in the first few days, before it went off. From then on, they ate preserved or dried foods, adding freshly caught fish whenever possible. Sometimes they killed an animal for meat.

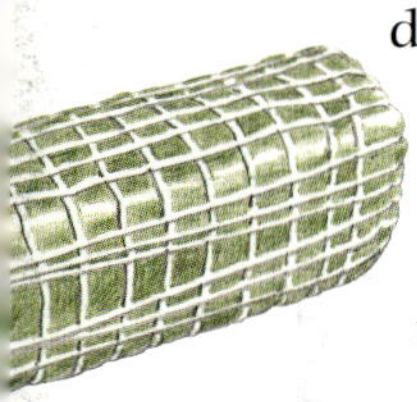

Fruit and vegetables

Fresh fruit: breadfruit, bananas. Fruit was also sun-dried on racks before departure, allowing it to be kept indefinitely

Fresh vegetables: taro, yams, sweet potatoes

Coconuts were an absolute essential for all voyages, providing coconut milk (a cool refreshing drink), coconut 'meat' (a delicious flavouring for other foods), coconut fibre (to make rope from, and to use as toilet paper – kinder to the bottom when wet!), coconut shells (dried and burnt in the cooking fire)

Meat and fish

Live dogs, pigs and poultry – sometimes in cages – were taken along and killed when necessary for fresh meat. Fish could sometimes be caught – but not always. Sometimes live fish were kept in bamboo cages tied to the side of the boat. Dried fish and shellfish would keep indefinitely

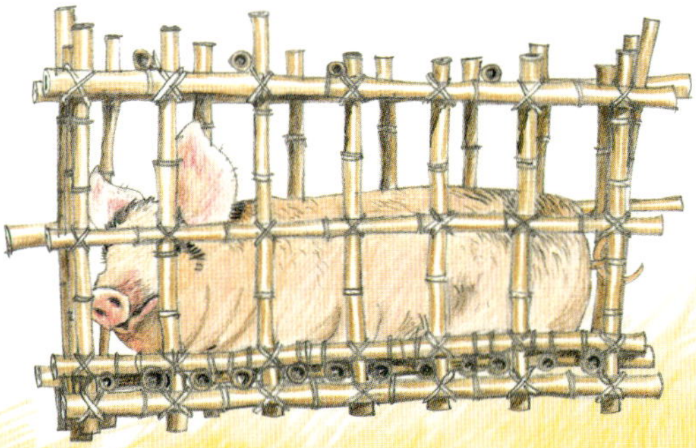

Drinks

Water was carried in large gourds, with wooden stoppers. Sometimes the sailors trailed these gourds along in the sea behind the boat, to keep the water cool. If it rained they could top up their supplies. If not, they had to be careful. Coconuts were kept cool in the same way. Left in the heat, coconut milk goes off quickly

The great navigators

The most extraordinary thing about Polynesian sailors was their ability to travel vast distances from one tiny island to another without compasses, clocks, computers or satellite navigation systems, reaching their target with pinpoint accuracy after a journey of perhaps days or weeks. How did they do it?

The *tahuna* (navigator) in Polynesian society was a person of great importance in the community. He carried a huge amount of information around in his head. Polynesians had no writing, but they had developed phenomenal memories.

A *tahuna* was assigned to every voyage, and he used a combination of methods along the way. The canoe would leave late in the day, setting a course by aligning the two prominent land features (trees, hills or headlands, say) that were appropriate for the particular trip.

The Polynesians constructed maps out of shells, twigs and bits of grass. Their maps often included an important element missing from ours – lines indicating the prevailing wave patterns

At sea, the stars were the *tahuna's* principal tool. He would identify one star near the horizon ahead, another near the horizon astern, and use those positions to keep the canoe on track. As the stars followed their nightly progress through the sky – some setting, others rising – so the navigator had to regularly select new horizon stars to guide him. If there were none, he would lie in the bottom of the canoe and line up two or three overhead stars. Many *tahunas* were experts on just one or two long complicated journeys, memorising long sequences of star maps, rather as we might learn a song or poem.

During the day he resorted to less accurate methods: the sun, and the direction of wind and waves.

Nearing journey's end, the *tahuna* kept watch for the telltale signs of land: differences in wave patterns, phosphorescence, and the colour of the water; the presence of birds, coastal fish, seaweed, floating leaves and driftwood; land clouds, smoke, and even the smell of land. Polynesians could detect land using these indicators, even if they were 40 or 50 km off course, long before they could see it.

Polynesians did have a set of directions like our north, south, east and west, but theirs were based on common wind directions, so they were fairly inaccurate and, of course, they varied from place to place.

Canoe ladders

n Hawaii there were no calm lagoons and asy passages out to sea, so people often ad to launch their boats straight into the ounding surf, sometimes off rocks. To do his they developed an amazing ontraption called a 'canoe ladder'.

The poles of a canoe ladder were bout 1.5 metres apart, with rungs every .5 metres. Most of the ladder was firmly ed down onto the rocks, with the bottom ew metres 'hinged' so it would rise and all with the waves.

For launching, the paddlers would sit n their canoe which was held by people n either side standing on the ladder. hey worked their way down the adder into the surf and then vaited for a big wave to ome. At exactly the right moment they pushed the boat off, allowing the wave to drag it away into deeper water.

Recovering the canoe was even more exciting. The paddlers had to select the right wave, then surf in on it, while people waited on the ladder to grab the canoe as it was washed up between them, holding it against the pull of the receding wave, then quickly dragging the canoe further up the ladder away from the waves

Polynesian Boats for All Purposes

The *thamakau* – an island speedboat

The Fijian *thamakau* is a classic Polynesian outrigger canoe. This is a small one, built for fishing and general transport in the lagoon and around the island. Many *thamakaus* were (and are) much bigger – up to 35 metres long with a crew of 40 – and could take as long as five years to build. Travelling at dazzling speeds, they played a major part in the exploration of the Pacific Ocean. They are still used for trading between distant islands.

Sail

The crabclaw or oceanic lateen sail was used so commonly throughout the Pacific that it has become a sort of symbol or logo for Polynesian seafaring. It was traditionally made from woven or plaited flax or pandanus leaves, but today cotton, canvas or woven polythene is used

Outrigger attachments

These ranged from the very simple to the very complicated, and were always carefully designed to spread the load and cushion the shocks of constant battering. Illustrated, from left, are outriggers from New Guinea, the Solomons, and a very common arrangement found throughout the Pacific Ocean

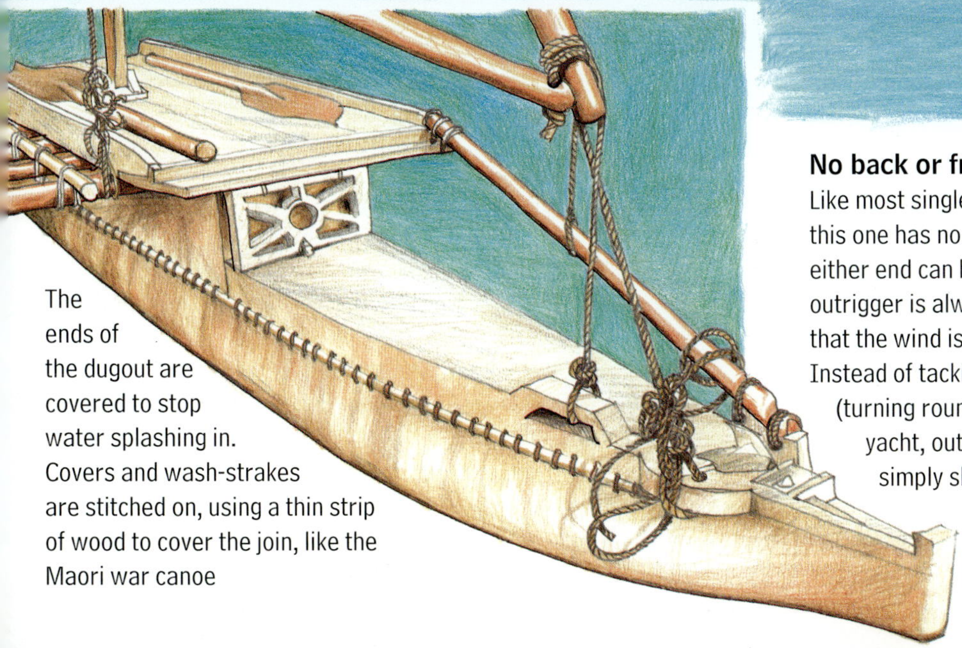

The ends of the dugout are covered to stop water splashing in. Covers and wash-strakes are stitched on, using a thin strip of wood to cover the join, like the Maori war canoe

No back or front

Like most single-outrigger canoes this one has no bow or stern – either end can be the front. The outrigger is always on the side that the wind is coming from. Instead of tacking or jibing (turning round) like a modern yacht, outrigger canoes simply shunt backwards and forwards

Facts and figures

Length: 5.9 metres
Width: 0.36 metres
Width including outrigger: 1.8 metres
Depth: 0.72 metres
Sail: Crabclaw or oceanic lateen
Number of people: up to 8 crew and passengers

A *vaka faimanu*

The *vaka faimanu* (it means 'boat designed like a bird') is the standard ocean-going canoe built on Tikopia Island in the Santa Cruz group. This one has a special story. When master boat-builder Pu Nukutapu and some companions were shipwrecked and stranded in the Banks Islands, over 200 km from home, they set to work and built this boat from the available materials.

Later it was used regularly to net flying fish at night, using coconut-leaf flares to attract the flying fish.

Facts and figures

Length: 10 metres
Width: 0.7 metres
Height: 0.9 metres
Sail: Crabclaw or oceanic lateen

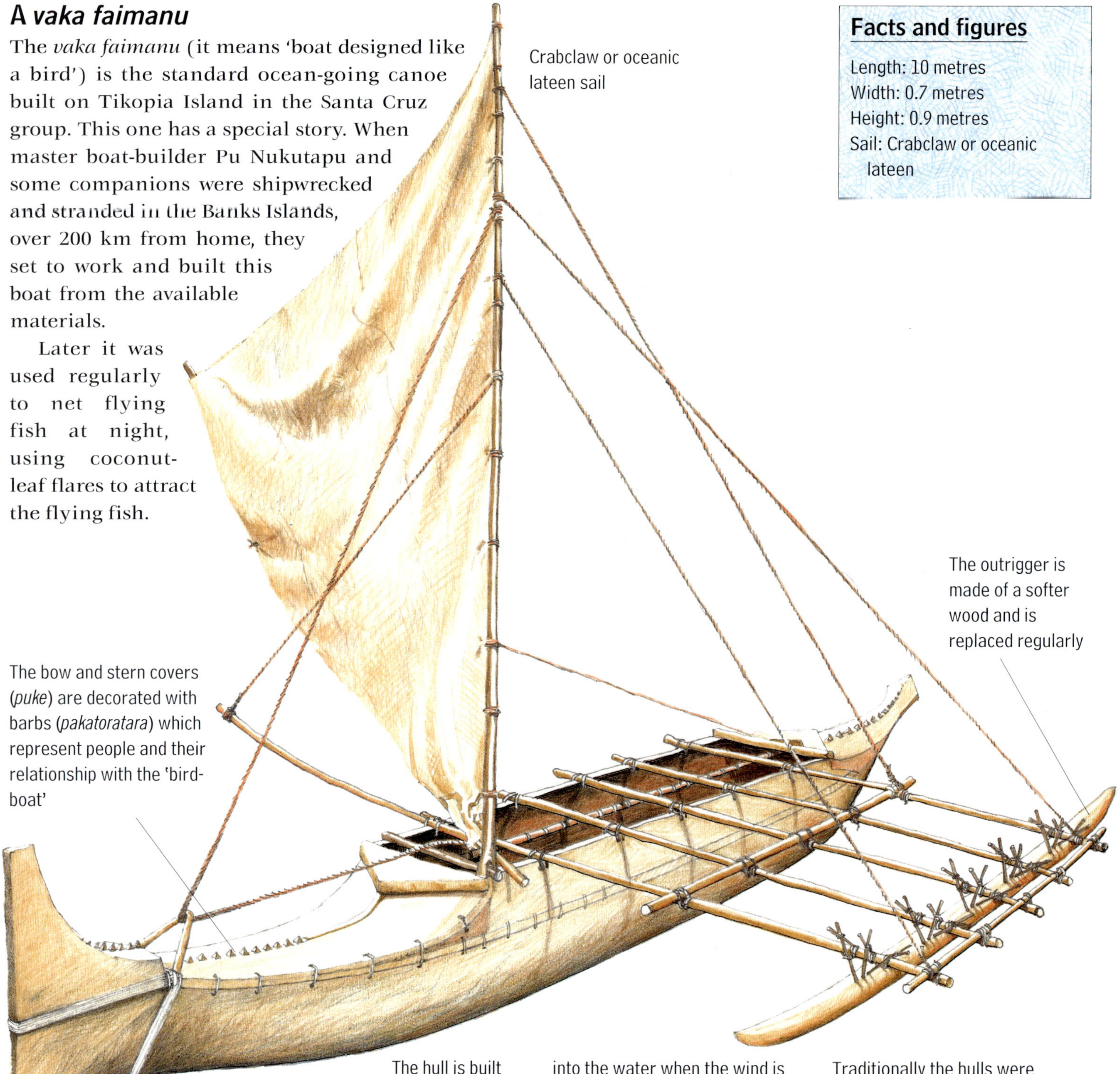

The hull is built from a single log of *te petau* – a hard, light, insect-resistant wood. The outrigger side of the hull (left side) has a slight bulge which stops the outrigger from digging into the water when the wind is coming from the opposite side of the boat. Unlike many outrigger canoes, this boat has a bow and stern – it is not designed to shunt backwards and forwards.

Traditionally the hulls were rubbed with algae from the reef to protect the wood. These days they are painted with enamel paint. These boats normally have a very long life.

A rough-water specialist

Illustrated here is a small outrigger canoe from the Reef Islands, built for punishing work in rough seas.

The dugout is almost completely covered to prevent waves splashing in. The single outrigger is made from two pieces of wood instead of one, and it is elaborately fixed to the booms with no less than 13 carefully arranged prongs!

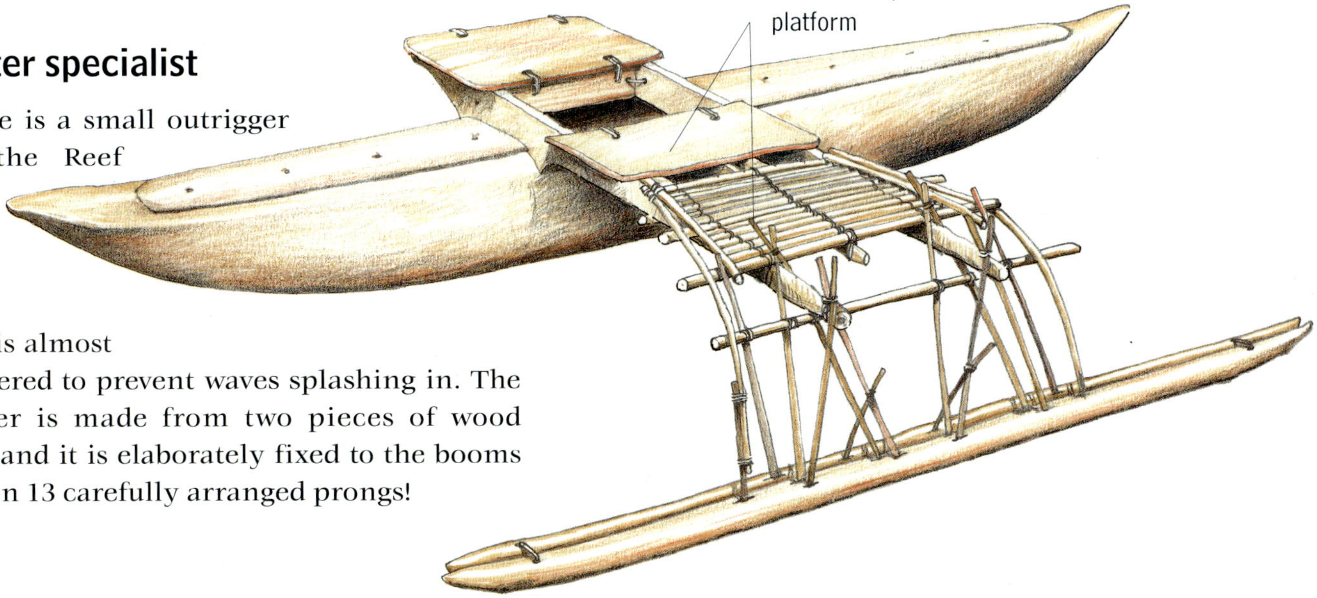

A *vak katea*

This small double hull is a modest version of the great voyaging canoes described on page 16. It is from the Cook Islands. Normally it has a crabclaw sail of woven pandanus leaves, but the crew paddles as well. This view is looking forward from the stern (back end).

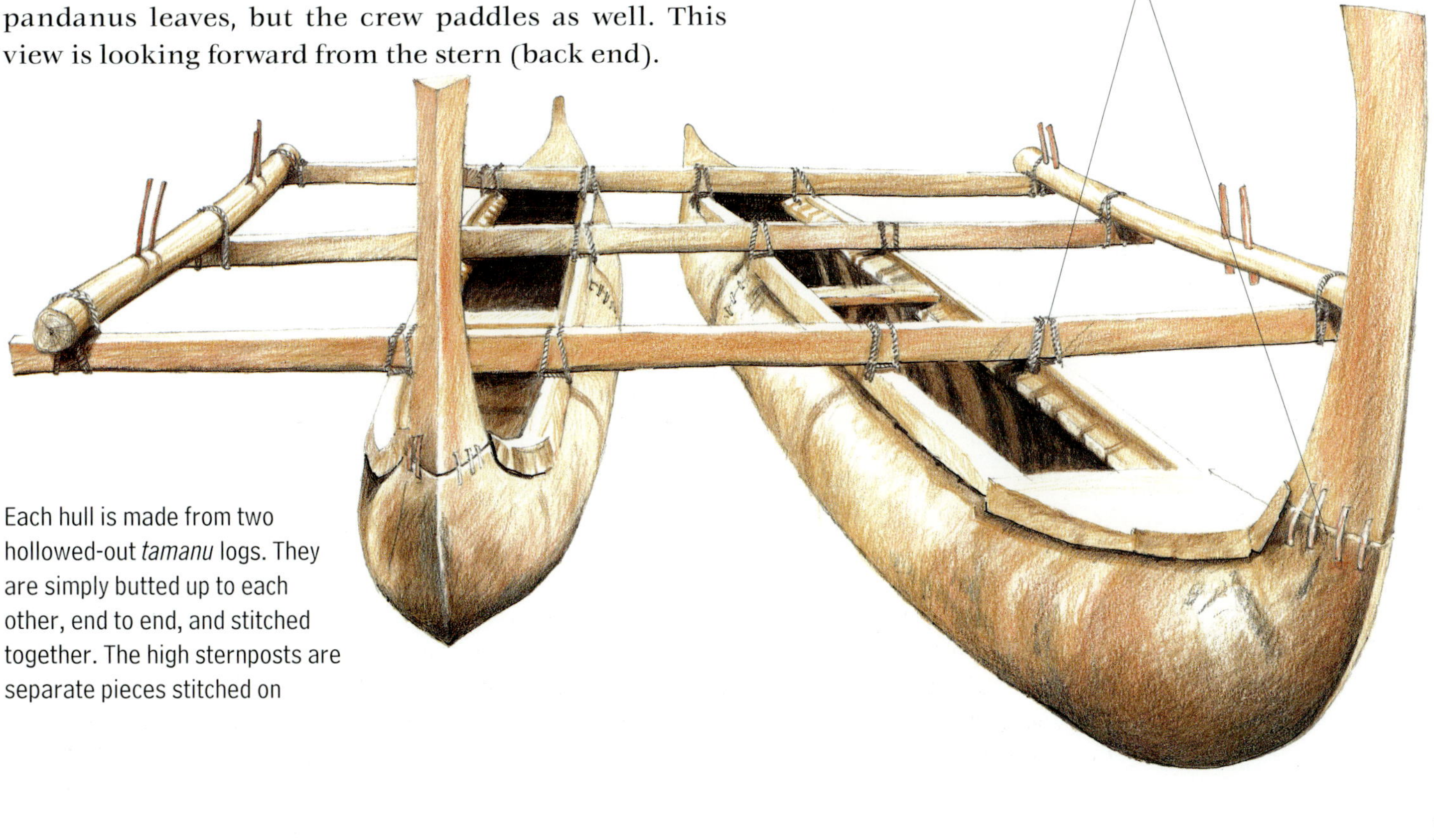

A *waka pahi*: big, strong and wet!

The Chatham Islands (Rekohu) lie about 800 km east of New Zealand. They were originally discovered and settled by another Polynesian group, the Moriori, at about the same time as the Maori were arriving in New Zealand. Here the conditions were different again. There were no large trees like *kauri* and *totara.* There weren't even many small trees, but there was plenty of flax and bracken, and the strong leathery seaweed we call kelp. These materials could be used to make the extraordinary boat shown here.

First the Moriori dried out the materials over smoky fires before soaking them in whale oil – something they had plenty of. Next they tied them into long bundles, which were then fixed to a wooden frame.

These boats were light, buoyant, stable and able to take a fair bit of punishment from the rocky coast and wild seas of the Chatham Islands. They were quick to make and easy to repair. But water flowed through them all the time, making them slow and heavy after a while, and the rowers were continually soaked. (By the way, the Moriori were the only Polynesians to use oars rather than paddles.)

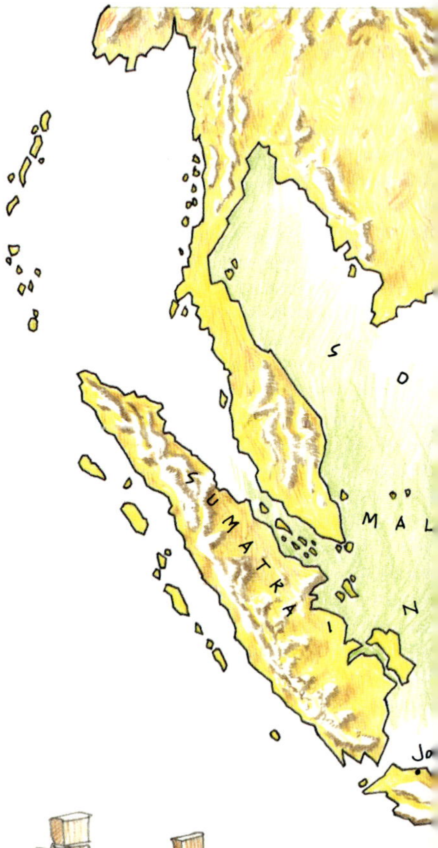

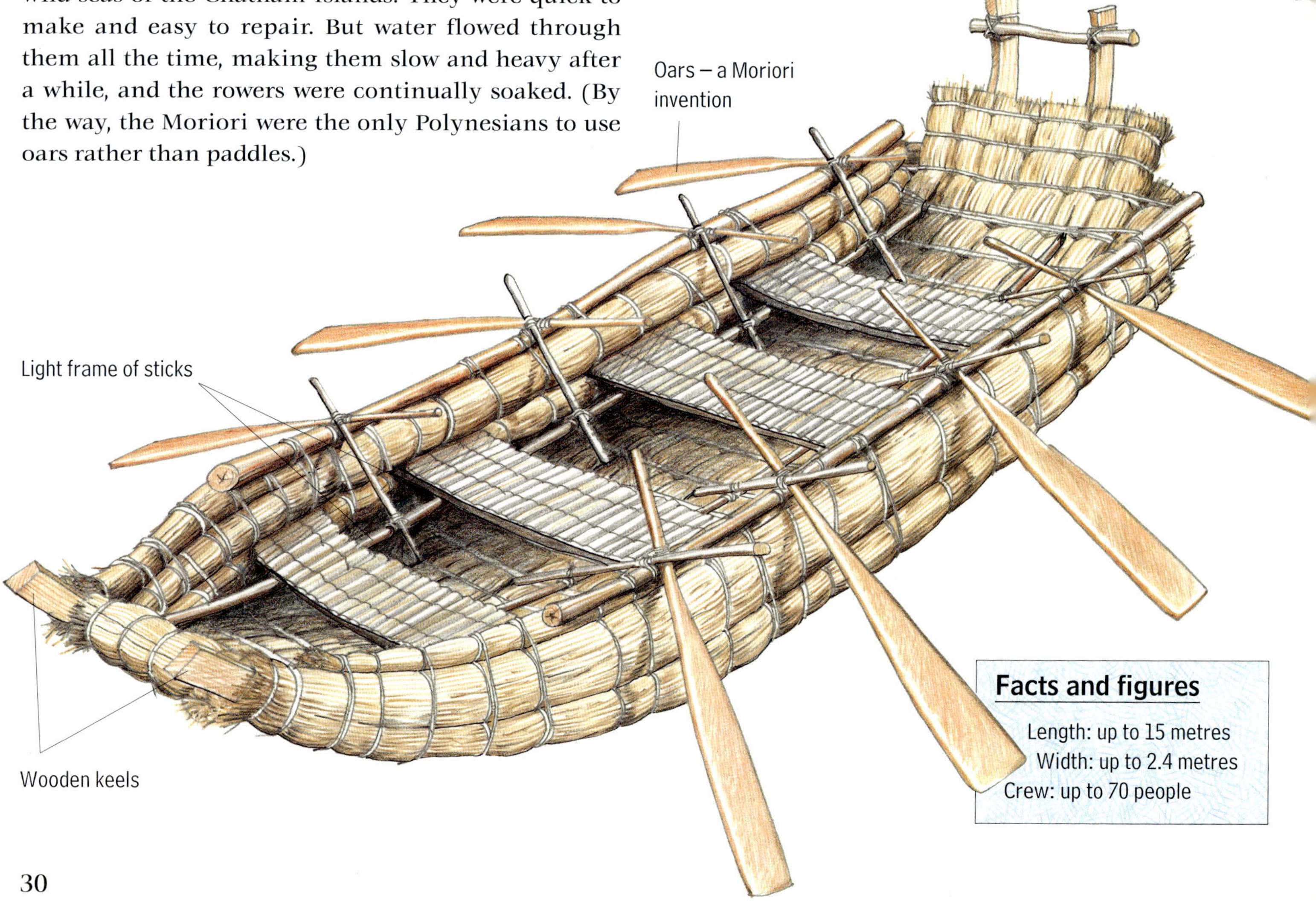

Facts and figures

Length: up to 15 metres
Width: up to 2.4 metres
Crew: up to 70 people

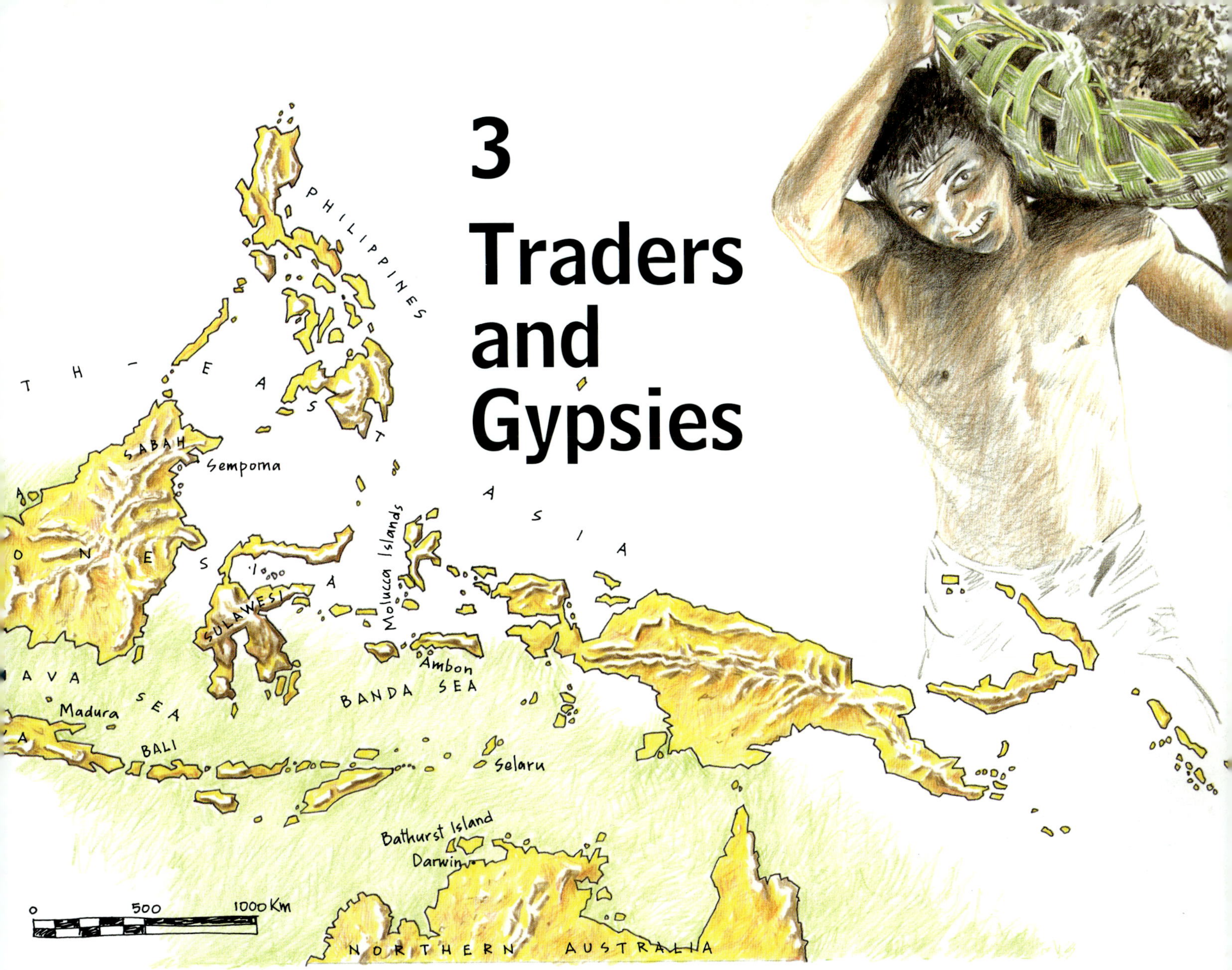

3 Traders and Gypsies

WE BEGAN this book with the very first movements of people out of Indonesia tens of thousands of years ago. In this last chapter we're going back to see what happened to the people who stayed behind. What kinds of boats did they develop to suit their world of islands?

South-east Asia has always been rich in some of the most precious products nature can offer – beautiful timbers, spices, intensely vivid dyes, silk, pearls and medicines. For centuries there has been an extensive local network of boats collecting these goods from thousands of far-flung islands and selling them to the outside world.

Praus of Indonesia

Jakarta's old harbour, the Kali Besar, is jammed with praus as far as the eye can see, while more queue at the entrance waiting for an empty berth

IF YOU VISIT the busy ports of Indonesia today you can still see hundreds of praus – the sturdy yet graceful little sailing ships that island people have been using as cargo carriers for over 1000 years.

They owe their success to the 'trade winds' – those regular-as-clockwork south-easterlies that blow through the region from April to October, and north-westerlies that take over from November to March. For centuries huge numbers of boats have used the south-east trade winds that blow from northern Australia up through Indonesia to Malaysia, Vietnam and the Philippines for six months, and then an equally large number would sail back the other way. These winds made ocean travel safe and predictable – merchants knew exactly when to expect their goods. There was very little risk of

Each region builds its own distinctive style of prau with its own colour scheme.Three are shown here: a *leti leti* from Madura (left), two *prau penisi* from the Java Sea (centre) and a *prau patorani* from Sulawesi (right), but there are dozens of others

delay or serious accident. The prau network linked up with larger ships – at first with junks from China and dhows from the Arab world, later with slow Dutch, Portuguese and English sailing ships from Europe. Today they continue the work, carrying the same kinds of goods to major ports, to be loaded into modern freighters for transport to Australia, America, Europe and Africa.

Today's trade is mainly in timber. A large prau can carry up to 200 tonnes of timber from the remote rainforest into Jakarta. On the return trip the cargo could be anything from flour or cement to washing machines or beer.

Many praus now have engines, but the reliability of the trade winds still makes sail power an attractive free option.

The boat with a belly button: the *Hati Marege*

The *Hati Marege* is a replica of a nineteenth-century *prau padewakang* built by Konjo boat-builders in a famous boat-building region of Sulawesi. It was given to Australia by Indonesia as part of Australia's bicentenary in 1988.

This kind of prau was used by Macassans from South Sulawesi to go fishing for trepang (sea slugs) in the waters off northern Australia. About 1000 men in 50 praus fished these waters for six months every year.

Quarter-rudder
(above) Instead of one rudder in the middle of the stern, praus had two 'quarter-rudders', one on each side. There seems to be an unnecessary clutter of strings and bits of wood around the quarter-rudders, but I'm told that each one has its own special purpose. Rudders are up to 6 metres long

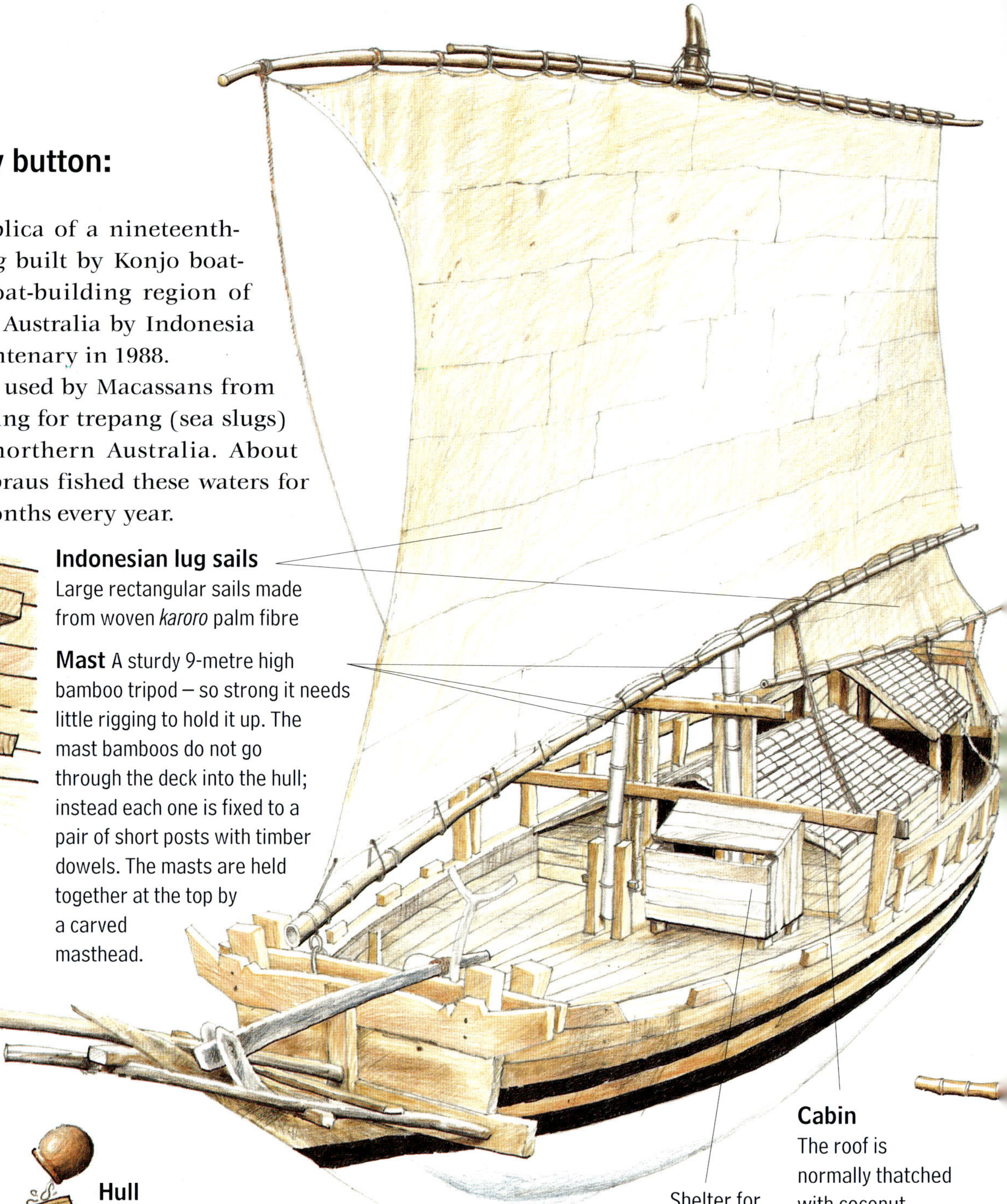

Indonesian lug sails
Large rectangular sails made from woven *karoro* palm fibre

Mast A sturdy 9-metre high bamboo tripod – so strong it needs little rigging to hold it up. The mast bamboos do not go through the deck into the hull; instead each one is fixed to a pair of short posts with timber dowels. The masts are held together at the top by a carved masthead.

Cabin
The roof is normally thatched with coconut leaves

Shelter for cooking fire

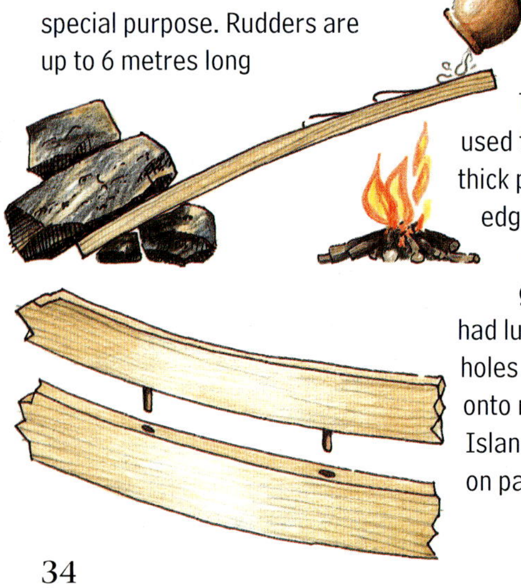

Hull
The Konjo boat-builders used fire and water to bend the thick planks before joining them, edge-to-edge, with hardwood dowels. They caulked the gaps with bark. The planks had lugs (sticking-out bits with holes in them) for later fixing onto ribs, like the Solomon Islands war canoe on pages 12-13

When all the planks were in place they fixed the ribs – 12 main ones, like the ribs of a human body. A boat is thought of as a living thing and boat-builders try hard to copy some of the features of humans. The *Hati Marege* even has a belly-button!

The hull is sealed with a mixture of lime and coconut oil

Facts and figures

Length of hull: 14.25 metres
Width: 4.28 metres
Depth: 1.43 metres
Crew: 20
Time to build: 9 months

Like a rusty Holden ute: the *Sama Saja*

The *Sama Saja* is a rough-and-ready home-made boat from Selaru in the Molucca Islands. It's a bit like a rusty Holden ute from the Australian outback. It has bits and pieces tacked on here and there – I particularly like the sliding window shutters. It was used for every possible job: carrying pigs to market, taking the kids to school, going shopping, visiting friends, carrying building materials for a new shed, and trading.

Australian Customs officers seized the *Sama Saja* in 1986, when she was making a trading trip to Bathurst Island, near Darwin. Indonesian sailors have fished in northern Australian waters and traded with Australian Aborigines for hundreds of years, but today Australian laws greatly restrict these activities. Many boats have been seized and destroyed, and their crews arrested and sent home.

Facts and figures

Length: 5.25 metres
Width: 2.9 metres
Depth: 1.07 metres
Sails: Gunter rig
(a European style)

A Sea Gypsy Houseboat

WE'VE ALL HEARD of the gypsies who live in brightly painted caravans and roam the backroads of Europe, stopping for a day or a week at a time in some farmer's paddock or public park. It's always seemed a very appealing idea to me – living in a caravan, always on the move, a bit like being in a circus.

Well, here in the island-studded waters of South-east Asia we have our own gypsies – the Bajau people. They live their entire lives on their boats, take no notice of national boundaries or governments, and catch their dinner with a fishing line. They go ashore only occasionally to trade – bartering fish for rice, tools and spices – or to repair their boats. The children don't go to school. They speak their own language, incomprehensible to those on shore, but similar to that spoken by other Bajau people thousands of kilometres away.

The Bajau houseboat illustrated here is called a *lipa lipa*. It is from the Semporna region of Sabah.

Facts and figures

Length: 7.54 metres
Width: 1.42 metres
Depth: 0.35 metres
Sail: Indonesian lug
Crew: one family

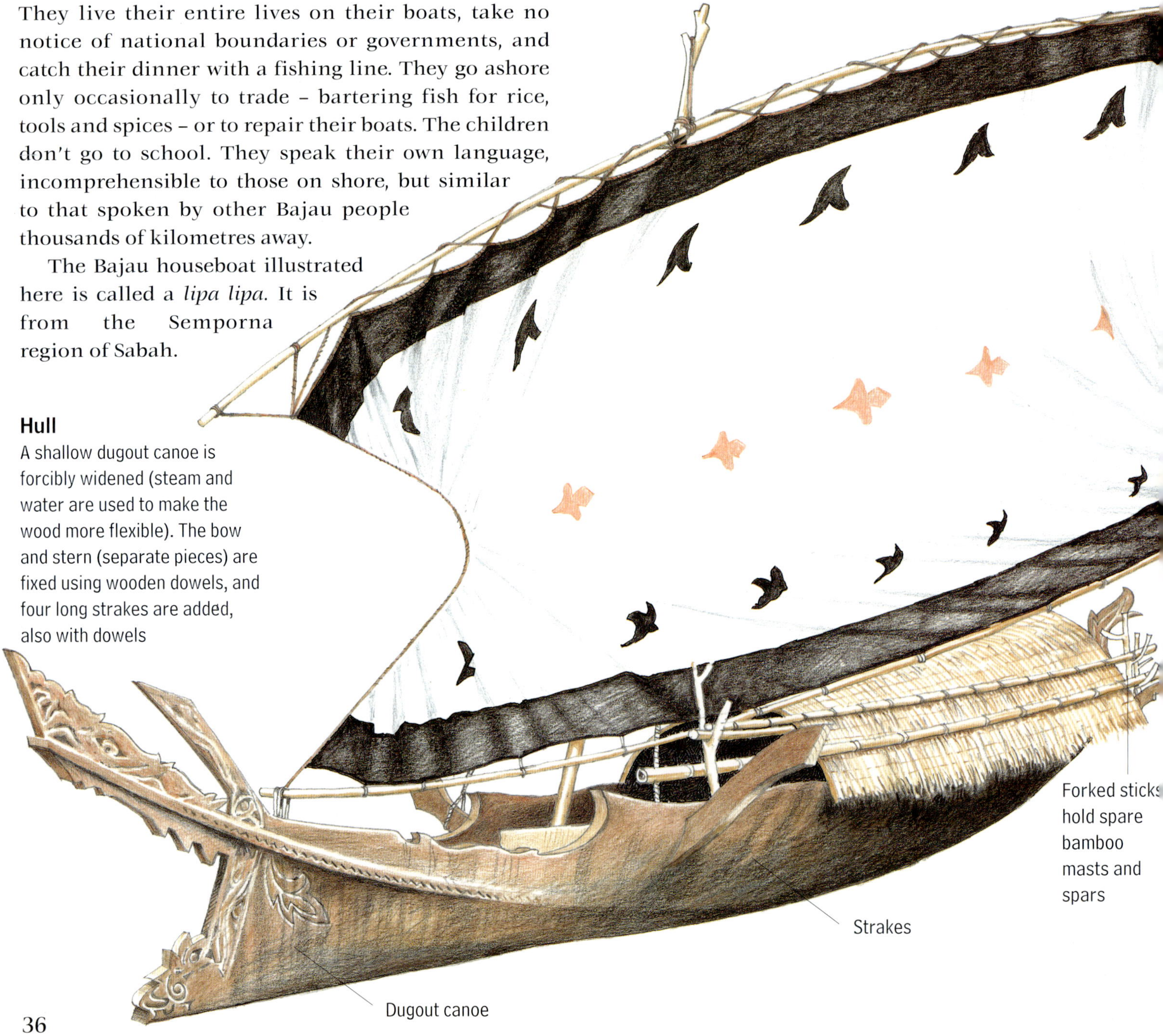

One small cabin serves as a bedroom for all the family and as a living room during wet weather. Soft mats are spread around on the split bamboo floor. Near the bailing well, a large flat earthenware dish holds the cooking fire. A wok rests on three stones with perhaps a delicious fish curry gently simmering. Bajau people eat two meals a day.

The cabin roof, made of palm leaves, can be easily removed and set up on the beach as a temporary shelter. Bajau use the ocean for washing and going to the toilet

Recently, many Bajau people have built houses to live in – but they still avoid living on dry land. Their small communities of 20 or 30 houses are built far out to sea, often on the edge of fringing coral reefs, where they can run their own lives with little interference from government officials, and where there are plenty of fish!

A *JUKUNG* FROM BALI

ANYONE who's been to Bali for a holiday has seen and probably sailed one of these. The *jukung* is a fast double outrigger built for fishing and fun in sheltered waters. It's a dugout made from a single tree (a quick-growing softwood called *belalu*) with outriggers made of bamboo. In the stern it has the traditional Indonesian quarter-rudder, like a prau, and a natural forked branch, partly to hold the rudder and partly as a storage rack for spare masts and spars. It is painted regularly to prevent rot.

Facts and figures

Length: 6.9 metres
Width: 0.46 metres
Depth: 0.73 metres
Sail: crabclaw or
oceanic lateen
Length of outriggers:
10 metres
Overall width including
outriggers: 4.88 metres
Time to build: 6 months

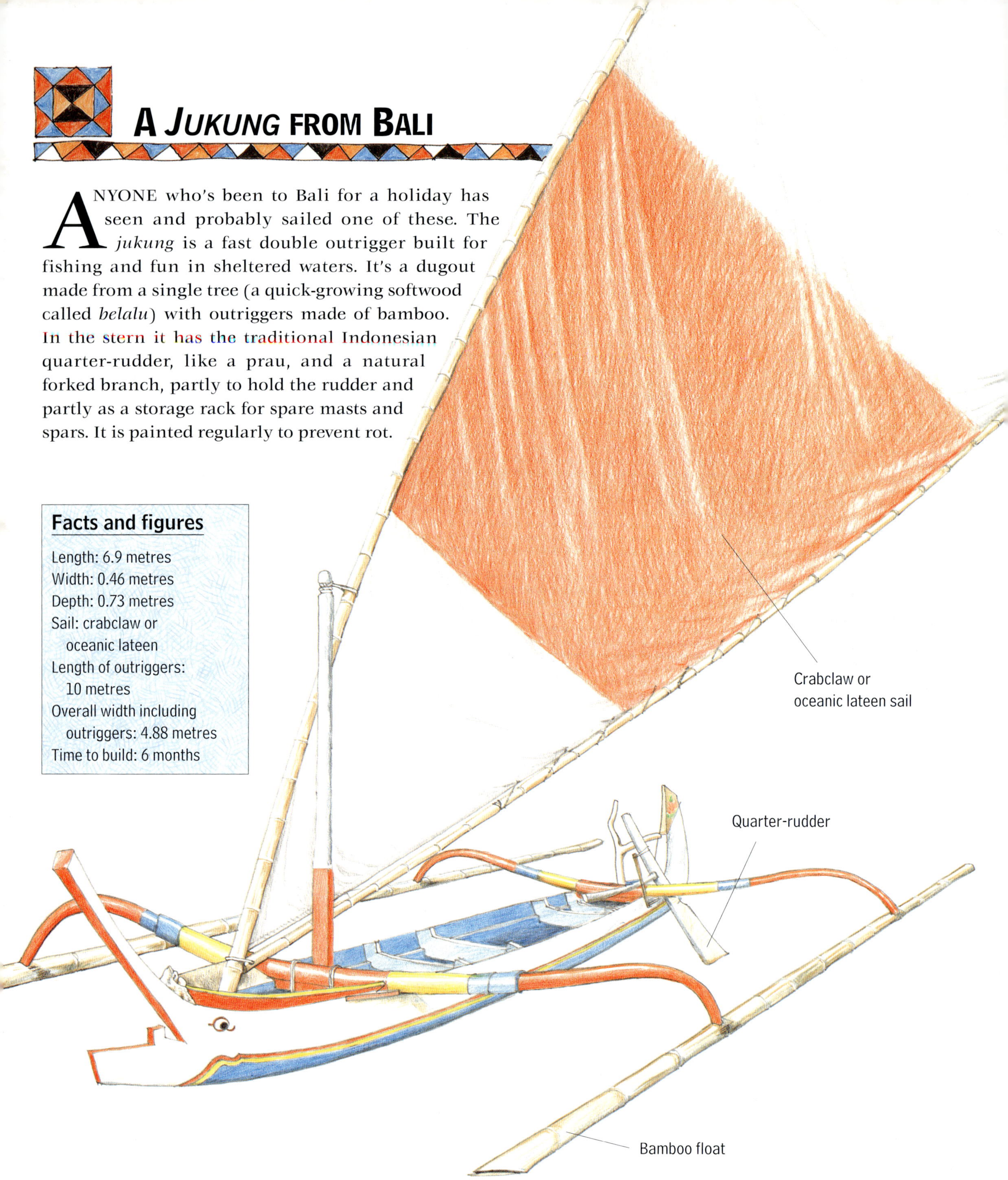

Glossary

adze tool for flattening and smoothing the surface of wood

algae seaweed and other water plants

anchor heavy object used to moor a boat, to keep it in one spot

bamboo giant woody grass with a hollow jointed stem

bail scoop water out of a boat

boom a pole with one end fixed, used to hold the bottom edge of a sail

bow front end of a boat

canoe narrow keel-less boat, pointed at both ends, propelled by paddles or a sail

catamaran boat with two hulls, side by side

caulking waterproofing material used to fill gaps between boards in a boat

cover strip thin piece of wood used to cover the joint between two boards

cyclone violent storm with strong winds

dhow Middle Eastern sailing ship with lateen sail

dowel headless pin, usually wooden, used to hold two pieces of wood together

dugout canoe a canoe made by hollowing out a log

float a small floating log fixed to the ends of several poles or booms sticking out from a canoe. Float and booms together make an outrigger

gourd dried and hollowed-out shell of a pumpkin, pawpaw or similar fruit and vegetable, used as a bottle or container

hull the outer shell of a boat or ship (not including masts, sails, cabins)

jibe to change direction in a sailing boat with the wind behind you

jukung outrigger canoe from Java or Bali

junk flat-bottomed Chinese sailing vessel with sails stiffened by wooden battens

keel the 'backbone' of a boat – a strong piece of wood running from bow to stern underneath the boat. The hull is built on this

lashing tying together with cord or rope

lime green citrus fruit, like a lemon

mast long upright pole that holds sails up

navigation a system for working out how to get somewhere

outrigger a light frame or float extending out from the side of a canoe to make it more stable

prau Indonesian sailing vessel

quarter-rudder rudder fixed to one side near the back of a boat instead of right at the back in the middle

rigging ropes used to control masts, booms and sails

rudder wide, flat piece of wood or metal attached to the back of a boat, used for steering

sails

scarf joint a strong joint between the ends of two pieces of wood, made by cutting them at an angle

stern the back of a boat

strake a plank fixed to the sides of a boat to make them higher and stop water splashing in

tack to change direction while sailing against the wind

trade wind consistent, predictable winds that always blow at certain seasons in the tropics

wash-strake see *strake*

INDEX

Printed in the USA
CPSIA information can be obtained
at www.ICGtesting.com
LVHW061940100324
774010LV00015B/209

9 798890 219923

I AM WITH YOU ALWAYS

(The Sequel)

I AM WITH YOU ALWAYS

(The Sequel)

PHYLLIS PRITCHARD

ISBN: 979-8-89021-991-6 eBook

ISBN: 979-8-89021-992-3 PaperBack

ISBN: 979-8-89021-993-0 HardBack

In loving memory of Mary Ellen Frusher
from her entire family who number many.
This book is for you Mom.

January 27, 2002

St. Mary's Hospital

Milwaukee, Wisconsin

"Kat, did you see that adorable doctor who just walked by in the hallway?" questioned Maggie, hoping to avert Kat's attention for a moment and add a little humor to the conversation for her sister's sake.

"Um, for God's sake, Maggie, I am a little bit busy here, and I don't give a damn who's in the hallway. How long will this go on anyway? I can't take too much more of it," groaned Kat.

"Depends."

"On what?"

"The baby. He'll come out when he's good and ready. and not a moment sooner," declared Maggie. "Oh swell. If he's as stubborn as his father was, he's going to take his good natured time then," bemoaned Kat. "How many hours has it been now, Maggie?"

"Six. And for goodness sake, calm down. Take in deep breaths and blow them out slowly like we practiced," Maggie ordered.

"Maggie, in case you haven't noticed, I have been doing just that for the last six hours and five minutes now. How in the hell did you manage to go through this torture when you had your three kids?"

"It got easier with each birth. By the time Chad came along, he came out so fast after my water broke, that if Marshall and I would've been a couple of minutes later arriving at the hospital, he would've landed on the sidewalk head first. This is a wondrous event with bringing a baby into the world. Stop the complaining so you can remember it for what it's truly worth," suggested Maggie.

"Easy for you to say since I'm doing all the work here. You want to trade places with me and then tell me how 'wondrous' this 'event,' as you call it, really is? I thought all women forgot what the pain was like anyway?" questioned Kat.

"They pretty much do, but they do remember the moments leading up to and after the birth. At least I did," Maggie explained.

Maggie, with a grin on her face, decided that her best bet was to keep her mouth shut for the time being, considering the mood her sister was in. She took the time to reflect on all that had happened to Kat leading up to the present time. To think that her sister had four angels living with her, and one was a general in God's army of warrior angels named David, the father of her son, who was almost ready to be born now. As Kat related the story to her many months ago, it seems David was sent to earth from God to inform Kat that she was to write a book for him, telling the world of catastrophic events that would occur if mankind did not change their ways. David was to protect her from demons whose job it was to prevent Kat from writing that book anyway they could. And to think her baby sister had to keep this all to herself until the time was right to tell her!

"Maggie, ah Maggie? Are you still with me here?"

"Yes, Kat, of course," replied Maggie, who was still partly in her own little world of daydreaming. "What's up?" she quipped.

"Funny! I thought you were supposed to be my backup here and say soothing words of comfort in my time of chaos," grumbled Kat.

"Chaos, Kat?"

"I couldn't think of a more appropriate word at the moment for the condition I'm in."

"Maybe try the word 'labor.' That, I think, would sum it up pretty accurately."

"Please don't start making me laugh. I might get the breathing thing and the laughing thing mixed together and then what would happen?" Kat asked.

"Never know. Little David might come out sooner just to see what all the commotion is about," answered Maggie.

Kat was in labor for another four hours before little David decided it was time to be a part of the world. He took his first breath along with two loud wails to let everyone know that he has arrived, which scared Kat to no end. "Maggie, why is he crying? He's not supposed to cry until the doctor slaps him on his behind. So why is he crying, Maggie?" wailed Kat in near hysterics.

"Kat, take it easy. Some newborns do come out crying, and from what I hear, little David sure has a good set of lungs."

"He's okay then?"

"Yes, Kat, he looks fine. The nurse will tell you herself after she checks him over. Don't worry."

After the routine procedures of cleaning him up, clearing his throat, weighing him and measuring his height, and, of course, taking his footprints, which were carried out by the attending nurse, she put a diaper on him and wrapped him in a receiving blanket. As a final touch, she put on a little blue cap to cover his head. He was now ready to lay in his mother's waiting arms.

"Ms. O'Brien," said the nurse, "your baby is a normal, healthy boy." She gently handed Kat her son.

One look at his face brought back the exact image that David had showed her before he had to leave: what their son would look like when born. Seeing the same wavy black hair and blue eyes as his father had brought tears streaming down her face.

"Isn't he beautiful? And he is the spitting image of his father just like he told me he would be," gushed Kat.

"Yes, he is. Maybe a little more wrinkled than his father was, but he sure is, without a doubt his father's son," laughed Maggie.

Maggie understood what was going on in her sister's mind, so she decided to leave mother and son alone to get acquainted. She returned to Kat's room about a half hour later and found little David sound asleep and his mother looking down at his face in awe. "Oh Maggie, it's over and he's fine. Thank God on both counts," stated Kat, with a wide grin of pride on her face.

Just then a nurse walked in and questioned with a raised eyebrow, "Ms. O'Brien, do you plan to nurse your son?" Kat didn't miss the gesture with the eyebrow and was in too good of a mood to take offense, because she is a Miss, so just answered with a curt "no" and left it at that.

"Well, Sis, I'm going to get out of here and go home and see how my brood is doing and see if the house is still standing. Is there anything you want or need when I come back tomorrow?" questioned Maggie.

"Thanks for asking but I can't think of anything," assured Kat. Maggie leaned over to kiss David and Kat and said her good-byes and left.

Kat felt a fleeting sense of loneliness with her sister's departure and then closed her eyes from sheer exhaustion. Her quick snooze was interrupted by another nurse entering her room with a bottle. The nurse explained to her the ingredients and the name of the formula and then instructed her on how to hold the bottle and burp the baby after every two ounces. She was a natural at all of the tasks, which gave her a little bit better sense of security with the care of her son.

She was talking to her son when a voice said, "Hi, Honey, how are you feeling?" She looked up to see her mother standing there with a big balloon with the word *newborn* on it in one hand and holding an overly stuffed teddy bear in her other arm.

"Mom, I didn't expect you to come until later tonight."

"I cancelled my outing as soon as I heard the good news, and I came right over. I certainly wasn't going to miss seeing my newborn grandson before he left the hospital. Maggie said that everything went pretty well."

"Not bad," chuckled Kat.

"Let me get a good look at little David. May I hold him?"

"Of course, Mom, but watch his head."

"Kat, I gave birth to you, Maggie, and your two brothers, so I think I know what I'm doing."

"I know you do, Mom. Sorry I said that. Guess I'm getting a little paranoid from lack of sleep."

"Oh Kat! I'm not saying this because he's my grandson, but he is beautiful. Evidently he does look just like his father, like Maggie said, because he sure doesn't resemble any of us."

"Maggie told you about David?"

"Yes, she did. Heaven forbid if I'd get the whole story from you with being as closed mouth as you are. It would be a cold day in hell first, before I got all of the facts from you, Katherine."

Mom only calls me Katherine when she's upset with me, surmised Kat, *and this must be one of many times that she is.* "Look, Mom, I was really going to tell you everything, but the time was just not right with all that has been going on in my life."

"I know, Honey. Maggie told me about the entire ordeal. You're not angry with her now that I know are you?"

"No, Mom, I'm not angry at all. I'm too excited about that little guy you're holding to be anything but happy."

"Good," her mother said as she handed David back to Kat. "Once you get home and settled, you'll be seeing more of me."

"I'm glad, Mom. I really am, because I've missed you."

"I've missed you too. All right, honey, I'd better be on my way, so that you can get some rest. Call me when it's convenient for you to have me over," informed her mother.

"Will do, Mom."

The nurse returned shortly after her mother's departure to take David away so that Kat could get the proper rest that she needed.

"Where are you taking him?" questioned Kat, with a trace of sheer panic in her voice.

"Don't worry, Ms. O'Brien, I'm taking him to the nursery where the other babies are kept. He will be fine. You need to get some sleep now. You've had a long, exhausting day."

"Yes, I know you're right," yawned Kat. "Please take good care of my baby, will you?"

"Of course, Ms. O'Brien. Don't worry. He's in good hands."

Kat was down for the count practically before her head hit the pillow.

Kat was waiting for Maggie to come and pick her up. She wandered over to her hospital window and looked out in amazement at the winter wonderland before her eyes. A fresh layer of snow blanketed the already four inches of snow on the ground. With the sun's rays shining down, it looked like little diamond sparkles dancing on the newly fallen snow. The old St. Mary's hospital across the street lent a beautiful background with the small, round green wreaths with the candles in the center, placed in every window facing the street. She remembered going with her mother to see her grandmother there as a teenager. She remembered walking up the grand staircase leading to the second floor and walking into the room where her grandmother lay, and noticing the built in fireplace against one of the walls. It was something to see, in her eyes, because she really appreciated the craftsmanship and the old oak wood of days gone by. The

entire complex was breathtaking. Whenever she looked at the beautiful North Tower lighthouse across from St. Mary's, it was as if she traveled back in time to an era with horses and buggies and the old glorious mansions so well known on the east side of the city. How wonderful it would be if she could go back in time, if only for a week, to see for herself the wonders of living before the turn of the century, she thought.

Kat arrived home with Maggie and David in tow after spending two days in the hospital.

"Are you sure you're up to seeing Marshall and the boys later on today?" asked Maggie. "All four of them can't wait to see David."

"Of course, it's fine. I have to start somewhere with sharing my baby with others. It might as well be right away today. You know, Maggie, I was thinking while in the hospital, remember how I used to call David, 'Davy'?"

"I sure do, and it irritated the hell out of him," Maggie recalled.

"That was my intention," chuckled Kat. "Anyway, so that there is no confusion with which David we are talking about, I was thinking that maybe we all should call the baby Davy. What do you think?"

"Sounds all right with me. Matter of fact, I'd prefer it that way," confirmed Maggie.

"Of course, down the road, I'll then have to figure out at what age we stop calling him Davy and go back to David."

"That's a long way off yet, Kat."

"I can't tell you how grateful I am that you have chosen to stay with Davy and me for a couple of weeks, so that you can show me the ropes. That should give me enough time to get into the swing of things."

"No need to thank me. I'm more than thrilled to help with Davy. It's been a long time since I've been around a baby. I'm so going to enjoy this," Maggie informed her.

"By the looks of the kitchen, Maggie, I'm all set to do whatever a person has to do to take care of a baby."

"It's a lot, Kat, but you do need a lot of things to take care of a newborn. I know from experience with going through it three times."

"How did you ever manage with three boys only two years apart? It had to be pretty hard. Of course, you had Marshall to help you."

"It was hard at first until I got myself into a routine. That's the whole secret to success with babies. As far as Marshall was concerned, he was absolutely useless."

"What do you mean useless?" Kat questioned.

"He didn't hold or touch any of the boys until they were about six months old. He had this strange notion in his head that they were all made of porcelain, and if he held any of them and accidentally dropped one, they would break. Don't get me wrong, after they were six months old, he got over his phobia and was a good father and couldn't do enough to help me with them," enlightened Maggie.

"I never knew that about Marshall," noted Kat.

"That's because we didn't want to spread it around. He's still a little sensitive of the subject even now," finished Maggie.

Kat gave Davy a bath, which she admitted later to Maggie that it was one of the top scariest things that she ever had to do. With Maggie continuing to look on and giving directions when needed, Kat dressed and gave Davy a bottle and lay him down for a nap.

"You did fine, Kat."

"Do you really think so? You're not just saying it to make me feel good about myself?"

"No, you're a natural," Maggie responded.

Later, there was a knock at the door and before Kat could get to it, it opened. She heard a very familiar voice say, "Can we come in?" It was Marshall and the three boys. "We didn't want to ring the doorbell and take the chance of waking up the baby, but we didn't have to worry, because the door was left unlocked," stated Marshall.

"That's alright if you would have, because he's awake," answered Kat, realizing that from now that she wouldn't be so careless with the front door.

"Now be careful, boys! He's just a little baby so don't touch him unless Aunt Kat says you can," ordered Maggie.

"Look, Mom!" exclaimed Chad, Maggie's youngest son. "He grabbed my finger and isn't letting go. He's got quite a grip there for a baby."

"Alright, all of you, back up and give Kat some breathing room," commanded Maggie. "Chad, you come over here by me and give Timothy and Chris a chance to look at him," Maggie ordered again.

"Ah gee, Ma! He didn't want to let go of my finger yet, and you made me move away," argued Chad.

"He grabbed your finger by accident, you dork. Babies can't see when they're first born," interrupted Timothy, the second born of the three boys. He nuzzled his way in next to his aunt Kat. "Uh, he's really little and kind of wrinkled," surmised Timothy.

"All babies are little and wrinkled when first born," said Chris. "If you laid for nine months in the same position, you wouldn't look so smooth either, little brother. He is handsome, Aunt Kat, and I'm not about to call a boy beautiful like my mom does," stated Chris with a wide grin of pride on his face.

"Alright, boys, back away and let me have a real good look at my new nephew. Can I hold him, Kat?" asked Maggie.

"Of course you can hold him," agreed Kat as she carefully handed him over.

"Oh my! You are beautiful," repeated Maggie.

"Handsome, Ma! Not beautiful," retaliated Chris.

"Oh look, Kat! He grabbed my finger too," she noticed. "Well, little guy, you finally made it, and you do your father proud to be sure. He has to know you're here," exclaimed Maggie.

"He knows," assured Kat.

As Maggie handed Davy back to his mother, Maggie's husband Marshall came over to see his new nephew.

"Would you like to hold him, Marshall?" questioned Kat.

"No, I don't think so. Maybe later when he's a lot bigger. It's been a lot of years since I held my sons, and I don't want to hurt him by trying."

Kat turned to Maggie and gave her a quick wink.

"And so far, no one has asked what you plan to name him or have you already?" asked Marshall.

"Yes, I have, Marshall. His name is David after his father. David Michael Gabriel Thomas O'Brien."

"That is really quite appropriate," stated Maggie, knowing full well the importance that the four angels had been in Kat's life.

"Well, Kat, now that my brood has gone home, what should we do while Davy is still taking a nap?"

"I started the book again about three months ago, because I figured it was about time that I got back to it."

"Alright! How far have you gotten with it?"

"Three more chapters."

"Well, three is good. Actually, that's not bad. One chapter a month sounds about right to me," informed Maggie.

"No, it's not, Maggie, and you know it. But thanks for trying to cover up your disappointment."

"My hesitation was not, because I'm disappointed in you. You have had quite an unusual life for the past year, to say the least. I wouldn't have been able to write one chapter, let alone three, after all you have been through," Maggie confirmed.

Kat led Maggie to a little alcove off of her living room where she set up her computer and two small filing cabinets. One for "accepted" material and one for "don't know yet" material.

"How's it going then?" questioned Maggie.

"Here. Read for yourself and then tell me what you think. You have to be honest with me, Maggie, or everything could turn out disastrous. I might think a sentence or a certain word sounds good and you could think it's awful. You could have the correct opinion, but unless you are willing to tell me the truth as to how you see it, it goes in the book 'as is.' Here's all six chapters, so that you can refresh your memory with the first three that we started together six months ago," Kat enlightened her.

As Maggie sat down on the sofa in the living room, Kat went into the kitchen to make a fresh pot of coffee. She still drank an abundant share of it, but in her defense, she never took up smoking again. David told her that she never would, and so far he was right. Kat had to chuckle to herself with the memory of her smoking habits. It was getting to the point that every new move that she made, she lit up. That might be a little exaggerated but not by much. David was right when he told her that she was a chain smoker. *Unbelievable how a small object like a cigarette could dictate a person's life to such a powerful degree*, she thought. As she returned to the living room with two cups in hand, Maggie was just putting the script back into the folder.

"Thanks, Kat."

"Well?" Kat asked.

"I think it's really good so far. There are a few words that I might have said differently, but other than that, I think you have a good script. We can go over it together. Two heads are better than one you know," informed Maggie.

Kat took the script and put it down on the coffee table.

"Have you thought of a title for the book yet?"

"I was thinking of calling it *The Angel And The Redhead*. What do you think?"

After a few seconds went by, Maggie said, "I like it, and it is appropriate since David was an angel and you are a redhead. Yes, I really do like it."

"Well, I'll stick with that title unless we can come up with something different that we like better," assured Kat.

"Kat, are you all right?"

"Yes, why?"

"You have that look in your eyes that tells me you have a concern. What is it?"

"Unbelievable how you can dissect me in just about every situation," laughed Kat.

"Practice," Maggie told her.

"Want another cup of coffee, Maggie?"

"Yes, please."

"Let's go into the kitchen where we can sit at the table and talk," suggested Kat. "I don't know if I can write this book. Look how long it has taken me to write six chapters."

"It never ceases to amaze me how strong you can be one minute and then, with the blink of an eye, turn everything around into negative thinking, Kat."

"I never asked for any of this responsibility. Sometimes I wonder how I'm going to accomplish all of the things God wants me to do, when I can't even handle the confusion and doubts that I face almost on a daily basis."

"Maybe you're right. But if it were me, I'd take this as an honor and a privilege. He chose you. Think of that, Kat. Just you and no one else in this whole wide world to do his bidding."

"I know you're right, Maggie."

"Maybe you have writer's nerves," suggested Maggie.

"What in the world do you mean by that?"

"I'm not quite sure myself. Maybe you don't have any confidence in yourself, thus you can't write this book the way you think it should be written. Okay, Kat. What else is it? Afraid you don't have enough education in your background, or that you won't use the proper words to get your message across?"

"Maybe."

"That's what the dictionary is for. Look up a word and see if there's a better word to use in its place, if that's what you are worried about. Fancy, eloquent words that no one knows the meaning of, unless they have the dictionary handy to look them up as they go along, is not your style. Write the way that makes you comfortable with yourself and from the heart. Don't fret when an idea doesn't come to you for a day or two or maybe even longer. It will eventually come to you."

"Why are you so sure of that, Maggie?"

"Because the proof is in the pudding, and God wants it that way. That's how I know."

"You're just surmising what God wants or doesn't want."

"Maybe. But in this case, I don't think so, Kat."

"In the pudding, huh? Why not in a fruitcake or chicken soup or maybe even in the—"

"I see what you're getting at," interrupted Maggie with a laugh. "And I have no clue whatsoever why it's in the pudding," she further acknowledged.

"Thank you," stated Kat.

"For what?"

"For helping me get myself off of my 'feeling sorry for myself' kick. I've been on one for quite some time now. It was nice being away from here for even a few days, because I wasn't bothered," she informed Maggie.

"What do you mean?" Maggie wanted to know.

"The demons."

"You haven't talked to me about them for so long that I took it for granted that they disappeared," Maggie stated.

"Nope. They're still with me and always will be until I die."

"You're starting to scare me, Kat."

"Sorry, Maggie. I didn't mean to."

"Now it's your turn to be completely honest with me, Kat. I can't help you if I'm left in the dark about what is going on."

"I know. I kept things from you in the past, because I wasn't allowed to tell you and then when I could, I didn't, because I didn't want to frighten you. And I'm still doing it," explained Kat.

"I'm willing to take the chance of being scared in order to help you in anyway I can. You know that, Kat."

"I know, Maggie. And from now on, I will tell you everything. I promise."

"Please don't tell me that they are still trying to kill you like they did in the past?" Maggie questioned with a calm demeanor, but dread in her heart with the fear of what Kat's answer would be.

"Ever since they killed me and David brought me back to life, they have not been allowed to touch me physically again, but they can say and do anything they want to in order to drive me stark-raving mad. That's their goal, Maggie."

After Kat hesitated for a split second, she knew that she had to tell her sister everything about her future and her son's future if she expected help—and she needed help. There was no way she could handle that future by herself and besides, she was told that Maggie would be there with her and for her in that future.

"Well, Kat. Maybe you're wrong and just maybe we can come up with a solution or some way to stop them. Maybe I could put a scare into them. I'm more than capable and very willing to do it."

"No, Maggie. That won't work, because you'll make them even angrier and more agitated, and then there's no telling what they will do to retaliate."

"I see. They can constantly torment you when they want to, but you have no recourse to turn the tables back on them, Kat?"

"Exactly. I was told to handle them by just saying 'no' and then say the Lord's Prayer and try harder to think of something else to block them from my thoughts."

"Mind over matter then?" Maggie wanted to know.

"Kind of, yes."

"Does it work?"

"Most of the time but not always. They try almost constantly to sidetrack me by interfering with my thoughts and choosing what they want me to think," declared Kat.

"These so-called spirits are very good at what they do then?"

"Yes, definitely."

"Do you know how many are around you at any given time? Say, right now?"

"No, Maggie. Could be one or ten or even more. I never know."

"What do they really want from you, or better yet, what are they trying to accomplish by always goading you?"

"For one, to try and prevent me from writing this book. And to think that I always thought David was totally annoying," chuckled Kat.

"I think you may have just found your answer on how to deal with these bas—"

"Demons, Maggie," interrupted Kat quickly.

"Oh yes, demons," replied Maggie with clenched teeth.

"How?"

"With a sense of humor. I doubt if they know how to deal with something like that. Maybe even sing a song or start laughing when they are at their worst. Throw them off balance and don't let them know just how much they are bothering you, or that you fear them. They probably feed on that," concluded Maggie.

"I have no fear for myself anymore, but I do fear what they may try to do to my son now that he is born."

"What do you mean by your son? Why would they want to harm an innocent little baby like Davy?"

"I'm not sure. I do know that David told me that our son would be a general of an army that would fight against the Antichrist. So maybe it's not only for the book itself but also for that reason. That's why I

have to learn to decipher between what they put into my head and what are actually my thoughts that I'm thinking and then figure out which is which."

"What do you mean?" Maggie asked.

"I have actually written three pages of nothing but garbage that they snuck into my thoughts. I'm getting better at detecting their tricks though, but I have to learn not to be so gullible."

"I don't think it has so much to do with being gullible but rather more like a little insecure with your abilities or doubts in yourself as to just how much you can deal with," analyzed Maggie.

"Maybe you're right."

"Well, Kat. I have that dentist appointment later this afternoon like I told you about earlier. I suppose I had better start getting ready to go. I really feel guilty about leaving you and Davy alone so soon. I tried to cancel after you had Davy and set up a new appointment, but they are booked solid for months, and they wouldn't be able to get me in again until—"

"Go," interrupted Kat. "And don't worry about Davy and me. We'll be just fine."

"I should only be gone for about an hour and a half at the most. You can call me on my cell phone if something comes up, okay?" Maggie suggested.

"I will, Maggie. Take your time, and if there's anything else that you need to do, go ahead and do it. You don't have to sit with us twenty-four hours a day. Besides, Davy should be awake shortly, and I'll be busy with him anyway."

Kat tiptoed into Davy's room to see how her son was doing. He was laying in his bassinette looking so peaceful. She laid on her side on her bed and propped up her pillow with her head resting on her hand to get a

better look at him. As she stared at her son, tears began to form in her eyes and she whispered, “Oh, David, our son is so beautiful. A miniature of you, whom I will love for the rest of my life, just as I love you and always will. He is the living bond between us, my love, and I will thank you every day for giving our son to me.”

Kat felt a strong sense of not being alone when a voice whispered to her, “Hello, Mistress Kat. It is I, Michael.”

“Oh, Michael, is it truly you?” questioned Kat, somewhat startled.

“Yes, Mistress Kat.”

“Is Gabriel with you also?”

“No. He was needed elsewhere and was told to stay behind this time. I am the one God chose to start guarding Master Davy when he is born. He is a handsome little fellow, to be sure, and a mirror image of the General when he was born.”

“You were there in Heaven when David was born?”

“Oh yes. I was there. It was my duty as an Archangel to watch over him for as long as I was needed.”

“Until he had to leave us, you mean?”

“Yes, Mistress Kat, until then.”

“I have really missed you, Michael. How long have you been with us, and why didn’t you let me know sooner that you were here?”

“I have been with you all the time, like it was planned, before the General left us, but I did not let you know. As long as the demons could not hurt you, I was to stay in the background and look after you.”

“Michael, will you please follow me into the kitchen where we can talk instead of whispering?”

"Of course."

As Kat sat down at the kitchen table, Michael replied to both of her questions. "I was here the minute that little Davy was born, but I didn't want to interrupt the joyous moments you were having with your family."

"You know, Michael, I love you and Gabriel dearly, and I would not have made it through the hard time I had when David left, if it hadn't been for the two of you."

"Thank you for the kind compliment, but I think you underestimate the courage and stamina that it took for you to go on. I know how much you still love the General. Knowing you were with his child certainly did more wonders for you than anyone could have imagined, and the General knew that that would be the case."

"Do you really think so?"

"Yes, I know for certain that he knew that you would be a wonderful mother to his son in every way. I truly think that, and the fact that he loved you deeply, helped him to deal with knowing he had to leave you, Mistress Kat."

Kat, with a terrible dread that came over her with the usage of the past tense of the word *love*, became nearly hysterical. "Michael, you said 'loved.' Does that mean that David is dead? Please don't tell me, Michael, that he is."

"Oh, Mistress Kat, I did not mean to imply that the General is dead. Please forgive me. I did not mean to distress you in anyway."

"Then he is alive?"

"Yes, Mistress Kat, the General is still alive."

"Have you seen him since he left here?"

"No, we have had no contact with each other since then."

"But, Michael, you said before that you and David were very close and that you saw each other a lot."

"That has changed, Mistress Kat, since—"

"Since the Counsel found out about the two of us," interrupted Kat.

"Yes," was all Michael had to say. Kat felt the uneasiness coming from Michael and knew he did not like talking about that incident regarding David to her.

"Michael, would you please do me a favor?"

"If it's at all possible, yes, of course I will."

"When you see God and talk to him, please tell him for me that David has been on my mind constantly. There hasn't been a day that has gone by since he left that I haven't thought about him."

"He knows, Mistress Kat. The Heavenly Father knows everything."

"Then he must know that a true love only comes along once in a lifetime. I was blessed by him when he sent David to me, and I pray to him everyday asking that he keep David alive on the other side. Because, Michael, if David is not there when my life finally ends, I don't want to exist without him. I pray to God everyday that in his infinite wisdom and forgiveness, that he will follow David and me to be together for eternity. But if that is not possible in his eyes, and if I have a choice, eternity will not be for me."

He was stunned by her directness. *She truly does love the General even more than anyone of us knew,* thought Michael.

Kat was about to prepare supper while still conversing with Michael, who was sitting at the kitchen table. She was just starting to peel potatoes while the pot roast that Maggie had made earlier was warming in the oven, when Michael jumped from the chair that he was sitting on and told her, "I sense demons in the backyard. Stay close to Master Davy!"

Before she could reach Davy's bedroom, she heard a high-pitched, piercing cry emitting from his bedroom that had a sharp and vivid effect on her senses. As she reached the door, which was ajar, and hit it open further with such force that it slammed against the wall, she ran to Davy's crib and was horrified as to what she saw. A large house cat was lying down across Davy's face. She started tugging at it but to no avail. With leaving the kitchen in such a state of panic, she didn't realize, at first, that she still had the paring knife in her hand. She took the knife and plunged it fiercely into the back of the cat. Nothing. She did it a second time with more force, and the cat vanished into thin air. Kat picked up her terrified son, who was gasping for air, and cradled him in her arms. She started to say soothing words to him, which helped to gradually return his breathing to normal. He started to cry uncontrollably, so she walked with him and continued swaying him in her arms, humming a tune while tears streamed down her face. With the combination of all the things that she was doing, Davy's crying started to subside and eventually slowed considerably, and she didn't let herself think of what could have happened, if she were even a few seconds later in getting there.

As she started out of the bedroom with Davy still nestled in her arms, Michael asked, "Is the little one alright?"

Kat had a hard time trying to converse, because she was still so distraught over what just happened, but answered, "Yes, Michael. He seems to be all right now, but he is still terribly frightened. It was them, the demons, wasn't it? But how? Or did a cat get into the house somehow without me seeing it?"

"No, Mistress Kat. It wasn't a real cat, but one of them turned into a cat."

"I don't understand. They have always been invisible, but this animal was real. When I stabbed it the first and second time, I hit something solid. It was a form not just thin air."

"It was real, Mistress Kat."

"But how? How can that be? It just doesn't make sense."

"They can change into any form that they wish to. They just haven't done it before and always stayed invisible. There were ten in the backyard, which was a diversion that lasted long enough for me to handle, so that the one could get to Master Davy."

"Another diversion, huh? It was a diversion that caused me to die, remember, Michael?" snapped Kat, not realizing how sarcastic her tone of voice was until she realized what she had just said. "Oh, Michael, I'm so sorry. None of this was your fault. Please forgive me," begged Kat.

"I understand, Mistress Kat. There is no reason to apologize. No mother should have gone through what you just did."

"Oh my God, Michael. How are we going to protect him if there are too many of them for us to handle, and they can change into anything they want to be?"

"Please calm down, Mistress Kat, and I will explain. I have the power to destroy any amount of them. Be it one or fifty, it does not matter how many. They have now made themselves known and what they are here for. They also know that they will never be able to divert me again. I will now stay with Davy at all times and never leave his side. They cannot harm him as long as I am with him, and I will be with him from now on."

"But this is his first day home, and they tried to kill him. That will mean my son will have to be guarded for who knows how long. Maybe until he dies."

"Please, come into the kitchen with me, and I will explain. After this incident, it is now time for you to know and understand how all of this pertains to Master Davy."

As Kat followed Michael, Davy began to calm down completely and was even starting to fall back to sleep. She continued to sway back and forth with soothing motions. As she sat down at one of the kitchen chairs with Davy still in her arms, Michael started to explain. "Remember,

Mistress Kat, when we went for a walk together, and I told you about the General starting his training as a warrior angel at the age of seven?"

"Yes, Michael, I remember. But what does that have to do with what just happened here with Davy?"

"Everything. You see, Mistress Kat, your son was chosen by the Heavenly Father to fight the armies of the Antichrist before and until the end of Armageddon. He will be a great general, and the youngest one in history."

Before Kat answered, she looked down at her sleeping son with an overwhelming sense of relief that he was safe in her arms. "Yes, I know all of that. Before he had to leave, David told me in the letter that he wrote to me."

"What else did the General tell you?"

"He told me that I must have him baptized in the Waters of Life at the age of seven. I told him that I would have him baptized by Father Daniels at my church, but he told me it was not enough. When I questioned him why, he asked me to promise him that I would do it, and when the time came, I would understand why it was so necessary."

"Yes. You see, Mistress Kat, not only do the warrior angels start their training at age seven, but they must also be baptized in the Waters of Life at that age."

"But why? What is so important about the Waters of Life, and what does that have to do with Davy? He certainly isn't going to start training to be a general at the age of seven."

"No, of course not. Not down here. But he will be a general for the Heavenly Father and must be baptized in order to receive divine intervention," he further explained.

"You're starting to lose me here, Michael. Divine intervention means what?"

"The Heavenly Father will intercede and give young Davy his divine protection. After he is baptized, no one, and I mean no one, will ever be able to harm him again."

"Even the demons?"

"Especially the demons," he assured her

"Let me get this straight. Davy will be protected after he is baptized but until then, we have to protect him."

"Correct."

"So from now on, until he is baptized, they will continue to do their best to kill my son?"

As Michael hesitated, Kat said, "Please, Michael, tell me everything you know. As his mother, I have a right to know everything."

"Yes, Mistress Kat, you do. They will attempt to kill Master Davy again. But we will never know how many times, when or how, until they try again."

"Oh, Michael. If it involved just me, I could learn to handle and deal with it, but being my son…I just don't know."

"You must have faith and trust in the Almighty One, Mistress Kat. That is what will help you to deal with all of this. Trust me."

"I trust you, Michael, and I know you are right about God, but this is my son, and I feel so helpless. What about David? Now that this has happened to his son, surely God will let him return again and help us?"

"No, Mistress Kat. The General will not be allowed to return, no matter what."

Kat felt so dejected, lonely, and drained of emotion, even though she knew that she had to fight back and do everything that she could do to keep her son from harm. Just as she was about to enter the living room, she heard Maggie coming in through the door in the kitchen.

"Hi. It's me. Is anybody around?"

"Hi, Maggie. Yes, I'm coming."

"You know, Kat, I'd rather go and see a doctor any day than to the dentist. I'm later than what I thought I'd be even with just having my teeth cleaned and one cavity worked on. I went in looking and feeling fine, and now I look like I've been in a fight with no feeling in my mouth or lips. Kat, what's wrong?" slurred Maggie after seeing the look on her sister's face. "You look like you've seen a ghost."

"I wish I had. It would've been a hell of a lot better than what we just went through. You want a cup of coffee?"

"No thanks. I wouldn't even be able to feel the cup. I'll wait until later. And what do you mean you wish that you would've seen a ghost, instead?"

"Sit down, Maggie, and I'll tell you everything that has happened since you left. Just like I promised I would. Remember, no secrets?"

"Yes. So what did happen while I was away? Those damn spirits again?"

"No. This time it was the demons."

"Alright, Kat, no fooling around," stated Maggie with a quiver in her voice, knowing it must have been bad by the look of her sister. "Tell me everything that happened and don't leave anything out."

As she related the dreadful experience, Maggie sat quietly with a look of rage on her face that quickly increased with the continued telling of the entire ordeal. "For God's sake, Kat. What are you going to do, or better yet, what can I do to help with all of this?"

"Just what Michael said we must do."

"What about Gabriel and that other angel that was here before? Can't they come back and help?" asked Maggie.

"Thomas," informed Kat.

"What?"

"The other angel was named Thomas."

"Right, whatever!" added Maggie.

Kat began to explain why Gabriel and Thomas couldn't help, even though she also thought that Gabriel would be here with Michael.

"Sorry, Honey. I didn't mean to sound so insensitive, but this is way beyond comprehension, and I'm so afraid for you and Davy."

"Don't be. I know it is easier said than done, but we have to keep focused and stay strong to get through this."

"Right," said Maggie, while nodding her head in disbelief. "We can do it, Kat. We just have to stick together."

She didn't sleep much that night with having to keep an eye on Davy and thinking about what should be done concerning him when it was time for her to go back to work. She and Maggie had discussed before he was born who would take care of him. Maggie, of course, kept insisting that she could handle it. But with what occurred with the demons, she didn't want to put her in harms way. They can't harm her anymore, but who was to say that they wouldn't try to do it with Maggie. She couldn't and wouldn't take the chance of that happening.

She arose from her bed, glanced at her sleeping son, grabbed her bathrobe hanging behind her bedroom door and donned her bedroom slippers. She was about to turn off the nightlight but changed her mind instead and tiptoed out of the bedroom. As she entered the living room, she could see a light shining from the kitchen.

"Good morning, Kat. Couldn't sleep either, huh?"

"Not really. I spent most of the night peering at my son to make sure everything was all right."

"The coffee is just about ready," informed Maggie."

"It's still pitch black out. What time is it anyway?" asked Kat.

"Five fifteen in the morning"

"Ugh. I'm wide awake now, and with coffee in me, I'll never get back to bed anytime soon. I'll have to take a nap this afternoon when I lay Davy down for his," yawned Kat.

"Want a doughnut, Kat?"

"I sure do."

As Maggie grabbed a box from off of the counter, Kat poured two cups of coffee and said, "Oh my goodness sake. There must be a dozen of the most tantalizing looking doughnuts that I've ever seen in there. They all look so yummy that I don't know which one to choose."

"I'm sure they do look scrumptious to someone who only has Twinkies and Snoballs lying around," Maggie laughed.

"Don't knock my choice of snacks, Maggie. They suit me just fine," chuckled Kat.

"Maggie, let's get off the subject of sweets and get serious for awhile."

"Sure. What's on your mind?"

"As I said before, I didn't sleep much last night worrying about Davy, so I had a chance to do a lot of thinking."

"As to?" Maggie wanted to know.

"About you caring for Davy after I have to go back to work."

"You don't think I'm capable of taking care of him?"

"Of course not, nothing like that. As a matter of fact, you'd be the only one I'd trust with his care."

"Then what are you getting at?" Maggie wondered.

"I don't want to put you in harms way and besides, you have Marshall and the boys to take care of. That would be a huge responsibility with just that, let alone watching a baby for more than eight hours a day."

"I'm willing to do it, Kat. Marshall and the boys are certainly old enough to take care of themselves. None of them ever wants a decent breakfast and, for dinner at night I'll make menus ahead of time and put them in the freezer, so all that they will have to do is shove it in the oven. Pretty much of a no-brainer there," confirmed Maggie.

"I know, Maggie. You're a rare breed when it comes to taking care of your family, always have been, and you'd be wonderful with Davy, but that's not the point here. I can't trust those demons to leave you alone, and I will not take that chance with you. Not you, Maggie."

"I understand your concern, Kat, but I should be all right with Michael watching Davy all the time, so why would they be interested in doing me harm?"

"David once told me that they can be very cunning and vindictive. I know you, Maggie. The first time that they try to scare you or do some ill prank on you, you'll let them have it—verbally. I was always warned not to get them agitated, because all hell could break loose. I didn't listen to David in the beginning and would swear a blue streak to get back at them, and it just made things worse. Look what one did to me while I was in the shower."

"I understand perfectly, but I want to help you in every way I can, or I'll feel totally useless," stated Maggie.

"Don't. I know you will be here for Davy and me when we need you, and you can visit every day, before I go to work if you want."

"Alright, Kat, tell me this. You don't want to put me in harms way, but yet you will knowingly let some unsuspecting woman, who has no idea what goes on in this house, come here and take care of him. Think about it. It's not right. I think you should calm down for a couple of days, and we'll talk about this again and come up with a solution."

That night while lying in bed and watching her son sleeping peacefully, Kat knew that she had to put this entire horrifying ordeal behind her and reclaim the strength that she would need to protect her son until God took over. Knowing Maggie's characteristic traits, she knew that she would never be able to talk her into anything. Actually, for sure, it would be the other way around. Maggie was right though, after she had some time to think everything over. She knew that it wouldn't be appropriate behavior on her part to put a stranger in danger either. She felt completely drained. It was time to try and get some sleep, for her son would be awake in a couple of hours. With that last thought, she slept.

Maggie heard Davy fussing from her bedroom across the hall two hours after Kat went to bed. She waited a few minutes but didn't hear any movement, so she rose from her bed, put her bathrobe and slippers on and walked quietly into her sister's bedroom. Kat was in a totally deep sleep. Maggie lifted Davy out of his crib and carried him into the kitchen where she warmed a bottle of formula. She went back into her bedroom and sat in a rocker and began to feed Davy and whispered, "Well young man, you're right on time. It's been exactly two hours since your last feeding." When all was finished, she went into Kat's bedroom and laid Davy on the changing table and changed his diaper.

As she was about to put him back into his crib, Kat, in a flash, sat straight up in her bed and looked around the room. When she saw, Maggie, she was still a little disoriented and said, "Maggie, what are you doing here? What's wrong?"

"Shhh, Kat. Nothing is wrong. You didn't hear Davy and I did, so I fed and changed him. He is back in his crib and is fine."

"Oh, Maggie! I didn't hear him. How could I have not heard him?"

"Kat, calm down. You were exhausted and still are. Go back to sleep and don't worry about Davy. I'll continue to get up with him until morning."

"But, Maggie....."

"Kat, I'm fine. If I have to, I'll take a nap tomorrow afternoon."

"Maggie, thank you. And this will never happen again. I will always hear my son from now on," assured Kat.

"I know, Sis. Now go back to sleep. You need it."

Kat awoke the next morning at eight feeling like a new woman and ready to face any challenges that might come her way. The first one would be Maggie. She had to tell her that she still did not think it was wise for her to take care of Davy and her own family. In Kat's estimation, it would be just too much of a burden on her. She checked the crib and found Davy sleeping peacefully. She dressed quickly and headed toward the kitchen where she knew she would find her, probably cooking up a storm.

"It smells unbelievably wonderful in here. What are you cooking? Or better yet, what are you up to?"

"Now, Sis, I can't imagine whatever you mean by that statement," chuckled Maggie.

"Right. I believe that about as much as I believe that the world is flat."

"I thought it was," informed Maggie. "I thought I would cook some meals ahead of time and put them in the freezer and have them ready to thaw and eat whenever we wanted them. And I made a special cake in celebration—"

"Of what?" interrupted Kat.

"Of me taking care of Davy, of course."

"Now, Maggie. We were supposed to discuss that today," recalled Kat.

"What's to discuss? It's already settled."

"But—"

"No buts about it. I am very willing and very capable of taking care of Davy and my family all at once. I see no problem with any of it."

Kat knew that she was probably wasting her time and fighting a no-win-situation, but she had to try one more time to convince Maggie that she felt it was better to hire someone outside of the family. "Listen, Maggie, I feel that it is my responsibility to—"

"I know what you're going to say," interrupted Maggie, "and I appreciate your concern about my welfare, but I am the better choice for the care of Davy regardless of the damn demons, and you know it."

"Alright, Maggie. If you're going to be stubborn about this and continue arguing with me until you're blue in the face, I have a suggestion that I think we can both agree on."

"Which is?"

"I'll agree to you taking care of Davy, if you do it on a trial basis."

"What do you mean 'trial basis'?" Maggie wondered.

"We'll go a month at a time, and if I see any wear and tear on you, because it is getting too much for you to handle, and I know you won't tell me if it is, then we call for outside help. Agreed?"

"Do I have a choice to disagree?"

"No."

"Alright then, I agree."

"Promise?" Kat asked.

"I promise, Kat."

"Oh no you don't. You have to cross your heart, just like we did when we were kids, and then I'll believe you completely."

"Alright! I promise," said Maggie as she crossed her heart as Kat requested, just like when they were kids.

Maggie was up early as usual to make sure her husband and sons Chris, Tim and Chad started the day off with a good nourishing breakfast. After they left and she was able to sit down and have a full cup of hot coffee, she thought about today being March 6 already. Her eldest son Chris would turn eighteen on March 20. It seemed like only yesterday that she held her first born son in her arms on the day that he was born, she reminisced. She thought to herself, *I had better get on the ball and start planning, because I want this birthday party to be so very special for him. Maybe Kat can help me and come up with some ideas.* Maggie decided to give her a call.

"Hi, Sis. It's me. How are you and Davy doing?"

"Just fine and you?"

"I'm okay."

"Just okay, huh? When you say it like that, it tells me something's cooking. You worried about anything?"

"No, Kat. I didn't mean to sound so negative, sorry."

"What's to be sorry about? Everyone has a right to have a bad day, but the way you just sounded, yours is evidently just starting. So what's really on your mind?" Kat questioned.

"You know that Chris will turn eighteen this month?"

"Yes, on the 20th, right?"

"Right. Eighteen is a special birthday, and I really want to make it very special for him, since he hasn't heard from the Air Force Academy yet and is down in the dumps. But as of now, I don't know what I'm going to do. Have any ideas?" Maggie asked.

"Sorry, Maggie. Off hand, I haven't got any ideas. You want to come over and we'll discuss it, and maybe between the two of us, we'll come up with a brainstorm or two?"

"You're not busy then?"

"Nothing out of the ordinary."

"Okay, Kat. I'll be over in about an hour. Is that all right with you?"

"Fine, Maggie. See you in about an hour."

Within the hour, Maggie was ringing Kat's doorbell.

"You know, Maggie," said Kat as they started for the kitchen. "To me, having a party for a girl would be a lot easier than for a guy. With girls, if you kept the number down to only her closest friends, you could have a sleepover."

"Sleepover? Don't you think that they would be a little old for that at the age of seventeen and eighteen?" wondered Maggie.

"Not really. I think girls love sleepovers no matter what their age. You could order pizza, open presents, then have cake and ice cream, and let them stay up all night talking about boys or whatever. That way, they'd entertain themselves just like we did when we were young and went to them. All you'd have to do is put up with the noise," chuckled Kat. "But since you went and had all boys, it's going to make it harder to come up with an idea."

"I know what you mean. When they were kids, all I had to do was invite some of their friends over to play some games, open presents, eat cake and ice cream, like you just said, and then send them on their way. Chris is a wee bit old for games," Maggie insisted.

"Not if it was with girls too. I made some notes and want to run them by you and see what you think," relayed Kat.

"What do you mean 'girls'? What are you up to, Kat?"

"Don't let your mind go wandering in the wrong direction, Maggie. Just hear me out and see what you think. If you don't like my idea, we'll have to come up with something else. There's always the possibility of everyone going to the indoor ice skating rink or roller skating, but maybe a few of them don't care for either, so I came up with a plan to invite only

Chris's closest friends and their girlfriends, if they have one. If not, tell them to invite a girl just like they would for prom night. They all have to be paired off for this to work, even Chris. Does he have a girlfriend right now?"

"I gave up keeping track of Chris and Tim's girlfriends a long time ago, but I can find out. Then what?" Maggie asked.

"Tell the guys to pick someone that they know of or admired from the past or from an era that they would have liked to have lived in, and have them dress according to the way that people dressed in that era. Their girlfriends would have to dress according to the era that they decide on also. You'd have to come up with a costume for Chris to put on later when he discovers what is going on. Now, what costume do you think Chris would want to wear if he had a choice?" questioned Kat.

"I don't even have to think twice on that one. Zorro, of course," answered Maggie. "He loved Zorro as a kid, and we bought him a costume for his seventh birthday. I think it was his seventh. It came complete with the black cape, hat, silk blindfold with two slits for the eyes, and of course, the sword. He was ecstatic. Took him only two days to make 'mayhem of our house,' though."

"What do you mean 'mayhem with the house'? What could a rubber sword possibly do?"

"It wasn't rubber but plastic with little teeth etched in the tip. He tried to 'Z' everything in the house before I finally caught him in the act."

"Oh no! What did the little scamp do?"

"I'm not sure what he started with, but surmised later that it may have been the toss pillows on the couch and loveseat. He then made his way to practically all the shades in the house and finally did his dastardly Z with the wallpaper in all three of the boys' bedrooms, which was the perfect thing in his eyes, because there were Z slits from top to bottom. Thank goodness that only one wall in each of the bedrooms was wallpapered. Needless to say, his Zorro days were over and he moved on to Superman, instead," laughed Maggie.

"That story is hilarious," Kat laughed.

"Now, yes. But at the time, I could have killed him when I caught him in his bedroom putting on the final touches to his wallpaper."

"So where are we supposed to have this costume birthday party at? My house?"

"Not unless you want to do all the prepping, cooking and cleanup."

"No. I'm not that gung-ho with an eighteenth birthday party."

"There are plenty of nice restaurants in the area where you can rent a room for any occasion. They will supply whatever food you want to choose, be it a meal or pizza, whatever. After the meal, have cake and ice cream and then have him open his presents. Maybe even hire a disc jockey for the entertainment, which would add a nice touch to the entire evening. It could turn out to be a lot of fun for all of them, especially the patrons in the restaurant, seeing a bunch of kids file through in costume heading to a private room. Knowing you, Maggie, you will insist on a chaperone, so let it be you and Marshall, who should also be dressed in costume to fit in with the entire theme. So what do you think?"

Maggie didn't answer Kat immediately, because she had to think about all the suggestions that she had just given her. "I don't know. With the cost of renting costumes and a present, that could turn into a lot of money that these kids would have to spend."

"I'd tell them to forget the present and only go with an inexpensive gag gift if they want to. And as far as costumes, there's a small shop that I know of, and I will give you the address where to find it. They have terrific sales on rentals during the off seasons. Kids their ages are innovative. They might even come up with their own idea for a costume. Make sure you tell Chris' girlfriend what you have for him to wear, and make sure that you also tell everybody that this is definitely a surprise party, so 'mums' the word. You and Marshall and all the kids should be at the restaurant at a certain time, and have Chris drive Tim and Chad there and arrive a half hour or so later," explained Kat further.

"Won't he wonder why we're not all going to go as a family?" Maggie questioned.

"Not if you make up a story that something came up, and you and Marshall will have to meet them there for dinner."

"You know, you might be right. It just might work and be a lot of fun for everyone involved and this way, Marshall and I won't have to worry that his eighteenth birthday could turn into a night of drinking, instead. You're going to come too, aren't you?" Maggie asked.

"No. Davy and I will come over on Sunday with Chris' presents. Make sure you take the camcorder with you for the party. We'll watch it when we come on Sunday, if that's all right with you."

"That'll work. Then he can open the presents from Marshall and me, too at that time. Thank you so much, Kat. I would never have thought of anything like this."

As it turned out, the party was a huge success, and one that Chris would never forget. There were a lot of laughs and crazy costumes, especially Marshall and Maggie's. As a comical twist, Maggie was Elmer Fudd and Marshall, of course, was Bugs Bunny. His costume was made complete by having a real carrot hanging from his mouth whenever he didn't have food in it.

The next big event for the family was to be Chris' graduation from high school on June 7. He had the foresight during the beginning of his freshman year to approach his guidance counselor in regard to his plans to join the Air Force Academy in Colorado Springs, Colorado, when he was finished with high school and ask him what he needed to do in order to attain that goal.

"I know one thing for sure," Mr. Davis told him, "you can't send out a resume of yourself requesting their acceptance. It doesn't work that way. My understanding is that you have to have the backing of one of our state's representatives, either a Congressman or a Senator to vouch for you. This means that he or she thinks that you are a worthy candidate to

meet the Academy's very tough criterion set down by their high standards of perfection. You have a 3.8 GPA up to now, and by the way, keep it at that or higher. You are one of the star players on our football team, but this alone will not get you into the Academy. I suggest that you join their JAFROTC Program, and I'll do some checking to get you in touch with the right person, because the instructor is located within one of our host high schools. He will get you started early as to what you must do until your senior year arrives. I'll get back to you when I get all the information for you."

"Thanks, Mr. Davis. I really appreciate your help."

"That's my job, Chris: helping our students the best way that I can."

Chris worked hard and studied hard throughout his four years of high school, because he was not going to let his dream, the one he had since he was a kid, of wanting to become a pilot, slip through his fingers. Prior to March 1st. and before graduation, he received athletic scholarship offers from four universities throughout the country. He had yet to hear from the Academy as to whether he was accepted, even though he did everything that was required of him.

He went back to talk with Mr. Davis. "Hang in there, Chris. The process of joining the Air Force is a lengthy one. With your background, I'd say you're a shoe-in."

Maggie would have preferred he would have chosen the University of Wisconsin, because he would be close to home, but then realized that it was his life and his dream, and that he had to follow that dream.

That night after supper, Chris went into his bedroom and spent the next couple of hours checking over all the copies that he had made of all the information that he had in regard to the requirements of enlisting into the Air Force Academy, hoping he successfully fulfilled each requirement. He started to go through all the pamphlets and booklets that his recruiting officer gave to him at their first interview and checked off each requirement that he accomplished with a red pen. After checking further, he found the

date he filled out a form sent to his Congressman and State Representative requesting nomination to the Academy. His records showed he filed his nomination with both on March 5 of his junior year and received a letter back from his Congressman on August 10 of that summer telling him of his official candidate status for admission to the Academy. That was one letter that made him sweat over the outcome until the day he received it in the mail, Chris recalled. With all the material that he had reread on the Air Force requirements, he came to the conclusion that he had a very good chance of being accepted. All he could do is wait, he realized, before he closed his last folder.

Chris received his letter of appointment from the Academy on March 27, one week past his eighteenth birthday. His dream was about to come true but only because he made it so.

Kat was due back to work after her twelve weeks of maternity leave were over. There wasn't anymore demon activity since that first day when she brought Davy home from the hospital. She arose early, so that she could spend as much quality time with her son before she had to leave.

"Oh, Maggie, my son is now three months old and I've been with him the entire time. How in the hell can I go back to work and leave him now?"

"Kat, calm down. You knew this day would come eventually, and you know he's in good hands."

"I know, but it still doesn't help. I don't know if I can get through the rest of the day and night without seeing him. Not even once."

"You're going through what every mother that works has had to go through for years. Trust me. It will be hard the first week or so, but you'll get used to it after you get back into the swing of things with your job."

"Yeah, I know you're right. Now let me run through everything with you before I go."

Maggie had to chuckle to herself. Here she was with three teenage boys, and Kat's going to tell her all that has to be done to take care of a little baby while she's gone. *I'll let her go through her instructions for her sake*, thought Maggie.

"There's six bottles of fresh formula in the fridge that I made this morning and remember to burp and change him after you feed him. Now, his diapers are on the second shelf of the changing table, along with freshly washed T-shirts and pajamas. His bibs are in the second drawer on the left side below the cupboards in the kitchen. Is there anything else I might have missed?"

Before Maggie could respond, Kat continued, "Alright, Maggie. Now this phone number is to my boss Dan's personal cell phone. I'm giving you his number, because I won't be able to hear my cell ringing over the noise of the knitting machines. In case of an emergency, call Doctor Rollins, whose number is here on the cupboard door, and then call me right away at work, okay? Have you got all of that, Maggie?"

"Yes, Kat. I understand everything and don't worry, Davy's in good hands."

"Yes, I know he is, and thank you, Maggie, for all that you have done for us," said Kat as she kissed her sister on the cheek and then her son and rushed out the door, because she had tears starting to form in her eyes. She called home during her two breaks and half hour lunch from work to check and see how Davy was doing.

The arrangement with Maggie taking care of Davy was going along smoothly, just as she told Kat it would. She left on Friday nights to return home after Kat came home from work. Kat didn't like her driving so late at night, but Maggie insisted and told her that she would be fine. She spent the weekends with her family and then came back to Kat's each early afternoon on Monday. She took Davy to her home whenever she had something extra to do during the week when Kat was at work and also to let her family see more of him. Marshall and her three boys pitched in with doing things at home: the dishes, doing their laundry, vacuuming,

and dusting—to Maggie's complete surprise. Everyone had a chore to do and did it without complaint, so that their special little nephew could have their mom staying with him.

"Hi, Maggie. It's me, Kat. I was thinking, have you, Marshall and the boys got anything planned for Memorial Day weekend?" Kat asked over the phone.

"No. Marshall will be spending the entire weekend getting caught up with negotiations, contracts, and so forth for his job, because he and I are going on that well needed vacation all by ourselves in less than a month that you and I discussed. The boys have their own plans with friends. Heaven forbid if they'd stay home on a holiday weekend with their mom and dad," complained Maggie.

"So is it still going to be a romantic getaway for just the two of you as you planned?"

"Yup. I have my see-through negligee already purchased, and, of course, a few more surprises in mind for my very stoic husband. He won't know what hit him once I get him on that ship," laughed Maggie, with a mischievous look on her face. "All I have left to do is figure out a plan to rid him of his cell phone just as we are ready to leave home, so there will be no interruptions, whatsoever. Before this ten day cruise to the Bahamas is over, he had better be so enamored of me, or I'll kick his sorry butt over the railing and into the ocean and come home alone."

"Oh, Maggie. I know Marshall loves you very much, and maybe you're right. He needs a little assistance with the ardor aspect of your marriage."

"Not a little assistance, Honey. An extremely big push is what my husband needs. Did you find someone to take care of Davy while we're gone?"

"Yes, my neighbor Sharon's younger sister Amy. She's in her third year of college, and her classes will fit in with my work schedule perfectly. I've met her only once but she seems really nice."

"So what's this about Memorial Day? You have specific plans in mind?"

"Yes, I thought if you have nothing going on that maybe you would like to take a ride with Davy and me up to Wautoma to see the cottage. We can stay the entire weekend, just overnight or, if you want, drive back on the same day. It's your call."

"I think that's a great idea. I'd love to. We can't come back the same day though, Kat. I think that would be too tiring for everyone. Wait a minute! How do you know that cottage is still for sale? It's been over a year since you were last up there with David," recalled Maggie.

"I called Helen a couple of months back and asked her if it was still for sale and it is. I made arrangements with a Ms. Karen Scholes, who is with Home Is Where The Heart Is Realty, and she will have all the documents and papers to be signed, ready and waiting for me at one o'clock on Saturday afternoon."

"Wee-bit-mushy for a real estate name," laughed Maggie. "Let's do it. It will be fun."

"Then it's settled. We'll leave early Saturday morning and kind of play it by ear, if we stay two nights or not and come back on Monday. Is that all right with you?" questioned Kat. "Sounds good to me. I think it would do all three of us good to get away for a weekend together," Maggie said.

On Thursday afternoon, Maggie came a little earlier than usual to talk with Kat about their trip to Wautoma. As Maggie walked into the kitchen, Kat was just finishing with feeding Davy. She approached Davy and plopped a big kiss on his forehead. "Afternoon, precious." She then proceeded to kiss Kat on her head and said, "Hi, Sis, excited about Saturday?"

She went to the cupboard for a cup and poured herself some coffee and sat down at the table across from Kat, waiting for an answer.

"Yes and no," answered Kat.

"And what is that supposed to mean?"

"I didn't get much sleep last night with thinking about the cottage. That was *the* most romantic six days that I spent with David, aside from the fighting that we did in between, of course."

"From what you told me afterward, I'd say 'battling' is a better word."

"I guess you're right," responded Kat with a forlorn look on her face.

"Oh, Honey. Is this trip going to be too much for you with all the memories of David?" Maggie wanted to know.

"I really don't know. But I'm sure as hell going to go anyway. I've wanted that cottage from the first time that I laid eyes on it. Just maybe it will help me to cope, knowing that at the lake is where Davy was conceived. It feels like I am actually bringing David's son back to him. That may sound really crazy, but that's the only way I can truthfully express what I feel."

"Why didn't you tell me of your plans before this?"

"You were so wrapped up with your own plans with getting Marshall to pinpoint an exact date to go on this cruise, and with all the arrangements that you had to make, I just felt that I had to wait and tell you later when I thought the time was right. If you would have been busy this weekend, I still would have gone alone."

Kat had a hard time concentrating at her job on Friday with the anticipation of going back to the lake. She also felt a dreadful emptiness come over her with the realization that David would not be there with her this time.

Again that night she slept restlessly, but surprisingly she woke up feeling in good spirits. With knowing what Wisconsin weather could be like, she took no chances and dressed Davy in summer wear, because it was such a beautiful warm morning with the sun shining so bright and not a cloud in the sky. She also packed practical clothes: jeans, long shirts, a coat, a hat and mittens. It amazed her and was totally crazy to her that they made jeans to fit a soon-to-be four month old.

She had about a half hour of spare time before Maggie would arrive, so she sat conversing with Michael at the kitchen table. "Michael, even though we are leaving the house and going somewhere else, you will still be with us, right?"

"Of course, Mistress Kat. Wherever Master Davy goes, I go. May I ask you a question, Mistress Kat?"

"Yes, Michael, of course."

"Like, Miss Maggie said, will you be able to handle going to the lake with remembering all that went on between you and the General?"

"Yes, Michael, I'm sure I can. It may be a little hard at first, but I'm a survivor, remember? You said so yourself at one time."

"Yes, Mistress Kat, indeed I did."

Maggie arrived right at nine o'clock in the morning. With Davy strapped into his car seat, the luggage put into the trunk, and the baby on board, the four set out for Wautoma.

What an absolute beautiful spring day, thought Kat. The sparsely branched trees of winter were now cascaded with a fresh array of colorful leaves. The frozen ground was thawed and blanketed with green grass and the beautiful array of wild flowers, some struggling to poke their way through the ground, and others almost in full bloom along the roadside, was a beautiful sight to behold.

"Well, let's see. Chris has less than a month to report to the Academy and then he's on his way to becoming a pilot. That's great," pronounced Kat.

"What's so great about it?" questioned Maggie, with an irritated tone to her voice. "I'm sorry, Kat. I didn't mean to jump all over you."

"Maggie, I thought you came to terms and accepted the fact that Chris joined the Air Force?"

"I thought I had, but as his departure date gets closer and closer, I find myself freaking out more and more. I read over all those brochures that he received from them, and it's going to be a living hell for Chris."

"Maggie, you and Marshall sent him to Colorado Springs last summer for that summer camp, so that he could live on the base for a week and get to know his surroundings and what's expected of him physically and mentally. I know it was rigorous for him, but after coming home, he didn't squawk about it did he?" "No."

"Well, see. That could have been his out for him, but he chose to finish the rest of the requirements and go for it. I'm personally very proud of my nephew. Those kids will learn discipline, duty and respect. Not much of that floating around in the halls at other places of learning, and he will be a better person when he comes out."

"I know. I keep telling myself the same thing, but..."

"But you don't want to lose your baby boy. He's not a boy anymore, and he certainly will be a man when he's finished with the Academy in every aspect of life. Let go of the apron strings and give your son the freedom to make his own choices in life. Are you going to see him off?"

"No, I don't think I could handle it. Marshall and the boys will be there."

"Maggie, for crying out loud, put your own feelings aside and think about how Chris might feel if his mother isn't going to see him off. He wants and needs your approval with this."

"You're right, I know. Hearing it the way you put it, I guess I have been selfish with only thinking of how I feel."

"When you start feeling down about Chris, recite the Air Force motto that you told me about. You never know, it might help," Kat suggested.

"Integrity First, Service Before Self and Excellence In All," recited Maggie.

"That-a-girl! Besides, you and Marshall will be going on that cruise shortly after Chris leaves, and that will help to take your mind off of him for a little while. A nice getaway will do the trick, and besides, you'll have an extra bonus with this trip with Marshall wanting to jump your bones," roared Kat.

"Really, Kat! You sure can come up with some off-the-wall statements, and this is one of your more terrible ones," declared Maggie, but within a few seconds, she joined her sister in laughter with the thought of Marshall doing just that.

They reached Wautoma at exactly eleven thirty in the morning. Kat had been leery of driving during the first holiday after winter, knowing there would be a lot of people heading out of the city. The traffic wasn't heavy, so she suspected that a lot of vacationers headed north on Friday night already.

"Want to stop and have some lunch now, Maggie?"

"I don't care, Kat. I'll leave it up to you."

"I'm opting to stop and maybe have a sandwich, and feed Davy, and change him before we have to go and see Ms. Scholes."

"That's fine with me. I could go for a cup of coffee anyway."

They chose a restaurant on the main drag of Wautoma. Looking out from her car window, Kat could see the café curtains in red-and-white checkered material hanging in the windows with the sign, "Millie's Place," and she thought this might be the right atmosphere for them. As they walked through the door, Kat was in awe of the entire setting. The counter was right out of the fifties era with the gray Formica counter top and chrome stools with red Naugahyde upholstery. The booths, with high backs, were made from new oak, along with the table in between, which was topped with the same red-and-white checkered material that adorned the windows. Each booth had a mini replica of the old standard jukeboxes with the turnstile that listed the records that could be chosen to play right from where you sat for twenty-five cents for three plays, just like

the price in the fifties. Kat couldn't get her quarter out fast enough and flipped through the selection of songs, all from the fifties and sixties, of course. She slipped her quarter into the slot and pushed the knobs inward and selected her three songs that she waited in anticipation to hear. The jukebox lit up and started to play the selected songs within seconds with a toned-down volume so as not to disturb the customers, of course. Kat was in seventh heaven. Her favorite music genre was Country Western, but her second favorite was music from the fifties and sixties.

"Isn't this place fabulous, Maggie?"

"Yes, Kat, I must say it certainly is. Look at the large soda dispensers at the counters and the napkin holders, right down to the salt and pepper shakers of that era. I saw pictures of the real thing, and this is about as close as you can get to it. Remarkable!" said Maggie.

Kat and Maggie ate their sandwiches, shared fries, drank their coffee and continued to look around in amazement at the coke memorabilia and pictures on the walls of movie stars that were famous in the fifties. Kat tried to feed Davy his strained peas while she took bites of her fries, but Davy wanted nothing to do with them. She finally gave up trying and brought out a bottle from her diaper bag. After she finished eating, she asked Maggie to watch her purse and headed to the ladies room with Davy in tow to change him. With that finished and the bill paid by Maggie, they headed for the real estate office.

Kat had the directions on how to find the place from Ms. Scholes per their last telephone conversation on Friday morning. It was off Main Street, and with the directions in hand, it was easy enough to find. It was going on at 12:50 P.M. when Kat, Maggie, Davy and Michael pulled into the parking lot. Ms. Scholes' office windows faced the parking lot, and she saw and presumed that this had to be Ms. O'Brien, because the office was normally closed on Saturday afternoons, as the three of them emerged from the car and walked over to the front entrance, a woman opened the door.

"Ms. O'Brien, I presume?"

"Yes, I'm Katherine O'Brien. Please follow me to my office and make yourself comfortable."

Kat sat in the chair with David directly across from Ms. Scholes' desk and Maggie took a chair next to her. As she started to remove Davy's coat and hat, he became a little fussy, so she retained his nooky from her diaper bag and slipped it into his mouth. He calmed immediately and sat back against her chest facing Ms. Scholes.

Maggie took a quick look around her office and found it to be decorated quite tastefully. She estimated Ms. Scholes to be about Kat's age and a very attractive woman with shoulder-length brown hair. She wore just the right amount of makeup for a business woman and was dressed in an impeccable jade green pant suit with a light green blouse underneath. As Maggie looked at her well-manicured nails, she noticed the wedding ring on her left hand.

As Ms. Sholes retrieved a pile of papers from her middle drawer, Maggie took the time to poke Kat and pointed at her own wedding ring. Evidently, Ms. Scholes was a Mrs.

"I guess the first thing on the agenda should be introductions. My name is Karen Scholes, and I would prefer that you call me, Karen. With as many years as I have been in this business, I find that first names have a tendency to make everyone feel more at ease."

"Well, then," said Kat, "my first name is Katherine, but I prefer to be called Kat. And this is my sister, Maggie."

"Kat and Maggie, I'm certainly happy to meet both of you. And who may I ask is this adorable little baby?"

"His name is David. We call him Davy for short."

"How old is he? And where did he get that beautiful wavy, black hair and those beautiful blue eyes from?" Karen wanted to know.

"He's four months old and he's a mirror image of his father," finished Kat.

"It says here that you are the one who is applying for the loan to buy the cottage. Is that correct, Kat?"

"Yes, correct."

"And the father will not have any say in any of this, so we will not have to have his signature on any of the documents?" asked Karen.

Kat knew that it was a reasonable question to ask, so took no offense from it and answered, "Davy's father is no longer with us. I will be the sole owner of the property."

"I see, and I'm sorry," responded Karen. Kat left it at that with no further explanation but only said, "Thank you."

"Well Kat, it was difficult to find any information on your elusive Mr. McDuffy in the beginning, but after a lot of research, we finally did manage to locate his only living relative in his home town of Spring Green, Iowa," stated Karen.

"I sent out more than six letters myself inquiring about Duffy and always received a letter back explaining that they were not able to give me any information on this person. I was about to give up until I called Helen, and she was the one that recommended I get in touch with you. She told me that if anyone can find Duffy's relatives, it would be you, Karen," explained Kat.

"She's a very sweet woman and I have known Helen for about six years now," answered Karen.

"I've only known her for about a year but agree whole heartedly with you," said Kat in reply. "How did you finally track down Duffy's family?" Kat questioned.

"I knew from talking with Helen that he served in Vietnam, so I went after his army records. That information is strictly confidential, so I talked to Judge Adams, who is a circuit judge for Waushara County. Wautoma is the county seat, so his office is right here in the courthouse. I told him

about Mr. McDuffy and the cottage that belonged to him and about your situation. Another couple had interest in buying the property also, but without Duffy's army records, we were unable to find out just where in Iowa he lived. I'm sure he mentioned it to some of his older cronies here, but no one could remember."

"I know. That's what Helen told me also," replied Kat.

"Well, anyway, Judge Adams came through for us, and we received the name of his hometown. There were no McDuffys listed in the phone book, so we hit another dead end. We have an affiliate office in Juneau, Iowa, which is about thirty miles from Spring Green. I made a call and talked to one of the real estate representatives named James Grishwald. It took about a week for him to get back to me, but he went to Spring Green and did some checking around. Seems Mr. McDuffy's only living relative is his uncle, which is his mother's brother. The ironic thing is, Mr. John Lamb lives only down the block from Mr. McDuffy's former home. It says here on the documents that he signed, giving his permission to sell the property, that he is eighty-three years old and lives alone. He knew from his sister that his nephew had owned some property in Wisconsin, but didn't know exactly where it was located."

"How sad! So he is the last one of the family that is still living?" asked Kat.

"Yes, he is the last one," replied Karen.

Kat looked over at Maggie and thought that she saw a tear developing in both eyes.

"Well, Kat and Maggie, I can say with certainty that this was one of the hardest properties to sell. By that I mean, with the two tragic stories that involved that little cottage, they are definitely two of the saddest that I have ever heard of. Like I told you over the phone, Kat, an elderly couple wanted to down size from their larger house and buy the cottage for their retirement home. It was the perfect size and location for them. Less than a month before the closing date, the husband died of a heart attack. Living in a small town like this, stories are told and retold and

sometimes are completely as far from the truth as you can get, but this one about Mr. McDuffy's life here, and the tragic story of his sweetheart, Rosemary, stayed the same. It seems, Kat, you were destined to have this little cottage on Rice Lake."

Karen gave Kat a thorough summary of what the documents that she was to sign entailed. She signed her name to every line as marked, and Karen handed over the title and keys to her cottage.

"Well, Kat and Maggie, that should just about do it. And, Kat, if you ever need my help again, please don't hesitate to call me. Maggie, it was certainly a pleasure to meet you."

"Thank you. And also you," said Maggie.

"This won't really be good-bye, Karen. Now that I will be living in the same town as you, mostly during the summer months, I'm sure we'll be running into each other now and then."

"You can count on it, Kat."

"Well, Kat," said Maggie as she got into the car and began to button her seat belt while Kat buckled in a sleeping Davy into his car seat, "if and when Marshall retires and we want to down size, I sure the hell don't want to go through any kind of closing like that one."

"I know what you mean. Pretty depressing, wasn't it?"

"That's putting it mildly," Maggie responded.

"Come on, Maggie. We need some cheering up. Let's stop for an ice cream cone or whatever you want at that Dairy Queen we passed on the way into town. I'm buying because you bought lunch."

"Sounds fine with me, Kat."

"We should probably pick a motel to stay at before we go out to the lake. With it being Memorial Day weekend, you never know what might be going on and how many people will be staying in the motels in town."

"You're right, Kat. We better, just to be on the safe side."

Kat and Maggie found a quaint little motel just a few blocks from Main Street. There were vacancies, so they registered and were given two sets of keys to room five. They retrieved their luggage from the trunk, Kat lifted Davy from his car seat, and they went in to inspect their surroundings. Everything was neatly arranged in the room with two double beds, a small refrigerator, microwave and of course cable television. Kat took the opportunity to feed and change Davy while in the comfort of their room. Maggie was checking out the channels for movies on cable while waiting for Kat to finish.

"Ready, Maggie?"

"Anytime you are."

As they were pulling out of the parking lot, Kat told Maggie, "I'd like to stop by and say 'hi' to Helen, and then we can leave the car by her and walk over to the cottage." Kat knew there had to be an entrance to the cottage other than via the beach, but they would check that out when they got there.

When they pulled into Helen's driveway, they could see her sitting on her porch reading. She glanced up and saw Kat and an infant heading her way, followed by another woman. Kat had called Helen ahead of time and told her that her sister would be coming with her. Helen surmised that this had to be Maggie.

"Oh my, Kat. It is so wonderful to see you again. And this little guy must be Davy." She hugged both of them at the same time and then turned to Maggie and introduced herself and shook her hand. "Come into the kitchen," instructed Helen as she closed the doors behind them. "Make yourself at home. What can I get for you to drink?"

"Coffee would be fine, Helen," replied Kat.

"Same for me," said Maggie.

"I see you still like your coffee, Kat," noted Helen.

"Figured I had to hang on to one bad habit, since I got rid of the other one," chuckled Kat.

"You did?" questioned Helen. "Finally gave up the cigarettes?"

"Yes. As a matter of fact, it was shortly after we left here last spring when I quit."

"Good for you, Kat. And what about you, Maggie. Do you smoke?"

"No. I never had the urge to try them. To be truthful, I can't stand the smell of cigarette smoke."

"Good," was all Helen had to say.

Kat realized her mistake with using the word *we*. She hoped Helen didn't catch it, because she never knew anything about David. *Actually, how could she? He was invisible,* thought Kat with a grin on her face.

"So this is little Davy. My goodness, Kat! He sure is beautiful. Look at that black wavy hair and so much of it for only being four months old. And those beautiful blue eyes. They are the same color as the lake in the summer. May I hold him?"

"Of course," said Kat as she handed Davy over to Helen.

"Oh my! Look at that big grin. He must be comfortable with me."

"I'd say. He's actually fussy as to who can hold him," answered Kat with amazement.

"Did everything go well with the closing?" inquired Helen, adding, "Karen is such a sweet woman."

"Yes, everything went well and yes, she really is a nice person," responded Kat.

"Are you still working?"

"Yes, I am. As a matter of fact, Maggie takes care of Davy when I'm at work."

"That's wonderful that you can have a family member watch your baby instead of a stranger."

"That's exactly what I told her. She thought it would be too much for me with my husband and three teenage boys, but so far everything is going smoothly. I love my sister very dearly, and I would do anything for that little guy you're holding, because I love him so much too," Maggie stated.

"Keep it up, Maggie, and you'll have me bawling in no time flat," responded Kat, but truly feeling what she just said. "My sister here is my Rock of Gibraltar, Helen. Always has been and always will be."

"I can see that the two of you love each other very dearly. How refreshing it is that the two of you can admit it so openly. It gives me a renewed feeling that maybe this world isn't quite as bad off as I thought it was," responded Helen.

"Helen, I'm truly sorry with your loss. Even though I didn't know Fred that long, he seemed like a very nice man."

"Thank you, Kat. Yes, he was a wonderful husband to me, and he was my best friend. It has only been three months since his heart attack, but life goes on. My only comfort now that he is gone is that we will be together some day and will never leave each other again."

"Will you continue to live here?" questioned Maggie out of curiosity.

"Oh yes, definitely. Fred and I had thirteen wonderful years together living here on the lake since his retirement. This is where I will die also."

Oh my, thought Kat. *We've got to get off of this subject or we'll have three women crying like a baby.* So she asked, "Helen, would you like to go with us when we walk over to see the cottage?"

"Thank you for the kind offer, but I don't think I'd make it very far with this bum knee of mine," she said as she began to rub her right knee for emphasis. "This little tyke is sound asleep. If you don't mind, I will lay him down on my bed while the two of you are gone and will keep a good eye on him until you return."

"Are you sure that's alright with you, Helen?" Kat questioned.

"Of course, I'm sure. It's no problem. Matter of fact, I've grown quite attached to this little fellow, and it would be my pleasure to watch over him. And this will give you and Maggie a chance to really look the cottage over. So take your time and don't worry about us. We'll be just fine."

"Thank you, Helen," said Kat as she and Maggie got up to leave.

As Kat and Maggie walked off of Helen's porch and down the stairs onto the cement drive, Kat suggested that they take their shoes off, if they didn't want sand in them. As Maggie was about to remove her second shoe and sock, she happened to see Mike and Sharon's house next door.

"Oh my, I wonder who owns that beautiful home?"

"That's my neighbor's Mike and Sharon's summer home. This is where David and I stayed for almost a week last spring."

"This is the place you stayed at?" echoed Maggie.

"Yes, isn't it gorgeous?" asked Kat.

"It certainly is—and big."

"*Huge* is actually a better word to describe their summer log cabin," chuckled Kat.

"Log cabin? I don't think so."

"Me either, when I saw it, but that's what they compared it to. Maggie, you wouldn't believe the inside."

"I don't believe the outside. I can't imagine what the inside looks like."

"When Davy and I come up after the cottage is finished, you'll have to come on the same weekend with me that Mike and Sharon are here, and she would be more than happy to show you their place."

"I can't wait. It's breathtaking."

As they continued down the beach, Kat took a quick look out over the beautiful lake. Helen came close to describing the color of it, when referring to the color of Davy's eyes, but it was even more beautiful than she described.

Kat pointed to a spot in the lake close to shore and told Maggie, "That's where David threw me in, clothes and all."

"You're kidding. He did that to you? I thought your average angel was supposed to be, I don't know, nice?"

"Oh, Maggie. That's too much. David was a general, remember?" roared Kat. "Nice?"

"Well, I thought he was," said Maggie.

"He could be very kind and considerate but most of the time, he acted like a general: dictatorial, a nagger to the hilt and down right annoying to the extreme."

"Yet, you loved him?"

"Yet, I loved him with all my heart," responded Kat with an audible choke and tears forming in her eyes.

"Kat, are you all right? You sure you want to do this now? Maybe we can come back again tomorrow."

"No, Maggie. I'm fine. I have to do this. I've always wanted this cottage since I first laid eyes on it. Now that we're here, we stay."

As they approached the gate to the white picket fence that Duffy had erected who knew when, Kat grabbed for the latch and was standing there with it in her hand. The fence was in a sorry state of decay, and the lawn that butted with the sand was no longer visible because of the overgrown, out of control weeds, foliage and bushes.

"Dear me," said Kat, "I never knew a place could fall apart so rapidly. I knew it was in need of repair when David brought me here to see it, but it wasn't in this bad of shape. Now the fence is still standing, barely, and the shutters are all attached, barely."

As they approached the back entrance, Kat could see that her estimation of the shutters was not overly exaggerated. One top hinge on all four of them was all that was holding them up. The stucco on the outside was in poor condition and would have to be repaired. They discovered that the screen door was in fairly good shape, but a small window within the top of the inside door was cracked in several places. After unlocking the door, they had a hard time pushing it open. *Probably warped*, thought Kat.

When they walked in, they met a barrage of cobwebs, which put Kat into a state of panic. Maggie, not being afraid of spiders, looked for something to knock them down with as they made their way into the cottage.

"We're in luck. I found an old corn broom lying on the floor behind that chair over there. I'll have these out of the way in no time. Just stay where you are, Kat."

She was not always in agreement with Maggie, but this time she sure wasn't about to argue with her. "Ugh!" said Kat, as shivers went up and down her spine.

As Maggie approached a door in the kitchen, she asked, "What do you suppose is behind here?"

"Probably a broom closet," answered Kat.

"Nope. Looks like a pantry to me."

“Really?” questioned Kat as she walked over to take a look. “I love pantries. Wish I had one in my house at home.”

After the two finished a thorough inspection of the entire place and were again standing in the kitchen, Maggie said, “Well, it has real potential, Kat, and could be fixed up to be a really charming place. It’s really deceiving from the outside as to the size of the inside.”

“I know, Maggie, it’s really in bad shape right now, but with some outside help to do the work, it could be a very special place for Davy and I to come to during the summer months.”

“What do you figure is behind here?” Maggie asked.

“I don’t know, maybe a storage closet,” answered Kat. “Oh for goodness sake. Of course! It’s stairs leading to the basement where the furnace and hot water heater are. Duffy did live here all year round, so he had to heat the place. Duh!” exclaimed Kat, mad at herself for overlooking such an important matter.

“Do you want to go down for a look?” asked Maggie.

“Are you kidding me, Maggie? Can you imagine what crawling creatures must be down there after being closed up for all these years? I’ll have workers go down and check everything out just in case Duffy stored anything down there. I’ll have to check with Karen and see if Duffy’s uncle wants any of his belongings or what should be done with them.”

As the two continued through the back door and back into the yard, Kat said, “It’s the last house before the woods begin about twenty yards to the left, so we only have one neighbor to the right. The houses are all spaced well apart, so that we’re not all sitting on top of one another, which is nice.”

“Do you think your property line goes all the way to the woods where the wide, sandy beach tapers off to almost a path meeting with those trees?” questioned Maggie.

"I don't know. I'll have to check out the abstract and see," answered Kat.

As they continued further into the backyard and reached the gate, Kat turned around to take one more glance at the cottage that David wanted her to buy. She raised one hand to shield her eyes from the sun while looking up at the sky and whispered, "Thank you, my love, for finding this place that has so much meaning to me and will some day have the same meaning to our son."

As they strolled back to Helen's house, they discussed what type of people were needed to get Kat's cottage livable again.

Helen had Davy on her lap and was sitting in a rocking chair overlooking the lake. He had a big grin on his face upon seeing Kat and Maggie, but he was still content to stay right there with Helen.

"Back so soon? Oh, it has been an hour and a half by my watch since you left."

"Yes. We wanted to really look the place over. I hope Davy was no bother."

"No. Not at all. He woke up about twenty minutes after the two of you left, so I changed him, fed him some applesauce and then gave him his bottle. He is one happy camper right now."

"Thank you so much, Helen. He looks very content sitting on your lap with you rocking him."

"All children love to be rocked, and Davy is no exception. It's one of the best ways to bond with a child. How about some coffee while you tell me all about Duffy's cottage?"

"If you don't mind, Helen, I'd prefer a Coke if you have it."

"Me too," said Maggie.

Kat lifted Davy off of Helen's lap and helped her up.

"All right, two Cokes it is. Maybe I'll join you."

As Kat filled Helen in on the details of Duffy's cottage, Maggie helped by adding things that Kat missed.

"We forgot to check out the roof," said Maggie. "Want to go back?"

"No. What's the sense? I plan to repair the entire cottage and I assume the roof is in as bad or worse shape than the rest of the outside."

"Even with all the repairs that are needed, it sounds charming, Kat," stated Helen.

"Yes, it is and will be even more charming when I've finished remodeling it. I'll hire local people to do the work, of course, because they live right here or in the area. Can you suggest a roofer, landscaper, plumber, electrician and painter? Also, I would like all new cupboards and counter tops in the kitchen, hardwood floors throughout and some new windows installed."

"Good idea, Kat, with the hardwood floors. I know from experience that it's easier to clean sand from a floor than if you carpeted the entire place, and I will make a list for you with phone numbers. All of these people are in this area and are very good at what they do. I'm more than sure that you will be satisfied with their work."

"I was also thinking of having a deck built in the back facing the water, but I will have to think about that one some more."

"If I may make a suggestion?" "Sure, Helen. Go right ahead."

"Go home and draw a layout of the cottage and take one room at a time and list what you want done in each room. This way, it won't be so overwhelming for you."

"Good idea. I'll do that with Maggie."

"Me?"

"Sure. When you and Marshall moved into your home, you had it remodeled to your liking and look how great it turned out. Two heads are better than one."

"Alright, Kat. I'll be happy to help."

"Well, Helen, thank you so much for all of your help and advice and again for taking care of Davy."

"It was my pleasure. Do you have any idea when you'll be heading home?"

"Since tomorrow is Sunday and Monday is Memorial Day, I'm assuming all of the places that I will need to visit will be closed, so we might as well head back probably around noon tomorrow after we eat breakfast. So take your time, Helen, and mail the names and addresses to me at home in Milwaukee."

"Nonsense. Stop by on your way home, and I will have the list ready for you."

"Alright. If that's okay with you, we'll stop before we leave for home."

"Good."

"See you tomorrow then."

Helen nodded her head in the affirmative and they said their good-byes and took their leave.

After Kat stopped at Helen's early Sunday afternoon, Helen gave Kat a complete list of everyone she would need plus the phone numbers of each of them.

"Thank you again, Helen. And I will keep in touch."

"Please do, dear. Now drive safely on the way home."

Kat grinned and descended the steps. As she got into the driver's seat and began to buckle up, Kat looked at Maggie, who gave her a thumbs up. She backed out of the driveway and the four headed home.

Kat just started to make a pot of coffee after laying Davy down for his early afternoon nap when the front doorbell started to ring.

"Maggie, for heavens sake. What are you doing here? You and Marshall just arrived home only two hours ago. Anxious to get over here to tell me first hand how your little scheme worked, huh? Come in the kitchen. I just made a fresh pot of coffee, and I'm dying to hear all about your vacation. And don't leave anything out, even if you think it's nothing at all, hear? So, come on, tell me, did everything go the way you wanted it to?"

"Well, kind of. Actually, too well. I think I've created a monster."

"Marshall a monster? Very doubtful, Maggie but tell me what happened anyway," chuckled Kat.

"Our plane trip to Florida went really well, considering how nervous I was about flying, since I have never been on a plane before. We stayed at a really nice hotel and left for the cruise ship early the next morning. We spent the whole day walking around the ship and taking in all the things available to do. Unbelievable how massive our ship was! We were on the seventh floor and there were still five more floors above us. For the evening meal, all passengers dined together—well, not all together, per say, because there were at least 3,500 people, not counting the ship's crew. Marshall and I both had cocktails with our meal, of course, and thinking back now, Marshall may have had one too many."

"What do you mean?"

"I'm getting to that. We went to the lounge area and continued to have a few more drinks when I realized it was going on midnight. It was really a great time at first, because Marshall said more than his usual three word sentences. I mean a lot more. Actually, he started coming on to me right before the dessert. He told me later that it was that wonderful, black, no back dress that I wore."

"You didn't. You actually bought that dress you said you were going to buy? I didn't believe you. I didn't think you would have the nerve to wear it," laughed Kat.

"Well, I did, and I did. Bought it and wore it, I mean. And I wish I never would have laid eyes on the damn thing."

"Maggie, what in the hell are you talking about? This was the whole idea of the trip: to get Marshall to notice you more and, um, see more of you," chuckled Kat with a devilish grin on her face.

"Well yes, I know, and he did, and he did, on both counts."

Kat rolled her eyes before saying, "Maggie, for God's sake, you're talking in riddles. Will you please start making sense?"

"All right, Kat. I'll give it to you right between the eyes. We barely made it back to our stateroom, before Marshall had the dress completely off of me."

"So? That's what you wanted, I thought?"

"Well, yes. But I thought he would maybe take a little slower approach to everything. I didn't even get a chance to wear that beautiful negligee I told you about."

"Oh, Maggie. You're something else. So did you enjoy the scenery?"

"What scenery? The only damn thing I saw the entire trip was our bed and the necessary trips to the dinner hall to eat and drink and back to our stateroom we went. Just like clock work."

"Oh my," is all Kat could say between bouts of hysterical laughter. "I'm sorry, Maggie, but I can't help but laugh. The way you've told the story is absolutely hysterical."

"Well, that may be so, Katherine Frances O'Brien, but tell me what am I supposed to do now?"

"What are you talking about, 'now'?"

"The here and now of course. He didn't stop his amorous 'things' just, because we left the ship."

"'Things', Maggie?"

"Yes, 'things.' And don't you dare ask me to go into detail with you. Oh God, listen to me. I sound like a raving maniac. But I'm not one, of course, Marshall is," stated Maggie, as she started to roar with laughter along with Kat.

"Maggie, I don't think I have laughed as hard in my life as I just have with your hilarious version of what happened between you and Marshall."

"Well, be that as it may, Kat, it is your sisterly duty to help me find a way to get Marshall to back off. I'm already worn out from him chasing me around the kitchen table like a dog in heat, whispering little innuendos in my ear about you know what, and we've only been home a couple of hours. If you never saw a person die from complete exhaustion, wait, and you'll see it happen to me or him, because he doesn't get a lot of exercise."

"Well, from what you have told me, it sounds like he has been exercising aplenty for the last ten days," replied Kat, ready to take off with another laughing jag and doing so after picturing the workaholic, extremely timid, Marshall doing the things Maggie claims to be true. "Oh my, my," said Kat, as she finally got her emotions under control. "I guess you do have quite a problem here. Marshall's no spring chicken, so maybe if you let him go on for—"

"Don't even think what I think you're thinking, Kat," interrupted Maggie.

"Either you help me, or I'll just have to move in with you, permanently."

"What I think you have to do, Maggie, is go home, sit Marshall down at the kitchen table and talk this whole thing over together. You never know, Marshall was not very attentive to you in the past, and maybe he thought he had to make it up to you. Maybe he is just as worn out as you, but now, he doesn't know how to stop."

"You really think that will do it?"

"Can't say for sure, but it's certainly worth a try."

"Yeah, maybe you're right. I better get going."

"Call me later and let me know how things went, okay?"

"If I show up on your doorstep in a couple of hours, you'll know your plan didn't work."

"If you show up on my doorstep in a couple of hours, then we'll have to come up with another plan, but try this first."

"Thanks, Kat, for listening to my ranting and raving."

"No problem. Don't forget to call me," said Kat as she walked Maggie to the door.

As it turned out, when Maggie called later, Kat's intuitions were correct. They decided when the time was right for both of them, they'd do it. In the meantime, cuddling would be just as good. Kat had to laugh to herself with Maggie's statement: "they'd do it." She and Marshall have been married for over twenty years, and Maggie still can't quite bring herself to say *make love* or *have sex*.

Kat hadn't heard from Beverly for quite some time so decided to give her a call and see, if they could meet for lunch together on a Saturday or Sunday afternoon, depending upon Bev's schedule. She quickly speed dialed Bev's number, and when the phone stopped ringing, and someone answered on the other end, Kat questioned, "Bev?"

"Kat, is that you?"

"Yes, it's me. How are you doing? Long time no hear," answered Kat.

"I'm just fine. How about yourself and little Davy? I thought you may have fallen off the face of the Earth."

"We're both doing alright. That's the reason I'm calling. It's been quite some time since we have seen each other, and I wondered if you would like to do lunch with Davy and me one weekend in the near future?"

After checking her appointment book, Bev replied, "How about two weeks from this Saturday? Will that work for you?"

"Yes. That will be fine. The psychic business must be doing pretty well for you. That busy, huh?"

"As a matter of fact, yes, for some reason. My clients are really starting to notice the changes in the weather: more tornadoes, hurricanes, droughts and flooding, which will get worse compared to the last decade. Even though it's ten years away, there is a lot of discussion with the media and talk shows about the Mayan calendar ending on December 21, 2012. People are starting to take an interest in it, because the speculation going around is that, since the calendar ends on that date so must the end of the world."

"I heard a little bit about it, but I didn't pay much attention."

"And what do you think, Kat?"

"Not sure. Maybe they were conquered by invaders from another country and all taken prisoners or made slaves as was the practice throughout history. Or some rival tribe or tribes finally got sick and tired of them using their people as sacrifices and decided to wipe them all out. Or could be the calendar maker died, and no one else knew how to continue on with his work," chuckled Kat.

"I like your last version the best," laughed Bev. "We have a lot of catching up to do."

"Yes, I know, and I'm sorry. Between work and with buying the cottage up north, I've—"

"You went ahead and bought the cottage?" interrupted Bev.

"Yes. Just last week."

"That's wonderful news, Kat. David told me that you would buy it sometime in the future. I didn't figure on it being this soon."

"He told you that?"

"Yes, Kat. He did, and he also said it would be one of the smartest moves that you ever made."

"Well, I don't know about that. It's going to cost me a bundle to get the place fixed up the way I want it."

"Are you having second thoughts?"

"No, not really. Just thinking out loud. I'm truly very happy with my decision to buy it."

"Well, Kat. I have to run. I have another client due in about fifteen minutes."

"I understand, Bev. So we're definitely on for Saturday, July 2, at the Pine Circle Restaurant on Division Road at four o'clock?"

"Yes, and I can't wait to see you and Davy. Do you think you can get there without getting lost?" chuckled Bev.

"I'm very familiar with the area, so I don't foresee any problems arising with that area of driving," laughed Kat.

"Good. Because every time you come out to Mequon to meet with me, you get lost. Remember?"

"Oh, yes. I remember all too well."

"Take care, Kat and give little Davy a big kiss and hug from his aunt Bev."

"Will do."

Kat and Davy arrived at the restaurant a little before four o'clock, and Bev's car was already in the parking lot. As she unbuckled Davy from his car seat and carried him into the restaurant, she spotted Bev at a table to the left and middle of the dining area. Bev immediately arose as she saw the two coming closer and took Davy from Kat's arms.

"Oh my, look at you. How you have grown, Davy. My goodness, Kat, he sure is the spitting image of his father," said Bev as she kissed him on his cheek.

As they sat down and Davy was strapped into a baby seat that fit over a chair, Bev put a little colorful bag with a ribbon attached to the top to keep it secure on the tray for Davy to see. As is his usual practice with things that are set down in front of him, he swiped at it, and it landed on the floor beside his chair.

"I hope that it's not breakable," said Kat with a twinge of embarrassment as she retrieved the bag off of the floor and handed it back to Bev.

"No," said Bev as she untied the ribbon, opened the bag, and took out the cutest stuffed puppy that Kat had ever seen. She squeezed one of its floppy ears so that it would make a barking sound.

Davy started to giggle every time it barked at him and when it quit, in his mouth went the little puppy's black nose.

"Typical kid," laughed Bev, "everything goes into his mouth."

"The main reason that I called you, Bev, was for us to get together, because I've really missed you, but also to ask you in person about David."

"What about David?"

"Will I ever be with him again while I'm still alive?"

"No Kat, you won't. You knew he would never be able to return to Earth."

"I know, Bev. I've been told that by you and Michael, but I was hoping that just maybe things could have changed and sometime down the road…"

"No. There will be no changes while you're still alive. As a spirit, there is a possibility that you will see him again. I think it will be very slim but possible."

"Oh, Bev. Do you truly believe that? Only a slim chance? Did David ever discuss with you what may happen to us in the future?"

"No. He never said a word to me about that. I think he considered it something that was very private between you and him. Kat, I know how much the two of you loved each other. Go with the knowledge that because of that love, there is a good possibility that you will be together sometime in the future. You have his son and you have a lot to do in the future. All your thoughts and actions must focus on accomplishing everything that you know you must do."

"I know, Bev. But I just had to ask one more time."

"Don't live in the past anymore, Kat. The memories you have of David are wonderful ones, but don't let those memories overtake every moment of your daily life. Focus on you and your son's future. That is where your happiness will lie, through your son."

After they finished their meal and Davy had a bottle, Bev and Kat talked about nothing in particular and went their separate ways and vowed to get together more often.

As the summer months dwindled away, Kat returned to the cottage five times by herself to see first hand the progress that the workers were making. She left Davy with Maggie for the weekends while she stayed with Helen, because of Helen's continual persistence that she do so. According to Helen, McDuffy's uncle decided that all the furniture and other belongings be donated to the local VFW Post in honor of his nephew, to do with as they wished. Helen kept her posted in between her visits as well.

It was nearing the end of October, and it was astonishing what they had accomplished. Kat decided to take Maggie, so that she could see for herself, first hand, all the things that were done that she had described to her for the last four months. Only a few minor adjustments had to be made, and the work on the cottage was complete.

As with the previous fall, the weather for this time of year was unseasonably warm. The leaves were in their glorious spectrum of colors, which made the drive north feel like a wonderland fit for a fairytale.

The four drove onto Helen's driveway, and they saw that she was waiting for them while sitting on the front steps reading a book. Helen closed the book and approached the car with great anticipation of seeing little Davy, who was not as little as he was the last time that she saw him. They said their hellos with warm hugs all around. Kat unbuckled Davy's seat belt and lifted him into Helen's waiting arms.

"Oh my! You have really grown since the last time I saw you young man and even more handsome," said Helen as she gave Davy a kiss on his cheek and proceeded to carry him to the house. Kat was a little leery that Helen would be able to carry Davy, since he was now nine months old, but her fears were unfounded, since Helen was up the stairs and into the house with Davy, before Maggie and her could retrieve their purses and exit the car.

"My goodness, Helen," stated Maggie, "You still look as good as the last time that I saw you. Will you ever change?"

"Well, thank you very much for the fine compliment, Maggie. I do try to eat properly, do my daily exercises, and keep a positive outlook on things. One or all of them must be the secret to the way I look."

"For me, it would be this place itself, because of the beauty and the pure serenity that I feel whenever I'm up here," stated Kat.

Helen sat down in Fred's favorite chair with Davy on her lap. She motioned for Kat and Maggie to take a seat on the couch.

"Helen, would you like to go over to the cottage with us and see the final results?"

"I would love to, Kat. The last time I was there was about three weeks ago. We can drive over since the front door is accessible now."

"Good. Let's get going," said Maggie. "I can't wait to see the end results."

Kat pulled into the two-car cemented carport located right off of the road.

"Oh my," said Maggie. "You thought about everything. I would never have thought about where to park the car."

"You give me way too much credit. Actually, I never thought about the car either. It was John, who did all the cement work that brought it up to me," stated Kat as she unfastened Davy from his car seat and lifted him into her arms.

Maggie was awestruck as soon as she exited the car.

A white picket fence encircled the entire cottage, front and back. A small sidewalk led to the new, main sidewalk to the house. A gate was installed from the carport and another one at the front of the main sidewalk leading to the cottage. The new sod was all in place, and miniature green and berry bushes were placed below the bay windows on each side of the sidewalk. A row of marigolds of several different colors, planted in front of the bushes, added such a lovely touch to the entire scene. The new black-shingled roof accented the newly repaired, painted, white stucco and the black shutters, which were the originals.

"Unbelievable," said Maggie. "After the great job they did on the outside, I can't wait to see what the inside looks like."

Maggie was shocked upon seeing the entranceway. "Wow! The paneling is gone and it just opens everything up, nicely."

"I know," said Kat. "All the paneling down the hallway was completely removed also, and all the walls throughout were re-plastered. All the floors throughout are simulated oak but look like the real thing."

"They are absolutely beautiful," stated Helen.

Kat continued on with explaining. "All the windows, except the bay windows, which were still in good shape in the living room, were replaced throughout. The only thing replaced in the bathroom was the window and a larger mirror with a new medicine cabinet, which replaced a small stainless steel one. The back entrance and sunroom are a replica of the front entrance, minus the alcoves.

"Really, Kat. I can't believe my eyes. This is the same place we looked at in early spring?" questioned Maggie as they entered Kat's bedroom and saw an oak, four-poster double bed adorned with a beautiful white chenille bedspread.

"I haven't seen one of those in years, especially not with the beautiful, delicate design this one has. All we have now are mostly comforters. Where did you get it from, Kat?" asked Maggie.

"Helen gave it to me as a cottage warming gift," said Kat. "It will be one of my cherished possessions from now on."

"I received it from my mother as a wedding gift, among other things," explained Helen. "It's been stored away in my cedar chest for years, and I thought it would be perfect for Kat, after she described her bedroom furniture to me."

As they entered the kitchen, Maggie's eyes became as large as basketballs with the sight that she was looking at: the new cupboards were done in oak, and a sage green Formica top resembling granite enclosed the stove, refrigerator and two stainless sinks, which were all on the same wall as was the door leading to the basement. A butcher block was also installed six feet in front of the sink, and a wood frame was attached to the ceiling above to hang pots and pans. Two new windows were installed and it finished off the remodeled kitchen. With a quick look across the room, Maggie noticed the door leading to the basement had a deadbolt lock with chain and asked, "Are you expecting company?"

"I know it may be a little overdone, but it will give me peace of mind knowing no one comes up from the basement unless I open the door," chuckled Kat.

As the three stepped down from the kitchen into the sunroom, three newly installed full-length windows showed the breathtaking view of the lake.

"So what do you think, Maggie, Helen?"

"It's absolutely adorable," agreed both women.

"Like I said before, Kat, the whole place is unbelievable. I personally wouldn't want to leave it," stated Maggie.

"I know. In my wildest dreams I never thought it would turn out this charming," answered Kat. "The workers did a fabulous job."

"Is this still all-year-round now?" asked Maggie.

"Yes. A new furnace and hot water heater were installed, and the heating system was all refurbished with new heating vents and registers," explained Kat.

"Where did you get all the furniture throughout?" Maggie questioned.

"Some from estate sales, but most of it was purchased from that furniture store about three miles outside of town."

Kat invited all the men who worked on the cottage along with Helen to the best fish fry dinner in town, or even for miles around, according to Helen. She vied for the drinks also, because she was so very happy with the final results of the cottage. Everyone involved with the remodeling did an excellent job in her opinion, and this was one way of showing her gratitude. She inserted an extra bonus check also into the envelope, along with the final payment due each man.

"That little outing we just went to had to cost you a pretty penny," stated Maggie, after they returned to the cottage.

"I know, but these guys were complete gentlemen the entire time it took to remodel this place, and everyone of them knew what they were doing and did their job very well. Each one gave me a discount because so

much had to be done, so that was the least I could do." Kat chose not to tell Maggie about the bonus checks.

Kat put Davy down in his crib in her bedroom and Maggie slept in Davy's bedroom.

"I think I'll turn in," Maggie said after spending an hour talking with Kat.

"Are you?"

"No. I think I'll stay up for a little while longer." Kat sat on a lawn chair on her patio with her legs bent and feet touching the seat of the chair with a shawl wrapped around her shoulders. She looked out over the lake, and instantly the memories of David and her flashed in her mind and said, "I only knew you for about three months, but I will love you my entire life. What do you think, Michael? Can David hear me?"

"Could be, Mistress Kat. Could be."

"You know, Michael, it is so unbelievably peaceful up here that it's hard to contemplate that there is so much chaos, hating and fighting going on in the world with the two planes flying into the Twin Towers, the war in Afghanistan, unrest in most of the Middle East and terrorists throughout the world. Will we ever have any period of time when there will be peace in the entire world before Armageddon?"

"No, Mistress Kat. There won't. Mankind is on a collision course with itself. All the things that you mentioned will continue up to and during World War III, which will start with the country your people call Iran firing guided missiles at the land of God's chosen people, Israel. Within a few short months, the United States will get involved, because your country and Israel are close allies."

"Are you allowed to tell me when World War III will start?"

"Yes, of course. On December 25, 2020."

"Is that the start of the End of Time that's written about in the Bible?"

"No, Mistress Kat. We have been into the End of Time already with the attack on the Twin Towers and the undeclared war with Afghanistan as only two major events out of many to come, until the start of Armageddon."

"I'm worried about Maggie's boys. Depending upon how long the war in Afghanistan lasts, there's still the possibility of Chris, Tim and Chad being called for duty. Will all three go to war with Afghanistan?"

"Yes, Mistress Kat. They will. But all three will survive to fight the Antichrist with Master Davy leading them."

"Michael, I was told by David that I will be a prophet in the future, so why haven't I seen all of these things happen before they actually occurred?"

"You know and have seen some things that will occur in the future, but you will find the answer to your question in the letter that General David wrote to you."

"Something I overlooked?"

"Yes, Mistress Kat."

Back at home, Davy was growing by leaps and bounds, and Kat knew he was getting to be a little too much at fifteen months for Maggie to handle, and Maggie agreed.

Kat made a list a couple of days later of all the agencies from the phone book that did in-home care for preschool children. There wasn't what you would call a whole slew of them, because day-cares are where most people nowadays took their children, while both parents were at work, or took the child to the caregiver's home. She checked the want ads and found two women that she would like to interview. She also placed an ad of her own.

With the want ads and the two agencies, she now had a total of four women. Kat wanted Maggie to be there over the course of the two days that it would take to talk with these women, as she needed her there to ask

questions that she herself might not think of. Kat's circumstances were a lot different, because she preferred to have Davy stay at home where Michael could watch him "one-on-one."

"Maggie, you don't mind sitting in on the questioning of the four women that I have for interviews today, do you?"

"Of course not. This may be very interesting."

The first woman to be interviewed was supposed to be there at 2:00 P.M. It was now almost at 2:30 P.M. and Kat told Maggie, "I don't know. This doesn't look too well to be late for a job interview. How reliable can this person be on a day-to-day basis if she can't be here on time?"

"I know, but we might as well hear her out, when she gets here if she gets here, as to why she is late, and see what she has to say about what she considers her qualifications to be in caring for a child," stated Maggie.

It was ten minutes later and Kat was just about ready to give up on this person when the front doorbell rang. She opened the door and there stood a young woman that she estimated to be about twenty years old. She was really quite pretty with a flawless complexion. She had blonde hair that cascaded to the middle of her back that Kat saw, because she bent over to retrieve a piece of paper that fell from the top of the books that she held in her left arm.

"Hi, my name is Susan Sheridan. Is this the residence of a Ms. Katherine O'Brien?" questioned Susan as she extended her hand to Kat and took a quick glance at the piece of paper that she now held in her right hand. Probably to check the address, Kat surmised.

"Yes, I'm Katherine O'Brien. Won't you please come in?"

"Thank you. And I must apologize for being late, but I haven't lived in Milwaukee all that long, and I don't really know my way around all that well yet. I transferred colleges after mid-semester break. I'm originally from a small town in Iowa called Hansen. Actually, we don't live in town but on a dairy farm about five miles out in the country. My parents are both dairy farmers."

Kat had to chuckle to herself at the dual mention of a dairy farm and that it was located in the country. Susan was noticeably upset, probably because she was late, thought Kat.

"Please, Ms. Sheridan, let me take your coat."

As Susan looked for a place to lay her books down, Kat took them from her, so that she could remove her coat, and then gave them back to her. She hung her coat inside the front closet and asked her to follow her into the kitchen. Maggie was sitting at the kitchen table drinking a cup of coffee when the two entered the doorway.

"Maggie," said Kat, "I would like to introduce Susan Sheridan. Susan, this is my sister, Maggie Ryan."

"How do you do, Mrs. Ryan?"

"Please, call me, Maggie."

"Please sit down, Ms. Sheridan," said Kat as she pulled out a chair across the table from where she and Maggie had intentions of sitting.

"Can I get you some coffee or a soda?"

"A soda. Diet, if you have it, will be fine, thank you. I must apologize again for being late. I left my apartment, which I rent with two other girls, with sufficient time to get here. That is, if I knew where I was going. I stopped at two filling stations for directions."

"We understand, Ms. Sheridan. Maggie and I have both been in that position, believe me," stated Kat.

"Please, Ms. O'Brien. Call me Susan, if you like."

"Well then, Susan. If that's going to be the case, please call me Kat, and my sister, Maggie. I never did like formalities, and this will make us all feel a little more at ease."

"Well, Susan. Can you give us a little history of yourself?"

After Susan left about an hour and a half later, it gave Kat and Maggie a chance to go over Kat's notes before the next interviewee was due.

"I really like her," stated Maggie. "She's sweet, wholesome, and she has a good head on her shoulders. And her choice of a career, nursing, is very commendable, and I think she would make a marvelous nurse."

"I agree. And with being the third oldest of ten kids, and having to take care of the seven younger ones for years, I'd say she has plenty of experience with children," noted Kat.

"Her classes coincide with your work hours all week, and if something would come up that she couldn't make it on a certain day or whatever, you'll have me as a backup," explained Maggie.

"Right. I think she is the one, but of course, we still have three more women coming, so it's only fair to meet them before I do make a final decision," stated Kat.

Kat was in Davy's bedroom as he was now awake from his nap, so Maggie answered the door at around 4:15 P.M. As Kat entered the foyer after putting Davy in his playpen, she assumed her mouth had to be hanging wide open, because she was not as good as Maggie at hiding her emotions. Hannah McDermott was the name Maggie told Kat as she introduced the two to each other. Kat surmised that Ms. McDermott's favorite color certainly wasn't blue, as she was dressed in pink from the bow in her hair down to the pink ankle boots with four-inch heels on her feet. Kat had a hard time differentiating Hannah's true age because of her dyed blonde hair that was of different lengths on both sides and sporting black roots, and her unbelievable amount of makeup on her eyes, and black lipstick, which matched the black fingernail polish on both hands. *Oh my*, thought Kat, *this is going to be very interesting*. Kat and Maggie were taught from a young age on to not judge a book by its cover, but this was certainly going to be a tough one to deal with or stay impartial to with her way of thinking, as to what this girl was all about. It just wasn't going to happen in Kat's mind, but she felt very strongly that she owed it to her to listen to what she had to say about herself and her qualifications to take care of a toddler.

As it turned out, Ms. McDermott just turned twenty-two years old, was currently unemployed by her own choice, did not have a driver's license, and was dropped off by someone who was parked down the block waiting for her to come out. They didn't know if her driver was male or female, as Hannah gave no indication to either gender. Kat knew Hannah was certainly not going to be considered for the position of taking care of Davy, so made short order of the rest of the interview and promised Hannah that she would call her either way when she made her decision, which Kat did the next morning, and told her that she had someone else in mind and thanked her for coming.

The third and last interviewee for the day came promptly at 7:00 P.M. Her name was Ms. Buleah DeMoore. She was retired, aged fifty-nine, and was the epitome of a circa 1960s spinster school teacher, which she was—a spinster, that is. As Kat invited her into the kitchen after helping her to remove her coat, Ms. DeMoore ran her white-gloved forefinger over Kat's table checking for dust. Kat figured that she must have found some after turning her hand over, because she uttered something that sounded close to a grunt.

I can't believe the agency sent a woman of her age, thought Kat as the three headed for the kitchen. She would never be able to keep up with Davy.

Kat went through the same routine of questions that she did with the previous two, even though she knew Ms. DeMoore would never work out, as she had a hard time keeping awake during the interview, which Kat kept to a quick twenty minutes.

"I don't know about you, Maggie, but this has been one very long and interesting day to say the least," chuckled Kat as the two sisters returned to the kitchen after escorting Ms. DeMoore to the door.

"There has to be a better word to describe this day than 'interesting.' With the exception of Susan, I'd say it was absolutely entertaining."

"Yeah, I know. If we told anyone about the last two, they'd say we were making the whole thing up. I'm going to fix myself a nightcap. Would you like one?"

"Sure. We both deserve one, after the day that we just went through."

The two sisters spent the next two hours enjoying their drinks and laughing almost throughout the entire conversation. They wondered what tomorrow would bring with the last woman to be interviewed and decided to call it a night.

The final interviewee arrived exactly at 3:30 P.M. the next day. As she opened the door, Kat realized there must be some mistake, for the person standing in front of her had to be no more than fifteen or sixteen years old.

"Hi, my name is Cindy Lancer, and I'm here in regard to the babysitting position that I read about in the newspaper."

Even though Kat figured there had to be some mistake, she invited Cindy in to interview her.

"Please, follow me into the kitchen where I will conduct the interview with you. Cindy, this is my sister, Maggie Ryan, and I'm Kat O'Brien."

"So very glad to meet both of you," said Cindy after nodding in reply to each of them.

"Take a seat here at the table across from us," suggested Kat.

"Thank you."

"Cindy, I'm going to get right to the point and ask you how old you are and did you read my ad thoroughly?"

"Yes, Ms. O'Brien. I did read your ad completely, and I am seventeen years old and a junior in high school."

"Well, Cindy. I'm not going to make any judgments in regard to your character, but I did request a mature person, someone in college or older."

"I know that is what the ad said, but I am very mature for my age."

"That may be so but—"

"Please, Ms. O'Brien," interrupted Cindy. "Please give me a chance to explain."

"Go ahead then."

"I will be very truthful with you, Ms. O'Brien. I am very mature for my age, like I said before, and basically, I'm a very shy person, and that is why it is hard for me to make friends at school. I am an only child, and I live with my only living relatives: my grandmother and grandfather. I don't know where I would be right now, if they hadn't taken me in to live with them when I was about two years old after my parents died in a car crash that killed both of them, instantly. The only consolation that I have is that they died together, because they loved each other so much. My grandparents are very loving people, but I need…" Cindy paused for a moment to think of the right words to say. "I need a connection with a family with children. I don't know if I'm expressing myself clearly to you, because it's kind of hard to describe the desires that I have in my heart. I'm really better at writing my feelings down on paper than to describe them verbally and—"

"Cindy," interrupted Kat, "why don't we all take a break at this point, and I will get my son up from his nap. I can hear him, and soon he will be letting me know that it's time to get him up," stated Kat as she left the kitchen nearly in tears.

Maggie wasn't in much better shape but asked Cindy, "Would you like something to drink, dear?"

"Yes, please. I would like some orange juice if you have it," replied Cindy, continuing with, "I don't drink coffee."

"A glass of orange juice coming right up," said Maggie, after rising from her chair and heading to the refrigerator. Shortly after, as she set the glass down in front of Cindy, Kat returned to the kitchen carrying Davy in her arms.

Davy was still pretty drowsy from his late afternoon nap but perked up as soon as he noticed Cindy sitting at the table. With one mad dash, he ran over to her, and begged her with his arms to lift her up onto her lap, which she did.

"Well now, looks like my son doesn't care how shy you are, and you have just made a new friend," remarked Kat.

"Sure looks that way," chuckled Maggie.

The three continued to talk while Davy sat on Cindy's lap. He was very content to be there with his thumb in his mouth. Cindy was invited to stay for lunch, which she accepted. The time flew by rapidly, but Kat knew that she had to make some kind of decision in regard to Cindy. She was just too young and inexperienced with the care of children, but she was so sweet and so very good with Davy.

Finally, Kat came to a decision. "Look, Cindy, I have decided that you are just too young to take care of Davy alone on a daily basis, but I have come up with a scenario that I think we all can be pleased with. How about if I pick you up on the weekends that your grandparents agree to, and the three of us—or even four of us, if Maggie hasn't anything planned—can help me with caring for Davy and any other chores that I might have to do around the house and outside too, of course. Or depending on how we feel, do fun things instead of working. Either way, I will pay you an hourly wage for being here. Does that sound okay with you?"

"Okay?" gasped Cindy. "Do you really mean it?"

"Yes, I really mean it," answered Kat, with a large grin on her face and a twinkle in her eye.

"Yes! Yes! Oh yes," replied Cindy with sheer delight. "I accept your proposal whole heartedly, Ms. O'Brien."

"All right, just one more thing I have to ask of you."

"Yes?"

"As long as we're going to be together, let's drop the formalities with names, and you can call me, Kat and my sister, Maggie, alright?"

"Yes, definitely, Kat and Maggie," chuckled Cindy in response.

"Good," answered Kat. "I will drive you home and have a talk with your grandparents about the arrangements that we have come up with and see if they will give you their approval. Do you want to go along with us, Maggie?"

"No thanks, Kat. I better get going home. Nice to have met you, Cindy. And I do hope I will see a lot of you in the future."

"Thank you. I do too."

Kat drove Cindy home and met her grandparents. She explained why Cindy arrived at her doorstep, and then let Cindy explain the rest of her story to them. They spent a good two hours talking with Davy sitting on Cindy's lap the entire time sucking his thumb, of course, in between his baby talk, which no one could understand but loved. They agreed to the arrangements to have Cindy come over to Kat's on the weekends when they have nothing planned. Upon their departure, both Kevin and Dolores hugged Kat and Davy, and Cindy wished they could stay longer.

As they were on their way home, Michael asked, "Mistress Kat?"

"Yes, Michael."

"I think you made a very wise decision with letting her be with you and Davy on the weekends. She needs you as much as you and Davy will need her."

"Do you really think so, Michael?"

"I know so. You will all be good for each other."

Just then, Davy popped up with, "Hi, Mike."

"Michael, Davy just said 'Hi' to you," replied Kat with an expression of total disbelief.

"Yes, Mistress Kat. Young Davy and I are quite good friends. As a matter of fact, I have been reading bedtime stories to him for about two weeks now."

"You mean he can hear you?"

"Oh yes, and he can also see me."

"See you? But how can that be? I've never been able to see you."

"The Almighty One thought it would be better if he could see and hear me because of his young age. This way, he will get to know me better and not be afraid. And Mistress Kat, before I forget, do you think you could get us some more reading material? We're on his last book."

"Oh my," laughed Kat, "I'm sure that can be arranged." *Wait until I tell Maggie about this,* thought Kat, who was still in shock.

As things turned out, Susan was the perfect choice to take care of Davy. She and Cindy were a big part of Kat and Davy's lives from then on. Susan was almost like a second mother to Davy as she continued to care for him during the week. She was very dependable and did extra little things around the house that Kat didn't expect but certainly appreciated and wanted to pay her extra because of it. Susan refused, saying she and Davy did those things together, and it was more like fun than work to her.

It was Susan's decision to make whether Cindy could come over and see Davy after school. As it turned out, she was there almost every day right after school up until the time that she had to leave to go home for supper. Her grandparents were in agreement with those arrangements and were content to stay home on most weekends, but when a special occasion occurred, then they expected Cindy to spend the time with them. She spent so much time at Kat's house that she was thinking of adding an extra room onto the house for her to live in.

She made a new rule: once a month they all should go to a movie, shopping, or out for a nice dinner together, on her. Maggie was also invited to go along and did, except on the Saturdays that she had other plans.

As time went on, the four of them—Kat, Maggie, Susan and Cindy—became very close and almost inseparable and came to care for each other dearly.

For Davy's second birthday party, Kat planned it to coincide with Chris' winter break from the Air Force Academy, as she had something up her sleeve in regard to Chris and Cindy. The entire family was there along with Bev, Susan, Cindy, and Cindy's grandparents, who were all considered family.

Susan and Cindy were sitting on the couch playing with Davy when the entire Ryan clan came walking in together. Kat introduced Susan and Cindy to Chris for the first time. Kat couldn't quite figure it out, as it wasn't really a standoffish reply from Cindy, but more like indifference afterward, even though she was friendly with her initial cordial response to him. She was now a senior in high school and had told Kat previously that she dated a few times, but wasn't really interested in any of the boys afterward. She was still a little shy around strangers but had come a long way in Kat's estimation from the time that she showed up on her doorstep until now. Kat didn't have time to think about the situation now, as she had a house full of people and Davy's party to attend to.

The party was going full swing and without a hitch, and everyone looked to be having a good time to Kat's relief. Chris spent a lot of time talking and kidding around with Tim and Chad, but as Kat noticed quite often, Chris kept an eye on Cindy's every move. He did approach her a few times, but the conversation between them was always short-lived.

While Kat was in the kitchen and putting the number "two" candle on the cake, Maggie walked in and asked, "Need any help with anything?"

"Not right now, but will you serve the ice cream after I give everyone a piece of cake?"

"Sure. I guess I can handle that chore without any trouble," chuckled Maggie, but further requesting of Kat that when she had a minute, she'd like to talk with her.

"How about when Davy starts to rip all of his presents open and then will later play with the boxes?" laughed Kat. "I'm really grateful to Marshall for recording the party so far. Is he getting tired of doing it?"

"Are you kidding? He's in seventh heaven. This way he doesn't have to make small talk with everyone."

As Davy started ripping the paper with gusto off of his first present, as Kat predicted, Maggie turned to her and asked, "What's with Cindy and Chris? I know my son, and I can see the interested look in his eyes when Cindy is near him, but she hardly gives him the time of day."

"I don't know, but I've been thinking the same thing from the time that I introduced them. I don't get it either. Chris is one hell of a good-looking guy with a super personality, and Davy is crazy about all your boys but Chris in particular. Must be his charisma!" noted Kat.

After the party wound down and everyone had left but Cindy, who offered to stay and help clean up after Kat laid Davy down for a well needed nap, the two were in the kitchen doing dishes.

Kat had every intention of doing a little snooping and asked, "So Cindy, do you think the party was a success?"

"I'd say yes, because it sure seemed to me that everyone was having a good time."

"What about you? Did you have a good time?"

Cindy thought that this was a strange question for Kat to ask but replied anyway with, "Yes, I had a great time, and your family members are all so nice."

"I think so too. What did you think of Maggie's three sons?"

"I think all three are very nice."

"It meant a lot to all of us that Chris was able to get back home for the party. He's such a nice kid, and Davy loves all of his cousins, but for some reason he sure favors Chris."

"Yes, I saw him playing with Davy more than Tim and Chad did. Does he like children in particular or just Davy?"

"I really don't know the answer to that question, but I suspect that any one who treats Davy the way he does, even though he is his cousin, must surely love kids."

"I suppose you're right."

"I know we never talked about this subject before, but do you see yourself getting married and having kids of your own someday?"

"I suppose I do."

Kat felt that she was getting no where at this point, so figured she would take the direct approach instead and said, "Chris seemed to be staring at you quite a bit today, and in my opinion, that told me he was interested in what he saw."

"You really think so?" questioned Cindy with an excited tone to her voice.

Now we're getting somewhere, thought Kat after seeing the expression on Cindy's face. "Yes, I really do think so." *Duh*, thought Kat. *That's it! Why didn't I think of this before. Cindy's interested, but like me, when I first met Jamie, I became tongue-tied and nervous and couldn't get away from him fast enough. With Cindy's shyness, she probably didn't know what to say or how to react to Chris, so avoided him as much as she possibly could. I'll tell Maggie what I've learned,* Kat decided, *and if they are actually interested in each other, then both of us have got to stay out of it and let the two of them carry it from here.*

Kat was right on the mark, for Chris did come over the next day to see Davy with the intent that he would like to spend as much time with him as he could before he had to go back to the Academy. Kat knew that Chris' motive was truly sincere in regard to Davy, but she also knew of his hidden objective: Cindy.

She stayed with Kat in the kitchen for the first half hour until Kat said, "I think I'll go and work on my book for awhile. Why don't you go in and see what Chris and Davy are doing?"

Another half hour later, Kat could hear three distinct voices of laughter coming from the living room. She told herself to stay out of it but after another hour, she decided Davy needed a nap so she took him into his bedroom to lay him down. While in there, she heard the two of them talking. Kat exited the bedroom with one big grin on her face and feeling smug as hell. As she entered the living room and saw the two of them on the couch conversing, she informed them, "I must get back to my book, so I will leave the two of you alone. Help yourself to anything you want from the kitchen. Left over birthday cake is the specialty of the day!"

The winter months flew by without a hitch as far as not having to deal with any demon activity since Davy was born. That and the fact that Kat had been working Saturdays for the last twelve weeks in a row, since Davy's second birthday party, because of an onslaught of special orders coming in from all over the country. There seemed to be no end in sight according to her boss Dan.

Kat sat in Maggie's kitchen on a Sunday afternoon during the early part of May sharing a piece of a five-layer chocolate cake for dessert with Davy. She figured she really didn't need it, especially with just finishing the wonderful meal that Maggie had prepared for her family and had invited Kat and Davy to join them. Kat turned to Maggie and informed her, "You know, Maggie, if Davy and I lived with you and ate like this every day, I'd hate to think of what we'd both look like by now."

"Well, thank you for the compliment, if I can assume that that's what it was, but we don't eat like this all the time, just on Sundays. It's the only day that Marshall, Tim, Chad and I can really spend a little quality time together, which consists of the four of us talking to each other in between chewing our food. And as soon as the meal is over, so is the quality time," laughed Maggie.

"I really think that you missed your calling. Between that fantastic meal you just made and this delicious homemade cake, you really should have been a chef. Mom's meals were always 'hasty and somewhat tasty,' so you didn't inherit your cooking skills from her, but—"

"Mom had four kids and a husband to take care of," interrupted Maggie.

"Maybe so, but you have three kids and a husband to take care of," interrupted Kat in return. "Does one more kid or less, whichever way you look at it, make the difference?" questioned Kat.

"No, Kat, it doesn't," chuckled Maggie. "Just like you don't care to cook, Mom didn't either."

"Well, that's a first. You discovered something Mom and I can agree about."

"Don't be cynical. You and Mom agree on a lot of things."

"Not while we're in the same room together. You still haven't answered my question. What's your secret to being a good cook?"

"There's no secret to it at all. You have to enjoy it first, and then everything from there just falls into place."

"No skill involved then?"

"Well yes, of course, there is skill involved, but—"

"I have absolutely none in the kitchen."

"That's because you don't have any patience. If it wasn't for the microwave, you and Davy would be eating out all the time or living on peanut butter and jelly sandwiches."

"Davy and I happen to like peanut butter and jelly sandwiches, thank you very much!"

"Kat, you underestimate yourself. You do pretty good in the kitchen."

"Right, Maggie. You want to give me an example?"

"The pot roast that you made a few weeks back with potatoes and carrots."

"As I recall, that roast was tougher than shoe leather and about as tasty."

"It wasn't all that bad," giggled Maggie.

"Right! As soon as I put my fork into the meat to hold it, so that I could cut it, the fork bent in half and I ended up cutting the rest of it with my electric knife. Now that's what I would call a really tender and juicy piece of meat," roared Kat.

"Well, it could be that your silverware was not of the best quality. Nah! It was kind of tough, I must agree, but…" Maggie couldn't finish her sentence or come up with any more excuses with remembering the incident all too well that Kat was referring to and started laughing so hard that she was in tears.

I don't believe those two, thought Marshall, with a grin on his face while he was in the den trying to get some paper work finished but was distracted by the noise coming from the kitchen. *Every time the two of them get together, this happens. Good! They both can do with some laughter right about now.*

"You seem to be in an exceptionally good mood today. Any special reason?" questioned Kat as she and Maggie started to calm down.

"Yes, as a matter of fact there is. We received a letter from Chris yesterday."

"Oh good! How's he doing?"

"According to him, fine. I'm really happy and proud of him, because he had the courage to try and make his dreams come true."

"Good for you, Maggie. Does this mean that you're getting better at dealing with Chris being away from home?"

"Oh yes, a lot better. I had to keep telling myself that my boys can't be here with Marshall and me forever. They have a life of their own to carve out, and whatever they do accomplish, will make us happy."

Out of pure nosiness, Kat asked, "Did he tell you of anything exciting going on with him, or has he met someone yet?"

"Every day is exciting for him, not only because of his involvement with the Falcon football team, but also, because every day that passes gets him closer to the time when he can start training to be a pilot."

"I have to say that the kid has guts. You couldn't pay me enough to get in an airplane. So when does his actual pilot training start? Does he know?" questioned Kat.

"The year after he graduates he will start. And according to what he has told us, that will take a whole year, and if he passes, that's when he will achieve his pilot status and go on for more training, if he chooses to do so."

"With Chris' determination, the word 'failure' will not be part of his vocabulary," stated Kat.

"I know. Even as a kid, if he had a goal in mind, he never gave up until he met it. As far as your other question is concerned as to whether he has met a girl or not, it has already happened."

"You mean it? He met a girl out there? Another cadet, I bet."

"No. Actually, we know her."

"Maggie, you're starting to confuse me. I don't know of any girl whose a cadet in the Air Force. So what are you talking about?"

"I'm talking about Cindy."

"Our Cindy?"

"Yes. With every letter that we receive from him, he inquires if I have seen her or know how she's doing."

"Maggie, those could be very legitimate questions from Chris. He met her, liked her, and could be genuinely interested in her welfare. I wouldn't go making too much of it."

"Before I found out, my intuition told me that there's more between the two of them than meets the eye. And you know, Kat, my instincts are usually correct."

"Before you found out what?"

"The two of them have been corresponding on a regular basis since he was home for Davy's birthday party. I can read between the lines, and I think he is falling in love with her."

"What's so bad about that? You know and have come to love Cindy, and she's about the sweetest and most caring person that I've ever met."

"I know. I truly do love Cindy and think the world of her, but they're both too young."

"Poppycock! C'mon, Maggie. Love has no age restrictions. I don't care if you're fourteen, like I was when I met and fell in love with Jamie or eighty. People do and will fall in love at any age."

"I think it was puppy love and infatuation with you toward Jamie."

"I agree that infatuation played a part in it, but I fell in love with Jamie at first sight. Even if he hadn't returned that love to me, which wasn't the case, because he did fall in love with me and we married, but because of the way that I loved him so deeply. That love would have lasted me a lifetime no matter how the circumstances in our lives turned out. A person can fall in love with another and not see him or her for the rest of their lives, and love can be one-sided; the other one may never know that someone did love them their entire life."

"This is different than Jamie and your story."

"How's that?"

"You saw each other every day. They haven't seen each other in over three months."

"Maggie, people who are complete strangers have fallen in love with each other. I read an article in the paper the other day about the rising matches between couples who have never met but fall in love while corresponding over the computer."

"Oh Kat, I don't believe that tripe for a minute."

"Tripe or not, it has happened."

"He can't fall in love now. He has another four years at least to finish with the career he planned, and if she would get pregnant, and a baby comes along, they'd have to get married. They'd have to find somewhere to live, and I don't think cadets can have wives living with them on the Academy, and—."

"Whoa, Maggie. For God's sake, calm down. You're blowing this whole thing out of proportion. Wasn't Chris only home for about five days when he was on leave when they met for the first time?"

"Yes."

"Chris may be a fast worker, but he isn't that fast. And besides, Cindy isn't the type to hop in bed with someone she just met."

"You think they did it?"

"Maggie, you're not listening to me. Yes, I'm positive they didn't do it," chuckled Kat at Maggie's reference to sex but not being able to bring herself to say it again. "If it's true that they are falling for each other, so be it. You can't turn love 'on and off' like a light switch, because of a time schedule. 'I will love you now but will stop and wait until after you become a pilot, then I'll start up again afterward,' isn't realistic."

"That's silly," stated Maggie.

"Exactly my point. Chris isn't about to let anything or anyone interfere with his plans, but that doesn't mean that he can't fall in love in the meantime because of those plans. And as far as Cindy is concerned, she's still in high school and plans to graduate and go on to college. She's as levelheaded as they come."

"Yeah, I guess you're right, Kat. I'm blowing this whole thing out of proportion."

"Damn right you are! Besides, if they do get married in the future, that will make you a mother-in-law, and then you can stew about a woman taking your baby boy away from you," laughed Kat, after giving Maggie a wink. "On that final note, Davy and I are out of here. Thank you again for inviting us for supper. We'll talk later."

Maggie's second oldest son Tim turned eighteen on May 26, 2004, and was due to graduate in June. Unlike his brother Chris, Tim waited until the beginning of his senior year to make an appointment with his guidance counselor to discuss with him his plans to join the Marines upon graduation. Mr. Davis, who was still at the school for nearly thirty-five years was about to retire when school let out this summer. Over the course of those thirty-five years, he must have talked to thousands of kids and hoped that he was an influencing factor in helping to shape their lives, and if that was the case, his time spent here at this school was worth every minute. As Tim knocked on Mr. Davis's office door, a voice replied from the other side, "Come in. Hi, Tim. You're right on time. Close the door and take a seat. By the way, before we get started, how is Chris doing in the Air Force these days?"

"He's been in for two years now, and from what his letters say, he's doing okay. Chris has always been a planner and did everything since he was a freshman to make sure he met all the requirements and also made sure that he was capable to join the Air Force. Unlike me, who procrastinates and likes to take the shortcuts whenever I can, because I don't have the patience to plan too far ahead. I just hope I haven't waited too long and could be running out of time."

"Good for him. He's got a good head on his shoulders and should go far in this world. So what can I do for you today, Tim? And what do you mean by 'almost running out of time'?"

"I want very much to enlist in the Marine Corp as soon as I can after school is out. I did some checking and discovered that I can and already have accomplished some of their requirements to enlist."

"I see. Let me get your files out," responded Mr. Davis as he walked over to a tall filing cabinet, opened it, and reached in for Tim's files. "I see that you have managed to stay out of trouble for the last three years. Good for you. Keep it that way!"

"I had no choice. Even though the opportunity was there, I was too busy playing football, basketball, and of course, studying," laughed Tim, putting studying last on his list of things he did. "I wasn't about to do anything stupid to get kicked off the team."

"Our team can't afford to lose a really good quarterback like you, so please keep your nose clean like you plan to." Mr. Davis caught Tim's statement with regard to studying very clearly and asked, "Are you taking the necessary courses and maintaining a good grade point in each? And out of curiosity, which sport of the two is your favorite?"

"Football, definitely. And yes, I have a 3.5 grade point average so far."

"You had one hell of a season your sophomore year when Chris was one of your receivers. That kid never missed the ball."

"I know. I threatened him with telling Ma if he did," smiled Tim, which brought about laughter from Mr. Davis.

"So you want to join the Marines? Do your parents know of your decision?"

"No, I haven't told them yet. I did tell my younger brother Chad, but I made him promise me that he wouldn't tell anyone about this, especially Mom and Dad. He did protest and told me it was only fair, and that they had a right to know."

"He's right, Tim. This is too important to keep from your parents."

"I know, but when Chris left home, Mom was depressed, which seemed to go on forever. I don't think I could stand to see her go through the same thing with me, not for a whole year, anyway. After the graduation party that she insists on having for me, I'll spill it to her."

"Well, Tim, I personally would handle it differently, but it's your choice to do what you feel is right. That is the key word here and is something you will have to deal with the rest of your life: choices. Believe me, I've been through it many more times than I'd like to admit. I do know one thing for sure, Tim: you have to be eighteen years old when you sign the final papers to enlist yourself. Because at seventeen, you have to have your parents' permission, like I said before. And if that happens, the service will then give you up to a year to enter, which is determined from the date the papers are signed, giving you time to finish high school. I know most of the requirements needed to enter, but that is better left to a recruiter to explain to you, whom I will put you in contact with. Give me a week at the most, and I'll get back to you, okay?"

"Sounds good to me, Mr. Davis, and thanks for all your advice."

"You're welcome, Tim. It's my job to give advice."

Mr. Davis came through for Tim in less than a week and gave him the name, address, and telephone number of the nearest recruiter in the area. Tim was on his way to becoming a Marine, something he always wanted to be since he was a kid.

The money coming in from all the overtime Kat was putting in at work was a profitable boost to Davy's college fund, but she was starting to get real tired of working every Saturday for the last four months. Very tired. And besides, she felt that it was more important to be with Davy as much as she could from now on, so she confronted her boss Dan to find out how long this mandatory bull was supposed to last.

"Dan, you told me almost a month ago that there's a good possibility that our workload will finally come to a halt. Next week will be a month

and personally, I've had it! I do have a life outside of this place and a son to raise."

"I know, Kat. You're not the only one who is unhappy with the heavy workload that we've put everyone here through, but it was necessary. We couldn't afford to lose our steady customers and new ones, because our girls didn't want to work the overtime. The owner, Mr. Phillips, informed us over a month ago to hire outside help and train them for third shift, because, as I said before, there's no end in sight yet."

"So what does that mean for the first and second shifts? Do we keep going as we have been with working Saturdays until God only knows when?"

"Well, I don't know about God's schedule," chuckled Dan at Kat's nonconforming attitude, "but another two weeks of working on Saturdays should do it. By then, the third shift should be trained enough to do their part in easing the load with no one working overtime anymore."

Damn! thought Kat. *There goes three days off for Memorial Day weekend.*

With Tim's graduation from high school coming within the next week, Kat figured that she had better call Maggie and see what she should give him for a gift. She didn't know if he wanted anything special or just give him the old standby: money. She also wanted to offer her help with his party, because Maggie was always there for her when she needed help with anything.

"Hi, Maggie. It's me. Just calling to find out how Tim's graduation party plans were coming along and I was wondering, if you needed any help? Also, what should I give him for a present?"

"How about a going away present, instead?"

What now? thought Kat. *I've never heard Maggie so angry*. "Dare I ask what's going on?"

"I'm sorry, Kat. I didn't mean to bark at you like that. None of this is your fault."

"I'm glad to hear that, but if it helps you any, bark away. Now, what's not my fault?" questioned Kat with trepidation as to what Maggie would soon tell her.

"Tim's leaving shortly after graduation and—"

"Cool," said Kat, not really understanding the word *leaving*. "Are you and Marshall sending him on a trip for his graduation? So what's the problem? Doesn't he like where you're sending him?"

"No, Kat. We're not sending him on a damn trip! He went and signed up for the Marine Corps right under our noses. He didn't say a damn thing to us, because he knew that I would act like I'm acting, and he couldn't stand to see me act like I'm acting," responded Maggie, with choking sounds and sobbing at the same time.

Oh brother, oops! thought Kat, so she quickly responded before she hung up the phone with, "I'll be right over, Maggie. Sit down and calm down!"

When she arrived, she heard two loud voices coming from the den. She walked into the kitchen and there was Maggie baking a pie.

"I just talked to you not even a half hour ago, and I come speeding over here in my car, driving like a maniac, because I was so worried about you, and I arrive and find you baking?"

"Yes, well, I have to do something to keep myself busy when I'm upset."

"Are you upset enough to come over and clean my house for me? I can't even remember the last time I dusted the furniture, and the only reason I'm keeping up with the laundry is because of Davy," smirked Kat.

"Kat, this is not a laughing matter. It's a very serious turn of events for Marshall and me."

"C'mon, Maggie. Lighten up a little. There is no serious matter that can't be worked out."

"Easy for you to say, because it's not your problem."

"True, but if everyone involved calms down, talks normally to each other without yelling, and discusses the situation rationally, a solution is sure to follow."

"Always the optimist, huh, Kat? I'm sorry," said Maggie, after realizing the words that just came out of her mouth. "You're here to help me and give me some advice, and I'm taking all my frustrations out on you."

Kat ignored the dig from Maggie, because she knew that she didn't mean it and she hadn't realized until now just how distraught her sister really was.

"So how long has the war between Marshall and Tim been going on in the den?"

"It started just shortly before you called."

"Look, Maggie. Maybe this wasn't such a good idea for me to come over here, so I'd better leave now and talk to you later."

Before Maggie could reply, they both heard the front door slam and then there was silence throughout the entire house. Marshall entered the kitchen shortly after.

"Hi, Kat. I'm sorry if you caught any of that tirade going on between my son and myself."

"No problem, Marshall. I was just telling Maggie that maybe this is not a good time for me to be here right now."

"Nonsense," said Marshall, as he pulled up a stool closer to the counter next to Kat. "You're family. And besides, three heads are better than two. A quiet discussion between the three of us may make a world of difference in alleviating Maggie's and my fears for our son's future and the disappointments that we feel right now because of his actions. It may bring down the high volume of tension that is permeating in the air right now for the two of us."

"Before I can contribute my opinions to this conversation, I need to know all the details," stated Kat.

"You want to tell the story to Kat, Honey? Or should I?" Marshall questioned Maggie.

"I guess I should, because I was the one that found the evidence and started this whole mess in the first place," informed Maggie, and she continued with, "I began to wash the bedding in all three bedrooms, and once I started, I decided to strip the beds completely. I figured that I might as well turn the mattress on each of the beds too. That's when I saw the booklet and a copy of his signed enlistment papers under the mattress. It seems that our son approached his guidance counselor at the very beginning of school this year and asked him for his help in contacting the Marine Corps to make known his wishes to enlist when he turned eighteen. He made Chad swear that he wouldn't breathe a word of his intentions to anyone, the least being Marshall and me. He told us the reason he did not tell us right away was to save us the heartache and worry that we would feel, especially since one of our boys is already gone from home. The counselor found a recruiter and made an appointment for Tim to meet with him as soon as possible, which turned out to be within three days. Tim met with him and was given a verbal list and a pamphlet listing all of the requirements needed to be accomplished by a person seeking to be a recruit in order to be accepted by the Marine Corps."

"I hope you don't mind if I interrupt again," said Kat, "but I thought you had to have your parents' permission to enter any branch of the service."

"We always thought so too, until we experienced Chris' enlistment into the Air Force Academy. If you are seventeen, you do have to have permission from your parents, but if you are eighteen, no," informed Maggie.

"Tim told me he worked hard his entire senior year making sure he met those requirements, which I have to admit that I'm very proud of our son for taking the initiative that was required of him. I'm still mad as hell with him for not telling us a lot sooner of his plans," interjected Marshall. "Go on, honey."

"At the last parent-teachers' conference that I went to, Tim's grade point average was 3.7," informed Maggie.

"I guess he takes after you, Marshall. Smart as a whip," interjected Kat.

"So if Marshall is the brains of this family, what am I?" asked Maggie, with a pretend injured expression on her face.

"Betty Crocker," replied Kat, with no real expression on her face.

"Don't you dare laugh, Marshall James Ryan," warned Maggie.

"I didn't know your middle name was James," said Kat.

"Yeah, it is. My middle name is for my father's oldest brother, and my first name is after my father's father: Grandpa Marshall."

"You never told me that, Maggie."

"Well Kat, somewhere along the line, it must have slipped my mind," retorted Maggie.

"All right, girls. The break is over," informed Marshall, thinking a little squabble between Maggie and Kat could follow at any minute.

"I just have one more thing to say," said Maggie. "I could kick myself for not recognizing that something was different about Tim lately."

"What do you mean, sweetheart?"

"Our son was always at the mall like clockwork, checking out the girls after football practice, but he started volunteering, like Chris did at the Soup Kitchen. Unlike Chris, our son Tim is very aware of his good looks and always used them to his advantage with chasing after those girls. Gads! The evidence was right there under my nose, and I wasn't aware of it. I thought that he maybe forgot about himself for a change and was thinking of others, instead. When all along, that community service helped him to get into the Marines."

"I detect a slight measure of cynicism here, Maggie," commented Kat.

"Rightly so, because I'm still mad at him."

"Before we continue, I better call Cindy and ask her if it's okay for me to be here a little longer. It's only fair. Just because she was by my house at the time of your phone call, Maggie, doesn't mean that I should take advantage of her willingness to watch Davy until I get back home."

"Go ahead, Kat, and make the call," said Marshall. "Even though you may have to leave, I do wish you could stay, so that Maggie and I can get your input into all that has been discussed so far and also with the rest of the information yet to come. We do value your opinions. Right, honey?"

"Right! We certainly do, Kat."

"Well, thank you both. That's really nice of you to say."

Kat called Cindy on her cell phone and was told that everything was fine with her and Davy and that she didn't have any plans for the rest of the day.

"Good! When I get home," responded Kat, "I'll take the three of us out for supper. Thanks, Cindy. With Kat's phone call finished, Maggie went on to say, "I'm not going to bore you with all the details written in this pamphlet" that she held it up in the air for emphasis as to how angry that she still was, "and I will just give you an idea of some of the requirements, because Marshall and I have read the entire thing already."

After giving Kat a fundamental idea of what the Marine booklet entailed, Marshall requested of Maggie, "Look back on those enlistment papers over there to see if Tim wrote down any occupational fields that he would be interested in."

"Okay," answered Maggie while skimming through the necessary papers to find the answer to Marshall's request. "Here it is under Enlistment Options Program, which guarantees well-qualified applicants an assignment to one of 130 occupational fields. Okay that's it, I'm done," informed Maggie. "Here, Marshall, you can look over the rest if you want to," Maggie said, as she handed over the pamphlet.

"I don't know about you guys, but this is pretty much all Greek to me," inserted Kat.

"I agree 100 percent," admitted Maggie.

"What do you think, Marshall?" asked Maggie.

"I'll save my opinions after I see the test score results," informed Marshall, knowing full well after reading Tim's choice of jobs that after his son was highly trained, he had his sights set on the intelligence aspect of the Marine Corps according to the rest of his enlistment papers.

"Well," said Kat, "Tim is a real bright kid, and I suspect that he knows his own mind, and if this is what he truly wants for his future, so be it. We all have choices to make during our lifetime, and this evidently is Tim's choice."

"I know what you are saying, Kat. It is definitely Tim's right to make a choice as to what he wants to do with his future. I only hope my son knows what he is getting himself into here," stated Marshall, with a worried frown. "And I definitely will make an appointment with his recruiter to find out for myself."

"Well, Guys, I best be getting home. Would the two of you like to go to dinner with us? My treat." questioned Kat.

After Marshall and Maggie exchanged glances, Maggie replied with, "Thanks for the offer, but I think we'll take a rain check. It's best for us that we talk a little more about this Marine thing."

"I completely understand," said Kat, before taking her leave.

Tim returned home within two hours from the time that he left. This gave him a chance to really think about the discussion that he and his father had prior to his storming out of the house. *I guess he was right,* concluded Tim. *I had no right to base my decision upon telling my folks about enlisting in the Marine Corps solely on how I thought they would react. Mr. Davis was right with telling me that they had a right to know right from*

the start. Upon entering the house, he found Marshall and Maggie in the kitchen about to eat supper.

Marshall was the first one to speak with, "Hi, Son. How are you doing?"

"Okay. Look, Mom and Dad, I'm really sorry if I hurt the both of you with the way I handled things."

"Are you hungry?" asked Maggie. "I made plenty to eat."

"Yeah, I'm starved."

The three talked while eating and carried on a conversation with each other for almost another two hours. The air was cleared with Tim relating everything that took place since he first met with Mr. Davis. He informed them how everything turned out. He passed with flying colors all of the physical requirements and scored high on all of the aptitude tests and opted to do his basic training at San Diego, California.

"Since you told us all this information, I guess it won't be necessary for me to make an appointment with your recruiting officer," explained Marshall.

"You were really thinking of doing that?" questioned Tim.

"Damn right! You're a very important part of our life, Tim. I wasn't about to let our son go into the Marines without knowing all of the facts. You should have told us of your plans long before now and maybe, just maybe, we could have met with your recruiter and helped you with your planning and final decisions. That's what parents are here for: to help their children in anyway possible," answered Marshall, with a visible tear starting to form in one eye.

"Your father's right, Honey," inserted Maggie, both eyes tearing up.

"I'm so sorry that I caused all of these problems between us. As Aunt Kat would say, I really made a bad judgment call."

With that last statement from Tim, three people had a smile on their faces, which led to them hugging each other very tightly and for a long time.

"I can set up an appointment with my recruiter, whose name is Charles Ross, so that you can meet him and ask him any questions that you have of him. Does that sound fair and help to ease the situation any?" questioned Tim.

"It's definitely a good start for your mother and me, so that we can get as much information as we can before you have to ship out. Which is when?"

"Three weeks after school is out is when I have to report."

Three weeks is not a long time for us, thought Marshall and Maggie.

"We'll have to make the most of the time we have together, agreed?" asked Marshall.

"Agreed," is all Tim was capable of saying, with the angst that the three of them were experiencing. Within a few days, Marshall and Maggie had their chance to meet with Tim's recruiter and ask their questions, which helped to alleviate some of the anxiety the two of them were dealing with together.

Maggie promised that she would keep a strong fortitude for Tim's sake through his graduation, his party, and the final count down of the three weeks until it was time to leave. She kept that promise very amicably, even with his departure from the airport. Marshall, Maggie, and Chad said their good-byes to their son and brother, and watched as he left the room and disappeared through the tunnel to the plane.

With not being able to sleep and knowing it was late, Maggie made an extra effort to quietly leave their bed so as not to awaken Marshall. She slipped on her bathrobe, left through the backdoor and sat on the back porch. When all the pent-up emotions were set free, she sobbed uncontrollably until there were no more tears to shed.

Marshall heard Maggie leave and then cried quietly until he finally fell asleep.

It was going on three weeks since Tim left and almost the end of July, and Kat had not seen Maggie. She talked to her sister over the phone but purposely stayed away, so that she and Marshall had time alone to make the adjustment on their own. She said her good-byes to Tim the afternoon of his graduation party, hugged and kissed him, and then she wished him the best of luck with his future endeavors. Maggie had asked her to join them the night before his departure for dinner at a newly opened restaurant, but Kat declined, feeling it was better for all that they have their last night together alone. She would miss Tim with his loveable characteristics, but right now her heart went out to Marshall and Maggie. She praised her sister in her mind as to how she put on such a brave front for everyone's benefit, but she knew for a fact that it would take Maggie longer to get over the circumstances with Tim having to leave. Not completely, because of him, but with the combination that her two boys were now gone from home. *Someday, I'll have to face the same situation with Davy, and then I'll truly know first hand what Marshall and Maggie are going through*, thought Kat. She missed her sister terribly.

Kat decided to give Maggie a call and see if she'd like to join her for dinner, which would give them a chance to talk.

"Hi, Maggie. It's me. How are you and Marshall doing?"

"We're doing all right. That meeting that we had with Mr. Ross, Tim's recruiter, really enlightened us as to what the Marine Corps is all about. It's still a little lonely around here, but we have Chad and with every day that passes, it gets a little easier to handle. What about you? How are things going for you? And Davy, how's he doing? I sure miss the little guy."

"We're doing great, especially since I don't have to work any more Saturdays."

"That's good! I really think it was starting to wear you down, Kat."

"It was, but that's behind me now. What do you think of the two of us getting together on Saturday and having dinner somewhere nice? Or are you tied up with anything else?"

"Nope. Marshall has another new client flying in from Florida, and he has to take him out for dinner and discuss business. Chad will be working at the Soup Kitchen on Saturday afternoon and evening until it closes for the day."

"Soup Kitchen, you said? What is that?" questioned Kat, not knowing for sure if that is what Maggie said to her.

"Remember I mentioned it to you in regard to Tim's enlistment into the Marines? Chris was the first one to start working there as a community service, then Tim and now Chad. It is called The Soup Kitchen, and they prepare and serve delicious homemade meals to the homeless. We'll talk more about it when we get together, alright?"

"Sounds good. How about at 5:00 P.M.? Davy and I will pick you up, because the restaurant isn't that far past your house, or is that too early for you?"

"No, of course not, 5:00 P.M. will be fine. See you then."

Kat decided to wear a white sundress with black polka dots and a matching short sleeve cuffed jacket, which went to the middle of her back and could be tied just above the waistline in front. She wore a pair of white sandals with black polka dots across the instep and sported a white purse, with you guessed it, black polka dots. She very seldom dressed up and this was really a treat compared to her usual attire of jeans or shorts.

"I look like something straight out of the forties, but I like the way it all goes together," said Kat to Davy, just before he made a quick attempt to pull one of the polka dots from her purse.

Davy was dressed in black cotton slacks with a short sleeve cotton shirt, which sported an attached little black bow tie. His black tennis shoes had Velcro straps and little lights that only lit up when he walked and scattered light around his shoes. *I assume that is the reason he runs around*

the house all the time, so that he can watch his shoes blink off and on, laughed Kat to herself.

"Alright, you handsome young man, are we ready to go?" asked Kat as she lifted Davy into her arms. She grabbed her purse and his spring jacket, which was hanging on the front doorknob where she put it earlier, so that she wouldn't forget to take it. She checked to make sure that her keys were in the front pouch of her purse, and the two were off to meet with Maggie.

While driving to Maggie's, Kat put in her Conway Twitty disc. She looked in her rearview mirror and saw the big grin forming on Davy's mouth when Conway began to sing. *Guess I got my kid hooked on Conway*, chuckled Kat. Davy's vocabulary was getting better, but still limited, so as Kat sang along with the words, so did Davy with his own version of the song. The two made quite a sight.

"Hi, Sis," said Kat as Maggie opened the door to the front seat to get in. Maggie changed her mind when she looked at Davy in the back seat and decided to open the door and give her young nephew a big kiss and hug. He was just as excited to see his aunt Maggie and responded warmly.

"He remembers me."

"That's because he has the memory of an elephant," laughed Kat. "Well, of course he remembers you. It's only been three weeks or so since he last saw you."

"I know, but I was a little scared that he might not."

When the three were shown to their table and Kat had Davy settled in the child seat, they looked over the menu with great anticipation, because everyone was very hungry.

"What are you having?" questioned Maggie.

Kat, without hesitation, said, "I'm going to have a steak. This is a special occasion, so I'm going to order the filet mignon, or the T-bone, or the Porter House. Oh shit, now I'm not sure which one to order."

"Oh shit," replied Davy, pointing at a picture on the menu.

"Oops, I've got to learn to watch my vocabulary around my son."

"I'd say," agreed Maggie, following with a little speech about how young people Davy's age are so impressionable and repeat everything they hear.

"Is that spaghetti and meatballs that he's pointing at?"

"Yes."

"Is that what you're going to order for him?"

"No. He just likes the picture; it's colorful. Davy's choice for a good meal is chicken fingers and French fries with lots and lots of ketchup."

"I think I'll have the seafood platter," said Maggie. "It comes with a little bit of everything."

Ever since she was a kid, Kat always liked her food hot. But by the time she cut Davy's chicken fingers and poured plenty of ketchup onto his plate, her steak and baked potato were just warm. "At least I had a hot bowl of chicken soup," chuckled Kat, after sharing it with Davy and giving him every other spoonful after she blew on it.

"You're giving him more ketchup?"

"Yup. He's nuts about it. Look how many chicken fingers and French fries are left, but the ketchup is gone." Kat proceeded to give Davy a little more and then said, "He'd be satisfied with just the bottle of ketchup and nothing more."

"Where'd he learn to like ketchup so much?"

"Who knows? It wasn't from me. I prefer mustard," replied Kat.

"So, Maggie, what's this about The Soup Kitchen? I can remember you saying something about it during our conversation with Marshall when you found out about Tim joining the Marines. Tell me all about it."

"Well, like I told you over the phone, Chris started to work there first as a community service, which was one of the qualifications to get into the Air Force Academy while in high school. That, or having a part time job. I'm really glad that Tim and Chad followed in his footsteps, as the opportunity gave them a well-learned lesson on how to appreciate and help the less fortunate. At first they thought it was a drudge, but they really became happy to be there, because of all the interesting people that they met."

"Chad is working there also?"

"Yes, because my third son has decided to join the Navy when he graduates from high school."

Kat started to choke on the coffee she was sipping when Maggie told her this and inquired, "You're kidding, right?"

"No, not at all."

"You're taking this news pretty well."

"After experiencing Chris and Tim's little scenario with the service, Marshall and I are getting to be quite the pros with dealing with our sons' choices in life."

"It really didn't surprise me with Chris and Tim's choices, but Chad? I figured he would go onto college for ten, twelve years or more, and become that brain surgeon or rocket scientist that we talked about years ago with the brain he's got."

"He certainly could have, for he's been a straight A student since he was in romper room."

"Romper room?" grinned Kat.

"You know very well what I mean, Kat."

"Preschool."

"Right, whatever!"

"Alright, Maggie, fess up. You don't sound too happy with Chad's decision to join the Navy, am I right?"

"I'm not sure what I feel. I just know it's his decision to make and that Marshall and I have to go along with it."

"If Marshall would have been on the ball, he could've given you a couple of girls and one boy instead of three boys. Then the only decision you'd have to go through is if their husbands were good enough for your little girls or not."

"I'll be sure and relate what you just said to him."

"Oh, Maggie! It isn't the end of the world. Personally, I'd be a very proud mother, if my three sons chose the armed services for a career. Do all three plan to make it their career choice?"

"Yes, and the only consolation Marshall and I have is that now we know ahead of time what Chad's plans for his future are."

Kat figured it was time to get off of this subject so said, "Tell me more about this Soup Kitchen. Is that the name of it?"

"Yes, The Soup Kitchen is what it is called. Well, I worked there one weekend to fill in for one of the volunteer mothers who had the flu. It's highly organized with all volunteers, and they serve very nutritious meals that are made right there."

"Sounds wonderful."

"It is. Matter of fact, I was asked if I would like to become an assistant to the director."

"Are you thinking about doing it?"

"Yes, but I haven't quite made up my mind yet. Some of the volunteers are very dedicated and help as often as they can, and some just do it once or twice and then quit. It's hard to keep steady volunteers, and that would be my job: to round up volunteers and help with inventory."

"Inventory?" asked Kat as she removed Davy's clean plate and looked for a Wet One in her purse to wipe Davy's face, hands, neck, and wherever else there was ketchup.

"Yes," continued Maggie, "flyers have to be sent out and phone calls made to request donations of money or food to stock the pantry, which has to be done on an almost daily basis. Inventory has to be kept of who and what people donate and how often. This would be my job, if I accept. Plus to try and find people to volunteer their time."

"That sounds like a lot of work for you. What do the other volunteers do?"

"They help cook the meals, serve them and then clean up afterward. Why do you ask? Are you thinking maybe of volunteering?"

"Now, Maggie. Don't put words into my mouth. I was just curious, and that was the reason for all the questions. Besides, I can't cook, remember?"

"You wouldn't have to cook. There's two wonderful ladies by the name of Martha and Ginny, who are probably in their early sixties, vie with each other to come up with the best recipes. And they're great cooks to boot! If you volunteered, all you'd have to do is wait for the person to walk in front of you, and then you'd take a big spoon and dunk it into a large pot of mashed potatoes and plunk it on their plate, which is set on a tray for easier maneuvering. You can also use large tongs with which to pick up the meat with. Or you'd be in charge of the vegetable of the day with the same routine as the mashed potatoes. Simple. No brainer! The cleanup would be the same as you do at home after cooking a meal but on a larger scale."

"Why are you looking at me like that, Margaret Mary Ryan?"

"Like what? I clearly don't have any idea what you mean."

"Yeah, right! That's your 'I'll con you into doing it sooner or later' look that I know so well."

"Now, Kat. So when can you start?"

"Next weekend be okay?"

"You really mean it?"

"Yeah, why not? Do I have to do it both days?"

"No, of course not. Only if you want to or have the time to."

"Wait! What do I do with Davy? I can't expect Susan or Cindy to babysit him either Saturday or Sunday of every weekend."

"On the weekends that they can't babysit, bring him with you."

"Oh sure! They'd love to have a two-and-a-half year old running underfoot all day and getting into everything."

"The kitchen is completely closed off except for the opening in the wall where the food is served, and that is blocked off with counters to slide the trays. He only has access to where they eat their meals."

"I don't know, Maggie. It could really end up being a disaster with Davy running around."

"Just bring him once and see how it goes and then take it from there."

As it turned out, Davy stood next to Kat hanging onto her leg for dear life for about the first thirty minutes, and then an elderly gentleman started to converse with him and actually coaxed him to come out and have some ice cream with him. With ice cream being Davy's favorite dessert, the man had a friend for life.

Kat didn't take Davy with her every Saturday, only the days that Susan or Cindy couldn't watch him. All the volunteers and the homeless people looked forward to seeing the little scamp and told Kat so whenever Davy wasn't with her. Kat began taking Davy with her every Saturday that she could make it, but stayed home with him on Sunday's, so that she could have one full day alone with her son.

Kat came up with one of her brainstorms while doing dishes one early Sunday evening and couldn't get Maggie on the phone fast enough to tell her all about it.

"Hi, Maggie. It's me." Kat didn't give her a chance to say anything in return and started to rattle off with the main reason that I called was to see how you were doing but also to tell you something. Now don't laugh with what I'm about to tell you, okay? I've always had this insatiable need, or whatever you want to call it, to learn to ride."

"Ride what?"

"A horse, of course. What else?"

"Kat, are you nuts?"

"Maybe, but ever since I was a kid, I wanted to learn to ride a horse."

"Have you ever been on a horse before?"

"At the moment, not that I can recall. So what do you think?"

"I don't know what to think, except maybe that you are totally crazy and will probably end up killing yourself."

"Could be, on both counts, but I'm going to go for it. I located a riding stable about twenty minutes from my house. Want to join me?"

There was absolute total silence on the other end and then Maggie said, "I think I may be a little too old to be getting on a horse, but—"

"That 'but' sounds to me like you might be considering it. Look how much fun it could be! C'mon, Maggie. Let's take a crack at it. What do wc have to lose?"

"Maybe our lives, because of a broken neck for starters. Oh, Kat, I don't know. It sounds so reckless and scary."

"If we don't like it after the first time out, we can just not go back. Simple as that."

"You've talked me into some really screwy ideas before, but riding a horse? I don't think…Oh, what the hell! Let's do it."

"You really mean it?" Kat asked excitedly.

"I may regret it, but yeah, why not? It might turn out to be fun."

"Good. I'll call the guy back and tell him that two of us will be there on Tuesday instead of just one."

"Tuesday? That's only two days away. Maybe we should postpone it for a week or so and—"

"No, you don't," interrupted Kat. "If we wait, we won't do it, and you know yourself that that is what will happen."

"Alright, alright! Make it for Tuesday. What time?"

"Two o'clock in the afternoon."

"Don't you have to work?"

"No. I plan to tell Dan on Monday that I'm taking off by using one of my vacation days."

"I see. Do we have to bring anything with us?"

"Like what?"

"I don't know. A saddle or maybe spurs," laughed Maggie.

"Whatever trips your trigger."

"Very funny," chuckled Maggie, at Kat's reference to Trigger.

Maggie wasn't about to tell Marshall of Kat's crazy scheme, for fear that he might have her institutionalized. When she approached Kat's door on Tuesday at around 1:00 P.M., a feeling of apprehension came over her, but it disappeared as fast as it came. Then she was filled with a sense of calmness, which left her looking forward to this outing. *I'm calling it an outing*, thought Maggie. *A disaster waiting to happen would be more like it.*

The two of them arrived at the stables twenty minutes ahead of time to check the place over. It was a beautiful August afternoon. The temperature was mild with a slight breeze and perfect for riding. The main house and the surrounding area was a sight to behold. Picturesque was a better word, for the beauty of the place with the brightly colored red barn, the large stable for the horses, and clusters of trees expanding as far as the eye could see. A maze of white fencing weaved in and out over the entire width and length of the property, which was a good distance, in Kat's estimation.

"Heavens! This driveway from the road to the house is longer than the block that I live on!" exclaimed Maggie.

"I know. It's quite long, but it sure is beautiful."

Kat drove her car to the back of the house according to the posted sign and parked. A large dog, whose breed was anyone's guess, came running from around the corner of the house straight to the car, and stopped dead in his tracks by Kat's door, barking up a storm.

"I guess we don't dare get out of the car until someone comes," Maggie told Kat.

"He might be friendly," chuckled Kat, "but I for one am not going to try and find out. They sure don't need an elaborate alarm system with him around to guard the place. I wonder what kind of dog he is?"

"I have no idea," answered Maggie. "All I know is he's as big as a bear and looks like one with all that black fur."

Just then, a tall lanky man with long brown hair tied in a ponytail appeared, wearing jeans and cowboy boots and sporting a mustache. Maggie estimated he was around forty, and with his command, the dog took off running from whence he came.

"It's okay to come out now, ladies," he stated as Kat was starting to open her door. "Don't mind Ham. He looks mean and can be toward strangers, but deep down he's just a big baby."

"Ham?" questioned Maggie. "That's an unusual name for a dog."

"Rightly so. My wife named him after me, because that's what she thinks I am: a ham. Welcome to the Double J, ladies. I'm Jake Reed and my wife's name is Jodie, thus the Double J," laughed Jake.

"Glad to meet you, Mr. Reed," replied Kat as she shook his hand. "This is my Sister, Maggie."

"Hi, Maggie. The pleasure's all mine and please, call me Jake."

"Alright, Jake. As I told you over the phone, Maggie and I have never been on a horse in our lives, so I guess that makes us real beginners."

"Actually, the word is 'tenderfoot,' but since there are two of you, the correct form of the word should be 'tenderfeet,'" chuckled Jake.

I really like this guy, thought Maggie. *He's joking around to put us a little more at ease, and if that's the case, Kat and I must look terrified.* "I suspect that by the time we're finished here, our feet won't be the only things that will be tender," Maggie joked.

"You most likely have a good point there, Maggie," answered Jake, with a grin on his face.

"Since both of you are new at this, I certainly won't put you on broncos," smiled Jake, "but will start you off with two of our gentlest mares."

"That's very kind and wise of you, Jake," giggled Kat.

"Okay, ladies. If you'll follow me to the inner corral, I'll introduce you to the two mares that you will be riding: Daisy and Molly."

"Introduce? Like, Daisy and Molly, this is, Maggie and Kat?" Maggie chuckled.

"Exactly. The key to a successful ride is to get to know the horse that you are riding. That horse needs to know just how you feel toward it. Either you show you like it or you show indifference. However you treat

your horse, the horse in turn will treat you the same. A little kindness such as calling the horse by its name, patting its head, whatever, and the horse in return, will do what you want it to do. Horses are very smart animals. In fact, they're smarter than some humans that I know, and some have an attitude, but they are usually the ones that are highly spirited. That is not the case with Daisy and Molly, so you don't have to worry."

After Kat and Maggie made their introductions to Daisy and Molly, they were ready for the next step: getting on the horse. Jake mounted his horse, Charlie, after talking to him and giving him a treat of some sort. The sisters couldn't make out what it was. He then dismounted with instructions for Charlie to stay, and then he could help Maggie and Kat mount their horses, if need be.

Maggie was the first to mount with Jake standing back aways, but close enough for him to get at her if she started to fall. She put her left foot into the stirrup like Jake showed them. She then grabbed the saddle horn and pulled herself up and swung her right foot over Molly's back and plopped down directly in the middle of the saddle. She looked down so that she could see her right foot and proceeded to insert it into the right stirrup. *That wasn't so bad*, she thought, but continued to keep a strong grip with both hands on the saddle horn.

Now it was Kat's turn. She put her left foot into the stirrup, lifted herself up and came straight down. "Oh, that was wonderful," laughed Kat. With the second try, she did the same thing. "Okay, what am I doing wrong?"

"You're trying too hard for one thing. You might try slowing down with elevating your body, which is leaning too far to the left and put more of your weight on the stirrup. Lean into the horse just a little bit before you swing your right leg over."

Kat tried again and managed to get her right leg over Molly, but came pretty close to falling off of the other side, if it weren't for her quick reaction of grabbing the saddle horn. She squirmed her butt until she figured that she was in the middle of the saddle and hung onto the saddle horn for dear life, just like Maggie did.

"Alright, ladies! Release your grip on the saddle horn, for I can see both of your hands are turning white. We'll sit here for a few minutes, so that you can get the feel of being at this height off the ground. Now, with both hands, take the reins and hold them like this. Not too tight or too loose. If you pull toward you, that is a signal for your horse to stop, if we were in motion, but we're not, and that will confuse the horse. If your grip is too loose, the horse will most likely put its head down and start grazing until you figure out what you want to do," chuckled Jake. "We will go at a slow pace until we get through the fencing and into the wide open space. We'll then rein in our horses and stop, and I'll give you more instructions. To get your horse to move, lightly tap both of your heals at the same time against their flanks, like this."

Jake took the lead and, surprisingly, Kat and Maggie followed. *They were doing really well for their first ride*, surmised Jake.

"This isn't bad at all," sighed Kat. It's easier than she imagined it to be. Her confidence was building. Maggie thought along the same lines, but unlike Kat, she was thinking about the trotting and wondering how fast a horse will go while trotting.

As they approached the clearing, Jake started to rein in Charlie and came to a stop. Kat was enjoying the scenery instead of paying attention and came pretty close to running into Charlie when she reined in Daisy to a stop. Maggie did fine because she was paying attention!

"Alright, ladies," Jake started to explain. "Like I said before, we will only trot. Galloping would be the next stage and full out running, the final stage. But since you are beginners, we will take it slow, so that you can get the feel of going from walking to trotting. Don't fear that your horse will take off running. Charlie here is the lead horse, and Daisy and Molly are well trained to follow his lead. All right, here we go!"

Maggie and Kat both grabbed the saddle horn with their left hands and hung on to the reins with their right hands, which was a natural reaction when you fear you may fall off the horse. It was a little unsettling, this trotting business, for both of them at first, but the longer they rode, the more confident the both of them became. They did this for a good

half an hour when Jake held up his right arm and reined in Charlie. Kat saw enough westerns on TV to know that when the officer in command held up his hand, the rest of the calvary stopped. She did fine and so did Maggie.

"Now, each of you will tell your mount to go left."

Maggie and Kat had a baffled look on their faces, telling Jake that they didn't know what the hell he was talking about.

Jake giggled to himself and started to explain, "You don't actually verbally tell your horse to turn. You do it with your reins and move them like this." Charlie turned to the left and stopped. Jake turned on his saddle and told Kat, "Now you try. Good! Maggie, now it's your turn. Great! Nice going, ladies. You're doing just fine!"

His next instructions for them was to repeat the same motion one more time, so that they would be heading in the direction, which would take them back to the stables and to start trotting again.

When they approached the fencing, Jake held up his right arm again and stopped. "Now we will continue at a slow pace to the inside corral just like we did when we came out."

When inside the inner corral, Jake stopped Charlie and dismounted while giving Maggie and Kat instructions on how to do it, properly.

"Remove your right foot from the stirrup, lean your body forward toward the horn and grip the horn with both hands. With your left foot still in the stirrup, slowly bring your right leg up and over your horse, which will transfer the weight of your body onto the left stirrup and down to the ground. Leave your left foot in the stirrup, and when your right foot comes in contact with the ground, this is the position both of your legs should be in. Slowly remove your left foot from the stirrup and set it on the ground. There! You've just learned to alit your horse. Well done, ladies!"

While Jake walked the three horses into the stable and handed the reins to a young man inside, Kat and Maggie had a chance to discuss with themselves what their next move would be regarding taking more lessons or quitting.

"So what do you think, Maggie? Do you want to continue with more lessons?"

"Do you?"

"Yes. I was petrified at first, but I want to continue. I really enjoyed it."

"I never thought I would say this, but I enjoyed myself too. So yes, I want to continue, also," agreed Maggie.

"Well, Jake. It looks like you have two 'tenderfeet' ready to take more lessons," laughed Kat.

"Good! With all kidding aside, I could tell by the looks on both of your faces that you were nervous and scared when we first started, which is natural, but you both did extremely well for your first attempt at riding a horse."

"You really think so?" questioned Maggie.

"Yes, I really think so. I've been in this business for many years and have seen capable riders and ones that will never get the hang of it, and I don't beat around the bush and will always tell them the truth one way or the other."

With that said, the three went into Jake's house to sign up for more lessons. He told Kat and Maggie that if for any reason that they wanted to quit the lessons, they could. This is not a contract where they would have to pay for lessons not taken.

"I don't run my business like that. Since you both want one lesson a week, we do have a policy that you can ride as many times as you wish per week but not on Sundays, and only at my discretion with determining

that you are capable at that point in time. I will always be your instructor, but later on when you come to ride on your own time, someone else will accompany you for a small fee, which covers the cost of the care and feeding of the horses and also to help with the pay of my two hired hands. If you agree with the terms, ladies, we have a deal."

"That sounds fair to me," said Kat, "but I do have one question to ask."

"Ask away," responded Jake.

"I work second shift and can't be taking off from work once a week to go riding, so is it possible to sign up for lessons during the morning hours?"

"Of course. You pick a day of the week and the hour, and I'll fill your names in the schedule book at those specified times. You show up and we go riding. If at any time you can't keep the appointment, we would like to be notified the day before, unless you become sick, then we would appreciate a call at least an hour before your lessons telling us if that is the case. I suspect that both of you want to sign up for the same day and time, am I correct?"

"Definitely!" answered Maggie.

With that information shared, Maggie and Kat shook hands with Jake, and told him that they would see him next week on Tuesday morning.

As they left the house and headed for the car, Maggie turned to Kat and said, "Well, we did it. We're coming back. Any regrets?"

"No. I really think once we get the hang of things, we might just do okay."

"I hope so," replied Maggie with a hint of uncertainty.

With working seven days a week, riding lessons on Tuesdays, and volunteering at the Soup Kitchen almost every Saturday, Kat's weeks flew by as quickly as the blink of an eye. Davy settled down and was having fun at the Soup Kitchen with the attention that everyone showed him, thus prompting Kat to now take him with her every Saturday.

After their sixth riding lesson with Jake, she and Maggie were confident to go out with one of Jake's assistants. Jake was in agreement, because the two became very capable with their ability to ride and were becoming excellent riders. They were now riding twice a week and loving it! Little did the two know at the time, that in the future, their knowledge of horseback riding was a necessity for what lay ahead for them in that future.

One night toward the middle of September after putting Davy to bed, Kat was sitting in her front room with a cup of coffee and working on the final chapters of her book when her mind wandered back to this past summer and all the things that occurred: Tim's birthday party in May, his graduation from high school and joining the Marines. Chris made it home for Cindy's graduation party from high school, which Kat planned and had at her house with Cindy's grandparents' approval. She recalled that Maggie's intuition was correct: the two were falling in love. Maggie had talked her into volunteering at the Soup Kitchen, and now she loved it. The two of them were so scared but went through the process of learning to ride a horse. Now neither she nor Maggie would change that experience in a million years.

Kat couldn't believe Cindy and Susan had been with her going on a year and a half already. *God gifted Davy and me when he sent Susan and Cindy into our lives*, surmised Kat. Susan went back home to be with her family for her twenty-first birthday back in July. Maggie, Cindy, Kat and Davy spent a whole day with her the day before doing whatever she chose to do, and then they took her out for a nice dinner afterward.

Susan started her senior year in college to get her nursing degree, unless she decided to advance her nurse's training; then it would be two more years. She met a real nice guy named Stephen in her junior year, and the two were crazy about each other. Susan took him home to meet her parents, and Kat figured that wedding bells would be ringing sometime in the near future.

Kat only made it to the cottage twice during the summer for a three-day weekend. Once was with Davy and the second time with Cindy and Davy. It was totally relaxing just sitting on the beach, swimming,

fishing and going out for dinner every night. Davy actually caught the biggest fish when they went with Cindy. She would sit on the pier with Davy between her legs and let him cast out the line. The three of them would sing songs while sitting and watching the bobber in the water. She knew they weren't supposed to make noise while fishing, but just sitting there was not holding his attention for too long. She will never forget the surprised look on his face when the bobber disappeared under the water. She started to reel in the fish or what she hoped was a fish, and then plopped the thing on the floor pier. Cindy took the hook out and Davy, not being one bit afraid, went over to the fish and tried to get it in both of his little hands. He managed for a second, and then dropped the fish too close to the edge of the pier and it disappeared. He started to cry until Kat had Cindy put another worm on the hook and assumed the same position with Davy as before. Nothing happened. Thank goodness Cindy had her cell phone handy with the first fish, for she took a couple of pictures of Davy trying to catch it. Some day Kat would be able to show him the big fish that got away, because they now had proof.

She planned to take Cindy and Davy again to the cottage. She promised herself that she would bait the hook herself and take the hook out of its mouth, because it was about time that she learned.

The weather, for nearing the end of September, was still gorgeous with temperatures in the middle seventies. Kat called Helen and told her of their coming plans, and that they should make sure to get together. Cindy stayed over with Kat on Thursday night so that the four of them could get an early start. After arriving before noon and unpacking their clothes and groceries bought from the store in town, she made her routine check of looking for any crawling or flying varmints, dead or alive! To her total relief, none were found this time.

Kat and Cindy were sitting under the umbrella on the patio while Davy played with his beach ball. Helen had taught Cindy how to knit and she was going at it with real vigor, Kat noticed. But she couldn't figure out what it was supposed to be that she was making and didn't want to embarrass her by asking. Kat had only one chapter remaining with her book and was getting anxious to finish it. A friend from work volunteered

to edit it for her, but she insisted that if she did, she would let her do it only if she could pay her for her time. She wasn't about to take advantage of a friend with that large a volume of work to be edited.

As they both sat there engrossed with their own doings, they heard the gate latch open and looked up to see Helen standing there leaning against a cane.

"Helen, for goodness sake! Wasn't that a real risk you took by walking over here in the sand with your bum knee?" questioned Kat.

Helen stepped inside the gate and proceeded to make sure the latch was hooked. As she turned, before she could say anything, Davy ran over and began to hug one of her legs in greeting. "Well, hello there, young man, and how are you?" asked Helen.

"Fine," replied Davy.

Helen looked over at Kat as she began to chuckle and said, "His vocabulary is starting to broaden. Well, good! How have the three of you been doing?"

"Just fine, and you?"

"I've been just fine. I had my sister Eleanor and her granddaughter Charlotte come and visit, and they stayed for two weeks. The three of us were on the go for the entire time. I was never so tired in all my life, but we sure had fun together."

Kat responded with, "That's wonderful, Helen."

"And what about you, Cindy? I heard from Kat that you are now in college? What do you plan on doing with your life?"

"I'm not sure yet, Helen. I haven't made a concise decision yet."

"Well, that's promising," laughed Helen with Kat catching on with her statement, but it went right over Cindy's head.

“Would you like something to drink?” inquired Kat.

“Sounds good. I’ve developed a thirst walking over here and looking at nothing but sand. Got any lemonade?”

“Sure do. Made a fresh batch just about an hour ago.”

“I’ll get it,” said Cindy.

“Well, Kat. I’d have to say that you’ve come a long way from that young woman that I first met staying at Mike and Sharon’s house.”

“A lot has happened to me since then, I can say that with certainty.”

“Then everything is really going well for you?”

“Yes, Helen. It certainly is.”

Cindy returned with a glass of lemonade for Helen and upon seeing it, Davy ran over expecting a sip.

“Davy, you have your own,” Kat scolded, while pointing to his little plastic cup still sitting on the table.

“That’s okay,” declared Helen. “His is probably warm and I have no trouble with sharing.” As she put her glass to Davy’s mouth, to her surprise, he took a few good slurps and spilled none.

After Helen stayed for a little over an hour, she decided it was time for her to get back home.

“We’ll walk with you,” Kat said, and Davy walked between Cindy and Helen, holding onto their hands for support.

As they reached Helen’s driveway, Kat turned to Helen and asked, “We plan to go for a fish fry tonight. You want to go along?”

“I’d love to,” responded Helen with excitement.

“Okay, good. We’ll pick you up around 5:00 P.M. then. Is that fine with you, Helen?”

"Yes. I'll be waiting."

The four had a really good time dining out. The food was exceptionally good and the conversation was even better. After dropping Helen off at around 7:30 P.M., the three went home and turned on the TV for entertainment. A comedy was on and so they watched it until 8:00 P.M. and then Kat put Davy to bed in her bed. Cindy would sleep in the spare single bed in Davy's room.

"Interested in a game of Scrabble for money?" Kat questioned Cindy.

"Sure. I'd love to."

As it turned out, Cindy's final score was 309 and Kat's was 225. "Well, that was eventful," smiled Kat. "Here's your fifty cents that I owe you."

"No. That's alright. You don't have to pay me."

"Yes, I do. We bet fifty cents and Kat O'Brien never reneges on a bet, even if it was a stupid one to make on my part," she laughed.

"Well, I think I'll turn in if it's alright with you," stated Cindy.

"Well, of course it is, Honey. You turn in anytime that you want. You don't have to ask my permission."

"Good night then."

"Good night, Cindy. Sweet dreams."

It was early enough and such a beautiful warm night out that Kat decided to go sit in one of the lawn chairs. The sky was clear, not a cloud to be found, and the stars looked like small diamonds sparkling on black velvet. It was almost as if they were superglued to a piece of black felt, she believed. The lake was calm, and the lights that were positioned around the circumference of it, reflected the mist from the lake, making it to look like small little clouds hovering over it. She stared determinedly at the lake to see if she could see Duffy and Rosemary sitting in their rowboat, when a voice interrupted her daze with, "What a perfectly beautiful night, don't you think, Mistress Kat?" asked Michael.

"Oh, Michael," responded Kat, a startled look on her face.

"I'm sorry, Mistress Kat. I didn't mean to frighten you."

"That's alright, Michael. I was daydreaming. And in answer to your question, yes it is absolutely beautiful out. Helen once told me that in the fifteen years that they lived here together, before Fred passed away that they were sitting on their porch and all of a sudden out of nowhere, the Northern Lights appeared in the sky. Helen said it was such a spectacular spectrum of colors and shapes flickering back and forth, and that it was almost impossible to describe. A person had to see for themselves to appreciate the beauty of it. I hope Davy and I will be allowed to see them sometime when we're up here."

"You will, Mistress Kat."

"You sure?"

"Yes. When Master Davy is past his ninth birthday, the two of you will be sitting here just as we are, and you will see the Northern Lights for yourself."

"Michael, I know the two of us are hardly ever alone to talk, and I'm truly sorry."

"Don't be sorry, Mistress Kat. I know how busy and hectic your life can be at times."

"Michael, do we die and nothing is on the other side for mankind? Or do we go to hell or heaven, depending on what kind of life we lived?"

"No. You don't actually die; your soul leaves the body and enters a state of euphoria."

"Why? Because it got rid of the excess baggage that it was carrying around?" she reasoned.

"No. The soul is free to do anything that it wishes to do."

"Such as?"

"Well, for example, it can divide itself into any amount of parts that it wishes and be in many places at the same time."

"You're kidding."

"No. Actually, it's the truth. The soul, through thought, can find itself moving through the universe in a flash, trying to fulfill that thought to wherever or whatever it wants to be."

"Is there a hell?"

"No, Mistress Kat. There is no hell. That word and concept was first used many, many years ago to keep the masses in line and under foot, so that they would not think differently from those who set the rules and laws down to be obeyed. The entire thing was accomplished through fear."

"Kind of like, if you don't abide by this law set down by us, who know of the truth, you will go to a made up hell."

"Exactly."

"So a few ruled the masses with deceit and mandatory rules set down to keep them in line and to dupe them as to what was really the truth. Unbelievable!"

"Yes, that's what happened, Mistress Kat. Your part in God's plan is to raise your son with the intention of preparing him to be a great leader."

"I don't have the foggiest notion as to what I'm supposed to do in that regard."

"Patience, Mistress Kat. The things that you will need to know in the future will come to you in due time when the Almighty One determines you can handle them."

"So, you're saying that he doesn't want to clog my mind with too many details all at once, correct?"

"Correct."

"Well, that makes sense."

"The Almighty One knows what he is doing. Always has and always will."

"Well, Michael, on that note, I think I'll turn in. Goodnight!"

"Goodnight, Mistress Kat!"

The weekend at the cottage went by far too fast. Everyone had a good time, and they couldn't ask for better weather.

Thanksgiving was next Thursday and Maggie informed Kat that she and Marshall were invited to one of his close client's home. Chad didn't want to go and stayed home and ate pizza, as he wasn't crazy about turkey anyway.

Cindy's grandparents invited Kat and Davy to their house, but she declined saying that she was taking her mom out for dinner. Kevin and Dolores would not take no for an answer and insisted that she should bring her mother along also. She agreed to go, because she had met both of Cindy's grandparents at Cindy's graduation party and liked Dolores tremendously.

Dolores prepared quite a spread. She was a wonderful cook from the "old school" and everything was absolutely delicious. When Kevin, Kat and Cindy volunteered to clean up afterward, this gave Dolores and Megan, Kat's mom, a chance to talk.

"You have a wonderful daughter, Megan. Kevin and I think the world of her, for what she has done for our Cindy. She accepted her into her life and her heart. And Cindy is absolutely crazy about her and Davy."

"Even though my daughter and I don't always see eye-to-eye on some things, I do love her dearly and agree with you, Dolores. Kat is very special."

"She was the reason for our Cindy meeting and falling in love with your grandson, Chris. What a nice boy he is! Kevin and I think the world of him."

"I know, and so do I, and not because he's my grandson but because it's true. He turned out to be a very fine young man, and I'm so proud of him."

Dolores caught Megan completely off guard with her next question.

"Do you think that Kat will ever get married again? It would be wonderful, if she could find a nice man who would be a good husband to her and a good father for Davy."

"Kat marry again? I'd love to see it happen, but it's very doubtful," chuckled Megan. "She loves her life just the way it is."

The entire evening was as wonderful as the Thanksgiving meal. After saying their good-byes, Kat dropped her mom off and she and Davy headed home.

Kat finally finished her book. She was very satisfied with the results and titled the book *The Angel And The Redhead*, but evidently the many publishers that she sent her transcript to didn't share her view. She was turned down six times. Christmas was just around the corner, and she was waiting to hear back from number seven. *That would make a great Christmas gift, but I'm not going to hold my breath*, she thought.

Horseback riding was over, because of the wintry weather, but she drove out to the riding stable once a week just to visit with Daisy and Molly. She still worked at the Soup Kitchen every Saturday and loved it. The regulars Kat knew so well now were such loving and caring people, and she never heard one complaint from any of them about the hardships that they faced on a daily basis. Maggie was doing so well as assistant to the director that when Charlie decided to retire and give up his position, he asked Maggie if she would be interested in taking over the entire operation. She said yes without any hesitation. Charlie still planned to volunteer his time but on a part-time basis.

Kat scrambled to get her house clean the way she wanted it and to get the Christmas tree and decorations put up. Davy helped with everything except the cleaning, of course. He was excited about decorating just like last year when the tree was completely done. As usual, she procrastinated with everything but gifts, which she started buying in the summer, because she had so many people to buy for. She was running out of room in every high place that she could think of to hide the presents to keep Davy from finding any of them. She invited Grandma, Bev, Marshall, Maggie, Chad, Susan, Steven, Kevin, Dolores and Cindy. Tim couldn't make it home but Chris could, and everyone had to keep it a secret from Cindy, because he planned to surprise her. Twice Kat came pretty close to letting it slip out. She ordered food to be catered in, as she wasn't about to cook and possibly screw it up on such an important holiday. All she had left to do was go to the liquor store and restock her liquor cabinet.

Some of the guests started arriving at 5:00 P.M. It got to be at 6:00 P.M. and she started to set the food out buffet style, because they were due to eat at 6:30 P.M.

"Where's, Chris?" Kat asked Maggie.

"I don't know. I told him to be here at 6:00 P.M. Calm down, he should be here pretty soon."

"Do you think his plane is late?" wondered Kat.

"I hope not. He was due in at 5:15 P.M., and since you're not all that far from the airport, he should've been here by now."

Everyone started to move away from the door except Cindy and Davy, because they wanted Cindy to be the one to open the door when Chris arrived. Cindy didn't notice anything, because she was busy playing with Davy near the Christmas tree, which was close to the front door. At exactly at 6:15 P.M. the front door bell rang, and Cindy looked around to see if anyone else was going to answer it. Since everyone was talking, and not seeing Kat or Maggie, she decided to get up and answer it herself. When she opened the door, there stood a very handsome Chris in his Air Force

uniform with a huge bouquet of red roses in his hands. Cindy screamed and jumped into the arms of the one that she loved with all her heart. Tears streamed down her face immediately and continued even through the long kiss that they shared. When they stepped into the living room, loud clapping and shouts of "Surprise!" rang out from their loved ones.

It was a festive night for everyone, and one that none of them would ever forget. After dinner, many gifts were handed around and opened, but no one enjoyed the party more than Davy. The chatter started to subside after all the gifts were opened and the words "Thank you" echoed throughout the entire room. Kat and Maggie started to sing a Christmas song and everyone joined in. Marshall had a wonderful tenor voice and sang "Oh Holy Night," which caused many eyes to mist. Kat waited to serve dessert, because everyone was too stuffed from before with all the food that she had set out.

A few yawns were heard, so Chris thought that he had better make his move now. He was sitting next to Cindy on the couch and began to rise. To everyone's surprise, he turned to Cindy, got down on one knee, and pulled out a beautiful little box from his pant's pocket. He proceeded to open the box and took out a little jewelry case, opened it, took Cindy's left hand in his and slipped the ring onto her finger. While still holding her hand, he declared, "Cindy, I fell in love with you the moment that I first laid eyes on you. It was truly 'love at first sight' for me, and I will always love you until the day that I die. Will you do me the great honor of becoming my wife and making me the happiest man in the world?"

You could hear a pin drop, because everyone in the room was speechless since Chris told no one of his plans. Cindy was dumbstruck and could hardly get an audible *yes* from her mouth, because once again, she began to cry. Her hugging and kissing Chris, did get her point across to everyone that she accepted. Tears of joy were shared along with hugging, kissing, handshakes and words of "Congratulations" from all.

After everyone was gone and Davy was put to bed, Kat sat in her favorite chair with a drink in her hand remembering all that occurred this wondrous night.

"Michael, are you here?"

"Yes, of course, Mistress Kat."

"This was about the greatest Christmas that my family and I have shared together."

"I am truly happy for all of you. Such a loving family you have! There are many things to be grateful for."

"You're sure right on that count. I have a wonderful son, family, a good friend in Beverly but not—"

Michael knew who she was about to mention so finished her sentence with, "The General."

"Yes, Michael, I have spent every waking day since he left thinking about him, but it seems that holidays are harder for me to get through. Can you understand what I'm saying, Michael?"

"Yes, Mistress Kat. I understand completely. From what I have observed since I have been with you, your holidays down here can be very festive and joyful but also very lonely when the festivity stops and then you seem to be all alone. But that is not the case, Mistress Kat."

"What do you mean?"

"The Almighty One is here with you now and everyone throughout the whole world every day. So you see, Mistress Kat, no one is ever truly alone."

As Kat took the last sip of her drink and rose from her chair to go to bed, she turned and said to Michael, "You sure have a way with words, Michael. Thank you! I mean it from the bottom of my heart. And Michael, Merry Christmas to you."

"And to you, Mistress Kat," replied Michael, even though Archangels don't believe in holidays.

Kat, Davy and Michael spent Christmas Day at home alone. She planned it that way to be with her son and the angel that they both loved dearly. They played together with the many toys that Davy received from everyone, and she saved a few special gifts that she bought for him to open today. Only one remained still high on a shelf in the closet that she would save for another Christmas when Davy was older and could understand who it was. She had an artist do a sketch from the memory Kat had of David when he revealed himself to her, and then had it painted onto a canvas and put it into an 8x10 inch frame. The likeness was unbelievable, and even Michael was astounded by the portrait. It was truly David.

Chris had five days to spend with Cindy until he had to return to the Academy. Not much was seen of the two during those five days, recalled Kat.

New Years came and went, and everyone helped Davy celebrate his third birthday with a party. His vocabulary increased and was easily understood, and his questions to Kat and Michael flowed like a raging river. They barely gave an answer to one question when another one followed, rapidly.

"My baby boy talks faster than I do," laughed Kat. She was very proud that he could recite his ABCs and count to twenty, already. He loved to have Michael and her read books to him, and he was fascinated by anything to do with the military. Kat didn't pay much attention to it, thinking it was a boy thing.

Kat's favorite time of year arrived rather quickly in the wake of the dreary, harsh months of winter. She loved spring, for soon everything would start to show signs of life and start to grow and blossom. In a few weeks, she could start working in her yard again and was really looking forward to doing just that.

She made a mental note to herself to call Jake and see when Maggie and her could start riding again. She hadn't visited Daisy and Molly for quite sometime, because of winter and found herself really missing them. The Soup Kitchen was running smoothly under Maggie's tutelage. There were several weekends when Kat helped out on both Saturday and Sunday.

Besides Chad's regular appearance on Saturdays, Susan and her boyfriend Steven and Cindy joined the force of volunteers. Kat even conned her mother into helping in between her bus trips to the casinos.

Plenty of birthdays and anniversaries came and went with more to come in the summer months ahead. *I spend more money on all these occasions in a year than on my property tax here and on the cottage*, surmised Kat, but she wouldn't do it any differently. Family is too important.

She thought ahead to summer and the cottage that they hadn't spent any more time there than a few long weekends. She was going to make sure it was different this summer and took a week vacation from work in June, July, and August, with another five days left. She wasn't quite sure when she would use the remaining five days, but had to before the year was up.

This was an exceptionally great day for Kat, for she heard from the thirteenth publisher, who finally accepted her manuscript and agreed to publish her book that Maggie and her worked so hard on to finish. It was also her last day of work before she started her vacation. Ten glorious days off with nothing to do, because the Fourth of July fell on a Monday this year, and she didn't have to go back to work until the fifth. She had Davy's and her suitcases all packed already on Wednesday, her mail held by the post office until her return, and her neighbor Mike volunteered to mow her grass. Everyone had Helen's phone number in case they needed to get in touch with her. That was the final thing that she checked off her to-do list. She went to work with great anticipation, for early Saturday morning to arrive when she and her son would be heading to the cottage for a well deserved vacation.

Chris was due home on leave for two weeks, and Kat was thrilled that she picked the right week to take off as it coincided with his leave. She originally invited Marshall, Maggie and Chad to come up and stay for as long as they wanted to, but Maggie said that it was still undecided if they could make it or not. She then asked Cindy, if she and Chris would like to come and stay for awhile. Cindy wanted to stay home until Chris came home and told Kat that after contacting Chris that she would call her and

let her know, if and when that they decided to come. Kat and Davy drove to the cottage, not knowing for sure who might come or when, or maybe no one would come, which was all right with her. Davy and her would make their own fun together.

As it turned out, Maggie couldn't make it, but Chris and Cindy wanted to come. They decided to drive up on the following Thursday and leave on Sunday, so that they could be back home to celebrate the Fourth of July on Monday with the rest of the family.

Chris and Cindy arrived around at 11:00 A.M. on Thursday as planned. They found Helen, Kat, and Davy in the backyard on the patio sitting and talking around the table. Well, Kat and Helen were, while Davy was playing in the sandbox in the yard. Chris had to laugh to himself at seeing him in a sandbox when he had a whole beach full of sand to play with. Kat caught the look and chuckled, "Davy and I were out wading in the water and played on the beach earlier this morning, and his sandbox is here in the yard, so that I can take a breather once in awhile."

At seeing Chris and Cindy, Davy couldn't get to them fast enough. Chris picked him up and twirled him around, and as Davy began to laugh, so did everyone else. He then handed him to Cindy as he sat down on a chair. Cindy greeted Kat and Helen just after putting Davy down. He grabbed her hand and headed to the fence and pointed at the water and asked, "Want to swim, Cindy?"

"I don't know, Davy. We'll have to ask your mom when you can go into the water."

By the time Cindy and Davy returned to the table, Kat had already introduced Chris to Helen. Davy jumped up on Chris' lap while Cindy sat and joined them and asked for lemonade. Kat returned with more drinks and plenty of snacks to go around.

"The two of you are in luck," indicated Kat, while putting the snacks on the table.

"Why is that, Aunt Kat?"

"I went into town on Tuesday and purchased a Weber grill, and Helen was kind enough to come over and help me put it together, so that I can cook steaks on it for all of us tonight."

"Aunt Kat," laughed Chris, "a Weber grill only has four sections to it: the lid, the drum, the legs and the grate that goes on the inside, and you had to have Helen's help putting it together?"

"He's got the Ryan family dry wit," whispered Kat to Helen, but loud enough for Chris to hear after catching the innuendo where the grate went.

"Everyone tells me that when it comes to humor, you and I are two peas-in-a-pod," retaliated Chris with laughter.

"What do they know?" roared Kat.

After the laughter died down, Chris asked, "So, Aunt Kat, have you ever cooked on a grill before, or are all of us going to be your guinea pigs for tonight?"

"Funny! I'll have you know," she responded, and after long hesitation, replied, "no."

"After we put it together," continued Helen, "I asked her where the bag of charcoal was. She told me to watch Davy and that she'd be right back," teased Helen, almost falling off her chair with laughter.

"Alright, alright!" giggled, Kat along with the rest of them, knowing full well that they were enjoying themselves immensely because of her.

"I thought you had a grill at home on your patio?" inquired Chris.

"I do, but it's just for show. I really should turn the lid over and have it for a bird bath, just to get some use out of it."

"I'll cook the steaks on the grill if you want, Aunt Kat," chuckled Chris while admiring his aunt for her candor.

"Good!" she answered with a sigh of relief.

"Cindy," said Helen, "Kat told me that you and Chris became engaged on Christmas Eve. She also repeated to me the words that Chris declared to you of his desire to ask you to become his wife. The story brought me to tears. How wonderful for the both of you! Congratulations!"

"Thank you, Helen. How very kind of you to say," responded Cindy.

"Did you run into any traffic coming up here?" questioned Kat.

"No. As a matter of fact, once we drove past Waukesha, it was clear sailing. I hope it will be the same going back," stated Chris.

"It should be alright," interjected Helen, knowing from past experiences that the holiday traffic going back toward Milwaukee is worse on Monday.

"Look, you two, the day is beautiful, not a cloud in the sky, the temperature is in the mid-eighties, and there's a beautiful lake out there just waiting for you. Why don't you take advantage of it and go for a swim? Helen and I will go inside and finish preparing the food that we plan to have for dinner tonight," suggested Kat.

"Are you sure, Aunt Kat?" Chris asked.

"We can certainly help and go swimming later," volunteered Cindy.

"Thanks for the offer, Cindy, but Helen and I have everything under control, so get your suits on and go have some fun. That's why you came up here, remember?"

"Alright, Aunt Kat, if you say so. Want to go for a swim, honey?" Chris asked Cindy.

"It sounds good to me, but what about Davy?" inquired Cindy.

"Davy will be fine with Helen and me, and we'll bring him out later when we are done. So go!"

Chris and Cindy spent about an hour and a half swimming and frolicking in the water when they decided to come in for a breather. Kat and Helen were finished with their food preparations, and Kat put Davy down for a nap, which only lasted an hour, and he was back outside ready to play.

"When we go back out, is it all right with you if we take Davy with us?" questioned Cindy.

"Of course it is. He loves the water."

After they rested for a while, Chris and Cindy walked to the beach with Davy hanging on to both of their hands. They walked him some of the way and then swung him in the air while holding hands with him until they reached the shore line, then walked with him into the water.

Kat and Helen watched the three of them playing in the water. Chris picked Davy up and carried him a little farther out into the lake where he stopped and put Davy over both of his arms and onto his stomach while Cindy showed him how to move his hands in the water as if he were swimming. Davy followed her every move, which pleased Kat to no end.

"Look at the three of them having so much fun, and Davy is so comfortable around the two of them. They will make wonderful parents some day," noted Helen.

"They certainly will, and I hope the two of them find all the happiness that they deserve in life," answered Kat. "My brother-in-law and sister did a wonderful job of raising their three sons."

If it were up to Davy, he would have loved to stay out there all afternoon with Chris and Cindy. Chris happened to look over at the cottage and saw Kat filling the grill with charcoal and said, "We must have been out here longer than I thought, so let's head back."

He carried Davy on his shoulders all the way back to the cottage. Kat took Davy and dried him off and dressed him in shorts and a cotton pullover while Chris and Cindy took turns showering and changing into dry clothes.

An hour later, they were all sitting at the kitchen table enjoying a very delicious meal of steaks that melted in their mouths. Helen, Kat and Cindy cleaned up the kitchen while Chris played catch with Davy in the backyard.

It was going on at 7:00 P.M. and Helen said her good-byes and Kat walked her home. When she returned, there sat Chris and Cindy, fishing on the dock with Davy between Chris's legs. Kat sat on one of the benches that was bolted onto the dock and watched the three of them. There were very few people lingering on the beach or swimming. Kat was so relaxed and sat engrossed with her thoughts while watching Chris, Cindy, and her son, and thought how much things had changed since she had her baby boy. Her life took on new meaning for her since the day he was born when she lay there holding him in her arms for the first time. She almost lost him once and knew that she would never want to live if anything happened to him. She stopped daydreaming when she heard Davy giggle and saw Chris reel in the line and there in Davy's hands was a little fish about six inches long. Davy turned to his mother with the biggest grin on his face and walked over to show her what he caught.

Kat put Davy to bed when they returned to the cottage. When she reappeared, Chris and Cindy were huddled together on the glider looking at the beautiful array of stars shining brightly in the sky.

Chris was the first one to speak when he said, "I heard from Mom what a great setup that you have up here, Aunt Kat, but her words did nothing to really describe the beautiful setting and serenity of your place."

"I know, Chris. There's something enchanting and mesmerizing about it, especially at night when you sit here and look out at the lake."

The three continued to talk for another hour about how things were going for Chris at the Academy and Cindy's decision about the challenges of being in college and what her future endeavors would be regarding a career.

"Have you heard anything from Tim lately?" inquired Kat. "I received a letter from him about two months ago, and he said everything was

going fine for him. It was too bad that the two of you couldn't make it home at the same time after his basic training."

"Yeah, I know. I miss him and would have liked to have seen him."

Kat told them why she came here for the first time and how she came to buy the cottage, all without the mention of David, of course. She also told them the entire story about McDuffy and later how Rosemary became involved, and the tale about the two lovers being seen in a rowboat on the lake at certain times during the latter part of the day and into the night.

Kat was really starting to get tired, as it was a long day, so she said goodnight to Chris and Cindy and kissed and hugged them both. She explained about the sleeping arrangements: Chris would sleep on the pull out couch, which was already made up, Cindy in Davy's room, and Davy with Kat, just in case they were up earlier and then he wouldn't disturb Chris and Cindy. She asked if they would make sure that the doors were locked when they turned in.

The two lovers sat on the glider until the wee hours of the morning.

Kat and Davy were up earlier than Chris and Cindy, and Kat had to tell Davy quite a few times not to disturb either one of them. She fixed the two of them some breakfast and was cleaning up when she discovered Davy was missing. She heard some laughter from the living room and discovered Chris and Davy wrestling on the bed.

"I'm sorry, Chris. The little devil disappeared from me and evidently headed straight in by you to get you up."

"That's alright, Aunt Kat," stated Chris as he started to tickle Davy again. "What time is it?"

"A little after 8:00 A.M. Davy, you come with Mom so Chris can go back to sleep if he wants to," ordered Kat.

"No, no, I'm fine. Is Cindy awake yet?"

"I don't think so. She was smart enough to close Davy's bedroom door before she went to bed, so that he didn't have a chance to get to her yet this morning."

"I'll take a shower, if it's all right with you, Aunt Kat. Then get dressed and meet you in the kitchen in a half hour."

"Chris, it's not necessary to ask my permission. Just do whatever you want. C'mon young man, you're coming with me."

As Kat was leading Davy back into the kitchen and as they approached his bedroom, Cindy was just opening the door.

"Well, good morning, Cindy. I hope you slept well last night," she started to say when Davy begged Cindy to pick him up. "Chris is in the shower and my son and I will leave you now, so that you can get ready for breakfast. Clean towels and washcloths are in the bottom drawer on the right hand side of the vanity. Help yourself," she instructed as she took Davy from Cindy's arms.

Kat and Davy were in the kitchen preparing breakfast when Chris and Cindy appeared.

"Help yourselves to some coffee. The juice is already on the table if you prefer that and sit down at the table, because breakfast will be ready in a jiff. I hope you both like bacon and scrambled eggs."

"That will be fine," indicated Chris after concurring with Cindy.

"So what's on the agenda for today, Aunt Kat?"

"Anything the two of you want to do. It's your decision. It's supposed to be another warm, sunny day, so get out and enjoy it. There's local bands playing today starting this afternoon and running throughout the entire weekend in town at the park as part of the Fourth of July festivities. I thought maybe we could all go together later on, and then I'll treat us all to a fish fry tonight while we're still in town. So what do you think?"

"Sounds good to us, but please, Aunt Kat, let me pay for the fish fry. It's the least we can do for your hospitality."

"Not on your life! I invited you, you're my guests, and I pay," declared Kat.

Cindy helped Kat clean up the breakfast dishes while Chris and Davy played with a beach ball in the backyard.

"I hope you and Chris are happy, Cindy. The way the two of you look at each other, I can only surmise that that is the case."

"Oh, Kat. I've never been so happy and so much in love until I met Chris. He is all that I ever dreamed a man should be. Looking back, I know you had a hand in getting us together, and I'll always be so grateful to you."

"I promised myself that I wasn't going to get involved as far as you and Chris were concerned, but then I changed my mind. Now I'm glad I did, honey."

"Me too."

It was going on 10:30 A.M. when Chris and Cindy decided to change into their swimsuits and go for a swim. They came back for Davy later as they did the day before and took him out with them.

For a while, Kat watched the three having fun in the water and then decided to go in and make the beds and put out clean towels. She didn't have to bother, for everything was done. *They didn't have to do this*, thought Kat, *but how nice that they did.* She grabbed the book that she had started to read a few weeks ago and went back out onto the patio and started to read. She looked up at intervals, finding the three of them still enjoying themselves in the water. The beach was not crowded by any means, but the next day would be a different story. Her mind drifted from the pages of the book as she contemplated taking Davy out on the pier early in the morning to fish before it started to get crowded.

When the three decided to come in from swimming, they found Kat in the kitchen making lunch.

"You're just in time, everything is ready."

"We'll quick change into dry clothes and be right back," informed Chris.

"As long as Davy's things are in his room, I'll take him with me and put dry clothes on him too," volunteered Cindy.

"Are you sure?" questioned Kat.

"Positive."

The four ate their lunch and talked about what time they would like to take a ride into town and see for themselves all that was going on.

Just before 2:00 P.M., the five of them piled into Kat's car, because they needed Davy's car seat, and then they were headed into town. Traffic was heavier than normal, and they could see the crowd heading for the park. Kat found a parking spot within two blocks of the park and a bustle of excitement permeated the air as they followed the crowd. They found a flea market going on, rides for kids and music coming from somewhere in the distance.

Davy rode on all four rides while Kat, Chris and Cindy watched him go round and round and waved at him every time the ride approached them. He had no fear, whatsoever of any of the rides and sat on each with a look of pride in himself with a wide grin constantly on his face. As they walked through the flea market and checked out all the items sitting atop tables and on the ground, passing one seller after another, Kat spotted a vendor selling jewelry. She told them to go ahead and that she'd catch up with them, knowing full well that she would be a little while. She looked up and watched Chris carrying Davy on his shoulders and Cindy walking beside the two of them and all three were sharing a pink, fluffy cotton candy.

There were two bands playing at two separate locations within the park. It was good to sit down for a change after all the walking that they did and listen to the music, which was country western. Kat enjoyed herself immensely, but she could tell by the looks on Chris and Cindy's' faces that this wasn't exactly their cup of tea as far as enjoyable music.

She suggested that they move on, and the crowd was larger with the next band, which was playing rock-and-roll. They had to stand by the beer tent and Chris bought himself a beer, Cindy and Kat a Coke, and water for Davy. The crowd was really getting into the swing of the music, as some were starting to dance. Kat found herself tapping her feet to the music, as this was her kind of music also. Davy loved to dance and started to do it all by himself. It wasn't really dancing that he was doing but just moving to the music and doing his own thing, which brought stares and laughter from those around them.

While Chris leaned against a pole with his arms across his chest and watching the people, Kat noticed he was starting to really enjoy himself. Cindy had been moving her feet to the music and finally she gave in, to Kat's surprise, and asked her if she wanted to dance. Kat jumped at the idea, and Cindy, Davy, and her were dancing up a storm in no time. They listened to the band for about another hour and danced intermittently, depending on what song was being played. They then decided it was time to leave, because it was really starting to get crowded.

It was at 5:30 when they all returned to Kat's car, and she drove to the restaurant where they served the fish fry. After being seated, Kat and Cindy ordered a soda and Chris had another beer. Many laughs about the day's events were shared while waiting for the waitress to come and take their orders.

"Wow! This place must be pretty popular given the amount of people in here," declared Chris.

"It's so popular, because of the wonderful fish fry that they serve. It's always like this every Friday from the time they open until they quit serving, and you have a choice of any type of fish that you want," informed Kat.

The waitress came within a short time and took everyone's order. Kat chose a child's portion of the deep fried cod and French fries for Davy. She didn't have to ask for the ketchup, as it was already on the table. Their food was on the table and ready to eat within twenty minutes after ordering.

"Oh my goodness!" exclaimed Cindy. "Look how much that they gave us."

"Oh brother!" echoed Chris with the same sentiment. "I'm a good eater, but I doubt if I'll be able to finish all of this."

"What's leftover, you can zap in the microwave later. It never tastes the same as when you first eat it, but it's still good," informed Kat. Chris and Cindy, almost simultaneously looked over at her and watched the amount of ketchup that she was putting on Davy's plate.

"He's actually going to eat all of that?" inquired Chris.

"I hope not, but he loves the stuff, so who knows," mused Kat.

"By the time he's grown, he probably won't be able to stand the sight of it," inserted Cindy, knowing full well how much Davy loved ketchup.

After the meal was over, everyone was stuffed. Chris and Davy managed to eat everything on their plates, but Kat and Cindy had to quit with some food still remaining so they asked for two boxes to put it in. With the bill paid and Chris carrying Davy and Cindy carrying the two boxes, the five headed to the car and drove back to the cottage.

Back at the cottage and sitting around the patio table on what turned out to be a balmy summer evening, the three talked about the Air Force and Chris' plans for the future. Somehow they all got into telling about funny things that happened to each other in the past. One story was funnier than the next, and a very enjoyable evening was had by all three. Davy had fallen to sleep while sitting on Chris' lap, so Kat lifted him and carried him into the house and put him to bed. She came back out, and the three talked for about another hour when Kat decided it was time for her to turn in. She told them to sleep as late as they wanted to, and that she would make sure that Davy didn't disturb either one of them in the morning. She also told them of her plans to take Davy fishing on the pier, so that they would beat the crowd.

Chris and Cindy cuddled on the glider and enjoyed the glorious night and reveled in the time that they could spend alone together.

Davy woke Kat about 7:00 A.M. on Saturday morning. She really felt like sleeping a little longer, but knew that once he was awake, he was totally awake and would not go back to sleep. She figured that she had to get up before he started playing around and possibly wake Chris and Cindy. She dressed herself first and then Davy, and the two sat at the kitchen table eating a light breakfast. Before going out the door, she grabbed a light weight jacket for Davy and one for herself and put them on, because the weather was certainly chilly yet, because it was still early morning. For a split second, a strange feeling came over her before they went out the door, but she chose to ignore it. With rod and reel in one hand and hanging onto Davy with her other hand, mother and son were off for a morning of fishing.

As they sat down at their favorite spot on the pier, Kat pulled out a small Ziploc plastic bag full of cold worms. *I hope they're all dead*, she thought to herself, as she unzipped the bag and grabbed one of the worms to put on the hook.

"This isn't what I call fun," said Kat to Davy, just before the worm started to wiggle. She let out a light squeal and the thing fell from her hand into the water.

Just then, Michael began to laugh and told her, "If you keep that up, Mistress Kat, you're bound to run out of worms in no time."

Davy saw Michael right away and turned to him and stated, "Hi, Mike."

"Good morning to you, Master Davy," answered Michael.

"Do you think maybe you could bait the hook?" asked Kat of Michael, before she realized what she was saying and then said, "No, I guess not."

She tried two more times and was finally successful on the third try. "Now we're cooking with gas," she giggled, as she let Davy cast out the line. "He's really getting the hang of this fishing thing, Michael," she related, further explaining, "He'll sit real still here for a long time watching for that bobber to move."

"He will always be like this, Mistress Kat. It's embedded into his nature to do everything to perfection."

"Michael, he's not even three and a half yet."

"I know, Mistress Kat, but as time goes on, you will see for yourself that what I am saying is the truth."

"It's not that I doubt what you're saying, but the enormity of what you are saying. Davy will insist on doing everything to perfection from now on?"

"Yes, Mistress Kat. That is what I am saying."

"Well, all I can say is that he must have inherited that trait from his father, because I don't do anything to perfection," she confessed.

"You underestimate yourself, Mistress Kat."

"Maybe."

As Michael and Kat continued to converse with each other on the pier, Chris snuck into bed with Cindy. He tickled her nose, which finally made her wake up.

"Good morning, sleepyhead," said Chris with amusement.

"Oh! I thought you were somebody else," replied Cindy in a tone that almost made Chris think she meant it. Then she gave him a devilish look.

"You want coffee with your muffin?" asked Chris.

"Yes. That sounds good, and I'll get the butter."

Davy saw the bobber go under the same time that Kat did. She started to reel in the line, but the hook came up empty and Davy began to cry. Kat told him that she would put another worm on the hook and quickly did so and handed him the reel to cast back into the water.

A familiar voice from behind them caught Michael's attention. As he turned, there stood Thomas, who said, "I was sent here to tell you that you are being summoned to Heaven, and that I should watch over Mistress Kat and Master Davy while you are gone."

"Mistress Kat, stay with Thomas until I return, and Thomas, do not let Mistress Kat or Master Davy out of your sight. Stay with them constantly until I return, do you understand?" questioned Michael.

"Yes, Sir, I understand."

"Thomas, is it really you?" questioned Kat, with delight in her voice to hear from him again. "Have you watched much TV lately?" giggled Kat, remembering how he liked to watch TV in the beginning when he was with her, along with Michael, Gabriel and General David.

"What's TV?" Thomas inquired.

Kat started to say, "You're not Thomas," when all of a sudden, she let out a terrifying scream as she watched in horror as her son was being pulled by his feet off of the pier and into the water. She pushed herself away from the pier, jumped into the water within a second after him, and sunk to the bottom. In sheer panic, she saw her son flailing his arms and legs while a form was hovering over him and trying to hold him down. As she struggled to get closer, she could see that it was something with a long tail that was on top of Davy. *You can't have my son, you bastard*! she screamed in her mind. With her body filled with insurmountable rage, she lunged at it with all her might and with unbelievable strength, fought to get him off of Davy and wrestled him to the bottom of the lake.

Chris and Cindy were on their way to the pier when he heard his aunt Kat's scream. They both ran to the side of the pier where they normally sat, and Chris dived in and saw Davy at the bottom of the lake. He swam down farther and lifted his little body and made his way back to the surface where Cindy was waiting and grabbed Davy into her arms. Chris descended to the bottom again and out of the corner of his eye, he saw a horrible looking figure struggling in the water and saw Kat floating toward the top. He grabbed her around her waist and made a lunge for

the surface. Chris struggled as fast as he could. When they broke the surface, he lifted her with all his might into the waiting arms of two men who grabbed her by her arms and pulled her straight up. They then grabbed her by her waist and slowly laid her down on the pier. Chris hoisted himself onto the pier and began CPR on his aunt Kat's lifeless body. He could see Cindy doing the same to Davy and knew that she was very capable because of her training in CPR during high school and again in college. As they both continued to work frantically on Kat and Davy, Chris could hear sirens in the background. The paramedics came running onto the pier and took over for an exhausted and emotionally panic stricken Chris and Cindy.

Davy finally responded after what seemed a harrowing amount of time and began to cough and sputter water from his mouth and was turned over on his stomach, so that he could cough the water from his lungs. As Chris turned him back over, he began to cough some more and started to cry hysterically while flailing his arms and legs around in a struggle for freedom from what he thought was the water and the monster who wouldn't let him up. Chris sat on the pier and lifted Davy onto his lap while rocking and hugging him close to his chest and saying soothing words to comfort him. Tears of joy flowed from his eyes knowing that Davy was going to be alright and that he was starting to calm down. Chris looked over at Cindy sitting next to Kat with tears flowing like a waterfall down her face and saw one of the paramedics nod his head.

"No," yelled Chris. "Please, don't give up on her."

Davy looked into Chris' face and followed his gaze to where he was looking and began to struggle trying to release himself from his hold. Davy screamed, "Mama, mama!" over and over. For some reason, Chris released him and Davy crawled to Kat and laid his head on her chest.

"Mama, mama, wake up!" cried Davy over and over.

The two paramedics started to put their equipment away knowing that they couldn't do anything more to save her.

Helen pushed her way through the people standing on the pier and stood motionless as she saw Kat lying on the pier with Davy lying

completely on her chest. His face was close to Kat's and his little hands were on her face. He was still crying and struggling to say, "Mama, wake up! Mama, wake up!"

Cindy couldn't bare to see anymore and was about to try and coax Davy from atop of her, when Chris said, "No, Cindy. Leave him and give him a little more time to be with his mom."

Kat could hear her son call her name from what seemed in her mind a long distance away. "I'm coming, Davy. Where are you, Davy?" she called to him with a voice that echoed in her ears. "Don't cry, my darling. There's nothing to cry about. Mama will be there soon to get you. I'm coming, Davy. Please wait for me. Mama's coming to be with you." As Kat started to stir and slowly opened her eyes, she found herself staring into the face of her baby boy. Davy never turned his eyes from her face from the moment that he crawled onto her and saw her open her eyes. He looked at his mama and immediately stopped crying and began to smile. She was still in a dreadful daze and wondered if she were alive or dead. Her ears were ringing so loud that she could barely hear Davy ask her, "Mama, fish?"

Three people in the crowd started to laugh and cry at the same time. They saw their aunt and friend put her son's face into her two hands, kiss him on his lips and hold on to him for dear life.

The two paramedics came rushing back with a stretcher and asked Chris to remove the little boy, so that they could get to Kat.

"No," said Kat. "He stays with me." Davy laid his head back down on Kat's chest, and mother and son clung to each other.

"Hi, what's your name?" asked one of the paramedics as he kneeled down beside Kat.

"Kat, Kat O'Brien," slurred Kat with a raspy voice in response to his question.

"And this little guy, what's his name?"

"He's my Son, Davy."

"Hi, Davy. My name is Mark."

"Hi," responded Davy without moving his head from his mom's chest.

"Well, Kat. I can't talk for my partner here, who by the way is Charlie and is in the process of taking your blood pressure."

"Hello, ma'am," interrupted Charlie with a more subdued response than his partner Mark.

"Hi," Kat said and nodded her head.

"Like I started to say before, Kat, you have got Charlie and myself completely baffled as to what happened here. You have certainly changed my attitude with regard to the 'Man' upstairs. We both have witnessed a miracle here, and we will believe that unless we are proven wrong, which I doubt.

"Now, while Charlie continues checking your vital signs and checks for any broken bones, I will brief you quickly on what we plan to do to get you and your son out of here as fast as we can. Charlie is in the process of putting a large mat down next to you while giving me the signal that you have no apparent broken bones. But to be on the safe side, we will put a brace on your neck, which is pretty much standard procedure, so don't be alarmed."

Davy moved his head so that Mark could put the brace on Kat's neck.

"Now, Kat, I will ask you one more time if it is possible that you let Chris take your son from you?"

"No, Mark. I almost lost my son. He stays with me," repeated Kat.

"Alright, Kat, as you wish." After noticing the look on Davy's face, Mark said, "Alright, Davy, Charlie and I are going to take you and your mom over to that white truck over there." He wasn't going to use the word ambulance to a boy this young. "We'll take you to see a doctor that will be waiting to make you and your mom feel better, okay?"

"Okay," responded Davy, with a slight grin on his face.

"Kat, are you ready?"

"Just one second, if it's all right," uttered Kat, and said to Chris, "Please meet us at the hospital."

"Yes, Aunt Kat, we planned to."

The ambulance sped from the scene with sirens blaring to the hospital in Wild Rose, which was about eight miles away. Davy had heard sirens before and was quite excited to be riding in a truck with a siren.

As the two were wheeled into the emergency room, a doctor, whose name is Dr. Rasmussen, was waiting for them. Mark stood off to the side out of her hearing and told the doctor all that took place on the pier. They found no physical problems wrong with Kat, except for bruises that covered the entire length of her body and the claw like marks across her face and neck. He then told the doctor that Kat had been going in and out of consciousness from the time that they started to work on her up until now. When he called her name, she would come out of it and would respond. Then at some point, she would go back under.

Chris drove Cindy and Helen to the hospital per Helen's directions, as that is where she went to see her doctor whenever needed. Cindy and Helen stayed in the outer waiting room while a nurse motioned for Chris to come into the emergency room. He made it in time to thank Mark and Charlie as they were just about to leave.

"From what I have been told, I understand that you are the lady's nephew," declared Dr. Rasmussen.

"Yes, I am. Chris Ryan is the name."

"I'm Doctor Rasmussen, the emergency doctor on call. The patient is currently unconscious again. Do you think that you could coax her son off of her without any further stress on Ms. O'Brien, so that we can examine her?"

"Yes, I'll try," said Chris as he contemplated the seriousness of Kat going in and out of consciousness. *Why is that?* thought Chris.

"Come, Davy," said Chris in a soothing tone. "Mama is sleeping and Cindy and Helen want to see you, okay?"

Davy nodded his head and allowed Chris to lift him off of Kat and into his waiting arms.

A resident doctor did an examination of Davy and found him to be doing well, except that he had the same claw marks as his mother around his ankles and on both shoulders. After the examination, Chris carried his cousin into the waiting room where the three anxiously waited for word of Kat's condition. Chris related to Helen and Cindy what the doctor had told him.

It was going on twenty minutes now since Kat and Davy were wheeled into the emergency room when Dr. Rasmussen started his examination of Kat. He knew Mark and Charlie for years, and from what they described that occurred on that pier, and with the amount of bruises and the claw like marks on her face, and it just didn't add up. This could not have happened to her just, because she jumped into the water. By the looks of her, surmised Dr. Rasmussen, this lady was in one hell of a struggle with somebody or something. The physical marks would eventually fade from her body, but what troubled him the most was her emotional state, which he felt was causing her to lose consciousness. After he finished with his examination of her, the total time was now nearing an hour, and she still did not awaken. He called her name several times with no response. He ordered a CAT scan of her brain and wanted the results ASAP. They gave her an injection to help with any pain that she might be experiencing and made her comfortable. That was all that they could do for now until he could talk with one of his colleagues. Dr. Jack Stevens was a highly qualified psychiatrist and well respected within the medical profession. He would notify him if the results of the scan came out negative, then he would need his opinion. If not, he would seek the help of a neurologist.

Dr. Rasmussen went into the waiting area and found Chris with Davy fast asleep in his arms and two women with him. Chris introduced Cindy

and Helen. He sat down and explained what was being done for her and told them that he was waiting on the results of the CAT scan. If they wished to go home, he would call them. They opted to stay. As it turned out, Kat's CAT scan came back negative as far as any injury to her brain or head, and Dr. Rasmussen made the diagnosis that her present state of being was due to psychological trauma. He would keep her in emergency where she would be constantly monitored, and get in touch with Dr. Stevens to see when he could come and examine her to make his own diagnosis.

Dr. Rasmussen returned to the waiting room and told the three of them of his findings and that they all should go home and get some rest. He also told them that the nurse on duty would get in touch with Chris if there was any change in Kat's condition.

It was now going on seven hours since the last time that she was awake.

"Mistress Kat, it's Michael. You must come back and wake up. It's useless, Mistress Kat. You'll never find the General no matter how far and for how long you look. It was not meant to be yet. Please, your son needs you. Come back!"

Kat opened her eyes and didn't recognize where she was and in a panic, just like Davy did, started to flail her arms to protect herself from whatever it was that pulled Davy into the water.

"Please, Mistress Kat. Listen to me. It's Michael. You're safe. I'm here with you now."

"Michael? Is it truly you?"

"Yes, Mistress Kat. It is I."

"Davy, where's Davy?"

"He's safe with Chris and Cindy, and I must get back to him. But I had to get you to come back first."

"Come back? From where? I was asleep, Michael, wasn't I?"

"No, Mistress Kat. Your soul left your body in search of the General and then came back. You kept going back and forth in search of him until no one knew if you would ever come back after the last time that you left."

"Oh, Michael. You mean that I was willing to leave my son?"

"I don't think you really meant to, but the urge to find the General was so overwhelming that it took over your reasoning."

"Michael? Dare I go to sleep, or will I transgress back into nothingness again?"

"No, Mistress Kat. You will stay now, because you answered me and now know the reason you left in the first place."

"I don't remember anything after jumping into the water after Davy."

"It's all right, Mistress Kat. When you are home and feeling better, we'll talk about the whole incident."

"Whatever you say. But I want out of here, and the sooner the better."

"Let them see that you are awake. They will monitor you for the rest of the night to see if you continue to stay conscious, and if you do, they will most likely release you some time tomorrow if you insist on leaving. Now I must get back to Master Davy."

"Thank you, Michael."

Kat stayed awake the entire evening and into the wee hours of the morning even though she was so very tired. She couldn't quite explain what she was feeling that made her afraid of falling asleep, but there was an underlying fear that was hard to shake.

When Chris and Cindy arrived at the cottage with Davy after letting Helen off at home, they undressed Davy and got ready themselves for bed. Chris and Cindy tried to go over everything that happened and tried to figure out what really happened. They talked for two hours and then

called it a night. The three slept together on the pullout couch in the living room with Davy in the middle.

Kat finally fell asleep when the sun came up for maybe a couple hours or so when she heard the voice of Davy in the distance. *I must have been dreaming*, she figured, until she heard the voice again. She jumped up and put on the hospital robe and slippers and was headed for the door when it opened, and there stood Chris and Davy with Helen and Cindy following right behind.

Dr. Rasmussen came in when all five were still hugging and kissing one another. "You're awake, I see. Good."

"Yes, Doctor. I feel fine, and I want out of here."

"Don't like our hospitality?" inquired Dr. Rasmussen with a chuckle.

"It isn't that. The sooner I'm out of here, the sooner Davy and I can get back to the way we were."

"I will release you, Ms. O'Brien after you talk with Dr. Jack Stevens, who is one of the finest psychiatrists in these parts."

"Psychiatrist? I don't need a psych doctor."

"I didn't say you needed him. I just want you to talk with him. You have suffered a deep traumatic experience, and I want you to tell him all that you remember of it."

"Will that get me out of here then?"

"Yes, I will sign the release papers for you to go."

"Alright, I'll see him."

Doctor Stevens and Kat talked for over an hour. She still couldn't remember what happened to her after she jumped into the water. He told her there was no physical damage, but her brain was traumatized and to what degree, it was too early to know. She may recollect what happened

in a few days, weeks, or never. He did suggest that she seek help from a well-qualified psychiatrist in the Milwaukee area.

"Have any of you eaten breakfast yet?" questioned Kat, as she finished applying some of Cindy's makeup to cover up the claw marks the best that she could.

"Actually, Aunt Kat, it's almost noon and time for lunch. Didn't they feed you in that place?"

"I missed breakfast, because I was still sleeping, and they evidently didn't want to wake me. We left before lunch and I'm starving," informed Kat, all in one breath.

They stopped for lunch at Kat's favorite café and were seated and waiting for their orders to come. Chris was the first one to bring up the subject.

"Aunt Kat, do you remember anything that happened?"

"I have no recollection of anything after I jumped into the water after Davy."

"Do you think you ever will?" inquired Cindy.

"I don't know. Dr. Stevens told me that I may start to remember in a week or so, or maybe never. But I sure the hell am going to find out," insisted Kat.

"How?" questioned Helen, continuing with, "Not all of us were there at the same time and didn't see everything from the beginning. Chris told us that no one was on the pier except Cindy and him when he dove into the water."

Oh boy! thought Kat. *I opened my big mouth before I had a chance to think of my answer. I certainly can't tell them I'm going to find out from an Archangel.* Instead, she just said, "I'm sure I'll remember soon."

"If it's all right with you and Cindy, Chris, I'd like to get back home

today whenever you want to leave. I'd really appreciate it if one of you would drive my car. I can't guarantee if I drove that I'd stay awake until we arrived home."

"Would you want to close the cottage and stay with me tonight and then head home tomorrow?" Helen offered.

"Thank you for the kind offer, Helen. But I think as long as I have Chris and Cindy to help me get home, I had better take the opportunity."

"I understand,"

Chris drove Kat and Davy home in Kat's car while Cindy followed behind in Chris' car. Kat and Davy slept from the time that they made it out of town until they pulled into Kat's driveway.

"Don't tell me I slept all the way home?"

"Yup," laughed Chris.

"And Davy?"

"Out like a light."

"Wow! The two of us were great traveling companions."

"Don't worry about it, Aunt Kat. I'm glad you decided to come home today with Cindy and me. I'd hate to think of you all alone with no other adult and driving Davy and yourself home."

After Chris and Cindy helped her and Davy into the house and took their luggage in, they said their good-byes and left promising Kat that they would be calling to find out how she and Davy were doing.

She knew that they wouldn't have to, because as soon as her sister found out what happened, she'd be over in a flash. And she was. As a matter of fact, she didn't even finish unpacking the suitcases when the front door bell rang. As soon as she opened the door, Maggie was in her arms and holding on for dear life.

"Oh, Kat! According to Chris, we almost lost you and Davy. For God's sake, what happened up there? And your face! Look at your face and your neck! It looks like something clawed you. Who did this to you?"

"Maggie, calm down."

"How can I calm down when your face looks like a road map?"

"It's not all that bad."

"Have you looked at it lately?"

"Well, no. Not since this morning."

"Those scratches look deep and very red to me, Kat."

After going into the bathroom to look in the mirror, she had to agree with Maggie that they did look really awful. Actually, terrifying would be a better way to describe what her face looked like.

"How am I going to go to work on Tuesday looking like this? Even Cindy's makeup didn't really do a good job of covering up all these scratch marks."

"You'll just have to call Dan and explain to him what happened and see what he has to say. He's a nice guy, and I'm sure he'll understand."

"Maybe. But I've just come off of a ten day vacation and have to call in sick. Why?" groaned Kat.

"Look, now that I know that you are alright, maybe it would be better that I leave you and Davy alone. We can talk tomorrow after you talk to Dan, okay? Go lay down and get a good night's sleep. You look like you could really use it."

"Thanks, Maggie. I agree."

As she made Davy and her something to eat before going to bed for the night, Michael came into the room.

"Hi, Mike," exclaimed Davy.

"And hello to you, Master Davy."

"Michael, please. I have to know. Will Davy have nightmares for the rest of his life with what happened to him?"

"No, Mistress Kat. The Almighty one has taken away any memory of the incident. Master Davy will not remember a thing."

"Michael, can you tell me what happened?"

"Why don't you take your sister's advice and go to bed with Master Davy and we can talk all about it tomorrow."

"Yeah, maybe you're right, Michael. I think we'll do just that. I am really tired."

After washing Davy's face and applying some ointment on his shoulders and legs and doing the same thing to her face and neck to help heal the scratch marks, mother and son shared the same bed. They fell fast to sleep within minutes of lying down, and the time was only 7:00 P.M.

She awoke around 11:00 P.M. and took a couple of aspirin and lay back down. She had a fretful night's sleep with tossing and turning all night long.

Kat awoke around 6:00 A.M. on Monday morning and took the pad and pencil where she always keeps them in her nightstand drawer and started to write down the dream that she had. She didn't think it was of much significance, because she had already written down a set of catastrophic events that David had related to her and put into her book, as she was instructed to do. She also thought that the dream was a result of the emotional stress that she was experiencing.

She wrote down: (1) 3/2/2013—12:01 A.M. —Barcelona, Venezuela. A giant earthquake measuring 9.8 on the Richter scale will hit and leave everything in ruin throughout the entire city.

Davy awoke a half hour later and the two had breakfast together. Kat decided to join the family later in the afternoon to celebrate the Fourth of July. A little partying may be just what she and Davy needed right about now. He was playing with his toys in the living room, and Kat was cleaning the kitchen when Michael said, "Good morning, Mistress Kat. I hope you had a good night's sleep last night."

"Yes, Michael. I slept pretty well," she replied, thinking it was only a little white lie that she was telling him.

"Michael, I'm feeling pretty good, and too bad I don't look the same," she chuckled, "but I'm not going to let that keep Davy and I from having a good time this afternoon at Maggie's."

"Good for you, Mistress Kat. Don't let them take you down to their level."

"It'll never happen, Michael. Since we are alone, would you please tell me all that happened to us on the pier?"

"Yes, Mistress Kat, for you do have a right to know everything. Do you remember the part where Davy, you and I were sitting on the pier fishing and talking?"

"Yes, that I remember."

"Do you also remember Thomas appearing and telling me that I was being summoned to Heaven?"

"Yes."

"What was your reaction to Thomas, Mistress Kat?"

"I was so happy to hear from him and made small talk, and I asked him if he watched much TV lately and started to chuckle to myself, because that is what he liked to do while guarding me when we all first met, remember?"

"Yes, that he did. He was genuinely fascinated with that picture box."

"Right," she agreed with a laugh at Michael's description of a TV. "When he answered my question with 'What is TV?', for a split second I knew that it wasn't Thomas and started to tell him so, but that was when Davy was pulled into the lake. It was a demon who was disguised as Thomas. Am I right, Michael? And he's the one who pulled Davy into the water?"

"Yes, Mistress Kat. You are right on both questions. After giving Thomas instructions to stay with you and Davy at all times until I returned, I started to turn and move away when I had this undeniable feeling that something just wasn't right. I didn't get very far because of that, and when I heard your scream, I returned to the lake and saw Mr. Chris diving into the water. He was coming to the surface with Master Davy, and that's when I saw you fighting with the demon. I pulled you off of it, and you started to ascend to the surface, and that is when Mr. Chris dove into the water again and grabbed you. In my anger, and because I have grown to love you and Master Davy, I descended again and I killed it."

"Oh, Michael, I've been so selfish. I was so wrapped up with my own feelings and emotions since I first met you that I didn't even take into consideration what you were going through. Can you ever forgive me?" implored Kat.

"Nothing to forgive, Mistress Kat. Truly. And there's more that I must tell you."

"I'm listening, Michael."

"Master Davy drowned. Mr. Chris did not get to him on time."

"What are you saying?" questioned Kat, with an uncontrollable quiver to her voice. "Then he must have been brought back to life by Chris or Cindy, right?"

"No, Mistress Kat."

"Okay. Then it was the paramedics that arrived on time to revive him and who saved him, right?"

Michael shook his head.

"Michael, there's no one left, unless it was you."

"No, Mistress Kat. I do not have the ability to bring anyone back to life."

"Michael, please. You are confusing me. Who saved my son's life?" demanded Kat.

"It was the General, Mistress Kat. He saved his own son's life."

"What in God's name are you talking about? David was not allowed to return to Earth, because of what we did. You told me so yourself that God would not allow it."

"I know I told you that, Mistress Kat, because it was so at the time. But the Almighty One can and does change his mind on occasion. Nothing is ever written in stone," chuckled Michael.

"Except the Ten Commandments," smiled Kat in return. "Michael, I don't know what Davy and I would do without you, and I can truly say that the two of us love you dearly."

"Thank you, Mistress Kat, for saying those words. You don't know just how much meaning they have for me."

"Michael, when David saved Davy's life, did I know it was happening?"

"Yes, Mistress Kat. Your spirit and the General stared into each other's eyes for a split second just before he had to leave."

"Did we speak to each other?"

"No, Mistress Kat."

"Then when I saw that my son was okay, I left my body in search of David, and that is why I was declared dead at the scene. Is that what happened, Michael?"

"Yes, Mistress Kat."

"And when Davy started crying and calling to me to wake up, that was when I gave up looking for David and returned to my body to be with our son?"

"Exactly, Mistress Kat."

Kat had to sit there a few minutes and try to calm herself down, because she was shaking uncontrollably.

"Michael, Davy is only three and a half years old and has another three and a half years to go until he turns seven and will be under divine protection. Will they try to kill my son again, and will David be allowed to save him again, if the circumstances warrant his help?"

"I am sure that they will try again, but as to how many times, no one knows. I can't say if General David will be allowed to save Davy again or not, because it's not for me to know, Mistress Kat. All we can do is wait and see. I know that is very hard on you, but it is all that we can do."

Kat took the time to call Dan at home and not wait until Tuesday morning, which would be almost like calling him at the last minute to tell him that she would not be into work. There was no answer, so she left a message.

Dan called Kat back about a half hour before she and Davy were going to leave to go by Maggie's.

"Kat, is that you?"

"Yes, how are you doing?"

"Just fine, and you?"

"Well Dan, that's why I called you."

Kat went on to tell Dan a made up story of what happened at the lake and asked if she could have a few more days off to let her nerves calm

down and to let her face and neck heal a little more. She then could put makeup on to cover most of the scratches, so that she wouldn't have to explain to everyone at work, who were bound to ask what had happened to her. Dan was very sympathetic about what she and Davy went through, and told her to take the rest of the week off and not to report to work until the following Monday.

"Oh Dan, you are a lifesaver, and I don't know how to thank you enough for your understanding."

"Kat, you and Davy have been through a very harrowing experience. You need the time to deal with that. Call me if you need anything. And Kat, I mean that."

"Thank you, Dan."

She and Davy had a wonderful afternoon with the family. No one brought up a word about the incident. They knew it was just too soon yet for her to discuss.

That night, she fell asleep feeling better, but spent another restless night and woke up at the exact same time as yesterday morning: 6:00 A.M. She reached for the pad of paper and pencil. She wrote: (2) 6/7/2014 — 4:20 P.M. — Greenland. An earthquake measuring 9.3 on the Richter scale will cause the entire northeast section of land inward for a total of 150 miles to separate and fall into the Atlantic Ocean.

Kat had to get out of bed and go and sit in the front room to get her bearings straight, for she wondered if she was really awake or having a nightmare in regard to this dream. *What was going on?* pondered Kat, after reading this second message that came to her in her sleep.

Maggie was over early to get all the details of what happened to Davy and her. She told Maggie that she really didn't remember much, only what Michael related to her. She also told Maggie of her two dreams.

"Do you know how many of these dreams that you are going to have, or are these the only two?"

"I have no idea."

"They're similar to the other catastrophic events that you listed in your book. Maybe you're supposed to write another book."

"And what if I only have these two dreams? That won't make much of a basis to write a book."

"I don't know, Kat. Ever since David, Michael, Gabriel and Thomas came to protect you from those damn demons, your life, and now Davy's, is turning into a nightmare in the making."

"Yes, but I wouldn't change the experience of knowing and loving, David for anything in the world, no matter what."

"Well, if I were you and you get any more of these dreams, promise me that you will talk to Michael. He must know what is happening. He's an Archangel, for God's sake, and here to guide you. That's what you told me."

"I know, and I will talk to Michael if these dreams do continue. They have to have some significance."

"Well, Honey, I'd better get going. You want to go riding with me today?"

"No, I think I'll take a pass. Maybe next Tuesday, okay?"

"I understand, Kat. If you need anything, be sure and call me."

"Will do. And have fun with your ride this afternoon. Say 'hi' to Daisy for me," chuckled Kat.

"I'm sure she will be happy to receive your message," laughed Maggie. "Catch you later."

Mother, son and Michael had a wonderful day playing together. Michael and Kat took turns reading to Davy, and the day seemed to fly by. After putting Davy to bed, Kat sat down with a new book that she was anxious to start reading. She read until at 11:30 P.M. and had to force

herself to put the book down, even though it was getting very interesting and go to bed.

Kat awoke the next morning and just knew without having to look at her alarm clock that it was at 6:00 A.M. Yup, on the dot. *All right, what is this?* pondered Kat. *Why 6:00 A.M. every morning? Not 7:00 A.M. or at 8:00 A.M, but always 6:00 A.M. I've got to discuss this with Michael like Maggie said and see if he knows what is going on.* She wrote down: (3) 5/18/2015 — 4:16 P.M. — Portugal. An earthquake measuring 8.8 on the Richter scale will devastate the entire country.

As she made a pot of coffee and waited for it to finish brewing, Michael walked into the kitchen.

"Good morning, Mistress Kat."

"Good morning to you also, Michael. I've got something important to ask you, if you have time."

"I'll always have the time for you and Master Davy, Mistress Kat."

"I didn't mention to you before now about these dreams that I have been having, because I didn't know if they would stop or continue on. Seems like they are going to go on. Do you know anything about them?"

"Yes, Mistress Kat, I do."

"So what do they mean, and how many more will I have? Why always at 6:00 A.M. in the morning?"

"I am glad that you finally asked me, so that I can give you some insight as to what this all means."

"So you knew that I was having them?"

"Oh yes, Mistress Kat. I knew. There will be twenty-eight dreams, consecutively. Every night you will dream of a different catastrophic event until the twenty-eight are finished."

"But why? For what purpose?"

"You will once again warn mankind of these events that will happen, if they do not change their ways."

"Do you mean that God will make these things happen?"

"No, the Almighty One will not be the cause of these events, but he will not stop them either. You see, Mistress Kat, mankind will bring about all of these tragedies upon themselves, because of all the negative energy emitted by you humans toward each other. With the vast amount of negative energy being emitted, there is bound to be catastrophic events of this magnitude to occur throughout the world."

"So this is a warning?"

"Yes, Mistress Kat, a warning."

"Well, Michael. If these catastrophic events start to happen then I would think that mankind would heed these words."

"Not if, Mistress Kat, but when. And not all of mankind will believe what you have told them, but some will."

"Then what's the purpose in telling them in the first place?"

"Choices, Mistress Kat. They will be given the choice to believe or not to believe, and then act in accordance with their beliefs."

"So, Michael. Am I supposed to write another book?"

"Yes, Mistress Kat. And you will prophesize all of these happenings in the future and more. You are doing it right now in your dreams."

"What do you mean 'prophesize'?"

"You will talk to the world and relate the Almighty One's messages as they come to you."

"Michael, let's be realistic here. How am I going to 'prophesize to the world,' as you put it, when I'm terrified to get up in front of ten people, let alone a room full or a crowd? And besides, what would I tell them?"

"You will not be afraid to speak, because the Almighty One will be at your side at all times, and he will be the one doing the talking. You will be his mouthpiece."

"You mean kind of like Edgar Bergen and Charlie McCarthy? Where I'm the dummy and sit on God's lap and move my lips in accordance to the words that he is saying? And it actually will be his words that will come through?" chuckled Kat. "Sorry, Michael. This conversation that we are having here is starting to make me feel a little uneasy and when I'm uneasy, I crack jokes. It's my way of coping."

"That's all right, Mistress Kat," said Michael, not really understanding what she meant in reference to the two gentlemen and calling herself a dummy. "The Almighty One likes a good joke once in a while."

"Oh, Michael. You are something else."

"Mistress Kat, did you reread the letter that the General left you, and did you understand what he was trying to tell you?"

"You told me that I was missing something when we talked at the cottage. So yes, I did read David's letter that he wrote to me again. All that he told me was that I would be a prophet some day and that my psychic abilities will get stronger with each passing day. I personally think he is off on both counts, because if I had such psychic abilities, I would have known about Davy and the lake ahead of time, right?"

"You did know ahead of time, Mistress Kat."

"Michael, what in the world are you talking about that I did know? If that were the case, Davy and I would never have been on that pier that morning in the first place," emphasized Kat, with a little edge to her voice.

"I did not mean to anger you with what I just said, Mistress Kat. I guess I did not put the words in the right order while telling you what I meant to say."

"That's alright, Michael. I know you wouldn't hurt anyone for the world. I'm not really angry, and I'm sorry that I got a little huffy."

Kat knew from the lull in the conversation that he didn't understand what she was talking about, especially when she used slang words and phrases.

"Huffy means uptight, touchy, or offended." *Finally*, thought Kat, *he understands what I meant,* when Michael responded.

"Ah yes, offended. I did not mean to do that, Mistress Kat."

"I know," is all she said, because this conversation seemed to be going around and around. "Okay, Michael, please explain to me what you meant when you said that I knew what was going to happen."

"I did not say that you knew *what* was going to happen, but that you knew that *something* was going to happen."

"You lost me again, Michael," Kat responded, and getting more frustrated.

"You see, Mistress Kat, whenever an intuition or gut feeling occurred to you, you immediately dismissed it instead of exploring that feeling further."

Kat had to think back to that Saturday morning and realized Michael was right. When she grabbed the jackets before going out the door, she did remember an ominous, foreboding feeling come over her for just a second that left her with a sense of uneasiness, which only lasted for a second. She never thought anymore about it as they headed for the pier. She then related this information to Michael.

"That's what you meant isn't it, Michael? If I would have taken the time to regard those feelings and then obtain a better idea of what they

were trying to tell me, I wouldn't have taken Davy fishing. And that is what David meant when he said that my psychic powers, which are, in my opinion, gut feelings, would get stronger every day. I had to realize first that that is what they were and then deal with them, accordingly?"

"Right, Mistress Kat. That is what the General was trying to get across to you."

"Well! The bonehead could have made the letter a little longer and told me what he really meant," chuckled Kat, not really meaning what she was saying.

"That he could have, Mistress Kat, but he wanted you to think things out for yourself," giggled Michael, at the mention of the word *bonehead*, which was her favorite word used to describe the General in the past.

Kat and Davy went to the cottage for her two remaining vacations. They continued to fish and frolic in the water and play in the sand on the beach. She wasn't going to live in fear until Davy turned seven. She was extra cautious, and if her instincts gave her a warning, which they didn't, she would certainly heed that warning from now on.

Susan and her boyfriend Steven became engaged during the summer and set a wedding date for next summer, a year after Susan would graduate from college, and then she only had one more year left to get that administrative nursing degree. They asked Kat if Davy could be in their wedding. By the time that they married, he would be four and a half years old, and Kat agreed. Chris and Cindy hadn't set a date to marry yet. Kat assumed that they would wait another two years or more when Chris would be well established as a pilot, and Cindy would graduate from college with a degree in business. Chad will graduate from high school next summer and then go into the Navy. Tim loved being in the Marines and planned to make a career of it, as did his two brothers with their chosen services. Kat loved all her nephews but felt more of a bond with Chris, probably because of the closeness he and Davy shared.

Kat had twenty-five more dreams of the catastrophic events bringing the total to twenty-eight, and then they stopped. The ironic thing, in

Kat's estimation, was the fact that she continued to wake every morning at exactly 6:00 A.M. to write them down. Michael tried to explain the reason to her and told her something about at 6:00 A.M. being the only hour that coincided with the time difference on the other side or something to that nature. She wasn't quite sure what he said actually. She simplified it and reasoned it must be the same time that God arose from bed each morning, so she had to also in order to write down the messages that he was giving her. Before putting the list onto her computer and copying it to store in a safe place, she went over the entire list of events one more time:

(4) 2/10/2016 —12:10 P.M. — Guatemala. An earthquake out in the Atlantic Ocean measuring 10.5 on the Richter scale will cause a 230-foot tidal wave to hit the country and destroy everyone and everything in its path as will the remaining catastrophic events.

(5) 8/30/2017 — 12:04 P.M. — Spain. An earthquake measuring 8.3 on the Richter scale and every living thing, including people, will be destroyed.

(6) 4/21/2018 — 6:45 P.M. — Afghanistan. An earthquake measuring 10.6 on the Richter scale will hit and the entire country will disappear.

(7) 6/12/2019 — 3:25 A.M. — Canada. An earthquake measuring 8.7 on the Richter scale will hit Nova Scotia, Ontario, and Newfoundland, destroying all three Provinces.

(8) 4/16/2020 — 6:40 A.M. — Brazil. An earthquake measuring 10.2 on the Richter scale and starting out in the Atlantic Ocean will cause a wall of water measuring 276 feet high to hit and cover the entire country with water twenty feet deep.

(9) 8/23/2021 — 4:10 P.M. — Poland. An earthquake out in the Baltic Sea measuring 8.6 on the Richter scale will hit and cause a wall of water measuring 110 feet high to destroy the entire country.

(10) 5/3/2022 — 4:20 P.M. — Mesopotamia. An earthquake measuring 9.2 on the Richter scale will hit and destroy the entire country.

(11) 3/28/2023 — 4:00 P.M. — Greece and Sicily. An earthquake measuring 8.2 on the Richter scale will hit both countries and sink them into the Mediterranean Sea.

(12) 8/12/2024 — 1:23 A.M. — Czechoslovakia. An earthquake measuring 8.1 on the Richter scale will hit and destroy the entire country.

(13) 4/8/2025 — 6:10 P.M. — India. An earthquake measuring 10.5 on the Richter scale will hit under the Ganges River raising the entire river, thus flooding the country with twenty feet of water.

(14) 7/6/2026 —12:45 A.M.— Turkey. An earthquake measuring 8.9 on the Richter scale will hit and destroy the entire country.

(15) 1/10/2027 — 6:10 A.M. — Panama. An earthquake measuring 7.9 on the Richter scale will hit and destroy the entire country.

(16) 2/16/2028 — 3:12 P.M. — Hawaii. An earthquake beginning out in the Pacific Ocean measuring 10.6 on the Richter scale will hit and destroy Hawaii and the seven other islands.

(17) 7/12/2029 — 7:11 A.M. — Denmark. An earthquake measuring 8.3 on the Richter scale will hit and destroy the entire country.

(18) 2/23/2030 — 5:23 P.M. — Hungary. An earthquake measuring 8.5 on the Richter scale will hit and destroy the entire country.

(19) 2/8/2031 — 4:08 P.M. — Scandinavia. An avalanche of snow will bury the entire country.

(20) 8/4/32 — 8:05 A.M. — Persia. An earthquake measuring 8.7 on the Richter scale will hit causing a wall of sand to bury the entire country.

(21) 2/20/33 — 6:10 A.M. — Prussia. An earthquake measuring 8.9 on the Richter scale will hit for the second time and destroy the entire country.

(22) 3/2/2034 — 3:07 P.M. —France. An earthquake measuring 9.2 on the Richter scale will hit and destroy the entire country.

(23) 6/6/2035 — 1:10 P.M. — Antarctica. Extreme global warming will cause icebergs to completely melt and deposit tons of water into the Atlantic Ocean, flooding the entire continent.

(24) 10/1/2036 — 5:07 A.M. — Cuba. An earthquake measuring 7.8 on the Richter scale will hit in the Atlantic Ocean and will cause a tidal wave measuring 230 feet high, destroying the entire country.

(25) 6/7/2037 — 12:12 P.M. — Santo Domingo. Heavy rains will form mudslides ten feet deep, burying the entire country.

(26) 8/8/2038 — 3:20 P.M. — China. An earthquake measuring 11.2 on the Richter scale will hit and destroy the entire country.

(27) 10/14/2039 — 4:16 P.M. — North Korea. An abundance of rain will cause mudslides to bury the entire country.

(28) 7/27/2040 — 4:30 P.M. — Tunisia. An earthquake measuring 12.1 on the Richter scale will hit and destroy the entire country.

Kat couldn't believe her eyes when she read the list of catastrophes over again, and really understood the terrible amount of devastation and loss of life that will occur for so many years to come. She showed the list to Michael, and he concurred that all of these terrible events would truly happen in the future.

The following summer, Chad followed in his brothers' footsteps and joined the Navy right out of high school. By now, Maggie thought that she would be used to the idea of her sons leaving her one by one, but it wasn't so. With the realization that all her boys have now left home, she was actually more depressed than when Chris first left for the Air Force. Marshall was a big help with trying to get Maggie back on track by spending more time with his wife, which turned out to be a major plus in their lives. Maggie threw hints at Kat, but couldn't bring herself to tell her that the sex was wonderful. Kat had to surmise that on her own.

Kat, Maggie, Cindy and Davy drove to Hansen, Iowa, on Friday morning, the day before Susan and Steven were to be married in the

month of June. They stayed at a motel in Hansen on Friday night, and attended the ceremonial practice, and were then invited to the wedding rehearsal dinner at a wonderful chalet style restaurant and bar about seven miles outside of Hansen. The place was huge and would be the setting for the reception after the wedding.

The wedding took place at 2:00 P.M. in a little church in Hansen where Susan's parents were married. As the wedding march started, Davy was the first one down the aisle dressed in a black tuxedo with a red satin shirt and black vest that sported a red rose. He looked absolutely adorable and was a miniature of the groom, best man, and the rest of the men in the wedding party. He did his part very well, which made Kat so very proud.

Susan's five sisters were either bridesmaids or part of the wedding party in some form, as she couldn't favor one over the other of the older ones to be her maid of honor. Susan was a beautiful bride and truly a sight to behold as she glided down the aisle with her father to meet with her husband-to-be. Kat was awestruck. She wasn't that young, shy girl who appeared on her doorstep over two years ago anymore, but a beautiful woman who was about to be married. Tears of joy began to form in her eyes. The wedding reception followed the ceremony. It was really a gala affair with nearly one hundred people, and Kat and Maggie thoroughly enjoyed the music and typical shenanigans that occur at every wedding. Davy was in seventh heaven playing with Susan's siblings, especially his pal Billy. It was such a pleasure for Kat to meet Jim and Diane for the first time, and she invited the two of them to come and see her and Davy, if they would ever make it to Milwaukee.

Kat had made up her mind to get in touch with the neighborhood school to see, if she could get Davy enrolled into K5 kindergarten even though it would be about four and a half months later after school started that he would turn five on January 27 of the following year. She called the school and was told to set up an appointment with the K5 teacher, which she did. After Kat related to Ms. Jackson Davy's abilities in reading and math, Ms. Jackson was very interested in meeting Davy and set up an appointment to meet with the two of them two weeks before school was to start. Kat knew that she would have to give up her second shift job

at some time or another, and it looked like the time was now. She didn't relish going back on first shift after all these years, but Davy's welfare came first. She was sure that Davy would be accepted, so she asked Dan if there were any openings for her on first shift. There were three openings available and since Kat had seniority, she could choose which knitting job she wanted. The entire situation worked out great, because one of the first shift knitters was very anxious to get on second shift.

Once the Fourth of July arrived, the whole summer just seemed to slip away. Kat used up two weeks vacation, but wanted to save the fourth one for Davy when he entered kindergarten. She hoped her intuition was correct, for she made a big assumption with changing shifts with her job. She would use up her third week of vacation before she had to start on first shift by inviting Marshall and Maggie up to the cottage for the weekend. They accepted, to Kat's surprise. Maggie, of course, had been to the cottage a couple of times, but Marshall had not. Even though Maggie had told him about it, he was very impressed with the whole layout.

It happened that her neighbor Sharon and her husband Mike were up to their place the same weekend, and Marshall and Maggie got to see what a real log cabin house looked like. Marshall couldn't believe what he was seeing, and Maggie's mouth was open during the entire tour.

Kat took them to the famous fish fry and they all sat around the patio table afterward feeling very stuffed but content to be outside on such a warm, gorgeous night. They hadn't heard from Chad as of yet, because he was still in basic training at Annapolis. Chris had a half of a year pilot training under his belt already. Marshall and Maggie were so proud of him when he graduated from the Academy, and they were invited to it and toured the entire complex. He graduated with more honors and was the star wide receiver on the Falcon football team all four years. But the best surprise for Marshall and Maggie was that he was voted salutatorian, because of his 3.9 grade point average that he maintained throughout the four years.

"I always knew that kid had a good head on his shoulders and would go far in life," pronounced Kat.

"You've said that about all my boys," answered Maggie.

"I guess you're right. You two sure did a fine job with raising those kids. In this day and age, that's not so easy to do."

"We just guided them and they did the rest," stated Marshall.

"Well, whatever the reasons for their success are, I'm still very proud of all three of them."

The next morning, Kat awoke to find Davy missing from his bed. In a short-lived moment of terror, she ran into the living room and discovered only Maggie sleeping on the pullout couch. She opened the back door and saw Marshall and him sitting side by side on the pier fishing. Only then did her emotions return to normal.

The rest of the day was spent enjoying the water, warm temperatures, and swimming, as Marshall and Maggie were avid swimmers. The water was not Kat's cup of tea, and the only reason she was out there was because of her son, so she spent the time in shallow water pushing and pulling Davy on an inner tube. Marshall had Davy swimming a couple of strokes in no time, and Davy was thrilled at what he was doing. Before they all decided to come in, he swam five strokes on his own before he went under. Needless to say, Davy was ready to quit.

"You really should have him in a swimming class," suggested Marshall.

"What I really need to do first is get him into school," reasoned Kat.

As the four returned to the backyard and Kat opened the gate, Davy spotted Michael and said, "Hi Mike, did you see me swim?"

"Who is Mike?" Marshall questioned.

"His imaginary friend," replied Maggie, before Kat had a chance to answer.

Later that night after Kat put Davy to bed, the three sat at the table under the stars.

"This is what I call a real vacation," stated Marshall, and he continued with, "It's beautiful up here, and so very peaceful. You don't have to deal with crowds and an itinerary on a daily basis as you do with most vacations."

"I agree, wholeheartedly," said Maggie.

The three continued to talk about old times, fun times, and their children and then called it a night.

Kat hated to see her sister and Marshall leave early Sunday afternoon, as the time spent together was just too short as usual.

She decided to go back home on Thursday of the following week instead of waiting until Saturday. Her entire sleeping habits would have to change in order to get up early each morning and go to work. But she would have more quality time with Davy. Maggie volunteered to watch Davy at her house for the three weeks before school would start. If Kat couldn't find anyone, Maggie volunteered to come over each day to pick him up from school and then leave after Kat came home, which was usually a half hour later. She needed to find someone to pick Davy up from school until she came home each day. She certainly couldn't ask Maggie to do it indefinitely. *She has done so much for Davy and me already, it wouldn't be fair to ask her,* thought Kat.

She didn't sleep much on Sunday night worrying about the alarm going off and not hearing it. She arose at 5:30 A.M. and left the house at 6:15 A.M., which gave her plenty of time to drive to work and start at 7:00 A.M. to 3:30 P.M. She came home dragging for the first week.

She and Davy kept the appointment for Wednesday at 4:30 P.M. the following week to meet with Ms. Jackson. After testing Davy in arithmetic and reading, she was very impressed with him. It was unusual to have a child with his caliber of skills at such a young age. She assured Kat that she would talk with the principal the next day and saw no reason why he wouldn't be accepted. *This child should definitely be in school, and the rules can be changed with extenuating circumstances*, thought Ms. Jackson.

"Now, all I have to do is find someone to pick him up after school each day and stay with him until I get home from work," lamented Kat.

"That will be no problem," indicated Ms. Jackson.

"What do you mean?"

"We have a program here at school that started a couple of years ago, which allows parents to bring their children here and drop them off on their way to work and then pick them up after work. The hours of the camp are from at 6:00 A.M. until at 6:00 P.M., with a reasonable fee, of course. Depending on the size of the group, one adult to every ten children is the rule of thumb. Nutritious snacks and milk are served to each child at a designated time before and after school. The adults have them do their homework first, and if time permits before their parent picks them up, the children can then play games. Would you be interested, Ms. O'Brien?"

"I'll say! Yes, definitely sign me up. This is wonderful. The kids stay right at school where they will be safe."

"Let me see if Mr. Shimley, who is our principal, is still in the building. And if he is, I can talk to him right away and tell him about Davy, if you wouldn't mind waiting."

"Of course not."

Kat and Davy waited in the K5 classroom and looked at the educational paraphernalia hanging on the walls, the different reading pamphlets, and arithmetic pamphlets stacked neatly on top of a bookcase. She had an unusual amount of toys and learning toys scattered about the room, and Kat found Davy honed in on the toy soldiers lying in a box. *Right up his alley*, thought Kat. Ms. Jackson was gone for half an hour, and Kat surmised with hope that this was a good sign.

Five minutes after Kat's last thought, Ms. Jackson returned accompanied by a short, slightly stocky man wearing wire rim glasses.

"Ms. O'Brien, I'd like you to meet our principal, Mr. Shimley. Mr. Shimley, this is Ms. O'Brien, the mother of Davy, who I see is interested in our collection of toy soldiers."

"Davy, come over here please," requested Kat.

Ms. Jackson repeated the same introduction to Davy, and Mr. Shimley offered Davy his hand, which Davy shook.

Mr. Shimley looked directly at Davy and asked, "Would you like to go to school here, Davy?"

"Yes, Sir. I certainly would."

"A smart child with good manners," declared Mr. Shimley. "What a welcome relief. Well then, Davy, school starts the day after Labor Day. Welcome aboard."

"Ms. Jackson, if you would please finish up here, then I'll be on my way. It was nice meeting you, Ms. O'Brien, and I hope we see more of you in the future, because we need the parents to take an interest in their child's education. Davy, we'll see you on the fifth. Good day."

"Good-bye, Mr. Shimley, and thank you so very much," said Kat, with Davy following with his own good-bye.

"Do you have any more questions that you wish to ask of me, Ms. O'Brien?"

"Just one. What about lunch? Do they serve hot meals?"

"Yes, we do. At the beginning of every month, we send a menu home to the parents stating what will be served on what days. If your child doesn't like what is made certain days, he can bring a bag lunch from home. You only pay for the meals that are eaten."

"Well, Ms. Jackson, I want to thank you very much for all that you have done for my son, Davy and me."

"You're entirely welcome. I did it, because this young man should be in school."

Kat couldn't get home fast enough, so that she could call Maggie with the good news. She would tell her about the camp, which relieved her worries, because now she didn't have to try and find someone to take care of Davy. Life was starting to look up for a change.

Kat recalled how nervous she was with dropping Davy off for his first day of school and how excited Davy was to go to school. She went by Maggie to pass the time away, because she took off from work. She needed to be around her at this time and to talk to her, so that she wouldn't worry herself to death and, of course, to cry on her shoulder, for this was the first time that her baby boy was away from her.

"Kat, for goodness sake. Davy was not taken away from you. He's in school for the first time and he's probably having the time of his life. This feeling of abandonment that you're going through will pass. I give it a week," laughed Maggie.

"What makes you so sure?"

"I have three sons, remember? And I went through the same thing with each of them. Don't worry, he'll be just fine."

"I don't know. What if the other kids don't like him and—"

"Kat, you're making a mountain out of a mole hill. Davy's a good kid. What's not to like about him?"

"I know, and you're right. I'm being the overprotective mother here."

"Davy gets out at 3:30 P.M. right?"

"Yes."

"How about we go clothes shopping? I have to find a dress to wear to a dinner party at one of Marshall's co-worker's home next Saturday. You can help me pick something out and then we can do lunch. By the time you drop me back at home, it will be time to pick Davy up from school. What do you say? Kat, have you been listening to me?"

"Sure, Maggie. Anything you say."

She shoved Kat's purse into her arms, grabbed her own, and ushered her out the door.

Maggie always has the knack for cheering me up, thought Kat.

The dress she finally bought, after trying on five, was 70 percent off and fit her perfectly.

They had a lot of laughs while eating. Of course, Maggie and her always giggled a lot when they were together. That was only one of the special things between the two of them: laughter.

Maggie was right. As soon as Davy got into his car seat and buckled himself in, the conversation between mom and son was non-stop about all positive things about his first fun day at school.

Ms. Jackson insisted that her students read one book from the school library each week, which was a good learning process. One night after supper, Davy was reading a book about the solar system to Kat. When he finished the last page and closed the book, he turned to Kat and said, "Mom, I can tell you word for word what the book said," and he did.

Kat was dumfounded and inquired of Davy, "How long has this been going on, and why didn't you tell me before now that you have this ability?"

"Since I learned to read from you and Michael. I didn't say anything to you, because I thought that it happens to all kids."

Kat dropped the conversation at that point and told Davy it was time for bed. She immediately called upon Michael.

"Michael, you knew all along of Davy's photographic memory, but didn't tell me. Why?"

"I am here to observe and give advice when needed. You must find out on your own all of the things your son is capable of doing."

"So, does this mean I'm in for more shockers like this one in the future?"

"If you will please explain what the word 'shockers' means, I will then be able to answer your question satisfactorily."

"It means surprises. As in something I didn't know."

"Oh yes, Mistress Kat, there will be more surprises to come, even when he is a man."

"Oh great! Are all these divine abilities really necessary? He's only five and yet it seems my son is a miniature version of Einstein, Isaac Newton, General Patton and soon to be Nostradamus, all rolled into one. He's only a little kid, Michael, and I want my baby boy back."

"He is still your baby boy, Mistress Kat, but he is just starting to be highly evolved, and will be more so in his future. This has all been in the making from the day he was born. There is no turning back, only forward."

K5 was a wonderful learning experience for Davy and he made friends easily. As the year began to wind down, Davy became bored with his homework, yet received A and A+ on all of it and was reading at a third-grade level. His gusto with military battles continued, and he only wanted toys with military significance. Kat talked to Michael again about the fears that she had with his obsession with military paraphernalia.

During the last parent-teacher conference, which was before the spring recess, Ms. Jackson suggested to Kat that she enroll Davy into an extracurricular activity after school, such as one of the many sports available all year long. Davy joined the school baseball team, which most of his friends belonged to. Kat was told that he needed more challenges and maybe this would help.

Davy loved to play and was good at each of the sports that he enrolled in: basketball, baseball and soccer. He was good, because he challenged himself to strive for perfection. Some of the games were held during the week, but most of them took place on Saturdays, which cut into Kat's volunteer work at the Soup Kitchen. He had some friends that he would play with after school, but he was really close to a boy named, Johnny.

They were inseparable, but after a while, Kat caught on to how Johnny made all the decisions about what they would play, when, and where, while Davy went along with whatever he said.

After enrolling Davy in the first grade in August, she talked to Maggie to see, if she really wanted to join her and Davy on the trip to the Holy Land to have him baptized in the Waters of Life. She made an appointment to talk with a travel agency to find out, if they could book a flight sometime after Christmas and into the New Year when Davy would turn seven. Kat figured that the tourist season was over by Christmas, and that it wouldn't be a problem booking a flight. She was told that they had group pilgrimages or that she could go on her own. There were certainly advantages and disadvantages with both plans. There was a third option, which would be to go with a group for a certain amount of time during the day and then go on their own afterward. Kat requested a full itinerary from the travel agency giving her the dates, total number of days and cost of a trip. She preferred to spend only five days to a week, but nothing beyond. The travel agency would gather all the data for her and get back to her when they received all the pertinent information for Kat to look over.

Kat was making breakfast on Saturday morning in mid-September when Davy called out, "Mom."

"Yes, Davy. I'm in the kitchen."

As he walked into the kitchen, he informed Kat, "I made a new friend in school yesterday."

"How nice. What do you mean by 'new'? Did he come here from somewhere else, or was he always here and you hadn't met him yet?"

"He moved here from Minnesota. He's been in school for a little over two weeks now."

"You want to ask me my opinion about him, right?"

"How did you know?"

"Honey, I'm your mother, remember? Mothers know when their children are worried by something. I knew by the hesitation with your words and by the sad look that you have on your face when you talk about him. So what's up?"

"Well, his name is Larsen Erickson, but he likes to be called Lars for short. I've watched as the other kids have made fun of him since the first day that he came to school, because of the way that he talks."

"Minnesota is only one state away. How different could he talk from us?"

"I don't know. He talks fine to me, but some of the kids think he talks with a funny accent, and they make fun of his first name."

"Oh my. It's hard enough for a kid to attend a new school, but to be made fun of. That's awful! Shame on the ones who are doing it."

"I know, and that's why I went up to him at lunch where he was sitting by himself, and I asked if I could join him at the table."

"I'm proud of you, honey. That must have made him feel good."

"Not really. He totally ignored me when I sat down and started talking to him. After basically talking to myself for about ten minutes, I finally asked him what his problem was. He finally opened up and told me: 'I know you're friends with the rest of those guys so don't pretend that you want to be nice to me.'"

"Then what happened?"

"I said, 'Look Lars, yes I am friends with most of them, but I don't like the way that they are treating you, because you didn't do anything to deserve it. I thought after a few days that they would get tired of hounding you, but they haven't let up, and I'm sorry that this is happening to you.'"

"Then what happened?"

"I told him that my name is David O'Brien, and my friends call me, Davy and we started talking. Believe it or not, Mom, we got along really well. I mean, he told me all about himself and his family, and I started to tell him about myself but didn't get far because the bell rang. We walked back to class together, and after school, I walked with him to his house. He only lives ten houses from here down our block, and then I came on home."

"How did the other kids react?"

"They were waiting outside for us but didn't say a word to either Lars or me. They just turned their backs on us."

"So, now you think that they might turn on you for befriending Lars, right? Well, honey, I can tell you how I would handle it, but it has to be your choice on what you want to do. But if the situation gets worse and out of hand, then I will step in."

"So what would you do, Mom?"

"First, I want to tell you how very proud of you that I am. You did a courageous thing by making friends with Lars. And then I'll ask you: do you want a bunch of bullies for friends? Because that's how they are acting."

"No."

"Good. I wouldn't either. So you just answered your own question. You made the choice to befriend Lars against your other friends. Now, if they back down and stop picking on Lars, then give them another chance to be friends with him too. But if they don't, you don't need friends like them, because their next move would be for you to take sides: Lars or them."

"So kind of wait and see what happens then?"

"Exactly."

Just then, a knock at the backdoor revealed Lars standing there.

"Come in," replied Davy, and then he introduced him to Kat.

"It's nice to meet you, Lars, and welcome to Wisconsin."

"Thank you. It's nice to meet you too," answered Lars in a whisper and with his head bowed. As the two left to go play, Kat poured herself a cup of coffee and sat down at the table.

"Did you hear everything, Michael?"

"I certainly did, Mistress Kat."

"Pretty pathetic. My son is only in the first grade and he has problems like this already. What will it be like in the future? Kids nowadays get worse with their behavior as they get older."

"Master Davy did a fine thing yesterday. He and Lars will remain friends for the rest of their lives."

"Truly?"

"Oh yes, Mistress Kat. Even though at some point in their lives that they will have to part ways, they will continue to stay in touch with each other over the years, because Lars will never forget what Master Davy did."

As Kat learned later, Johnny, who was supposed to be Davy's friend, was the one who talked the other kids into being mean to Lars. As time went by, they started liking Lars, and because he wanted Davy to be friends with only him and wouldn't change his ways, Johnny was the one on the outside looking in.

It was late November and the temperature for the past few weeks was still in the fifties. Kat had yet to make up her mind which package deal she wanted for the trip to the Holy Land.

Kat was in the kitchen finishing up the lunch dishes one Sunday afternoon, and Davy was outside playing with his friends with their bikes over at the park. There was one extremely high hill with another one

below it that the kids loved riding over. There was plenty of room for the kids to brake after the second hill, which butted the sidewalk and the busy street beyond. She was just ready to hang up her dishtowel when an awful feeling of dread came over her and her stomach was hurting like hell. She didn't hesitate and took off running through the backdoor in the direction of the park, which was two blocks away. As she approached the busy intersection from across the street and continued running and weaving between the traffic, she saw Davy approaching the second hill. His bike seemed to be picking up speed, and he was frantically applying his hand brakes as he was reaching the bottom of the hill. He was on a collision course with Kat, but within five feet of hitting her, his bike came to a complete halt.

"Davy, are you alright?" Kat wailed, hysterically.

"Yeah, Mom. I'm okay. My brakes didn't work. Why didn't my brakes work, Mom?" cried Davy, knowing full well what could have happened to him, if he would have kept going and ended up in the street with all the traffic. "It was Michael who stopped me, Mom."

"Are you really here, Michael?"

"Yes Mistress Kat, it is me."

"C'mon, let's go home," uttered Kat, who was still shaken by the incident. Davy and Lars followed her while pushing his bike.

"Davy, why don't you and Lars go watch TV," instructed Kat as the three entered the kitchen.

Instead of her usual coffee, Kat proceeded to get a glass from the cupboard, poured a shot of whiskey into it, grabbed some ice and Coke from the refrigerator and sat down at the kitchen table.

"I don't need to ask you this time if it was them, Michael, because I know for sure that it was."

"Yes, your gut instinct told you."

"Yes. This time it was like someone took their fist and punched me right in the stomach. I didn't have to wait and analyze; I knew something was going to happen and soon. Michael, for God's sake, we still have two more months to go. After this failed attempt, they could try again and again to get Davy."

"Yes."

"That's it, I'm getting on the phone tomorrow after work and make those reservations, lock up Davy's bike, take him to and from school and keep him in the house until we go."

"You can't stop him from living his life, Mistress Kat," suggested Michael.

"Oh yes I can, Michael, and I will. My son will be in my sight at all times except when he's at school. And I'm going to move his bed into my bedroom," informed Kat. "They'll have to go through me to get to my son. The bastards!"

Kat kept the promise to herself and did everything she told Michael that she was going to do to keep her son safe from now on until he was baptized again.

Kat, Maggie and Davy were due to leave for Israel as planned on Wednesday, January 28, exactly one day after his seventh birthday. They would return home on February 2. Kat had the full itinerary, passports, plane tickets and hotel reservations. She and Davy were packed and ready way ahead of time. Since his seventh birthday fell on the twenty-seventh of January and they were leaving on the twenty-eighth, she planned on one heck of a party for him when they arrived back home.

Every day that passed meant one more day without any incidents. Kat was strung as tight as a string on a fiddle with waiting for the time when Davy would finally be safe and out of harms way.

Christmas was an exceptionally festive occasion this year due to the fact that Marshall and Maggie's three boys came home at the same time.

Everyone gathered at Maggie's for Christmas Eve.

On Christmas Day, Kat was in the kitchen before 8:00 A.M. making Davy and herself a special breakfast before they exchanged their gifts later that morning. Maggie and the rest of her family weren't due to come by Kat's until at 5:00 P.M. that afternoon. It wasn't going to be as elaborate as Maggie's party for Christmas Eve, but she had a catering service make up finger sandwiches, hors d'oeuvres of all types and plenty of drinks and desserts. As she motioned to Davy to sit at the table and eat his breakfast, Kat became very melancholy and close to tears. She had no explanation for it, and it only lasted for a few seconds.

Later that afternoon, she had time to spare before all the family were to arrive for the Christmas Day celebration at her house, so she decided to retrieve the notes that she had made a few days now as written for her new book. She was really starting to make strides, and she wanted to work on it as much as she could while her recently written thoughts were still fresh in her mind. She was into her notes for about half an hour when the front doorbell rang. When she opened the door, there stood Maggie with four large bags of colorfully decorated presents.

"Maggie, what is all of this?"

"Presents."

"Well, I know that, but why so many? You're spoiling, Davy as it is."

"That may be so, Sis but these aren't all for Davy or me. I'm just the delivery person. Some are from Chris, Tim, Chad, Marshall and me. Marshall, by the way, should be about an hour behind me in arriving, Where's Davy?"

"In the backyard playing. Well actually, trying to build a snowman from the three inches of snow that fell last night."

"I know I'm early, but I thought that I'd come sooner to see if there is anything that I can help you with."

"Thanks for the offer, but everything's a go. Here, let me help you with those and let's go into the kitchen. Feel like a cup of coffee?"

"You know me, I never turn down an offer of a cup of coffee," answered Maggie. The two only had a short time to talk when everyone started to arrive.

Everything was set out buffet style, which made it easy for everyone. Marshall served as the bartender until everyone had a drink, then he fixed himself a plate and a drink and joined the family sitting in the living room. The air was festive with talk and laughter, and in that moment Kat realized what the melancholy mood was earlier. What a wonderful family she had, and she was surely blessed, because of them.

"Mom, are you with us?" came a voice, which seemed a distance away. This made her snap out of her thinking of David and come back to reality.

"Why yes, of course. What is it, Davy?"

"Everyone is asking if you and I can open their presents now?"

"I don't see why not."

"Cool!" giggled Davy.

Most of Davy's gifts consisted of toys and clothing, which he could surely use since he was growing like a weed, thought Kat. Chad and Tim came up with some wonderful things from overseas wherever they were stationed or visited. Chad gave him a replica of an old wooden ship complete with sails encased in a glass bottle. While unwrapping his other present, Davy took a good look at the book titled *Famous Sea Battles Throughout History*.

"Thank you Cousin Chad," uttered Davy, as he reached out to his cousin and gave him a big hug.

"You're very welcome, Davy," answered Chad.

"What I want to know is how they got that ship inside that bottle?" questioned Tim. No one could answer him.

There was a carved ebony elephant from India, which Tim swore was very lucky, and a book titled *European Battles*. Davy's eyes were as big as saucers when he saw the book.

"Thank you Cousin Tim," replied Davy as he sat the book carefully down on one of the end tables and headed over to give his Cousin Tim a big hug.

"You're welcome, sport. Enjoy, because Mom told me how fascinated you are with battles," Tim said.

Next, Davy was handed a colorful bag from Chris. He opened a box and found a beautiful polished stone with a gold chain attached.

"I was in the Holy Land a few years back and walked into an antiquities store. Folded underneath the padding is a card claiming that this stone is part of the walk where Jesus dropped the cross and over the years, that same walk has become chipped. I had a hole burrowed into it so that you could wear it as a chain if you wanted to. There's two more items in the bag. Open the smaller one first."

Beneath the Christmas wrapping was a book titled *The Battle Between Good And Evil*, and in parenthesis below the title were the words "The Epic Fight Between The Archangels Michael and Lucifer."

"I found that while browsing through a dusty old bookstore in Florence, Italy, and I also know of your fascination with battles, so I bought it."

Davy couldn't believe his eyes. This was *the* first battle ever fought. He was near tears when he looked up at his Cousin Chris. Chris saw the look and quickly told him of one more present in the bag. As he tore away the gift-wrap, there before his eyes was a beautifully painted portrait of the Archangel Michael in full battle armor sitting atop a magnificent white stallion.

"Oh my," replied Kat.

"Oh, cousin Chris, I will cherish all of this forever! Thank you so very much," said Davy as he got up from off his knees and ran to his cousin Chris to give him a big hug and put the chain around his neck, which he wore for the rest of his life.

"You're welcome, Davy."

Davy continued with, "I couldn't ask for three better cousins than you. Thank you again from the bottom of my heart."

Davy was Chris' shadow for the rest of the night until he fell asleep in Chris' lap. Kat was going to wake him up, but Chris insisted on carrying him to his bed.

The party started to wind down, because everyone was getting tired except the three brothers, who continued to drink and talk about their chosen military careers.

Kat walked over to her three nephews and thanked them again for Davy's presents and kissed and hugged each one goodnight and called it quits, because she couldn't keep her eyes open any longer.

"Stay as long as you want. Just make sure the front door is locked before you leave. Merry Christmas to you, and goodnight."

"Merry Christmas to you too, Aunt Kat," said the three in unison.

Kat had the foresight to take another day's vacation, because she knew that the holidays would be hectic. As she walked into the kitchen the next morning, there sat Michael and Davy at the kitchen table. She said her good mornings and proceeded to get a pot of coffee going.

"You two are up early, any special reason?"

"Master Davy was anxious to get a good look at the books he received from his cousins."

"Yeah, Mom. We waited for you to get up so Michael can tell us of the battle between God's army and Lucifer's followers. We thought you'd like to hear it."

"I'll say I do," answered Kat, as she poured herself a cup of coffee and sat down at the kitchen table anxiously waiting for Michael to tell his story.

After Michael told the tale of his battle with Lucifer, Kat and Davy both were dumbfounded. Kat was the first one to break the silence.

"That was one hell of a story, Michael. Did all of what you just told us really happen?"

"Yes, Mistress Kat. Indeed it did."

"Michael, that portrait of you. Does it look like you?"

"It's uncanny, Mom, just how close that artist came to depicting Michael," interjected Davy.

"Yes, he did do a good job, Mistress Kat."

Chris, Tim, and Chad left at two-day intervals, which was good for Marshall and Maggie, instead of all three leaving on the same day. Chris went on for a second year with pilot training school and was involved with the training of other pilots. He was completely at home in the cockpit of any plane; it didn't make a difference. It was uncanny how he could fly any type of plane after a short period of training time. Tim never really changed. He was still that happy-go-lucky guy even though he was a no-nonsense and top-notch Marine. He never talked about the specialized field that he was in, and, of course, no one asked. Chad had two more years of training with the Navy. Maggie took pictures of all three of them and how handsome they looked in their dress uniforms. Those pictures were her prized possession and were proudly displayed on her mantle. This certainly was a Christmas to remember in both Marshall and Maggie's eyes.

January was half over and the clock was ticking down for Kat, Maggie, Michael, and Davy to leave for Jerusalem.

Kat awoke early to cook Davy's favorite breakfast for this very special day: his seventh birthday. She laid the bacon on a paper towel and covered it with a lid, and then proceeded to scoop up the pancakes from the griddle, covered them, and transferred them to a plate. She grabbed some silverware and decided to go and wake Davy. She didn't make it out of the kitchen when she heard him yelling, "Mom where are you?"

"In the kitchen, Honey. Sit down," she suggested, as she put the pancakes, bacon, butter, and syrup in front of him, and then proceeded to sing the birthday song to him.

"Thank you, Mom. That was cool," said Davy in regard to the song.

"Thank you for the unprompted compliment. I know exactly how I sound when I sing. So what is making you so happy this morning? The fact that it's your birthday?"

"Well yes, that too, but you'll never guess what happened to me last night."

"Well, let's see. Don't tell me you found another present lurking around that you missed after opening the first hundred or so at Christmas?"

"Oh Mom. I didn't have that many presents."

"Okay, I give up. What happened to you last night?"

"I had an out-of-body experience with Michael. He took me to be baptized in the River Jordan."

Kat's mouth opened and the silverware she was carrying hit the floor at the same time. It was a good thing that she had the plates on the table already, for they would be the next things dropped on the floor.

"And Mom, it was Jesus, Himself who baptized me in the River Jordan. He was standing in the water waiting for me."

"How do you know it was truly, Jesus?"

"Because he told me who he was. He said, 'My name is Jesus,' and he told me not to be afraid."

"Are you sure you didn't dream all this and woke up thinking that it really did happen?"

Before Davy had a chance to respond, Michael spoke. "No, Mistress Kat, he didn't dream it. He is telling the truth. It was an out-of-body experience with me just like he said, and it was Jesus of Nazareth who baptized him in the Waters Of Life, just like the General told you would happen when he turned seven."

"But Michael, I thought we were all supposed to go to Jerusalem and it would happen shortly after he turned seven?" Kat asked, confused.

"Yes, Mistress Kat. That was the original plan, but with what happened to Master Davy with his bike and what was going to happen to him yet, the Almighty One intervened."

"Davy, why don't you go and get dressed, because I would like to have a few words with Michael."

"Sure, Mom."

When Davy was out of hearing range, Kat wanted to delve further into Michael's statement, so she asked, "What did you mean when you said, 'What was going to happen to him, yet'?"

"The plane that the three of you would have been on would have crashed with no survivors."

Kat couldn't remember what happened to her after Michael spoke those words, but within seconds, she found herself sitting on the chair and slumped over the table.

When she was coherent enough to speak, she asked Michael, "You mean to tell me that they would have done something to the plane to make it crash?"

"Yes, Mistress Kat."

"Then it's all over, Michael? He won't have to be guarded twenty-four hours a day from now on?"

"That's right, Mistress Kat. It's all over. There can be no more attempts on his life since he has the Almighty One's protection from now on."

"What about you, Michael? Can you still stay with us?"

"Yes, Mistress Kat. I have been instructed to stay with you and your family for guidance from me if that is what you wish, and it will be for a long, long time to come."

"Michael, thank you from the bottom of my heart. You have given me the greatest present a mother could receive. You have given me back my son," declared Kat with tears streaming down her face.

"It was not I, Mistress Kat, but the Almighty One that you must thank."

"I certainly will, Michael. You can count on it!"

Michael saw the state that Kat was in and decided it was best to leave her alone with her thoughts. Instead of thinking, she called Maggie.

"You doing anything special right now?"

"Not really. So what's up?"

"Have I got a bombshell to tell you. How long will it take for you to get over here?"

"Since it's early, probably twenty minutes. Why?"

"It's too important to talk about over the phone, so I'll see you in a little while then," declared Kat, and she hung up.

Whenever Kat uses the word bombshell, she's usually not exaggerating, thought Maggie as she weaved her way through the traffic. Maggie came

to the back of the house as she figured Kat would probably be in the kitchen, and there she found her sitting at the table with what looked to be a drink in her hand. The door was unlocked so Maggie just walked in.

"Taking up drinking again?"

"No. I'm just going to have this one and that's all. No big deal. Want one?"

"No. It's a wee bit early for me."

"Suit yourself."

"You're starting to scare me, Kat. Because you're talking like you did when David was here: with sarcasm."

"That noticeable, huh?"

"Yes, very much so."

"I know I have to snap out of this, but I can't seem to shake it, because today is Davy's birthday, but—"

"Snap out of what feelings?" interrupted Maggie.

"Davy was baptized this morning and I wasn't with him or asked to be."

"What are you talking about? We're leaving for the Holy Land tomorrow."

"We don't have to now. It seems that Michael took Davy to the River Jordan to be baptized last night—a minute after midnight, to be exact."

"How'd he get him there? On his back, or flying nonstop both ways?" chuckled Maggie, to help lighten up the situation somewhat.

"I never even thought of asking how he did it. I was too busy sulking," answered Kat, totally ashamed of herself because of her attitude. "He was baptized by Jesus Himself."

"What? Get out."

"Yes. According to Michael and Davy, it was Jesus who baptized my son." *Oh my God!* thought Kat. "What an honor for this to happen to Davy. I sure better get my act together."

"I'd highly suggest it. I was really starting to look forward to the trip even though we had to fly," confessed Maggie.

"Yeah, I know what you mean. I was too," responded Kat.

"So why was everything changed at the last minute?"

"I'm not sure if you want to hear this, but the plane would have crashed with no survivors."

"You mean because of mechanical trouble or something?" questioned Maggie.

"Yes. But done on purpose by some demons. This was their last ditch effort to get rid of Davy. They were getting desperate."

"I don't understand."

"Three times those bastards tried to take my son from me and on the fourth try, they would have succeeded if God did not intervene to stop them. Michael said that the End of Times will start in a little over two years and that God would not let anyone or anything interfere with his plans for this world, which he has had before he created the Earth. Their plans were to kill my son all along, but that plane would have had 360 people or more aboard. Evidently, I'm assuming that God was not going to stand for that."

"Sounds that way."

"Maggie, I'm sorry I got you over here when I was in such a state."

"Don't be sorry."

"It's all over, Maggie, and that is what I have to be grateful for. Davy can go back in his own room and start having fun again with his friends, and I can settle down and stop being so paranoid."

"You had every right to be paranoid after what they put you and Davy through, and you before him."

"Oh Maggie, what would I truly do without you?"

"You're a survivor, Kat. And that's what you have always been and will continue to be. That's one thing that you can be sure of."

It never ceased to amaze Kat with how her life had changed since that first encounter with David over seven years ago already. He was still never far from her thoughts, and maybe that was what kept her going besides the love for their son.

Davy was completely safe now from anyone who wished to do him harm. To Kat's relief, this was the moment that she had been waiting and praying for since her son was born.

The big birthday bash that Kat had planned for Davy's seventh birthday was no longer going to take place, so she decided it would be better for just the four of them to be together on this special day in light of what took place earlier. She originally bought a few gifts for Davy to open today, and she had the party favors bought already and had the cake in the freezer.

Later on in the afternoon while Kat, Maggie, and Davy sat at the kitchen table with the party hats on and after they ate birthday cake and ice cream, Kat brought out three presents for Davy to unwrap. The first gift was three pair of jeans, three shirts, and a sweater from Marshall and Maggie.

"Oh my!" said Kat.

"Cool, Aunt Maggie. You bought me designer jeans."

"Yes, we did, and I hope they fit."

The second present made Davy sit up and pay more attention, for it was a complete set of army equipment including soldiers, tanks, airplanes, jeeps, and even a complete medical hospital unit like the one on the popular series, *MASH*.

"Wow! This is really cool. Thanks, Mom."

"This is also from Michael and not just me."

"Thank you, Michael," responded Davy while giving his mom and Michael a big hug.

"Um, you're welcome, Master Davy," answered Michael, surprised that Kat included him.

Kat informed Davy that she had one more special and very important present for him so proceeded to move the other presents aside.

As Davy unwrapped the box and opened the tissue paper, he found a picture of a man inside of a frame.

"This person looks like me, Mom."

"Yes, Honey. He does and should, because that person is your father."

"You knew my father?" questioned Davy without realizing what he had just asked.

She took the portrait from the box and set it upright on the table and said to Michael, "I guess this is the time to tell him about his father."

"Yes, Mistress Kat. It is."

Kat started to relay the details about his father to her son by saying, "Eight years ago, your father, whose name is also David, and who was the general in God's army of warrior angels at that time, came to Earth along with Archangel Michael here, and Archangel Gabriel and another angel

named Thomas. They were sent here by God to protect me and to tell me that I must write a book for God."

"Protect you from what, Mom?"

"Bad spirits."

"What kind of book?"

Kat was reluctant at first in giving Davy a copy of her book, because of the details in it, but the truth has to be given to him even at his early age, according to Michael.

"A book telling the world what will happen if they don't change their wicked ways," Kat relayed, as she took a copy of her book from the shelf and set it in front of Davy. "This is a copy of the book I wrote, which tells how your father and I met, what happened to him, and why he is not here today with us. I know you are very capable of reading it, and it will explain to you what happened between all of us. You can start reading anytime after I finish telling you the story about your father and what he was like.

"Your father started training to be a general at the age of seven which is customary in Heaven."

"He came from Heaven?"

"Yes, Davy. He lived in Heaven just like Michael."

"Wow! And he was only seven just like I am now?"

"Yes. He didn't become a general at seven, but he trained to be one, which he did become at the age of thirty-six. That's equivalent to our Earth years." *Oh boy,* thought Kat. *How am I going to tell this to a seven-year-old without tripping over my own tongue?* "Michael told me at one time that your father was the youngest general in Heaven's history."

"Cool!" announced Davy, eyes alit in anticipation of hearing more about his father.

"You know that generals have to be stern with their men and be the leader who gives the orders?"

"Right, Mom."

"Well, let's see," hesitated Kat, wondering what to say next. "I was a different person then than I am right now. What I mean to say is, I had no responsibilities except my job and no commitments to anyone but myself. I basically said and did anything I wanted to. This did not set well with your father. He was used to giving orders and having them obeyed, which in the beginning I never did. My actions and behavior were hard for your father to understand until he got to know me better, and I still very seldom did what he told me to do."

"Why?"

"Because I was stubborn and thought I knew it all, therefore I continued to do things my way, which was wrong. Eventually I came around and started behaving like a grownup should. Your father was a kind, gentle, and a very caring, spiritual being, even though he was a general. Actually, he had a very good sense of humor too."

"Did you start to like him then?"

"Yes, I did—very much so as a matter of fact—and I then started realizing I had better get my act together, and think about what I was going to say in the book that God wanted me to write."

"Did my father help you write this book?"

"Yes, Davy. I wrote the story and your father relayed the facts from God to me that went into the book also."

"So where do I fit in, Mom?"

Oh boy! thought Kat. *I knew he was going to ask that question sooner or later. Great! My son doesn't know the facts of life yet, and I just gave him a book to read that will tell him. Heaven knows this isn't going to be easy.*

"I couldn't have children of my own so—"

"Why not?" interrupted Davy.

"Because," hesitated Kat for a second to see what kind of explanation she could come up with. "Some women, like me, are unable to have children because of the structure of their bodies."

"Oh! So how could I be born then if you couldn't have babies?"

"Well, you see, Honey…" Kat hesitated until she finally said, "Your father and I grew to love each other very, very much, and because of who he was—a spiritual being—he was able to give me you. He wanted me to have his baby, so that I would know the joys of motherhood, and to see in you what your father looked like at different stages in his life."

"So, I look exactly like my father did now?"

"Yes, exactly."

"You aren't able to see Michael like I am, Mom. But were you able to see my father?"

"Not in the beginning. I could only hear him. But before he had to leave, he showed me exactly what you would look like when you were born and also showed himself to me for only a few seconds, so that I would know what he looked like. That is why I had his portrait painted for you, so that you could see what your father looked like too."

"Why did he have to leave us, Mom?" questioned Davy, with noticeable tears forming in his eyes.

"Because, Honey," answered Kat, as she moved toward her son to hug him in comfort. "There were circumstances that happened and your father was called back to Heaven. Right from the beginning, he told me that we were from different worlds and that he would never be allowed to stay here on Earth with us."

"But Michael got to stay. Why is that?"

"Because Michael is an Archangel and God told him to stay behind and watch over you and me. This is a great honor for both of us, sweetie, to have someone as great as Michael to be here with us."

"I know, Mom. And I really love him."

"Me too. Why don't you go and play with your new army toys for now, and later, after supper, we'll have some more cake and ice cream."

"Okay."

"Well, Michael. What do you think? Did I do a good enough job with answering Davy's questions?"

"Yes, Mistress Kat. You did a fine job."

"Michael, he's only seven. Was it really necessary for me to give him the book to read? I mean, he's going to know every little detail about David and me."

"Yes, Mistress Kat. It was necessary. You may consider him too young to know of these things, because of the taboo theories down here. There is no shame in what took place between you and the General, and Master Davy is a child of the Light now and must know everything about himself. It is the unwritten law according to the Almighty One. And Mistress Kat, thank you for the 'Me too.'"

"You're welcome, Michael. I meant it and it came straight from the heart," replied Kat, as she looked over at Maggie, who had tears in her eyes.

Davy continued to excel in school with academics and with sports. He had his nose buried in a book describing battles or in front of the computer checking out the facts relating to those battles in his spare time.

"There's a few underlying factors in regard to the victors of each of the battles that were fought throughout history," informed Davy, while on the computer one day.

"Oh! And what's that?" asked Kat.

"A good leader is a must. Someone who is in front and not behind the lines. This gives his men a sense of bravery and devotion for their leader who is right there with them risking his life also. Know your enemy, be familiar with the area, leave no room for error with your strategy and plans for the upcoming battle, and take the enemy by surprise if at all possible. Plenty of battles were fought with the victors being outnumbered. The greatest fighting forces were the ones that were highly trained and had the superior weapons and the best armor for their protection."

"Interesting," proclaimed Kat, as she walked around the chair and took a look at the computer screen showing the plans for a certain battle. There were diagrams of the battlefield showing unusual terrains and passes, and also arrows pointing in every direction with footnotes under each. She gave up. This was way beyond her understanding.

It was such a good feeling to Kat that the winter months had faded away, and that they were well into spring. Since the weather was nice, Jake opened the riding stable early. She and Maggie continued to ride once a week—more if possible—and became excellent horsewomen. They rode Daisy and Molly on occasion to keep up the friendship developed between the four of them.

Davy and Johnny never rekindled their friendship, but not because of Davy. He tried everything he could think of to get everyone back together again, but Johnny never wanted to and became a loner except for a few select friends that he chose. Meanwhile, Davy and Lars became closer. Within two years, Johnny's father was transferred with his job to somewhere in Texas.

Kat continued to work at the Knitting Factory and at the Soup Kitchen whenever time allowed. Maggie was doing a great job handling the huge task of running the business end of the establishment completely on her own.

Steven and Susan visited Kat in late summer on their way to see Susan's family in Iowa. They had two children: a boy named Casey who was

about to turn three, and a beautiful little girl named Katie—short for Katherine—who was about to turn one. Susan kept in touch with Kat and sent pictures of her children from the time that they were born. Susan was very successful as an administrator for a hospital in Appleton, Wisconsin, and Steven had his own insurance agency with three other partners. Susan also kept in touch with Cindy, and she visited them when she could get away from her part time job with working at a department store on the weekends and going to college during the week.

Davy entered the third grade in the fall and received good reports about his performance in school on notes sent home from his teacher. Even with knowing what Michael had told her a few years back, Kat still found it hard to believe the knowledge that was stored in her son's brain. She now had a soon-to-be eight-year-old who was a walking encyclopedia and a perfectionist to boot. Kat was worried with his continued obsession with battles, but in a conversation with Michael, he explained to her again what his future role in the world would be. He was born to be a general just like his father was, and he would play a major role in fighting against the Antichrist.

Kat's psychic abilities picked up a little bit and she was told by Michael to have patience. That was one virtue that Kat knew nothing about and never practiced. She always figured that would come some time way in the course of her future when she was in her sixties, maybe.

It was nearing the end of the first semester and Davy was in the fifth grade at the same school that he entered in K5. His teacher, Ms. Kimbel, sent a note home with Davy requesting a private conference with Kat that stated that she should call her and set up an appointment. Kat was a little confused as to the reason that she would want to meet with her, because Davy was a good student and well behaved in school. She called Ms. Kimbel and set up the appointment for 4:00 P.M. in two days.

She arrived at the school fifteen minutes early and found Davy in the gym playing basketball with a bunch of other kids. She went over to him and said that she would come back for him after meeting with Ms. Kimbel, and that they would be going over by Aunt Maggie's for supper.

As she walked down the hallway to Davy's room, she noticed the artwork hanging on the walls. All were done very well. Some were of cartoon characters or popular science fiction characters, but the one that impressed her the most was a beautiful landscape featuring a farm scene. Kat couldn't believe the detail. It looked almost like it was taken with a camera and enlarged. She moved closer to get a better look at it and discovered it was painted by Lars Erickson. She'd have to ask Davy about it later.

When she came upon Davy's classroom, the door was closed so she knocked twice.

"Come in, please," said a voice from behind the closed door. Ms. Kimbel was sitting at a long table grading papers and stood to greet, Kat.

"So nice to meet you again, Ms. O'Brien," greeted Ms. Kimbel.

"Same here," replied Kat.

"Please, pull up that chair and have a seat."

"Thank you," answered Kat as she laid her purse and car keys down on the table.

Ms. Kimbel fingered through a pile of papers in front of her until she found the one that she wanted and set it upside down on the table. She then proceeded through the next pile doing the same thing until she finished with the fifth pile of neatly stacked papers.

"These are the results of the tests that I gave to the class yesterday in the five major categories of study: reading comprehension, math, science, history and English." As she handed them to Kat, she informed her that these were the results of Davy's testing.

Kat accepted the papers from Ms. Kimbel and found an A+ in red ink at the top of each one, which brought about a grin to her face, because of the overwhelming sense of pride that she was feeling for her son right now.

"Is this the reason that you wanted to talk to me because of these tests?"

"These test results are part of the reason that I called this conference, but it is more in depth than that."

"In depth?"

"By that I mean, look at my notes in the margin of each page. Not only does he have a perfect score on each test, but you can see that his cursive writing is excellent for a boy. Most boys his age have a tendency to not care how they write. They just want to get it done. Also, look at the use of his punctuation marks. They are perfectly placed. I've taught the use of punctuation marks and cursive writing for only a short period of time, and David has it down pat, already. He's polite, well mannered and very likeable. He is the epitome of every teacher's dream student, and I'm not exaggerating one bit. What I'm trying to get across, Ms. O'Brien, is that your son is being stifled. He needs to be challenged a lot more than the fifth grade curriculum can give him. I did some checking on my own and found that David has maintained an A average since he started school here. What I'd like to do, Ms. O'Brien, is to have David tested to find out his IQ, and if my intuition is right, have him elevated to a higher grade level, which would be equal to his abilities. But your permission must be given in order to do this."

"My son just turned ten, Ms. Kimbel. What I'm worried about is his social ability to deal with older children on a daily basis, if he's switched to a higher grade level."

"Maybe two or three."

"Two or three? Oh no. That would put him in the seventh or eighth grade. I just can't see advancing him into that level. No, I won't have it."

"He wouldn't be in a regular school, but he would go to a speciality school for gifted children with highly trained teachers, who know how to deal with the academic abilities and the emotional abilities of prodigy children like David."

"It sounds like my son would be a guinea pig. I won't even consider that possibility."

"Ms. O'Brien, we're getting way too far ahead of ourselves here. I need your permission to have his IQ tested, and then we can go from there. If it is as high as I suspect, you then could meet with those highly specialized teachers and visit the school with David and have them give you a tour and give you all the pertinent details of what this move would be all about."

"What about sports? Davy is crazy about basketball over all the rest. He needs that outlet for emotional release. You said so yourself."

"Yes, I did. They offer all kinds of extracurricular activity, including all types of sports activities. This will be a two-part decision: yours and David's. Even though he is young, I truly believe he should have a say in the decision as to what he wants to do. Would you at least be willing to talk with the professionals after the results are back from the IQ test?"

"I guess it wouldn't hurt to hear them out. I appreciate all that you wish to do for my son, but I'm afraid if we go through with this, that he will somehow lose his childhood."

"I honestly can't address your concerns with that, because I'm not knowledgeable about the steps that are taken in regard to a child prodigy. But some children with high IQs have a tendency to be loners and lack certain social skills, but not David. He is very open with his thoughts, makes friends easily and is liked a lot by his classmates. I truly think he would adapt very easily, and that is why I suggest that you take each step slowly in regard to his wellbeing. Like you said, that is what is important here. If you agree, I will give you the name, address, and phone number of the person in charge of administering the test, so that you can get in touch with him or her if you choose to do so."

"It won't be given here?"

"No, I'm afraid not. It will be taken at the school that we just talked about and the results will, from what I understand, take at least two weeks to get back. You see, Ms. O'Brien, these professionals take their

steps in determining a child prodigy very seriously and have certain ways in determining if David will fit their extensive, extremely difficult qualifications."

"You mean that he could be turned down?"

"That is a possibility, but I think highly unlikely in David's case. Once he is accepted and assigned to a professional, it will be out of my hands, and everything discovered about David's abilities will be kept confidential between you and the school. But Ms. O'Brien, I would appreciate it, if you would tell me if you plan to carry through with this after the test results. I will be anxious until I hear from you."

"I definitely will keep you informed of my decisions."

"Thank you for that. Here is all the pertinent information that you will need to get started. Good luck to both you and David. And whatever the outcome will be, we can at least tell ourselves we gave it a try."

"David will remain here in this school then?"

"Yes. Until all the information is gathered by them and David is accepted, only then will he leave here."

"I want to thank you for the interest that you have taken in regard to my son, and as I said, I will keep you informed."

"That is all that I ask, thank you."

"Don't bother getting up. I can find my way out," assured Kat.

As she left the room and closed the door behind her, she felt numbed by what was all said between her and Ms. Kimbel. She would have to talk this over with Michael as soon as possible and get his opinion on the matter.

After spending supper with Maggie that night, it was getting late by the time that they arrived back home. Davy had gone to bed and Kat and Michael sat in the kitchen to discuss what Ms. Kimbel had told her.

Michael was there and heard every word between Kat and Ms. Kimbel, which he told Kat before their conversation.

"As I told you before, Mistress Kat, Master David not only has the Almighty One's divine protection since he turned seven, but also divine powers since he was born."

"I know that you said divine powers, but I thought that they would come later when he was to fight against the Antichrist."

"No. His divine powers will accumulate more and more the older he gets."

"Michael, I'm in for one hell of a rocky road in the years to come, am I right?"

"You could put it that way, but that is why I am here to guide you along the way."

"What do you think about all that Ms. Kimbel said to me about moving Davy ahead two or maybe even three grades, because she thinks he is being stifled while remaining in the fifth grade? I want my son to enjoy some of his childhood, because heaven forbid, it's going to be nothing but tragedies and sorrow in the years to come."

"This is true, Mistress Kat, but Ms. Kimbel is right. Master Davy is truly far beyond the knowledge that he is taught in the fifth grade. Far beyond. This is a special gift from the Almighty One and must be handled with a lot of thought on your part. He has evolved even further than that little boy of a few years ago, and he will continue to grow intellectually until the end of his life."

"Well, I told her that I would at least sit down with these professionals and hear them out, and I will. After the test results come back, I'm sure I will make the right decision for all concerned."

"You will, Mistress Kat. Of this you can be sure of."

Kat took Davy to meet with Dr. Jerome Malcolm, who was the head of the Sir Isaac Newton School for the Highly Gifted Children, within two weeks of Ms. Kimbel's conference with her. *They're really anxious to get my son under a microscope to pick his brain, and the school's name is quite appropriate*, thought Kat, with her usual trademark grin on her face, as they took the elevator to the fourth floor.

After a brief introductory meeting with six other people in the room, Davy was lead away to take his IQ test. Kat was told to ask them any questions that came to mind while they waited for Davy's test results. Little did they know that she made a long list the night before of what she considered pertinent questions.

She didn't know for sure just how much time had passed when she heard a door open and looked up to see a young man walk over to one of the gentlemen and whisper something into his ear.

"Ms. O'Brien, it seems that Dr. Malcolm wishes to test your son further, so we will call a recess for now and return when they are finished. There is a nice lounge area out into the corridor on the other side of the elevator. Just turn left and walk about fifty feet. There is a sign to follow and it has vending machines with all sorts of snacks and drinks and plenty of magazines to read if you wish to do so. Please make yourself comfortable, and we will send someone to fetch you when Dr. Malcolm returns."

"Thank you, that will be very nice."

She waited for what seemed an eternity and was thankful that she decided to bring her notes along for her book.

Finally, a young man entered the lounge and told her that Dr. Malcolm and the others had returned and were now ready to talk with her. As she entered the room, there sat Dr. Malcolm and the others seated on both sides of him while Davy occupied the same seat as before.

"Please, Ms. O'Brien, take a seat next to your son," requested Dr. Malcolm.

Kat looked over at Davy, who was as cool as a cucumber, while she felt like her stomach was tied in knots. Davy must have noticed her uneasiness so took her hand and gave it a squeeze and smiled at her.

"Before we get started with David's test results, I'd like to give you a summary of just how a young person's IQ is determined," relayed Dr. Malcolm. "Today's intelligence tests are based largely on the original test devised in the 1950s by French psychologist Alfred Binet. In order to identify students who would need extra assistance in school, the French government asked Binet to devise a test that could be used to discover, which students were in need of help. Based on his research, Binet developed the concept of mental age. Certain questions that he posed were easily answered by children of certain age groups. Some children were able to answer questions that were typically answered by children of an older age. These children had a higher mental age than their actual chronological age. Binet's measure of intelligence was based on the average abilities of children of a particular age group. The group that your son, David is in is a higher mental age than his chronological age. Are there any questions from either of you at this point?"

Kat looked at Davy, who was shaking his head no. She did the same.

Dr. Malcolm continued on with further explaining how he would test Davy to ascertain his IQ and mentioned something about a Bell Curve and a graph sloping upward and downward and a term pinpointing low and high standard deviation. By now, he really had her confused, as this lingo was way beyond her comprehension, but again he paused and asked Kat and Davy if they were still following him.

"Good. Now that you understand these terms, we can talk a bit more about how we interpret IQ scores." Again he continued on and when he mentioned Einstein's IQ of about 160, Kat perked up and became interested. He further informed all sitting at the table, "The highest IQ score ever tested belonged to a man named William James Sidis, who was considered a universal genius with an IQ between 250 and 300. I added a paragraph giving a little more detail about this gentleman," he further stated. "Now, getting back to David here. I just tested nineteen children

yesterday, and I added David's test to this group, thus making twenty as a total number of tests taken. With children, we test them with the five major subjects that are taught in most schools today: math, science, reading comprehension, history and English. I can tell you now, Ms. O'Brien, that your son scored high on each test. To be exact, very high. That is why I decided to try something different with David and test him in calculus, just for the fun of it. I gave him a calculus problem, and I can say I was truthfully astonished, for he came up with the right answer within fifteen minutes. Ms. O'Brien, just in case you don't know this, calculus is normally available for students to take in the last two years of high school."

Kat looked over at Davy who had a very wide grin on his face. She heard of calculus but never paid much attention to the subject since she barely made it through algebra. She was still stunned beyond words.

"To come up with David's IQ, I divided his mental age, results of the five tests, divided by his chronological age. The quotient is then multiplied by 100, or Ratio IQ. The average score of the five tests was 144 divided by 9, which is his age, and that equals 16x100, or 160. Your son has an IQ of 160. In light of the calculus problem that I gave him, that brings us to another whole development, which I will discuss with my colleagues here. In theory, with the calculus problem, your son is in the 160 to 160 plus IQ range, making him a very near genius or genius. After further study and discussion with the six panel members here, we will calculate our findings and will write you a letter with the results. Your son is highly gifted, Ms. O'Brien, and certainly has no business being in the fifth grade. In light of what we learned here today, we would be highly honored to accept your son as a member of our school, but you are the one that has to make that decision, Ms. O'Brien. We will notify you of our findings, as I said, which should take at least two weeks, which will give you time to think over all that transpired here and hopefully come up with a decision. At that time, if you decide to enroll your son with us, we will set up another appointment with you and David to discuss the details of enrolling in our school and will also take you on a guided tour. Do either of you wish to ask any questions or concerns at this time?"

Kat answered for both of them, for she and Davy would discuss at home what transpired here, and said, "Not at the moment, Gentlemen, but I'm sure that I will have tons of questions to ask if I decide to enroll David in your school."

"That's fair enough, Ms. O'Brien. So, I guess at this point, all that's left to do is for us to fulfill our part of the bargain and wait for your decision within the next two weeks. Thank you for coming, and it has been a real pleasure meeting both of you," said Dr. Malcolm.

"Thank you Gentlemen for your time and very informative information on my son's abilities. It has been quite an eye opener for me, to be sure," related Kat, as she and David arose to leave and said their good-byes.

When Kat and David entered the kitchen, she turned to him and said, "Okay kid, it's pow-wow time. Michael, are you here with us?"

"Yes, Mistress Kat. I am here."

"Good, because you said yourself that you were left behind to guide us, so start guiding and tell me what to do."

"The answer to that will be between you and Master Davy. I can give you advice, but the final decision will be yours to make."

"Okay, then answer me this, do you think that Davy really is a genius, like they claim?"

"Oh yes, very much so."

"Alright, now that we have that settled, just how many grade levels do I let them advance him?"

"I would wait and see what they suggest and make your decision then. Master Davy, you must have some input into this, because the entire matter revolves around you and what you wish to do."

"I can tell you this, Mom and Michael, if I have to spend one more day in the fifth grade, I'll go nuts."

"Is it really too easy for you?" questioned Kat.

"Yes, Mom. Way too easy."

"Alright, let's go under the assumption that they wish to move you to a seventh or eighth grade level. These kids are older than you, of course, but also bigger than you. Will you have a problem with that?" inquired Kat.

"Heck no! I think it will be all right as far as older kids are concerned. I can deal with them. I want to learn all that I can, and this school will be the start of that knowledge. I'm confused, though, why I'm not like all the other kids that I know."

"Because, Honey, you have been given a very special gift from God."

"Why me?"

"Why not you? Don't you realize what an honor this is? God chose you out of all the kids in the whole world to do his bidding for him, and that is why you have received his divine gift," informed Kat.

"What do you mean by his bidding, Mom?"

"Michael, do you want to answer this one?"

"Yes, Mistress Kat. I will. Master Davy, remember when you were baptized in the Waters of Life at the age of seven?"

"Yes. Jesus baptized me."

"Correct. The reason that he baptized you was so that you would receive the Almighty One's divine protection."

"Michael, when you say the Almighty One, are you referring to God? And why do I need protection?"

"Yes, the Almighty One and God are one and the same, and it is time for you to know why you received the Almighty One's divine protection in the first place. Do you know who the Antichrist is?"

"Yes, the Archangel Lucifer."

"Correct. He is living on the earth as we speak, and is ten years older than you are right now."

"Does he know who he really is?" questioned Davy.

"Yes, he has known all along. He will make himself known to the world in the year 2027 toward the end of WWIII and will take credit for ending the war. He will become the one and only world leader after that with the blessing of most of mankind, because they will believe him to be a wonderful being, who is here to help the world heal and seek peace, which he will accomplish."

"You mean most of the world will believe that he is the Messiah?" asked Davy,

"Yes, exactly. But in reality, he will plan and carry out his diabolical manipulation of the masses in order to take over the world and seek their approval by having them accept the sign of the beast—666—on their person. Little will they know at the time that they just handed over their souls to him, which was his goal all along: to take away all the souls from the Almighty One, who created them."

"Will he succeed?" asked David.

"Mostly yes. Billions and billions of people will fall under his spell and accept him as the true Messiah. The ones that don't, he will hunt down and force them to by threatening them with death. Out of fear for their own lives, people will tell on those who have not accepted them, and this will turn husband against wife, sister against brother and man against his neighbor. Fear leads to chaos and the world will experience it first hand: utter chaos."

"Where do I fit in, Michael?"

"You will be the youngest appointed general in the history of the United States and will enter a military school for your four years of college. Later, you will then lead an army on foreign soil. You, Master Davy, will be the

Antichrist's worst nemesis in the future."

"Is that one of the reasons why I'm so interested in battles?"

"Actually, the only reason."

"Where will I find an army to do all of this?"

"Yes, Michael. I'm very curious to learn the answer that you have to Davy's question," interjected Kat, for the first time.

"The Soup Kitchen, for starters."

"The Soup Kitchen? Are you kidding me, Michael?"

"No, Mistress Kat. I am not."

"Michael, these people are mostly elderly and down on their luck as it is. How can they even be considered to join an army?"

"I don't mean your regular elderly patrons. In time, there will be many people willing to join forces with Master Davy against the Antichrist, because of your prophesizing to the masses. The Soup Kitchen, in time, will be a front for volunteers that you will convince to join Master Davy's army, Mistress Kat."

"The time on the clock indicates that it's way past your bedtime, Davy. Get your pajamas on and brush your teeth. I'll be in to say goodnight," ordered Kat.

"But, Mom. It's just starting to get interesting. Can't I stay up for a little while longer?"

"No! We will continue this discussion some other time."

"Alright, alright, I'm going."

"Michael, did Davy really need to know all this information at this time?" questioned Kat, with a surly edge to her voice.

"Yes, Mistress Kat. He did. More and more information will be received from the Almighty One, so it is better for Master Davy to learn

the facts one step at a time, instead of all at once, which could be too overwhelming for him."

"I think the conversation we just had was way too overwhelming already, but who am I to say anything. I'm just his mother," said Kat, sarcastically. "Sorry, Michael," stated Kat, after she had a second to realize what she just said but more so how she said it. "That was uncalled for."

In less than the scheduled two weeks, Dr. Malcolm sent Kat a letter via mail. A date and time were listed in the letter to meet with him and his colleagues. Kat only had to verify if this would be convenient for her and Davy, which she did.

"Thank you for coming, Ms. O'Brien and David. My colleagues and I, after in-depth research into David's acquired grades since he started school, coupled with the results of his IQ testing, and after talking with the principal and all of his teachers at his school, have come up with what we think is a close estimation as to where David should be placed in the academic level that coincides with his mental capabilities. Therefore, we are all in agreement with placing David in the ninth grade of our school, if you so choose and are in agreement with us."

"Well, Gentlemen, I must say that I am shocked to say the least. I expected maybe two grade levels that Davy would be elevated to, but never four. This opens a new can of worms for me," related Kat, leaving her wondering why she said something so stupid in regard to the worms.

"That may be so, Ms. O'Brien, and I can clearly understand your concern with this move, but if David is put into any level below the ninth grade, he will be stifled again just as he is in the fifth grade."

God, I hate that word, thought Kat. "Gentlemen, you don't expect an answer from me one way or the other at this time, do you?"

"No, of course not, Ms. O'Brien. This is just too big of a decision for you to come up with an answer to right away. We suggest that you take a few days to think it over. If you accept our findings, then we will meet here again with the necessary paper work completed and ready for your

signature. This will be a very big step in your son's life, but one that we feel is necessary. Please keep that in mind when making a decision."

"I certainly will, Gentlemen. Thank you for your time, and I will certainly get back to you with my decision as quickly as possible."

When the three arrived home, they were more than ready to sit down and discuss Dr. Malcolm's decision.

"Who wants to go first?" questioned Kat. With a noticeable lull hovering in the air, she then asked, "No takers? Okay, I guess I'm first. I personally think all seven of them are off their rockers. Even thinking of putting Davy in the ninth grade is absolutely ludicrous, let alone suggesting it."

"But, Mom. You heard what Dr. Malcolm said at the end that I would be stifled again, if I am put into any grade lower than the ninth grade."

"Please refrain from using that word in my presence. It really corks me to no end," emphasized Kat.

"Mistress Kat, if I may say something."

"Of course, Michael. You're part of this family and here to guide us. I value your opinion."

"I think the most objective way to handle this ordeal is to take it apart. Namely, listing the pros and cons, analyze them, and then make a decision that will suit the wellbeing of Master Davy."

"Sounds fair enough," resounded Kat.

"I'm all for it," replied Davy.

"Davy, we haven't taken it apart and analyzed it yet," emphasized Kat. "You're jumping the gun."

"Maybe so, Mom. But the more I think about it, the better I like the idea."

"So, if I make a decision contrary to yours, Davy, I'll be the bad guy here, right?"

"Mom, I know what your biggest beef is. My age. Am I right?"

"Darn right it is! A nine year old in the ninth grade? I don't think so."

"If I may put my two cents worth in," exclaimed Michael, hoping to alleviate Kat's concern somewhat. "I think we need to set aside the age difference for now and focus on the benefits that Master Davy will receive by putting him in a grade level that coincides with his mental capacity. The Almighty One works in mysterious ways, and I can assure you that this is one of them in the making."

"So, what you're saying is that God wants this for Davy and if I say no, I'll be stepping on his toes?"

"I wouldn't have put it quite that way. But yes, Mistress Kat, this is part of the Almighty One's plan."

"Well. I guess that's that. Who am I to argue with God?"

"Do you mean it, Mom? I can go to their school?"

"Yes, Davy. I agree."

"Cool, Mom, and thank you," replied Davy as he hugged his mother and made a beeline for the back door to play with his friends.

"Cheer up, Mistress Kat," replied Michael after seeing the worried look still on Kat's face.

"I guess I have no choice, Michael. I was out-numbered three to one," chuckled Kat.

Kat and Davy toured his soon-to-be new school with Dr. Malcolm within two days of their last meeting. She was impressed with every aspect of the school, from the science lab, gym, cafeteria, and cleanliness of the rooms inside to the outside recreation facilities available. AJRROTC

program was also included, for those who wished to include the military as part of their education. Dr. Malcolm saw the pleased look on Kat's face while touring the school, but he still sensed a feeling of apprehension coming from Kat, so explained, "Our school is rated in the top ten of the nation with the sole purpose of evaluating and educating children with special abilities. This is strictly a school of learning, Ms. O'Brien, and we do not tolerate misbehavior from our students in any form."

"I'm certainly relieved to hear that from you, Dr. Malcolm. It sure puts my mind at ease, thank you."

Davy was due to start at his new school in two weeks.

To Kat's relief, Davy's first semester at Sir Newt's School, as the kids called it, was totally to his liking. He joined the JRROTC the very first day he walked in the door, and he was not stifled anymore, but challenged with his courses. It amazed Kat how he did his homework with a lot of gusto and was given a new calculus problem every day, which he accomplished solving, in Kat's estimation, in very little time. *Evidently, calculus is right up the alley of my son, 'the genius,'* smiled Kat.

Davy took the bus to and from school everyday, which was a relief for Kat, because she didn't have to drive him back and forth and try to fit it in with her work schedule. She left for work in the morning an hour before Davy met his bus, and she was home at the time that he was accept on days that he had JRROTC or sports activities after school, then she would drive and pick him up.

Kat stayed in tune with his grades and activities at school. With all the fundraisers held, she never baked so many cookies in her entire life.

Davy continued to help at the Soup Kitchen on Sundays, which included part of his JRROTC program of doing community service, because Saturdays were always a busy day for him with sports. Kat had no time for herself on weekends, so resorted to working on her second book during the week after Davy was in bed. Her first book was doing okay, but not like she dreamed it would, and that left her aspirations of

becoming a millionaire down the tubes. Maybe once she was done with the sequel, things might change for the better.

Chris and Cindy finally decided that it was time that they got married so set a wedding date for Saturday, July 2, 2011, of this coming summer. Kat didn't see a lot of Maggie lately, because she was deeply involved with the wedding plans.

Early one Sunday morning while Kat and Davy were eating breakfast, Davy brought up the subject of his first name.

"Mom, do you think maybe that you could stop calling me, Davy when we're around other people and call me, David, instead?"

Kat knew that this day would eventually come, but not quite this soon. She answered, "Yes, of course I can, David. So that there is no confusion with now calling you, David. how will anyone know who we are talking about with your father's name being the same?" smiled Kat with delight over her son's decision.

"Well, from now on, everyone can call me, David, and when they are referring to my father, how about calling him General David?" questioned David.

"That probably would be better than referring to you as David Junior or David number two," joked Kat.

"Ah Mom! Either one would be disgusting to say the least. It won't bother you to call me, David, then?"

"Of course not, Honey. Now that you're in the ninth grade, I guess it is time to stop calling you, Davy."

"Thanks, Mom. This means a lot to me."

Oh, goodness sake, thought Kat. *My little boy is now a little man. I've got to go with the flow.*

"I really appreciate this, Mom. I thought you would say no."

"You underestimate me, David. Things change and so must I. Listen to me, I sound like a philosopher," laughed Kat with a heavy heart, knowing that her baby boy no longer existed. She slipped a couple of times after that with calling him, Davy, but made a point to try harder with calling him David from now on.

Kat kept in touch with Bev by phone but hadn't seen her in over two months. She called her and they agreed to meet for lunch the following Saturday while David was at baseball practice.

"My goodness, Kat, how are you?" questioned Bev after giving her a hug.

"I'm fine, Bev, and you?"

"Never been better, and since we're together, it's even better. Does that sound right?" questioned Bev, with a smirk.

"Sounds alright to me."

"How are Davy and Michael doing?"

"They're just fine, but Davy no longer exists."

"What are you talking about?" questioned Bev, with a frantic look on her face.

"I'm sorry, Bev. That didn't come out quite like I meant it to. Davy now wishes to be called, David."

"I see. He's turning into a little man then?" questioned Bev, with a sigh of relief.

"Yup! He's my little man now."

"How precious!"

"Precious or not, that's the way it has to be from now on."

"Do I detect a little animosity here?"

"Yeah, a little, but I'm getting better at handling it."

"You should, if it pleases your son."

"I know, and it does please him to no end that his mother agreed with him."

"He's growing up, Kat, and that's a process that you can't do anything about."

"I've come to realize that, but a little tiny bit of me doesn't want to let go, but I am."

"Good for you. What else is new with you, Kat?"

"Since I talked with you over the phone only a couple of weeks ago and probably bored the hell out of you with telling you all about David, not much else has been happening."

"You didn't bore the hell out of me, as you put it, because I'm always anxious to hear about, Davy, excuse me, David and how he's doing. But actually, I knew ahead of time most of what you told me in the first place," laughed Bev. "I just enjoy your version of the stories. You do have a way with words, you know."

"Yeah, right! I am getting better at thinking before I open my mouth though," inserted Kat.

"Good! Because after I first met you, I had to hesitate and go over what you said just to make sure I understood you right."

"I was that bad?"

"Not really. Just kidding."

"Your sense of humor hasn't changed. Things must be going well with you then. Of course, you always were upbeat, Bev."

"Well, thank you for the compliment, but that's the only way to be. Never let a problem get you down so bad that you don't see a light at the end of the tunnel."

"Good advice, but sometimes hard to enact."

"Not when you have faith that tomorrow will be a better day."

"That's what I love about you, Bev. Your philosophical outlook on life."

Kat and Bev continued their light-hearted conversation throughout their meal and then said their goodbyes, and promised each other to get together sooner than two months time.

Spring dissipated rather quickly with summer fast approaching. Soon, David would be out of school, and Kat had another problem on her hands. Who could she get to be with David during the summer months on the days that she had to work? Even though her son was levelheaded and basically a good kid, the law required that a child had to be thirteen in order to be home alone. That problem was solved within two weeks of school letting out. With the large influx of kids signing with the JRROTC program, David's recruiter asked him if he could help with orientating the new recruits. David jumped at the idea. This would take care of the mornings, but there was still a few hours left in the afternoon. Kat came up with one of her brainstorms and called, Maggie.

"Hi, it's me. Could you use some more help at the Soup Kitchen every day during the week for a couple of hours in the afternoon until I get home from work?" questioned Kat.

"We can use all the help we can get, especially with Chris and Cindy's wedding so close at hand," relayed Maggie.

"Good. Because I'm volunteering, David. It's either the Kitchen or I'll have to hire someone for a couple of hours a day. I'm sure he'll opt for the Kitchen. Do you need any help with those wedding plans, Maggie?"

"Thanks for the offer, but no. Cindy and I have everything pretty much under control with the help of her grandparents."

"That's nice that they got involved," noted Kat.

"It's unbelievable how much help that they have been. We wouldn't be this far without their help," stated Maggie.

"Well, if something comes up and you need my help, let me know."

"I will, Kat."

Maggie, Cindy and her grandparents did a wonderful job with the wedding plans, from the bridal party dinner the night before, and the beautiful decorations in the church to the dinner and reception following the wedding itself. It completely left Kat in awe, especially during the ceremony with seeing her three nephews standing at the altar with Chris in his dress uniform, and Tim and Chad in their dress uniforms, and Cindy was the ultimate beautiful bride.

Later during the reception, the two sisters finally got a chance to talk. "You know, Maggie, this is one of the most beautiful weddings that I have ever been to. You and Marshall have to be very proud of your three sons."

"We certainly are, Kat. Don't all three of them look so very handsome?"

"Yes they do, and if I weren't their aunt and was ten years younger, I'd be after all three of them," chuckled Kat.

With Chris' time schedule with the Air Force, he and Cindy had a three-day honeymoon in Key West, Florida.

Two years had passed since Chris and Cindy's wedding. They both so wanted children. Cindy finally became pregnant, but at the end of twelve weeks, she had a miscarriage. It was devastating for the entire family.

"You're both young and healthy, and there is plenty of time to start a family," consoled Maggie.

As it turned out, Cindy had another miscarriage the second time she was pregnant, and to make things worse, her dear grandfather passed away of a heart attack a few months later. Maggie was worried sick over how

Cindy would handle the three terrible things that happened to her in such a short period of time. She knew how close Cindy and her grandparents were. After the second miscarriage, Chris and Cindy decided it was best for her to go to a specialist to determine why these miscarriages were happening. The tests all came back negative and Cindy was young and very healthy, so there was no physical reason why she miscarried twice. The doctor suspected stress and told her of his findings. Of course, she denied it, but Chris saw the gradual change in Cindy's personality after the first miscarriage. The many changes of location where they lived could have been a major factor in Cindy's behavior also, thought Chris. He told her that if she became pregnant again that she should go and live with her grandmother for the length of the pregnancy, so that she would have some stability in her life. Little did he know that he actually made things worse, for in Cindy's mind, she took his suggestion as a way of getting rid of her and that maybe he didn't love her anymore, because she couldn't carry a baby full term.

Within a year's time, Cindy became pregnant with their third child. Both she and Chris were elated and looked forward to a baby, but always had in the back of their minds of what may happen again. And it did. This was beyond reasoning for both of them, and Cindy suggested having her tubes tied and forget about having kids. Chris knew that deep down she didn't mean a word she was saying, he hoped.

While stationed in Colorado Springs again for an undetermined amount of time, Chris and Cindy received word that her dear grandmother passed away in her sleep almost one year to the day that her grandfather passed. Cindy knew in her heart that her grandmother died of a broken heart. She needed to be sedated to make it through the funeral. Maggie suggested that she stay with her as long as she needed to get her grandparent's estate settled, for Cindy couldn't bear to stay in their home without either one of them with her. She was grateful that both of them lived to see her married to Chris, but they never had a chance to see a greatgrandchild.

Maggie helped Cindy every day with going through her grandparents' belongings and getting their house ready to go on the market. Kat and David helped as much as they could. One late afternoon while Cindy was

going through a trunk that belonged to her grandmother, Maggie came into the room to see how she was doing when she caught Cindy in a deep trance-like state. Maggie freaked out and called Kat, and was grateful that she answered the phone on the second ring. Kat came over as quickly as she could get there, and between the two of them, they managed to bring Cindy back to reality. Neither Maggie nor Kat saw anything like it. Cindy was completely in another world of her own. Chris was notified and flew back home and stayed for a week. She seemed to come around with Chris being there, but as soon as he left, she became despondent and moody. It was an ordeal for all concerned to get her grandparents' house finished and ready to turn over to a realtor to be sold. Chris came back home again but only for a short time, as he received orders to report to another airbase. He loved what he did and was an ace pilot and could fly anything, but his wife was falling apart under the stress of the happenings that she had to deal with within a few short years' time.

Maggie's doctor suggested that she be institutionalized, just until she could get the help that she so desperately needed. Chris refused and came for his wife. Within a year's time, they moved twice. Cindy seemed a little better, but never the same as she was. His sweet, loving wife became moody and despondent and very suspicious that Chris was having an affair, because he was never home. She never bothered unpacking all of their belongings from their last move. When confronted by Chris, Cindy's answer was, "Why bother? We'll be moving somewhere else in six months."

Chris knew that she needed to lay down roots, but it would never happen for them with his job with the Air Force. He suggested that she get involved with the other officers' wives. She tried it for a short period of time, and then began to become paranoid with thinking that they didn't want her around, which wasn't true. Ruth, one of the wives, made friends with Cindy, and they seemed to connect, and Chris was able to relax a little and hoped that this friendship would help Cindy.

One night when Chris came home after a long day, he opened the door and found Cindy sitting on the couch with a drink in one hand, a cigarette in the other and watching TV with a hammer laying beside her on the

floor. Chris couldn't believe the carnage. She totally destroyed all the furniture, which was ripped to shreds with a pair of scissors and evidently used the hammer to pound holes in every wall. Anything breakable was lying on the floor. She looked up at Chris and explained, "Sorry, but I didn't have time to fix supper. I was too busy cleaning."

Cindy was institutionalized for four months in Colorado Springs and Chris went there every night to be with his wife. She seemed like the old Cindy when she was released. But Chris didn't want to take any chances and talked her into going home and staying with Maggie and Marshall for a while. He promised her that he would come home as many times as possible to be with her.

Cindy worked at the Soup Kitchen every day and she loved it there, which pleased Maggie to no end. Kat and David included her every time that they went up to the cottage for long weekends. Cindy improved every day, and Maggie associated it to keeping her busy and making her feel needed. She would fly to wherever Chris was stationed for a weekend now and then, and Chris flew home to be with her as much as possible.

David loved every minute of the entire four years that he spent at the prestigious Newt's School. Kat, in hindsight, knew her decision to enroll him there was the right choice. David was extremely challenged those four years and yet still maintained a 4.0 grade average. He graduated with the honor of being chosen salutatorian of his senior class and thus gave the salutatory address at the commencement ceremony.

He learned early on how to deal with kids that were older than him. He was no pushover. far from it in fact with his four years of training with the ROTC. And his karate lessons paid off for him. by earning him a brown belt. He came close to blows with a few other students at Newt's School, but succeeded in using a diplomatic approach to solving the issue at hand, for he could never figure out why people resorted to anger and violence when, with the right attitude, could solve any problem with diplomacy and tact. He was living in an extremely violent world where the former was the norm. Kat was elated beyond words and was so very proud of her son with what he had achieved at Newt's School.

David wanted a military training school for his four years of college. His dream was to go to West Point, but it would be nearly impossible to get him enrolled there, because of his early age. He picked five schools from across the United States and wrote resumes of his achievements to all five of them. All there was left to do was wait until he heard from each of them for acceptance.

It was nearing the end of June and Kat and David had yet to go to the cottage, because of the busy schedule with David graduating from high school and the big party that she held for him. She had planned to ask Maggie and Marshall if they would like to join them knowing that it would be a nice getaway for all of them when Kat took her first vacation during the second week in July. She just finished fixing David and herself breakfast, before they headed for the Soup Kitchen when the phone rang.

"Kat?" questioned a voice on the other end.

"Maggie, is this you?" There was a short lull then Maggie continued...

"It's...it's Marshall," answered Maggie. She was almost inaudible to Kat, because she was crying, hysterically.

"Maggie, please! I can hardly understand you. What's going on, and what did you say about Marshall?"

After a long pause, Maggie explained. "I went to call him for breakfast and found him in the den. He was slumped over his desk. I called the paramedics right away and they revived him in the ambulance for a short period of time when he looked straight at me and smiled and then he closed his eyes again. I just knew then that he was gone, Kat."

"Oh no! Are you saying that Marshall is dead, Maggie?"

"Technically. He's on life support. Oh, please hurry! I really need you now, Kat," sobbed, Maggie, again, and the phone went dead.

Kat knew Maggie and Marshall always went to St. Mary's Hospital when need be, and she hoped that she was right, because Maggie hung up the phone before she had a chance to ask. The drive seemed to take

an eternity for Kat in anticipation of being with her sister, even though she and David rushed to the hospital and arrived there within twenty minutes. They found Maggie in ICU with Marshall, who, as Maggie said, was technically alive, but only because the life support apparatus breathed for him. Maggie ran to Kat and hugged her for what seemed an eternity and sobbed all the while. Kat rubbed her back and tried to console her sister with soothing words in between her own sobs of grief.

Maggie calmed down somewhat and turned to Kat and David and explained, "I won't take him off of life support until our three sons are here to help me make that decision."

"I'll call all three of the services and find out how we can get in touch with them when we get back home," informed Kat.

"Okay, Kat, I'll leave that up to you, thank you!"

Kat and David stayed with Maggie for three hours and after the doctor on duty told Maggie that there was nothing she or anyone could do for Marshall now, convinced her to go home and get some rest and to come back later if she wished to.

They took Maggie home with them, and Kat finally convinced her to go and lie down in the spare bedroom, before the sedative that they gave her to calm her down took affect. When Maggie agreed, Kat made some phone calls to try and get in touch with all three of her nephews to tell them what had happened to their father. She spent the rest of what was left of the afternoon and into the evening before she reached each of her nephews, personally.

Someone from the Marines located Tim in Singapore, and his call came through to Kat first.

"Aunt Kat, it's me, Tim. All they told me was that Dad is in the hospital, and that I should call you for more information. What's going on?"

"Your father had a heart attack early this morning. He's on life support, honey."

"Oh my God! And Mom, how is she doing, Aunt Kat?"

"They sedated her before we left the hospital and she's sleeping now. When can you get back home?"

"I can catch a military plane from here to New York and then take a commercial airline home. It will probably take me a whole day of flying, though."

"Your Mom and I will be at the hospital early tomorrow morning and probably most of the day and into the night. Do you have a pen and paper handy so that you can write down my cell number when you get all the information about your flights?"

"Just a minute. Okay, I'm ready."

After Kat gave Tim her cell number, she told him to call as soon as he had all the pertinent information, and that she would pick him up at the airport.

"No need for that, Aunt Kat. I would prefer that you stay with Mom. I can rent a car and go right to the hospital."

"Okay, Tim. However you want to handle it."

"Does Chris and Chad know about Dad?"

"No, Honey. You're the first one to call me back. They do know by now that something happened and will be calling."

"Please take care of Mom for me, Aunt Kat."

"I will, Honey. Have a safe trip, bye."

Oh this is so very hard, thought Kat, as she hung up the phone.

Kat and David sat in the kitchen conversing with Michael. Kat broke down a few times even though she tried to convince herself to stay strong.

"Why did God have to take Marshall now, Michael, when Maggie needed him the most with their three sons away from home?" questioned Kat.

"The Almighty One did not take him away, Mistress Kat. It was his time to return to the Heavenly Father," informed Michael.

"What do you mean?" asked Kat.

"You see, Mistress Kat, everyone who ever lived chooses who they will be in their lifetime, and when and how they will leave it," explained Michael.

"You mean kind of like a contract?" interjected David.

"I wouldn't quite use that term," responded Michael. "But yes, that's another way of putting what I mean to say."

Kat told David it wasn't necessary for him to return to the hospital early the next day with her and Maggie if he had something that he wanted to do, because they would most likely be there all day and into the night.

"No, Mom. I don't have any plans and besides, I want to be there for you and Aunt Maggie."

About an hour later, Chad called. This conversation was similar to Tim's. He wanted to know what happened to his Dad and how his mother was doing and if Kat would be there with her until the three sons arrived home.

"I'm in between assignments right now, and I am stationed in Annapolis, aunt Kat. I'm at the airport now and should be home by midnight tonight."

"Do you want me to pick you up, Chad?"

"No, Aunt Kat. I'll rent a car and go to the hospital to see Dad and then go and stay at home. What time did you say you and Mom would be at the hospital tomorrow morning?"

"With the sedative that your Mom took, I suspect she will sleep through the night but will be up early and will want to get to the hospital as soon as we can. Why don't you meet us there at 8:00 A.M.? It will be a comfort for your mom having you there."

"I understand, Aunt Kat, and thank you for being there for Mom."

Kat's composure was starting to wane, so she quickly said, "You're welcome, honey. And have a safe trip. We'll see you tomorrow morning."

The Air Force commander caught up with Chris about an hour before he was ready to fly an old B52 bomber to Lackland Air Force base in San Antonio, Texas, and told him to call his aunt because there was an emergency with his father. Chris was beside himself and could barely dial the phone, as his hands were shaking so badly.

"Aunt Kat, it's me, Chris. What's wrong with my dad?"

"Honey, your dad had a heart attack this morning."

"Is he going to be all right?"

"Chris, your dad is on life support."

"Aunt Kat, that means—"

Kat couldn't hold back the tears any longer as she heard soft sobbing in the background. When Chris gained his composure, he asked her, "How is Mom doing?"

Kat repeated to Chris the same thing that she told her other two nephews. "She is highly sedated and is sound asleep."

"Aunt Kat, Cindy and I will drive to Denver and catch the first plane out that we can. It will probably be real late when we get into Milwaukee."

"Chris," instructed Kat, "go directly home when you get in. Chad will be here around midnight tonight, and then plans to go and see your dad at the hospital, and then go straight to your house. You and Cindy should

go there and then meet your mom and me at the hospital at 8:00 A.M. tomorrow with Chad, okay?"

"Alright, Aunt Kat. See you in the morning then."

Maggie was still sleeping when Kat and David decided to retire for the night. It wasn't that late, but the two were emotionally exhausted.

Even with having a good night's sleep, Maggie awoke in a trance-like state, as she couldn't believe or want to face all that was happening to her. The night was fretful for both Kat and David with thinking about Marshall and wondering how Maggie would be the next morning, especially with seeing two of her three sons at such a bereaved moment in their lives.

"Good morning, Honey," Kat said as Maggie walked into the kitchen. "I have coffee already made and will start breakfast for—"

"Just coffee for me, thanks. I don't really feel like anything to eat right now. Kat, were you able to locate my sons to tell them about their dad?"

"Yes, Maggie. I did talk to all three of them last night."

"Why didn't you wake me?" questioned Maggie, with a somewhat surly tone.

"Maggie, you were down for the count after that doctor sedated you and no one would have been able to wake you up, so I didn't even try. Besides, you needed to get a good night's sleep."

"I'm sorry, Kat. I didn't mean to jump all over you."

"That's alright, I understand. Chad arrived here around midnight last night, and Chris and Cindy didn't have a flight arranged yet when I talked to him, but he said that they would probably get in real late. They all stayed at the house last night, and I told them to meet us at the hospital at 8:00 A.M., because I figured that you would be awake before then."

"What about Tim?"

"He said that it would probably take him twenty-four hours to get here from Singapore. He should be home sometime tonight. He was supposed to call me back and let me know about when he would get here but probably won't be able to call until he's between flights." Maggie began to wobble a little before she had a chance to sit down, so Kat helped her to a chair and passed her a cup of coffee.

"When was the last time you ate?"

"I don't know. Maybe a day."

"Maggie, you can't go on without eating something."

"Yeah, maybe you're right. But just a piece of toast with maybe some peanut butter is all that I want. Did you eat?" questioned Maggie.

"Yes. I had the same thing you're about to have," chuckled Kat with the intention of lightening up the mood a bit.

"Is David up yet?" asked Maggie.

"Yes I am, Aunt Maggie," said David as he walked into the kitchen and kissed his aunt on the cheek.

"I'm ready to put the bacon on. How do you want your eggs?"

"I'm not really all that hungry. Maybe just a piece of toast with peanut butter will do."

"Chunky or smooth?" questioned Kat.

"I have a choice?" inquired David.

"You bet. This is a classy joint, I'll have you know."

Kat looked at Maggie and winked, which brought a smile to her face.

The three arrived at the hospital at around 7:15 A.M., so that Maggie could spend time with her husband alone before her two sons were due

to arrive. Kat and David waited in the lounge for Chris, Cindy and Chad to arrive. When they did at exactly 8:00 A.M., Kat had tears in her eyes but vowed to herself not to cry for everyone's sake. Greetings, hugs, and kisses were plentiful all around and when Maggie heard her sons' voices, she emerged from the ICU. Chris was the closest to her, so she went to him first. Kat and David stepped back while Maggie, sons, and daughter-in-law hugged each other in a tight circle and not a dry eye was to be found, because of the tearful reunion. Just then, Maggie's legs began to buckle out from beneath her and Chris caught his mother before she hit the floor and carried her over to the couch and laid her down. He grabbed her hand and started patting it and cried, "Mom, are you all right?"

Maggie opened her eyes and smiled at her son with a tear-stained face and began to rise while saying, "Yes, I'm alright."

"Please, Mom," begged Chris. "Lie down for just a little while longer."

Maggie did as her son requested and lay there with her eyes wide open and stared at the ceiling. Kat, upon seeing the state that her sister was in, went for help.

As the nurse approached, Maggie, she asked, "Mrs. Ryan, should I get a doctor?"

Hearing a strange voice brought Maggie out of her stupor.

"No, please don't call a doctor," she said, for she was fearful that he would sedate her, and her family needed her right now. She somehow found the strength to get her composure back and said, "I'm fine. Let's all go in to see your father together as a family."

Kat and David again started to back away when Maggie stated, "No, Kat, you and David come too. You're family."

Everyone took turns sitting with Maggie in Marshall's room, as she didn't want to leave her husband's side in hopes that he may come out of it and be all right again. When the rest went to the hospital cafeteria, they brought coffee and sandwiches to her, but she ate very little and dozed

for only minutes when Kat insisted that she try and get some sleep. It was heart wrenching for everyone to see the state that Maggie was in.

The day seemed to drag on for all and by 7:00 P.M., everyone was getting excited to see Tim who was due to be there any minute according to his call on Kat's cell when he talked to Maggie. David was the first one to spot him getting off of the elevator and ran to him and the two embraced.

"Hi, Sport. You've grown since the last time I saw you."

"You look great, Tim."

"Well, thank you for the compliment, sport," replied Tim, as he put his hand on David's head and ruffled his hair.

By then, the rest of the family was at Tim's side. He grabbed his mom and hugged her hard as he lifted her off of the floor. Tears had started to form in his eyes as he took a good look at his mother, who looked like she had aged twenty years. The rest of the family took their turn hugging Tim, and afterward Maggie led him aside and explained the severity of his father's condition, but that there was always hope that he will be fine. Tim and Maggie went into the ICU alone, so that he could be with his father. After about a half hour, Tim emerged into the corridor and motioned for Kat to come in.

"Aunt Kat, will you stay with Mom while I talk with my brothers about Mom's behavior?"

"Sure, Honey. I'll stay with her," answered Kat, not really understanding what he meant by the statement in reference to Maggie.

The three sons and Cindy conferred with Marshall's doctor and were told that he was not in any pain but also that their father had a massive heart attack, and that he was clinically dead. Only the life support is keeping him alive.

"We're going to have a hard time convincing our mother that there is

no hope, Doctor Ramsey, because the entire time that I was in there, she was telling Dad that he had to snap out of it and come back to his family," informed Tim.

"This is a natural reaction when a loved one is involved. Your mother is in complete denial and will not accept the fact that your father will never come out of it. It's up to the four of you to convince her that this is the best thing to do for your father's sake: let her husband go. I do suggest that all of you, including your mother, have to agree with unplugging the life support, because there may be resentment on your mother's part later on that the three of you went ahead and gave us your permission without hers," informed Dr. Ramsey.

It was nearing at 9:00 P.M. when all agreed that it was time to leave. Kat suggested that they all come to her house, because she knew that Maggie was not ready to go home yet with Marshall not being there.

"I've got a roast in the slow cooker and we can have hot beef sandwiches if the meat isn't stuck to the sides by now," she joked. It wasn't, of course, because she snuck out around 6:00 P.M. and ran home to check on it so that they could have hot beef sandwiches for a very late supper. All agreed and headed for Kat's house.

After supper, the three brothers went into the living room where the atmosphere became more light-hearted. Kat associated it with getting away from the hospital setting. Kat did converse with her three nephews at the hospital about Maggie, and told them that she too tried to convince her of unplugging the life support. She also informed them what Maggie had told her when she and David arrived at the hospital for the first time.

"Your mother said, 'I will not even consider taking him off of the life support until my three sons get here to help make that decision.' Somewhere along the line, my sister changed her mind and I suspect that it's, because you're all together again and now she's got this notion that it's just a matter of time before Marshall will wake up and you all can be a family again."

"So what can we do, Aunt Kat?"

"I don't know, but let's call it a night pretty soon. It's been a long day for all of us. We can try and figure out something tomorrow."

While in bed that night and talking with Michael, David brought up the subject of his aunt Maggie.

"If it was up to, aunt Maggie, the way she talks, Uncle Marshall will be on that breathing machine for only a short time, because he will wake up any minute now or whichever one comes first."

"No, David. It won't be long, only a few days so that everyone can say their good-byes."

"How do you know, Michael?"

"Trust me, I know."

"Oh, good. So, they'll convince, aunt Maggie, somehow."

"No, they won't convince her."

"But you just said that it would only be a few days."

"Yes, I did, and it will. It won't be they that will convince her, but you."

"Me? How can I talk her into it when no one else has been able to do so, so far?"

"Trust me, David. You and you alone will find the right words. Of this you can be sure."

The following morning, David walked into the lounge area of the ICU unit and found Maggie there by herself.

"Hi, Aunt Maggie. How are you doing?" questioned David.

"I'm okay, Honey," answered Maggie, with tears forming in her eyes with seeing him.

"I'll get right to the point, Aunt Maggie. I had a talk with Michael last night and he told me that I would be the one who would convince you to take Uncle Marshall off of life support and let him go. He told me that it is unbelievably beautiful on the other side where everyone goes when they pass on from this existence. He will be in a better place than this and will wait for you until it is time for you to join him. So you see, Aunt Maggie, that is where Uncle Marshall really belongs."

Late the next afternoon, Maggie approached her family and informed them that it was time to let Marshall go, because it wasn't fair to him that she wanted him to stay.

"You made the right decision, Mom. But what made you change your mind?" asked Tim.

"Not what, but whom. David and I had a long talk and I realized that what he was saying to me was all true. We must let your father go."

Marshall lasted less than two hours once the life support apparatus was removed, and his funeral was held three days later. One hundred and fifty people were there to show their respect, including Maggie's entire family consisting of her mother, her brother Bob, his wife Helen, her brother, Dan and his wife Shirley, which Maggie and Kat hadn't seen for three years.

Maggie stayed with Kat and David for two weeks afterward but then told Kat, "It's time for me to go back home."

"Are you sure?" questioned Kat.

"Positive. I can't hide out here forever. I have to go home and face the fact that Marshall won't be there with me."

Toward the end of summer after hearing back from all five schools, David accepted a four-year scholarship to the Military University. It was offered to him, because of his excellent grade point level and his abilities on the football squad. The Military University, which was associated with the army, was located in Norfolk, Virginia, and he joined the ROTC program offered. Kat had a hard time dealing with the fact that he chose

a school so far from home, but she had to realize that her son's academic abilities were not of the normal teenager but one of a young adult and to be happy and proud of him, because of what he had already accomplished and for being accepted at such an early age.

Kat and Maggie took a very needed five day vacation to New York City a few days after David left for college. They enjoyed the different landmarks immensely but had a hard time dealing with the hustle and bustle of the people and traffic. When they arrived back home, they drove to the cottage for a needed rest, and to celebrate the acceptance of Kat's second novel from the same publishing house that accepted her first novel. The two sisters not only enjoyed the weather, but each other's company with a lot of reminiscing, crying and laughter. The latter was the most important medicine for the two of them at this critical time in their lives.

Kat insisted that David call her every week for the first month that he was away at school to keep her informed of how he liked his school and every aspect of his education. Most of all: did he make any new friends? She knew this was important: having someone close to share every phase of his daily existence with, because he was away from home and so very young even though he had Michael there to watch over him.

Maggie vowed to herself that this was going to be a festive Christmas for her even though her beloved Marshall was gone. She had Chris and Cindy coming home for four days and Chad was staying for five, but Tim could not make it home. The holidays would not be quite the same for her without Marshall, but she was going to have some of the most important people of her life with her and that was all that mattered.

Kat was counting down the days when David would be home for the winter recess. It was hard for her when he had to leave for college. The trip to New York and to the cottage was a nice interlude until she and Maggie returned home, and now the house was really empty for the first time since David was born.

The weekends were the hardest for Maggie to adjust to and Kat considered the entire week hard enough to adjust to with the silence in her house day in and day out. She stayed busy with her job and now

worked both Saturday and Sunday at the Soup Kitchen along with Maggie. Both were putting the final touches on Christmas decorations before the holidays. This was a very festive time and the two were going to make sure that the homeless had a happy Christmas as they have done for the previous years. More people volunteered over the holidays than any other time of the year, which was great, because there was a lot of work to do. Kat was extra excited whenever David came home for the holidays, because she had some time to spend with Michael also.

"I love this time of the year, Michael. Everyone is in such high spirits," said David without realizing that he was talking a little too loud.

"I'm sorry, I didn't quite hear what you just said," informed Sam, the cab driver.

"I guess I was thinking out loud, sorry."

"Don't apologize. You'd be surprised at some of my fares that sit in this cab. Some talk, some cry, some don't talk, some are nice, some are grouchy, but all are good tippers, so I try and mind my own business. I didn't catch your name, Sonny."

"It's, David, and you are?"

"The name's, Samuel, but everybody calls me Sam."

"Well, Sam, I'm glad to meet you."

"Same here, David."

"You visiting folks here in Milwaukee or do you have other family here?" asked Sam.

"Both. I was born and raised here."

"You look kind of young to be wearing army sweats, David."

"I attend a Military University in Norfolk, Virginia. I'm home on winter break."

"You look pretty young to be attending any university."

David didn't want to explain anything to Sam so just said, "I look exactly like my father, and he always had a baby face too."

"Where does your father live? Am I taking you there now?"

"No, my father is gone."

"I'm sorry, David," replied Sam, when he realized that he may be getting too personal.

"It's snowing pretty good. Do you know how much we're supposed to get?"

"This is pretty much lake effect. But they did say between five or six inches. I don't like driving in the stuff, but I chose to live here and retire here, so I don't have a right to complain, I'm thinking. That address you gave me isn't residential. If I recall correctly, it's the Soup Kitchen."

"Right you are, Sam. You know the city pretty well then?"

"I should, 'cause I've been doing this for thirty years."

"That's a long time."

"Yeah it is. But everyone has to earn a living doing something, and I chose to drive a cab."

"Thank you, Sir," replied David, as they pulled up in front of the Soup Kitchen and he handed Sam his fare and a tip.

"Haven't been called that in years. Sounds pretty good," informed Sam, as he proceeded to get David's suitcase and duffel bag from the trunk. "Best of luck to you and enjoy the holidays. Oh, and yes, welcome home and have a Merry Christmas."

"Well, thank you, Sam. A Merry Christmas to you and your family also. Here, I'll get those," as he took his belongings from Sam and put them on the sidewalk. "It was a pleasure meeting you, Sam," replied David, as he was standing in the doorway of the Soup Kitchen and waving good-bye.

Sam nodded his head and walked to the driver's side of the cab and got in, tooted the horn, and waved back as he pulled away.

One of the older patrons grabbed David's duffel bag and said, "Here, let me help you with that, sonny."

"That's okay," David started to say as he looked up and saw that it was Henry. "Henry, how are you doing?"

"David, is that you? I Didn't recognize you."

"I'm fine, Henry, and you?"

"Same. Your mom's going to be surprised to see you here."

"Yeah. I figured she would be here working, so I just came here from the airport instead of going home."

"David, is that you?" questioned Maggie with a tone to her voice that made David think that they hadn't seen each other in years instead of only three months.

"Yes, Aunt Maggie. It's me. You look great."

"Well, thank you. And you look…ah, what word was I thinking? Oh yes…older." laughed Maggie.

"Is Mom around?"

"Yes, she's in the kitchen. We didn't expect you until tomorrow."

"I was finished with my classes and all the loose ends that I had to take care of, so instead of sitting around and being bored, I decided to come home early."

"Oh, David. Kat will be so surprised. She's really missed you since you have been gone."

"I know, Aunt Maggie. I've missed her too."

"Is Michael with you?"

"Yes, Aunt Maggie. He's standing right next to you."

"Oh," replied Maggie, a little startled. "How are you, Michael?"

"Just fine, Mistress Maggie, and you?"

"I'm all right, Michael. I haven't been called that since you left, so I forgot that you called me by that name," laughed Maggie. "David, go and surprise Kat before she comes out of the kitchen." She continued with, "Make sure that she doesn't have anything in her hands, because she has a tendency to drop things when she's startled," laughed Maggie.

David found his Mom leaning over the sink and peeling potatoes for the supper crowd.

"Hi, Mom."

Kat turned around with a startled look on her face and a paring knife pointed at David's stomach.

"Oh my God, David. Is that you?"

"Yeah, Mom. It's me, your Son, David."

"Oh you," laughed Kat, as she set the knife down on the kitchen sink, which relieved David, and then she embraced her son.

Kat held him at a distance so that she could get a better look at him and replied, "Look at you! You've grown."

"Mom, I've only been gone three months. I'm sure I haven't grown any in that short of time."

"You look taller, David," insisted Kat.

"I just talked to Cindy and she is making supper, so the two of you come over by me. Chris and Chad are there also, so we can all be together for the evening," informed Maggie.

"And Tim? What about him, Aunt Maggie?"

"My elusive son will not be home this time around."

As the three entered the front door to Maggie's house, they found Chris and Chad drinking beer while watching a football game.

"Aunt Kat and David, what a nice surprise," noted Chris as he stood to hug both of them.

"Good to see both of you again," said Chad, doing the same as his brother just did.

"It's really great seeing the two of you together," stated Kat.

"I'll say," echoed David.

"Sit down," requested Chris.

David took them up on their suggestion and practically crawled over the two of them to get to the other side of the couch.

"I think I'll go into the kitchen with Maggie and Cindy. Maybe there's something I can help them with," Kat said, as she left the room.

Even though their sons were now all living away from home, Kat and Maggie's lives were far from unfulfilled because of their jobs, Kat's volunteering, their continued riding with Daisy and Molly, flying to Virginia whenever feasible to see David and of course, they had the cottage to go to even during the winter months if they chose to do so. Chris, Cindy, Tim, and Chad returned home whenever they could to see Maggie, and David always came home for the holidays and, of course, during the summer months when school was not in session. He filled his days with volunteering at the Kitchen with Kat and with the local JRROTC program and coached basketball at the local YMCA. Life was good for the two sisters.

Rumors from all around the world hinted at a possible war in the near future, because the heads of the Super Power Nations could not negotiate

with Syria, Iran, or North Korea, even with the sanctions imposed on all three countries that have been in place for almost three years. The Taliban overtook Afghanistan in less than a year after all of the American troops were withdrawn from the country in the year 2018. The unrest in the Middle East continued, but with each passing day, it left death and destruction on a major scale in its wake. The world's populace was on a collision course and spinning out of control. It was just a matter of time when all the hatred, killing, and atrocities that mankind bestowed upon each other would come to a head—and it did.

It was Christmas Day, December 25, 2020. Maggie was up early as usual, and as soon as she heard the news, she tried calling Kat to see if she knew. *I know she's home*, thought Maggie as she was driving to Kat's house, after trying five times to get through to her over the phone. Kat's car was in the driveway, so she knew that she had to have used it to go somewhere and decided to go to the back door. She knocked three times with no response, so on the fourth try, she pounded on it. To her surprise, it opened. Maggie walked into the kitchen and found Kat baking, dancing, and singing along to some very loud Christmas music.

Maggie yelled, "Kat! What are you doing?" but received no response. She then went over to the DVD to turn down the volume. Kat turned to see what happened to the music and almost collided with Maggie.

"Maggie, for God's sake, you scared the hell out of me," scolded Kat, right before she dropped the cookie sheet with cookie dough, which now was spread across the floor.

"I'm sorry, Kat," laughed Maggie, "but I called you five times on the phone and got no response, so I came over here and knocked on your door as many times and it opened, so I walked in. Evidently you didn't hear me, but the neighbors had to hear your music two blocks away with it playing so loud."

"Well, I thank you for bringing my shortcoming to the surface, and I surely must apologize to the neighbors the first chance I get. So what's so important that you had to run all the way over here to tell me when you

could've told me later?" questioned Kat as she proceeded to gather the cookie dough from the floor.

"It's been all over the TV, and I can't believe that you don't know about it," stated Maggie, with an overly anxious tone to her voice.

"Calm down, Maggie. Know about what?"

"The President has scheduled a State of the Union address to the American people, and it has something to do with Syria, Iran, and North Korea. The commentators are suggesting war. Let's go into the living room, because he is due to start at 8:00 A.M."

"What? He can't declare war on anyone; it's Christmas," declared Kat.

"Evidently, he sees it differently."

"My God, Michael told me when I was at the cottage that WWIII would start on December 25, 2020, and would last for seven years. I can't believe I could forget something as important as that."

Kat then ran to David's bedroom door, pounded on it, and yelled, "David, get up!"

"Gee wiz, Mother, you sound just like my drill sergeant from military school. What time is it anyway?" asked David, who was still in a sleep mode and not wanting to wake up, because he arrived early this morning.

"David, get dressed and meet us in the living room," insisted Kat.

"Who is 'we,' Mother? I thought no one was here yet."

"They're not. They're all coming later this afternoon. It's just, Maggie."

"Well, thanks, Kat."

"Oh, Maggie, you know what I mean."

"What's going on?" inquired David.

"Get dressed. You'll know soon enough. Michael, are you here?"

"Yes, Mistress Kat. I am here with you and Mistress Maggie."

"Michael, you told me when World War III would start, but I can't believe that I forgot. Why didn't you remind me?"

"It was my duty to tell you once, but as far as you forgetting the date, it was because you did not believe what I was telling you to be true."

"Thinking back on that conversation between you and me, I think you are right. I didn't quite believe what you were trying to tell me, and since none of the predictions from each book has yet to happen, I guess I didn't believe that they were true either. Actually, I didn't want to believe, because I knew what it would mean for this world. It won't happen again, Michael, of that you can be sure."

"This is good, Mistress Kat. You must believe in everything that I tell you in the future, because it is coming directly from the Almighty One, Himself."

"Michael, is it true what it says in the Bible about God having to intervene with World War III, because mankind would annihilate each other, if He didn't and the human race as we know it, would cease to exist?"

"Yes, Mistress Kat. That is entirely true. The Almighty One will have to intervene in order for mankind to continue to exist."

"This war will be worse than the previous two then?" questioned Maggie.

"Yes, Mistress Maggie. It will be far worse than the two previous World Wars combined. The loss of lives and the damage to the Almighty One's creation will be incomprehensible to mankind. The world as you know it now will be but a shell of it's original self with total massive destruction throughout. The two of you must distance yourself from all the tragic future events that will take place, because neither of you can do anything about it. It's out of your hands."

"That will be easier said than done, but I do know what you are trying to tell us, Michael. In order to save our sanity, we can not let the future tragedies that we are about to face deter us from what we have to do in that future."

"Yes, Mistress Kat, exactly."

"Mom, what's going on?" asked David, as he walked into the living room with a doughnut in one hand and a glass of milk in the other.

"Looks like we may be going to war," answered Kat.

The newscasters reported that North Korea, which is slightly larger than the state of Indiana, pummeled Japan, which is smaller than the state of Montana, with nuclear warhead missiles. It happened so fast that Japan was not able to retaliate and was literally blown off the surface of the Earth. They then aimed missiles simultaneously to South Korea, an area combined with North Korea, which is slightly larger than the state of Indiana. Again, nothing was left standing and the loss of life was staggering and uncountable. Israel, which is about the size of New Jersey, was hit with missiles with nuclear warheads concurrently with Japan and South Korea, along with the United States' two Naval carriers, by North Korea, Syria, and Iran.

The planned attacks left the world in shock. *How did the Super Powers let this happen?* was the question of the day.

The newscaster continued, "This just in from our foreign correspondent, John Anderson: 'This is what just came over the newswire: From what we have seen, it has been verified that Japan and South Korea have been wiped off the face of the Earth along with one of our Naval carriers. There is extensive damage to the second one that was moored near Wanton, South Korea, in the Sea of Japan.'"

"John, if I may interrupt, the President is just walking into the press room. We will get back to you. We will now turn it over to Jerry."

"Yes, thank you. The President just walked in and is conversing with one of the reporters in the audience. The President."

"In light of the extremely despicable actions of North Korea, Iran, and Syria, I have declared war against these three countries and any of their allies, who may be involved with the overwhelming approval of both Congress and the Senate. Reports have come into the Oval Office stating that Israel has retaliated with their own means for further self-preservation. A force of one hundred thousand U.S. troops is being deployed as I speak, along with our three remaining aircraft carriers, stealth fighters, and numerous drones. It is a bleak day for our country and the world. It is beyond comprehension what our future will be like in wake of the knowledge that we now have of North Korea, Syria, and Iran having missiles with nuclear war heads. Our lives and those of the entire world will never be the same, but we have to unite with our allies and fight to secure our freedom and that of the rest of the world. May God help us all, thank you."

"There you have it, Kevin. The President's speech was short but definitely to the point."

Christmas that year was spoiled, in Maggie's eyes, because of the news, but she would certainly not be the only one affected. Chris and Cindy had to leave right away, because he received orders to report back to the airbase in Colorado Springs, Colorado. Minutes after Chris' call, Chad received the same orders telling him to return to Annapolis, Maryland.

Kat and Maggie flew to Virginia to be with David for his graduation ceremonies from the military university. He could be classified as a Second Lieutenant if he served in the army for five years afterward.

His original plan of going to West Point did not materialize for David, because he joined the army. He planned to go back home with Kat and Maggie for the two weeks that he had remaining before reporting for duty at Fort Bragg in Fayetteville, North Carolina with Special Forces. He had already worked out all the necessary details with the school as to which branch of the army that he planned to enter. Even though he was old enough and didn't need Kat's permission anymore, he still wanted his mother's blessing with his plans for his future.

David, why are you so adamant with joining the army? There's a war going on and as soon as you are out of boot camp, they'll send you somewhere to fight. I won't give my blessing and besides, your dream was always to go to West Point."

"I know, Mother, but I feel really sure about my decision to join the army. That's why I joined, because there is a war going on. I need to do this, Mother."

Kat gave in finally, but only, because she had a long talk with Michael and he reminded her that David would not be killed, because of God's divine protection, and that he still would always be by David's side.

It was early spring of 2022 when Kat walked into her kitchen.

"Michael! My God, you startled me. What are you doing here? You're supposed to be with David. Oh no, it's David, isn't it? What's happened to my son? Please—"

"Mistress Kat," interrupted Michael in a soothing voice. "Please calm down. I'm sorry that I startled you. Your son, David is fine."

"That was just about too much for me," smarted Kat, as she proceeded to wipe the tears from her eyes and tried to steady herself, as she headed for a kitchen chair and spoke in a raspy voice. "I have learned to deal pretty well with all the tasks that God has asked of me, but I don't know if I could go on, Michael, if I were to lose David."

"Again, I apologize to you, Mistress Kat. I did not mean to startle you in any way. You see, I have come to remind you of Scotland. It is very near to that time in which you and Mistress Maggie must take a trip over there."

"Michael, this is mind-boggling, and I can't believe God wants me to do this," stated Kat, remembering what Michael had told her in regard to Scotland. "How are Maggie and I going to go over to Scotland and build a garrison for David's army in one of their mountains?"

"You still have doubts even though all the catastrophic events that you predicted in your books are now starting to come true?"

"No, I believe God relayed all of those things to me, but what does that have to do with going to Scotland?"

"You certainly have little faith in yourself, Mistress Kat. You do have the ability to succeed with this part of the Almighty One's bidding, whether you think you do or not. You and Mistress Maggie will go to Scotland and pick out the sight that the garrison will be built on."

"And where exactly do we get the people from and the money to build this so-called garrison? And just what is a damn garrison, Michael?" asked Kat, with pure frustration with what was being asked of her.

"Basically a very large fort, and there are many small villages in the area. The men will be glad to take on the task for wages, which are hard to come by since this war started. The Scottish Parliament has three months left in which to pay back a loan to a bank in Switzerland, but it does not have anywhere near the monies to repay them, which will cause them, in time, to spiral into bankruptcy and financial ruin. Scotland is only one of a handful of nations left that continues to fight against, and have not fallen prey, to the Antichrist. But with possible ruin looming toward them, only the Almighty One knows what will happen. So you see, Mistress Kat, they will more than welcome your ideas, for they have nothing to lose and everything to gain with the building of a garrison in their country, which will give them the security that they need and desire to fight alongside with David's army. They will rebound economically as they were before the war started and they will be a great asset, for they are very righteous people and have strong beliefs in the Almighty One. The monies that you made on your two books since their release, coupled with the movie that will be made, will supply plenty of money to pay back that loan and to start the building project."

"That movie deal is still in the negotiating stage, Michael."

"It will happen, Mistress Kat, and you will negotiate a price to pay the Scottish government a yearly fee for the rental of their mountain."

"Right, Michael!" laughed Kat, with looking straight ahead and conjuring up the look he was probably giving her, which changed her attitude and she accepted his explanation of what is to take place.

"You will have to buy the materials from the surrounding larger cities and your nephew, Chris, with his cargo plane, will be the perfect one to transport the supplies," informed Michael. "You see, Mistress Kat, as I said before, this war is not like any other that mankind has had to face. The casualties of military and civilians will be so astronomical that they will be unable to keep an accurate account of the total. This war will be only one segment of the catastrophic disasters to come with The End Time. As I said to you before, you will be the Antichrist's most hated adversary. The Almighty One will protect Scotland, because of you, your son and followers for a certain amount of time until you pass on. Then and only then will the Antichrist be able to make war with your son and his army."

Kat told Maggie of Michael's plans for them to go over to Scotland. They talked about this before and Maggie came up with the theory that Michael may have mixed up God's instructions and he meant for someone else to do this.

"Nah, cop out! God meant you and me, Maggie. Let's get packing. We're going to Scotland. God help us!"

The plane ride over the Atlantic Ocean wasn't any fun for either sister. Actually, it was terrifying for both, but it had to be done in order to get to Scotland. Either that or it was to go by ship, and Kat was scared of water even more. She did her homework before they left and read as much as she could about the country: Highland compared to the Lowland, mountains, terrains, and waterways, temperature difference, and easy access by roads. She had the perfect place picked out in her estimation. *This isn't going to be easy*, thought Kat, *especially since neither one of us knows what the hell we're doing or supposed to be doing.*

As the two were walking the ramp from the plane to the terminal, Maggie turned to Kat and asked, "Kat, what are we doing here?"

"Good question, Maggie. I wish I had the answer. I guess we just have to leave all of this in God's hands. Even though we don't know what's going on, he does, and we have to have faith in him and then ourselves if we are going to make this work."

They were escorted to their room in the major hotel in Edinburgh and just as Kat paid the bell boy, the phone began to ring.

"How does anyone know that we are here?" asked Maggie, with a look of confusion on her face.

"It's the First Minister, a Mister Samuel Berkley," whispered Kat, in awe as she covered the mouthpiece with the palm of her left hand.

"God does work in mysterious ways," commented Maggie, with as much astonishment as was showing on her sister's face.

Samuel Berkley knew of their plans in regard to the garrison from David, who made a trip to Scotland while serving in Ireland and discussed everything with the Prime Minister in advance of their arrival. It was quite ironic in the Prime Minister's eyes that David's ideal location of the future garrison coincided exactly with Kat's, and that just about all of her ideas in regard to the garrison matched her son's exactly.

The two sisters felt very much at ease with the plane ride back to the States, because of all that was accomplished.

"Well, Maggie, we did it, or I should say God did it with a little help from my son," stated Kat, thinking back on everything that took place over their three week stay in Scotland. "But I never thought in a million years that we'd pull this off."

"Me neither. It's amazing, though, what can be accomplished with so much dedication by so few, for a project such as this one. The architects' plans were unreal considering the fact that they finished their blueprints of the garrison in a little over two weeks."

"I know, Maggie. Unbelievable how everything just seemed to fall into place with very little effort on the part of everybody concerned, but with

the condition that this world is in and deteriorating more and more each day at such a fast rate, there isn't any room for delay. The faster we get this accomplished, the better for everyone concerned on both sides."

Kat took the preliminary written draft drawn up by members of the Scottish Parliament to her lawyer and his law firm associates for necessary input and approval with her having the final say in regard to all the details from both sides. She acquired pertinent information regarding the monies already deposited in the name of Samuel Zachariah Berkley, First Minister of Scotland, with the same bank that now holds the paid loan. With all of this done, she was back in Scotland within a month with the final draft needed to get the ball rolling.

It was starting to get to be too much for Kat and Maggie trying to deal with all the minute details and the many trips back and forth, while overseeing the building of the garrison, the huge task of recruiting personnel on both sides of the Atlantic, and the need to run all aspects of the operations. They were trying to hold down their jobs, which they both loved and didn't want to quit. This was just the beginning of their life's work for God, which was priority. With many more years to come, they had no choice but to give their notice at their places of work as Maggie was now just as much a part of this as was Kat.

It was Wednesday afternoon, early fall, in the year 2022, and Kat was at work in the lunchroom enjoying the festivities planned by Dan and a few of her close co-workers for her farewell party. With his secretary whispering in his ear, Dan turned to his employees with the announcement that Washington D.C., was bombed only minutes before. Speculation was that it was hit with a nuclear warhead missile, but it was not yet confirmed. The entire plant shut down and everyone gathered in the lunchroom to watch a small TV that was mounted on the wall. The carnage was unbelievable with a preliminary estimation of at least three hundred thousand lives lost. Kat knew that news reports were at times exaggerated for effect, and she hoped that this was the case. She, like every one of her co-workers, was stunned. The war had lasted over two years already with no end in sight according to the newscasts, and it was not entirely to blame for the massive destruction throughout the United

States, but also due to Kat's predictions that took a greater toll on North America. The devastation to the world, coupled with Kat's catastrophic predictions that Michael said were starting to come true, left very little room for unscathed locations, and it was just getting worse on a daily basis. She recalled Michael telling her that the Bible predicted that if God did not intervene and shorten the years of this "evil age," the war would leave no flesh intact, and now it certainly looked like it was in the making. She rushed home in anticipation of more news reports that could tell the world what happened to the White House. She was glued to the TV when a knock on her front door startled her.

"Hi, I'm glad you're here."

"Me too. I couldn't stay home and watch this all alone, so I called the factory and Dan told me that you had left and that's why I came over here," explained Maggie. "Any more news about what it was?"

"No, not really. All the newscasters on the cable stations each have their own views, but nothing is confirmed yet. Want a cup of coffee?"

"If you don't mind, Kat, can I have a drink, instead?"

"Well, of course. I think I'll have one with you. Let's go into the kitchen and watch it from there."

"Fine with me," answered Maggie.

As Kat made the two drinks and sat down beside, Maggie at the kitchen table, another special report came over the screen. "It has been verified that this was not caused by a missile, but a small meteorite that hit directly in Rockville, Maryland, a suburb twelve miles north of Washington, D.C.," the reporter relayed.

"That's one of the predictions from the first book that you wrote, right?"

"Yes," was all that Kat replied to Maggie's question.

"Can we ask, Michael to make sure, Kat?"

"No, Maggie. Michael is with David, and he would not answer me anyway. He would have to be here in order to do so."

"I know that all of your predictions have come true so far, but I guess I was trying to go into a denial mode again, just like I did with all the rest that came true."

"I know what you mean, Maggie. But remember what Michael told us: we have to find a way to deal with all of this, because there is nothing we can do to stop it or change any of it in any way."

"I understand, but that doesn't make it any easier for me."

"I know. Do you want to stay here with me tonight?"

"I thought you'd never ask. Let's have another drink," suggested Maggie.

By now, David served a year in Iraq and didn't hesitate when his tour of duty was over and signed up for another one. He received a promotion to Major, because of his unusual abilities to coordinate and carry out special combat techniques in the line of combat duty. He was now stationed with the Special Forces unit near Kabul, Iraq.

Another one of Kat's predictions came true, leaving the District of Columbia obliterated with a radius of twenty-five miles in all directions, affected to some degree. Congress was not in session, but the rest of the populace in the area were killed, along with the President, Vice President, and Speaker of the House, who were in a meeting at the time of the impact. It was still unconfirmed at this date in time as to the exact amount of lives lost, comprising not only of the people working and living in the area, but also the unknown amount of people from the States and all over the world who were visiting as tourists.

David had yet to serve a full year of his second tour of duty, when his unit was on a special mission in the dead of night. They were sent to rescue ten Kurdish prisoners of war, two diplomats, three journalists, a CIA operative, whose identity was not yet known to his captors, but would certainly be known in a short period of time and a dozen or so

known civilians from all walks of life, who were caught up in the heart of this war for one reason or another.

David took a liking to Joe Owens of his unit, and in the course of their tour of duty together, they became good friends. It was Joe, who was walking ahead of him as they left the Apache helicopter and headed to the enemy compound a mile and a half in the distance. As they approached the compound and entered a courtyard, David, in a fleeting blink of the eye, could see a shadowy form off to his left, who had his gun aimed directly at Joe, who was now only a few feet ahead of him. Without hesitation, David reacted by throwing himself on Joe and was hit in the left shoulder. As he fell to the ground with his right leg extended into the air, that too was hit by another bullet. While still on top of Joe, David turned over and shot the man who tried to kill him along with another one of the enemy and then went unconscious.

Joe pushed David off of him and dragged him to a truck that was parked a few yards away. He checked David's bloodied shoulder and saw that it was a minor wound, but he had to apply a makeshift tourniquet to David's leg, because it was bleeding, profusely. He then proceeded to push David partially under the truck and out of sight. As David became conscious, he could see Joe running to the side door of the compound where he then disappeared. Before he went unconscious again, he could hear shouting and rapid gunfire in the distance. When he once again became conscious, he was being carried back to the awaiting Apache helicopter.

U.S. Army Post Hospital—Baghdad, Iraq Because of his bravery of saving another human being's life in the line of duty, David was to receive the purple heart in a future ceremony when he was able to accept it on his own accord. He also was told that he was to be promoted to Major General. These were not normal times, nor did normal circumstances apply with the promotion that David was to receive. Now was the time for him to call Kat and tell her what had happened to him. *Better to hear it directly from me instead of another source,* thought David.

"Michael, this is not going to be easy for me, because I know how upset my mother will be when I tell her of my injuries, which is understandable," declared David.

"I understand completely, but it must be done," answered Michael.

"Right, and the sooner the better," replied David as he dialed Kat's number.

"Mother? Hi, it's me, David."

"David, how are you?" questioned Kat, and in the same breath asked, "What's wrong?"

"Does there have to be something wrong, just because I chose to call my mother to find out how she's doing?" chuckled David.

"Yes, definitely. David, I get text messages from you on a regular basis, but this is the first time that you have called me in over a year. I repeat, what's wrong?" demanded Kat, with not really wanting an answer, for deep down she knew that her worst fears were about to come true.

"Well, Mom. I'm calling from an army hospital in Baghdad. I've been wounded and wanted you to hear about it from me directly instead of," said David, as he held the phone away from his ear, because his mother chose to interrupt with a voice close to a yell and shouted, "Wounded? You can't be wounded! You have God's protection and Michael is supposed to be guarding you. Put Michael on the phone, I want to talk with him," demanded Kat.

"Mother, please calm down. You know that's impossible, and besides, God's protection means I won't lose my life."

"Don't get technical with me, young man," retorted Kat, at the same time realizing just how much she was over reacting. "I'm sorry, Honey. I didn't mean to upset you, but if you were a mother, you'd realize just how I'm feeling right now," laughed Kat, having no idea why she just said what she just said to her son.

Hearing his mother's laughter, David inhaled a sigh of relief, for it would now be easier for him to tell her of his wounds. "I was wounded in my left shoulder and right leg, Mother. But I am recovering very fast and the doctors tell me that it will be a complete recovery. So you see, everything's going to be all right."

Kat caught the mention of doctors in the plural compared to doctor in the singular and continued with the question, "You said doctors instead of doctor. Why did you have to have more than one doctor, David?"

David could never hide anything from his mother. In his estimation, she just always seemed to know everything or had a suspicion about facts pertaining to everything about him, and this was no exception. But he was not going to let her know the news of the seriousness of his leg over the phone. He would wait and tell her in person, so he answered, "That's just the way things are done in the army, Mother," and he let it go at that. "I'm going to be sent State-side in a few weeks to Fort Bragg in North Carolina for a full recovery. Is it possible that you and aunt Maggie will be able to come and see me and be there for the ceremony, Mother?"

"Ceremony? What ceremony?"

"I'm to receive the purple heart and be promoted to Major General."

"Oh my God," exclaimed Kat, as her voice began to quiver with the realization that the purple heart is only awarded to servicemen for bravery in the line of duty or posthumously to those who died while serving their country. She recalled the words that his father told her about their son being a great general in God's army on Earth. "Oh David, I'm so very proud of you!"

The rest of the conversation between mother and son was light-hearted, which it needed to be, considering the reason for the phone call in the first place and further details of the ceremony were added by David.

"I don't care what I have planned. Maggie and I will definitely be there, even if we have to fly back the same day."

"Alright, Mother. I'll leave that part up to you."

David did not know at that time, but in the future, Joe would be one of his most trusted commanders in his army against the Antichrist. Because of the injury to his leg, David would never be able to return to full combat again. He was to be sent to Ireland in the capacity of teaching the Irish Republic Army combat military techniques that he knew and participated in so well over a short-lived army combat career.

David was home on leave for only two months prior to his next assignment over in Ireland. He was very tired of recuperating and was totally ready to get back into the swing of things minus the combat role, which he finally came to terms with.

"Hi, Maggie. It's me. Are you doing anything special right now?"

"You'd think I would be since it's Saturday and all, but no. So what's up?"

"The reason I'm calling is, because they said on the news that a crowd is gathering for a rally outside the courthouse this afternoon against that bill that the city's Common Council is supposed to vote on with the proposal of tearing down historic St. Mary's Church and replacing it with a civic center."

"What are they thinking?" asked Maggie.

"Evidently they're not. Maybe they don't believe a war is going on, only throughout the rest of the world but not here. Who knows what their reasoning is."

"I'll definitely come. Should I meet you there?" questioned Maggie.

"No. Why don't you come here and we'll walk over, because we don't know what the parking situation will be like. Come as fast as you can get your coat on and grab your purse. Is that too soon?"

"Of course not. I'll be over in about twenty minutes."

"Good. See you when you get here then, bye."

"David, Maggie and I are going to take a walk through the park over to the courthouse. See you later," yelled Kat, as the two sisters walked out the back door.

Since it was a beautiful day and the weather was warm for a change, the two sisters knew the walk would do them both good. As they neared the edge of the park, they heard loud applause coming from a small crowd that had gathered around a man standing on an inverted wooden crate addressing the people. He was saying, "He is the one that we have been waiting for: the true messiah, here to bring us peace for a thousand years to come. Don't be fools, your souls depend upon your belief that he is our savior. Bow down to him and accept his code of numbers telling him that you are and always will be a faithful follower of his teachings. He is your truth, your redemption—"

In that short period of time, Kat had heard enough of the lies that this man was feeding these people, so spoke up in a clear, loud voice, "This man, who calls himself Romanolf Musva, that he talks about and refers to him as your savior, your redeemer, your messiah, is a fake. He is the Antichrist in sheep's clothing. He's a configuration of the fallen angel Lucifer, and he is not here to rescue you from the troubles of the world but to add to them. He won't give you peace for as long as you live but just the opposite. He wants your souls as a vendetta against God. That has been his goal ever since God had him thrown out of Paradise. In reality, he is your worst enemy. Don't let him fool you into accepting his sign of the beast numbers 666 on your person. If you do, you will never see the face of your true God, the God who created you, the God, who has loved you all along. Don't be fools! Do you want a few days, weeks, months, years to live on this earth under his tyrannous rules, or do you want an eternal life with your Creator? Think what is at stake here. Don't let fear guide your actions. The greater fear will be if you accept him. Your body and soul will cease to exist once your presence on this world is over, and you become a pile of ashes instead, and you will lose the wonderful chance to be with your true God. You can be sure that you will return to dust and your name will be removed from the Book of Life. There's too much at

stake here for you now. Don't turn your backs on your Creator but bask in the glory and the knowledge that you will be with God for eternity if you are faithful to him. Of this, he promised, if you stay true to him."

At that moment, a large stone was thrown at Kat and hit her on her shoulder. Loud cries of "Blasphemer!" rang out in her ears. Maggie grabbed her arm and they escaped from the crowd through a row of trees linking the edge of the park.

"My God, Kat. What just happened there? Why did you say those things to make the crowd so angry with you?"

"I didn't, Maggie. Those were not my words coming out of my mouth. I don't know how to explain it. I could hear the words coming from me, but I was not thinking those words or speaking them."

"Kat, I was standing right next to you and your mouth was moving to the words. It was you saying those things."

"Michael, where are you?"

"Right here, Mistress Kat."

"Michael, please tell me I didn't say those words."

"You didn't, Mistress Kat."

"Well, who did then?"

"Remember the General in his letter to you telling you that some day you would be a prophet?"

"Yes, Michael. I remember, but what does that have to do with this?"

"You have been chosen by the Almighty One to be his prophet for The End Time. It was his words coming through you, and it will continue to happen until your life on this planet ends."

"Michael, I'm not sure that I want to hear or believe what you are telling me, not now with all else that is going on, but let me get this straight. You're saying that every time I open my mouth from now on that the words coming out of it will be God's words?"

"Not all the time, Mistress Kat. Only when you talk against the Antichrist to the masses and when you preach to the masses also."

"What exactly do you mean by 'preach to the masses'?"

"You will not only be a prophet for The End Time, but you will teach the word of God to the masses, and they will be His words coming through you. I told you this before, Mistress Kat. Another untruth in your eyes?"

"See, Maggie. I told you it wasn't me saying those things," quipped Kat.

"Kat, did you hear all the things that Michael just told you?" asked Maggie.

"Yes, Maggie, I did," answered Kat, with feeling terribly guilty about the words on her part that Michael brought to the surface. "This is all too overpowering for me right now. I'll have to think about what all Michael told us later when I'm alone and can get my head clear, which may only happen with a few drinks under my belt."

"That's not funny, Kat."

"I know. But some light-hearted conversation has to enter somewhere in this startling conversation we're all having, or I may, in reality, just lose my sanity."

"Those people had hatred for you written all over their faces, Kat," stated Maggie.

"This is just the beginning of the outrage that will be cast upon the ones who don't believe like they do that Romanolf Musva is truly the savior of mankind," informed Michael.

"Oh great, Michael. The next time I open my mouth to badmouth Musva, or whatever the hell his false name is, I may get pelted with some more stones, or better yet, shot at. Joyous rapture!"

"Don't get yourself in such a tizzy, Kat. You know how melodramatic you can get sometimes," warned Maggie.

"Don't forget, Maggie. You're my sidekick in all of this, so whatever happens to me, happens to you," smirked Kat. "And what the hell does tizzy mean?"

"I'm not sure. Mother always used that word. I think it may be English for upset."

"Who's upset? Do I look upset? Just because my hands are shaking uncontrollably doesn't mean I'm upset, right?"

"Kat, you're rambling," informed Maggie, with a worried look on her face.

"Got that right, sweetheart," answered, Kat, with a very large grin forming at her mouth.

"You did that on purpose by pretending to get all upset. I hate when you do that to me."

"Payback for telling me that I was the one saying all those things to that mob back there."

Michael just stood there nodding his head at these two with a grin on his face. He had been around both of them long enough to know what they are capable of saying to one another. In answer to Kat's original statement, Michael informed both of them, "You have the Almighty One's divine protection, remember, Mistress Kat? And as long as Mistress Maggie believes in what you are doing for the Almighty One, she too has his divine protection. It wouldn't hurt to have some precaution, when you are addressing the masses in the future."

"That's really some good advice, Michael," responded Kat. "Next time, Maggie and I will go incognito, when we address the masses!"

"Kat, for goodness sake. You can't talk to Michael like that. He's an Archangel of God," "I know, I know. I do apologize, Michael. I get a little crazy sometimes when things that I least expect to happen, happen," explained Kat.

"I understand completely, Mistress Kat, but you must be prepared, for it will only get worse in the future."

"Thank you for that tidbit of information, Michael. It makes me look forward to my future with great anticipation."

"Kat! There you go again."

"I'm sorry again, Michael. It's not fair to take it out on you." In her next breath came, "Let's go shopping, Maggie."

"After what just happened to us?"

"I think it's as good a time as any. Why not?"

"What about the rally?"

"With what just happened, I don't think the rally is of much importance to us anymore," assured Kat.

"Okay, let's go," laughed, Maggie, as the two of them headed across the street in another direction home as if nothing unusual just took place.

Michael stood there scratching his head and wondering about all that just happened and thinking about what the General said about Mistress Kat. "With an attitude like hers, she'll do just fine with the Almighty One's bidding."

Kat awoke from a restless night of tossing and turning, and after a failed final attempt to get some much needed sleep, she decided to give up and get up out of bed. She slipped on her robe and headed for the kitchen to brew a pot of coffee. As she sat at the kitchen table sipping a cup and

savoring the taste along with a chocolate chip cookie from the batch that Maggie made her, she took a moment to enjoy the peace and tranquil feeling that came over her that had eluded her for so very many months.

"Michael, are you here?" questioned Kat.

"Yes, Mistress Kat. I am sitting at the table with you."

"Michael, I must apologize again for how I behaved toward you yesterday afternoon. I was way out of line with what I said to you, and I'm truly sorry, if I may have hurt your feelings, as that is the last thing I would purposely do. I hope I didn't."

"No need to apologize, as you didn't hurt my feelings, Mistress Kat. And I know full well what you are having to deal with, and it is taking a toll on you. But you must remember that this chaotic world is only temporary, it won't be long before the Son of God will return and peace will finally reign supreme."

"Now that I have you alone, Michael, which hasn't happened much of late, I would like you to tell me more about this Romanolf Musva that you claim is the Antichrist. What exactly do Maggie and I have to do in regard to him?"

"He has already made his presence known in Europe and the Middle East. He comes as a fake messiah with the promise of attaining peace from this terrible war and billions of people will believe him, because he comes across as a youthful, good-looking, charming, very knowledgeable, peace-loving, human being, who has the ability to fulfill all of his promises through the eyes of the masses. He is not as well-known here yet, but as you and Mistress Maggie witnessed first hand in the park yesterday, his name is starting to take form here also."

"Ahh," sighed Kat as she tried to choose the words carefully and with as much meaning as needed for her own purpose to try and fully understand what is required of her.

"You hesitate, Mistress Kat. Even with knowing full well how successful you and Mistress Maggie are with fulfilling the Almighty One's wishes in regard to the garrison."

"I know, Michael. It's getting to be a bad habit with me with thinking that I am not capable of doing anything right that God asks of me. I also know, like you have been telling me all along, that I need to have more faith in myself and a little more self-esteem with regard to my attaining those capabilities."

"Yes, Mistress Kat. With that accomplished, you will find it easier to carry out the Almighty One's wishes, because you will see that you do have the needed ability to do just that."

"I really think you give me way too much credit, Michael. But I will agree with you for now. What other pertinent information do I need to know at this time, so that I will fully understand what's expected of me, and what I'm possibly up against? What's to become of us, since we now have a substitute capitol in Philadelphia and a makeshift government with the President pro tempore of the Senate now running the country, because he is next in line to do so according to the Constitution and the Presidential Succession Act of the Senate made into law in 1947? I had to look all that up, Michael, because I never would have guessed that position in a million years," chuckled Kat.

"Yes, Mistress Kat. I will answer your questions and I will give you all the information that the Almighty One relayed to me. As I said before, Romanolf Musva, the Antichrist, along with a spiritual hierarchy, who will himself spread lies to the masses, will both be very successful in fooling the majority of the populace into believing, who they claim him to be. Eventually, the ones who resist will be hunted down and forced to wear the beast's numbers on his or her person or face death. Man will betray each other either, because of their beliefs in the Antichrist, or because of fear of death if they don't. It's a no-win situation for mankind while living on this Earth, if they are not the true believers in the Almighty One. Only the faithful ones who become martyrs or survive the final days and stay true to the Almighty One, will be rewarded with eternal salvation."

"I get all of that, Michael. But I still don't understand my position in all of this."

"Patience, Mistress Kat. For it is very important for me to relay certain information first before I give you all the demands that the Almighty One expects that you and Mistress Maggie to follow. You see, the more you know about your greatest adversary, the better understanding you will gain on how to deal with him in your future. Remember what your son told you while in his youth, that when fighting a battle, the number one rule is to know your enemy?"

"Well, yes, I do remember that, Michael."

"And there is more that you should know. He is very cunning and will stop at nothing to obtain all the souls of the Almighty One's creation. That has been his revengeful goal all along: all of mankind's souls. It is a shame that mankind never learned to get along with each other, for war has never been the real answer due to the tirades of the previous rulers throughout the world toward each other. It has left misery and untold numbers of lives' lost in its wake, which is too great a price to pay when the end results will have solved nothing. But mankind does not know how to settle their differences any other way. History has proven that time and time again. What you must remember foremost, Mistress Kat, is that these two entities are not of human form, they only look like it. You must be steadfast and hardened with your determination to fight them. Show no mercy for they won't. It is not a game that you will be playing, until your time on this Earth is through, but you must continue to be strong in order to fulfill the Almighty One's dream for this world since he created it: faithful souls, who will have saved the right to join him as a member of his God-like-family in eternity. This is the true reason we have all existed since the creation. This is the true meaning of life, Mistress Kat."

"Wow, Michael! I have never heard it put quite like that, but since I know this all to be true, my attitude toward everything that has happened to me, and will continue to happen to me has certainly changed. He did really choose me, Michael, to do his bidding, for The End Time did He?"

"Yes, Mistress Kat. You are the chosen one for The End Time."

With the knowledge of all that Michael told her and the final understanding on Kat's part what was expected of her, she never waned again with her determination to see his final bidding through her accomplished, until the end of her life.

Kat and Maggie made one more trip to Scotland before they were to start their tour of the States and stayed longer than the norm, as they had to oversee the accomplishments made on the garrison and continue to recruit new personnel along with the swearing-in of allegiance ritual to their cause. She had hired very capable people from the beginning to be in charge of the overall operation, which proved true time and time again with each visit that they made, and the two sisters were now more confident in their capabilities in managing all the aspects for completion. Kat now had a clear vision of what was to be done on both fronts of the two countries, and had a renewed faith in herself, since her talk with Michael. "When faith is present, all things are achievable."

It was late spring in the year 2024. The entire complex was incased in the mountain range located in the Upper Highlands of Scotland near strategic waterways, roads, and plenty of forests to hide the terrains from an aerial view when hauling supplies. The finished project would measure close to twenty-five miles long by ten miles wide.

The work done on the garrison was unbelievable considering the amount of time that had passed since she and Maggie were there last. The entire first floor was completed with more than three-fourths of the second floor done and the start of the third floor already in progress. Over fifteen hundred people worked day and night to accomplish the results so far, but time was closing in on the opted deadline with little room to spare.

It was truly a massive undertaking considering the limited amount of time for its completion. As Kat and Maggie entered through the massive steel doors that served as the entrance, the installation of the intricate computer system and database, which would be the future brain of the

entire complex, would be installed shortly where they now stood to start their tour. Mathew, the head contractor-architect and ace carpenter, was to give them their final tour of the main complex only, for the entire tour would take a longer time than they had planned on since the complex was so vast in size. They had to allow for a final important meeting scheduled this afternoon with the Prime Minister to go over any loose ends or other pertinent information that need to be taken care of. A four-seated golf cart was used to transport the three around the massive corridors, which made up the major connections to the many rooms large and small that were the heart of the complex itself. Two of the cars, which would be part of the El Train System, stood parked off to their right. They resembled in looks and size of the smaller yellow school buses that were the trade mark of the school systems throughout the United States, except these had a metal pole on top connecting to an intricate power source of electrical devises similar to the old street cars that were a mainstay of San Francisco. This would be the transportation for the ten thousand or so people who would be the future residents and workers in the garrison.

The subterranean level held aqua ducts for water supply, a sewerage station to handle waste, and a sub-electrical station for all the electrical needs throughout. The El Train storage housing and depot were also situated on this level along with miles and miles of stored military equipment needed to run an army. A large stable with the capacity to house one thousand horses and equipment, along with a mid-size farm and butchery, finished off this level.

Kat and Maggie were shown blueprints and pictures of the typical one-bedroom apartments for single non-com men and women, and two-bedroom apartments for married couples with children. These housing units were situated at both ends of the mountain on the first level along with the huge room built exactly in the center to hold the data base and subsequent military objectives, which would be the heart of the entire operation. David's offices, along with other military offices and two large mess halls with adjoining kitchens for preparation of food on both sides, were situated around the database. The outer area consisted of everything that made up a small town: hospital, clinic, pharmacy, military police

department, fire department, grade school, high school, shopping mall, bakery, park, and small cafeterias located on all levels throughout the complex.

The second level consisted of two large community centers for gatherings, small library, theater, gym, workout facilities, and row apartments with one bedroom and efficiency apartments for both military and medical personnel.

The third floor roof consisted of large solar panels to catch the sun's rays needed for the two massive green houses extending almost the entire length of the garrison installed for the purpose of growing food. A large atrium in the center of the two greenhouses had a generous seating accommodation throughout and was sectioned off with large screening at intervals to give a more secluded atmosphere.

Yes, this truly was a massive undertaking, but a very necessary one, as this would be the heart of God's army fighting against the Antichrist, for many years to come and as long as it will take leading up to and part of Armageddon, and the return of the true Messiah, the Son of God.

This would be the last time Kat and Maggie would visit the garrison, for they now must continue with their commitment to God by touring the United States, so that He could preach to the masses through Kat. David left word for Kat and Maggie as to what needed to be done yet, as he too has been involved with the intermittent overseeing of the project, since he was stationed over in Ireland. He also has been recruiting members of his future army, and the preparations needed to insure that each one is a loyal follower of God and not the Antichrist. When his tour of duty in Ireland was completed, David moved into the unfinished garrison to oversee the final stages of work to be done, and to start the operation of running it. This included planning and implementing his ideas for setting up five main divisions of his future army throughout Scotland, Ireland, and England, with lesser army facilities stationed throughout Europe. He left a memo to Kat instructing her to remember to check for the mole on each recruited person, for it was so crucial to the success of his army: knowing that all the members were faithful to the cause.

It was early fall and Kat planned well for her strategy of touring the United States. She purchased an old Greyhound bus and made necessary adjustments, for the comfort of her and Maggie and accommodations for the driver's use. The whole idea of a bus was a good one, as it not only saved them the hassle of locating and renting motels, but to avoid the cost of those motels. She hired Fred, a retired police detective, ex-marine, and weekend racecar driver, whom she was well acquainted with, because he lived on her same block. His duties would be to do the driving and act as a lookout for suspicious behavior and basically a bodyguard at all of her speaking engagements. He lost his wife to cancer five years ago, and he never had children or close relatives to speak of only some distant cousins that he recalled so was more than willing to jump at the chance being offered to him by Kat. She mapped out a direct route through each state with instructions to use only major highways, not back roads of any kind. She knew distinctively, which cities and towns to speak at, and which ones to avoid and thus notified by mail the churches, civic centers, or the cities large enough to have a local TV station, requesting permission to speak there. She never really understood how she knew, but never questioned why. It was a huge undertaking, and one that they would not have been able to accomplish without recruiting the help of patrons from the Soup Kitchen, who were more than willing to help with the task of e-mailing permission slips throughout the entire country and keeping track of the organizations that returned those slips giving them their permission. With the hundreds of mailings sent out, all but a handful notified Kat by mail or phone that they would be happy with the opportunity for her to speak in their community. This gave her a renewed sense of self-worth, and the realization that just maybe she and Maggie could very well pull this whole thing off in the name of God. "Nothing ventured, nothing gained" was Kat's new motto to live by from now on.

On the advice from Fred, the two sisters each purchased a handgun for protection, and under his tutelage, they practiced handling the guns and shooting at targets at the place that they purchased their firearms. He also taught them the techniques that he learned of scanning the crowd and looking for anyone acting suspiciously. His rule of thumb dictated that anyone wishing to do harm to another, more times than not, would be

acting nervously in some way or form, such as moving from side to side, stepping in place, or even something as noticeable as biting their nails.

The sisters made sure that they kept in touch with Ellen, Maggie's friend, and the one who lined Kat up to meet with Beverly so many years ago, to keep them informed of what was going on in and around Milwaukee. This is how Kat found out the news of the passing of Beverly, shortly after they began their journey through the States. Kat had called Bev two weeks prior to their departure date to fill her in with the details of all that had transpired, since they saw each other last, and to send her an itinerary of all the dates, locations, and phone numbers where either she or Maggie could be reached. Her good friend and confidant would certainly be missed, as she was an exceptional part of Kat's life for all these years.

Kat and Maggie made sure that they listened to a cable news station on a nightly basis to keep them informed of what was going on in the States and the rest of the world also. This is where they originally learned that the Antichrist, Rudolph Musva, arrived in the United States shortly after they had left. In less than three months, he managed to talk Congress into foregoing the election process and name him Commander-in-Chief with the overwhelming approval of the American people. He was now President and had the authority to do as he pleases with his reign of terror just starting to take form. He needed the greatest Super Power in the World: the United States. He knew that this was where the largest and best-trained military existed and had access to untold wealth at his disposal. All government agencies ceased to exist as there was no need for any of them, because he was now the undisputed ruler with his own ideas on how he was going to have complete control here and then eventually throughout the rest of the world. Quite an accomplishment already for someone so young and he was only thirty-two years of age, born into a wealthy family from Warsaw, Poland. He had a vast list of academic accomplishments in his name, one of which was a Rhodes Scholar. He was fluent in speaking seven foreign languages, traveled extensively throughout Europe—his playground—and knew the Middle East like the back of his hand. Not a bad testimony for someone so evil who chose December 25 as the day of his inauguration.

"How ironic! Evidently the day of his rebirth in his eyes," surmised Kat. She was glad that she had God on her side.

The threesome were into their three month time period and closing in on Christmas. It was almost non-stop from Chicago, the first city on their itinerary. They zigzagged up and down the Mississippi Valley states, over to the Ohio Valley area, to the southern states, into the eastern coast States, and on up the eastern coast. They continued through New Hampshire, Vermont, the lower section of Maine, across to upstate New York, where they now were located. They decided to stop and spend Christmas Day in a quaint little town called Burlington, where the main street was so cleverly and festively decorated for the holidays. They would leave the day after Christmas, and head to Montreal, Canada where they were scheduled to meet with their contact, who would help them escape the States at a later date in time.

They left Montreal heading east then south until they came to North Dakota. They then zigzagged throughout the western States over to Washington, Oregon, and California where they veered into an easterly direction traveling back and forth entirely throughout the west and southwestern States until they reached Missouri. From there, they went north to Minnesota and finally back to Wisconsin.

"Well, Maggie. Another two hundred and sixty miles to go and we then should be home. We've been on the road close to six months, and I don't know about you, but I'll sure be glad to get off my butt and get my feet back on solid ground again," stated Kat.

"Am I missing something here? I thought that that's what we have been doing for the last six months: walking on solid ground. Actually, forty-eight states of solid ground," laughed Maggie.

"I meant, Milwaukee ground," chuckled Kat. "Maggie, I just thought of something. Aren't there fifty states? Oh God, don't tell me we have to go back out and cover two more?"

"You're pulling my leg, aren't you?" questioned Maggie, but she saw the expression on Kat's face, which didn't reveal any indication one way

or the other. This left her wondering, until Kat responded with, "Yeah. I have air time scheduled for both Alaska and Hawaii."

"You know, Kat. Thinking back at the entire overall experience, it's when we started to become well known due to the news coverage that we received, that was the turning point of the negative actions toward us."

"Yeah, I know. The longer we stayed out on the road, the scarier it was starting to become, even though only a handful of our rallies turned ugly, and became chaotic and almost out of control."

"Thank God we had Fred with us. Can you imagine what the two of us would have done on our own?" asked Maggie.

"Run like hell would be my guess," chuckled Kat. "Maggie, what's wrong?"

"Nothing."

"I can tell by the look on your face that you're thinking about it. It's over and done with. You've got to get it out of your mind."

"That'll never happen. I'll remember it until the day I die, because I almost lost you."

"Maggie, it was a flesh wound. Nothing more."

"What I can't understand is why he shot you."

"There's a lot of crazies out there, and this guy was the cream of the crop with a lousy aim," laughed Kat.

"That's not funny, Kat."

"The cops told us he had a history of mental disorders most of his life, and he didn't agree with what I was saying. Simple as that. I certainly don't hold it against him. He evidently couldn't help what he did."

The incident the sisters were referring to happened at a community center on the outskirts of Albuquerque, New Mexico. As the three pulled up at the Baptist church where Kat was to speak, a crowd numbering around twenty-five people was hovering outside with two fire engines stationed in the side parking lot. As Kat, Maggie, and Fred approached, a gentleman from the crowd came up to them and recognizing Kat from a picture and item of her in the local newspaper, and introduced himself as Charles Mann, pastor of the church. Upon questioning by Maggie on how the fire started, Pastor Mann said, "After talking with the fire chief, a preliminary investigation showed that it may have started in the kitchen, because that is where the thicker black smoke was billowing from. The fire damage is minimal, but the smoke damage is quite extensive because of the grease, I'm afraid. We certainly won't be able to hold your rally here, Ms. O'Brien."

"I understand. Would you like to cancel completely? Because if you do, I'll certainly understand," replied Kat.

"No, no please. We have been advertising your speaking engagement for almost a month now, and from the verbal responses that I have heard, there will be a numerous amount of people in attendance. It will be very disappointing for a lot of them if I would agree to a cancellation. We have a community center about two miles down the road that we can use instead of the church. I already made arrangements with the director after calling him when I saw for myself that the fire was completely out and that no one was seriously hurt. So you see, Ms. O'Brien, everything has been taken care of, and your rally can go on as planned."

"There's just one thing, Pastor Mann. How is everyone going to know where the rally is going to be held, or if it was canceled?"

"We have almost two hours before you are scheduled to speak, and I have already notified the three local TV and two of our many radio stations of the change. Plus, of course, word of mouth. This is a tight-knit community, and the word will travel fast. And besides, I left a note on the front and side door," chuckled Pastor Mann. "So you see, it's just fine."

A fleeting, nagging feeling left Kat doubtful, but she failed to see the warning, if you want to call it that, and agreed to the change. Even before the sound equipment was set up on the stage, and a piano was brought in to replace the church organ, and to accompany the church chorus in the singing of chosen hymns, the crowd was already starting to fill the chairs faster than they were being set up. Kat, Maggie, Fred, and Pastor Mann enjoyed a cup of coffee with a quiet, peaceful interlude in the office of the director, before the most frightful incident of their long journey was about to take place. Kat did not realize until later that, because she deviated from God's scheduled plans, she put herself, Maggie and Fred into a real life-threatening situation.

She was almost finished with her sermon and would then have an open forum, for the members of the audience to ask questions, just as she did with all her other rallies when saying the final words of, "Will you join me, your Heavenly Father, with my arms wide open to receive you in my kingdom as a righteous one against the Antichrist?" As she raised her arms in gesture to mimic the open arms part of her sermon, she heard a swishing sound followed by what sounded like breaking glass. Just then, a bullet tore through her left shoulder, felled her on the spot, and embedded itself into the back of a mirror hanging on the wall about twenty feet behind her, shattering glass in all directions. As Kat lay bleeding on the wooden floor, total chaos ensued. She could hear screams and chairs being toppled to the floor as the crowd scrambled to the exits. She then went unconscious.

Later on that evening as Kat was recovering from the surgery to repair the damage to her shoulder, she awakened to find Maggie, Fred, Pastor Mann, and a portly gentleman who looked to be in his early fifties talking with a doctor in her room. Maggie was the first one to speak, saying, "Oh Kat, you're awake. Good. How do you feel?"

"Don't know yet, Maggie," mumbled Kat, who felt like she had a mouth full of cotton and sounded like Marlon Brando from *The Godfather*. "Water. I need water."

"Doctor," called Maggie. "Can my sister have some water?"

"Ah, I see you're awake, Ms. O'Brien. How do you feel?" questioned Dr. Stone.

Kat could barely speak, so she just nodded her head *yes* as Maggie helped her sip some water from a glass and held the straw for her.

"This is Detective Williams from the Albuquerque Police Department who is covering your case. Do you feel up to answering any of his questions or would you like for all of us to clear out of here, so that you can get some rest?" questioned Dr. Stone.

"Stay," answered Kat in a clearer voice due to the water that she was drinking. "Whatever you gave me for pain is working, because I don't feel a thing. I'll be all right now."

Detective Williams went on to tell everyone in the room that the man who shot Kat was forty-two, never married, a loner, and had a history of mental disorders. He had seen and heard Kat speak on a special segment on *INN* earlier this month and hated her from the start. He never would have shot her inside the church, but when he discovered that she was going to speak at the community center instead, he grabbed his gun and had every intention of killing her.

"I would have to say that the Man upstairs was really watching over you, or you are one extremely lucky lady, Ms. O'Brien. Because of the movement of your arms extending upward and out and your head at the time tilting forward, those two movements saved you from a direct hit to your head."

After a few days spent in the hospital and another two days at one of the top hotels in Albuquerque, courtesy of the city, the threesome were back on the road again. Detective Williams told them that he would keep in touch and would inform them when they would have to return in order to testify at the trial against her shooter.

"Kat, Doctor Stone said that you would have been hit in the head if not for the position of your arms and head at the time. Why was your head bent so far forward?" Maggie asked, puzzled.

"There was a little boy about four sitting on his mother's lap directly in front of me. He had been waving at me as if to get my attention and was trying to say something to me, which I couldn't hear or understand. That is when I moved my head forward to see if I could hear him better with what he was trying to tell me, and that's when it happened. When you come right down to it, that little boy actually saved my life."

Only a handful of incidents, except for the shooting, were possibly life threatening, if it were not for the quick action from Fred. The real danger most of the time was the weather conditions that they encountered, having to deal with flooding, tornadoes, and snowstorms aplenty. The threesome still continued to preach the Gospel of God throughout Illinois, Minnesota, Iowa, and Michigan with broadcasts from the local Milwaukee stations transmitted to Alaska and Hawaii. Kat was invited to appear many times over the next year on *INN* and the other two popular news networks televised over the internet along with invitations to speak extensively in Europe, Australia, New Zealand, and China. It was starting to get dangerous for the threesome, as the more popular the Antichrist became, the more threats were made to them. Thus, it was time to return to the States and stay there for now.

Because of a lesson well-learned at Albuquerque, Kat never again strayed from God's future specific wishes of her by following his itinerary, not hers.

During the summer of the year 2027, the Antichrist continued to do a weekly broadcast of his State of the Union address to the people in order to keep them informed of his strides in ending World War III. He commandeered all broadcasting facilities throughout the United States and allowed only scenes of peaceful settings to be shown on television stations nation wide. These were supposedly true stories that were testimonies from his loyal followers on how wonderful their lives had changed for the good. This propaganda tactic helped to make his followers believe he was truly the messiah. He related that everything else was just wonderful and that his plans for ending World War III were almost complete and that peace would reign forever as long as he was in charge, and it did in a few months. In reality, more than three-fourths of the major cities in

North America were destroyed or left almost in ruins, because of Kat's predicted catastrophic events. And not by any major fighting, because his army fought overseas in Europe and the Middle East and not on United States soil. There was nothing "wonderful" about anything, anyway you looked at it. By now, he had taken complete control of all branches of the military, Wall Street, NASA (with instructions to forego any future space missions), and build state-of-the-art weapons of mass-destruction for his future use. He closed all banks and confiscated the monies and started a voucher system for everyone who were true to him. Poor and middle class became words of the past, as he provided a roof over everyone's head, food on the table, and a nice weekly paycheck in accordance with their job title. Yes, life was good according to Mr. Musva, and he was revered by most. That was the case for his faithful followers, who proved their loyalty by accepting the numbers of the beast on their person: a chip surgically implanted on the top side of one's left hand or individual numbers 666 implanted on three fingers of the right hand; the choice was left up to the individual.

He emptied out all prisons and gave the prisoners the choice to be his personal henchmen with special privileges for their services for as long as they lived or death if they refused. Needless to say, he had a well-established killing machine for the sole purpose to hunt down and force, or kill anyway they chose to, the one's who had yet to accept him for whatever reason. For in his eyes, there was no justifiable reason for not giving him their allegiance. For them, their lives were bleak and worsened on a daily basis. The non-believers also had to fight the elements the best way that they could as their homes were confiscated, and they were now left to the streets. Scrounging for food was done on a daily basis, as was hiding in constant fear of being caught. Trust was another word from the past and not practiced anymore for, as the Bible stated, mankind was now turning against each other: father against son, husband against wife, brother against sister, and the list went on. These poor souls stayed too long in their beloved America. They were now most likely to be captured and killed, as the underground railroad set up by some of Kat's followers two years ago, had become known to the Antichrist, and destroyed as recent as a few months ago.

Kat and Maggie were not exempt from any of the atrocities either, for when they had to sneak back into the United States with returning from Europe, they learned that their mother was taken away and killed. Their brothers, Robert and Daniel, who had a chance to get away with their families but chose to stay behind and fight with other members of the underground railroad, were also killed. Kat and Maggie's homes had been burned to the ground, and nothing was left for them but the clothes on their backs and their safe haven in the Soup Kitchen basement. It was all boarded up on the outside to make it look abandoned. They entered through a tunnel dug by volunteers years ago. It would only be a matter of time before they were eventually discovered. Musva knew that he could not do them harm, because of God's divine protection of his worse adversary, Kat, but that did not mean that he couldn't have them arrested and put in prison to rot. They were now on his "most-wanted" list of fugitives and must now find an alternative escape route out of the United States via Canada to Scotland where David was in command of his army and was stationed at the garrison. The Antichrist was after them with a vengeance, because of the souls who turned to God, instead of him throughout the world, because of Kat's speeches. He blamed her for all of it, for his objective was to have all the souls that God created, nothing less.

All airports throughout the United States were heavily guarded and all flights in and out of each state and in and out of the country were searched thoroughly, as were ports of entry to all waterways throughout, large and small. The southern border to Mexico and northern border to Canada were heavily guarded as well. It would be almost impossible to get through without detection.

A lot of connections and plans were made by Kat with their tour of the United States, because she knew that this would happen to her, Maggie, and Fred through Michael. The three were not exempt from any of the tragedies taking place now and all around them and all over the world, until they reached the safety of the garrison.

After three weeks of hiding, the intense search for them started to wane somewhat, and the due date was now upon them to make their

escape to Montreal. Kat, Maggie, and Fred left in the dead of night and crawled through the tunnel hidden in the basement to an opening in the nearby park that was heavily disguised by a wooded area in which a car was waiting for them. It was an exact replica of the minivans used by the Antichrist's police force and also equipped with a siren. It was stocked with plenty of food, water, stored gasoline, maps, guns and ammo, mechanical hardware, blankets, pillows, and toiletries so that nothing had to be purchased and possibly exposing their whereabouts. Each wore exact replicas of the uniforms and each had fake identification with picture as verification that they were part of that police force. Their underground contacts did a wonderful job of supplying the threesome with the necessary tools for their planned escape to Canada.

The Antichrist had no worries if it was just Kat and Maggie that he was trying to track down, but he knew from his informants that Fred Kramer, a highly trained ex-Marine and ex-police detective, was helping them to escape. That is why it was so imperative to find out something about their whereabouts, which left him wondering if they already made it out of the country, because they had plenty of time to do it by now. Little did he know that they had just started their perilous journey to Scotland.

Hoping that the Antichrist would think that they would take a direct route into Canada, which would be from Wisconsin into northern Michigan, they went south instead to Gary, Indiana, with Fred being the first one to start out driving. It took them longer than the allotted time with interstate driving, because they chose to take the lesser-traveled roadways all the way to Niagara Falls, New York. Kat took over driving then Maggie, who was behind the wheel when they reached the Falls after approximately seven hundred miles and fourteen hours of driving. The plan was to leave from there and try and escape over the border somewhere in the vicinity of Montreal, which was still another four hundred miles away. So far, "lady luck" was with them, for they only encountered two police vehicles that were heading in opposite directions in all that time, and they tooted their horns in recognition.

As the threesome stood at the railing overlooking the Falls, each was into their own thoughts as this would be the last time that they would

see their beloved America. A good size crowd was gathering, which was normal on a daily basis, because this was one of the most toured and beloved sights in the United States.

Maggie removed the glove from her right hand, so that she could retrieve a Kleenex from her coat pocket and dab at the tears that were starting to form in her eyes. As she looked up, she caught a young woman staring at her with a look that was indiscernible, as she then continued to stare at Maggie's hand. With a foreboding feeling, Maggie too looked at her own hand, and to her horror she realized the reason the woman was continuing to stare so intently: her fingernails were painted bright red, and they were very long and well manicured. The Antichrist's policemen, along with the women, had a reputation of blatant brutality, so Maggie caught on immediately and knew the police women would certainly not be allowed to have nor want the well-manicured hands that she just exposed to this woman. Maggie, with a nonchalant poke to Kat's side, gazed at her right hand for Kat to catch on. Kat, in turn, whispered to Fred and the three took their leave immediately. As Maggie looked back at the young woman before they entered their vehicle, she could see that she was surrounded by several people and all were actively celebrating something. As they drove away with Fred behind the wheel, Maggie was the first one to speak with, "Oh my God, I'm so sorry that this happened. This is all my fault. What are we going to do now?" Maggie asked, with a distraught and fearful look on her face.

"Maggie, calm down. It's not your fault. We both have long nails. It never entered my mind either. Besides, you were the one that reminded me not to wear perfume or hairspray. It's something we overlooked and can't do anything about now," responded Kat.

"Hopefully they all are part of a wedding party, and that woman will be too engrossed and preoccupied to really analyze what she saw until later or not at all," suggested Maggie, not really believing what she just said.

"That's a good possibility," responded Fred. "My guess, though, is that she may be too fearful to get involved at all and will forget the whole thing."

"What now?" asked Kat. "Are we still going to try and cross at Montreal?"

"No, I personally don't think we should. There's just too many of Musva's goon squad around here. I think we should go with our alternative plan and head to Maine and cross over there with the hope that it's not as heavily guarded as the Montreal location must be if this is any indication," surmised Fred, as he veered easterly from his northern location.

"I agree," added Kat.

"Whatever you say," responded Maggie.

With Kat's earlier calculations, the distance from Niagara Falls to their destination of Topsfield, Maine, was approximately seven hundred and eighty-two miles. But as before, the threesome would be traveling the lesser-traveled roads and it would probably take them approximately twelve hours of almost non-stop driving if the weather conditions were in their favor. The police radio was listened to intently now for any reference to the three fugitives scrambling to the Canadian border in hopes of eluding the Antichrist.

The three were approximately five hundred miles from the Falls with Kat driving now and Maggie in the passenger seat and Fred in the back sleeping, when the flash came over their radio. Their cover was blown, but the information had them possibly holed-up somewhere between the Falls with Montreal as their cross-over point, because they were spotted going north from the Falls by an onlooker.

"Fred," stated Maggie.

"I'm awake and heard it. Kat, take that next road to the right. I think the sign said Highway Z, and pull over by that row of trees," ordered Fred.

As he exited the back seat, Kat turned to Maggie and said, "I don't know about you, Maggie, but I can't take much more of this with not knowing if the next turn in the bend could be a road block just waiting for us. I hate that bastard Musva with a passion for taking away our country and

our God given freedom to live in it. And, if we make it out of this alive, I swear that I will do everything in my power to make his life a living hell," scowled Kat.

"I know, Honey, I know," responded, Maggie, with a soothing voice. "I don't think that would bother him though, Kat. For that's where I think he likes being in. Hell, that is. He's been there so frickin' long by now that I assume he likes it," laughed Maggie, which left her unable to finish the rest of her sentence.

"Oh, Maggie. I needed that," laughed Kat. "Thank you."

"What's so funny, ladies?" questioned Fred as he re-entered the backseat.

"Just some funny chit-chat between two sisters," answered Maggie.

"I suggest we all take a breather here for a moment and have something to eat, drink, and go over our plans for when we hit the border," informed Fred.

As Kat exited the driver's seat and Maggie was on her way around the van, as it was her turn to drive, Fred intercepted her and stated, "Maggie, I know you really don't care to drive at night, so why not let me take over?" Fred suggested.

"But Fred, you haven't had all that much sleep, and besides, it's only fair that I take my turn," responded Maggie.

"That's all right. I'll be fine, Maggie."

"Okay, if you're sure that that's what you want to do, Fred."

He had an ulterior motive for taking over the driving, for even though they still had close to four hundred miles to go, he wanted to be behind the wheel if any trouble ensued. And it did, about a hundred miles down the road. He faced very little traffic since he took over driving, which was a plus, but now a siren rang out and headlights overtook the vehicle as Fred began to pull off to the side of the road.

"Get down on the floor, Maggie, and cover up with that blanket. And Kat, follow my lead and stay cool," ordered Fred.

Fred had taken out his revolver and placed it next to his right side on the seat, and hid it from view under his coat. He now rolled down the window.

"Evening," said the patrolman. "Can I see some identification? Where are you headeded this time of night?" he questioned, as he shined his flashlight in Kat's direction and circled it around the backseat to see if there were any other passengers.

"Evening," responded Fred and Kat in unison as they both handed over their identification along with their badges.

It was hard to determine if they were going to pull this off as Fred couldn't see the reaction on the officer's face, because of the flashlight when looking over their identifications. He put his right hand on his revolver again just in case he had to use it.

"As you can see, officer, by my badge, I am a special agent with the police force and my partner and I are heading due north. After persuading an informant, nicely, we were told that the three fugitives will cross over at Edmundston, New Brunswick," explained, Fred, with a laugh in reference to the persuasion of the informant.

The officer laughed in return, knowing full well what Fred was referring to, but then proceeded to the back of their vehicle to check the license plate while shining his flashlight extensively throughout the back of their SUV. Fred turned to Kat and whispered, "I don't think he's buying any of this, but just a warning to you both: if he tries to go for his vehicle to radio in for help, I will have to kill him," replied Fred.

"Step out of the car, now! And you on the other side of the seat, freeze, and don't move," ordered the officer as his gun came into view. He was directly in front of Fred's door with his gun aimed at Fred through the open window.

Fred, without hesitation, made a move to open the door in hopes of averting the officer's attention, while with his right hand, he grabbed his gun and pointed it at the officer's chest and fired. He was dead before he hit the ground.

Kat and Maggie both were too stunned and taken aback with fear, as they watched Fred turn off the lights to both vehicles and drag the body of the officer to the front of their vehicle.

"Come on, ladies. Snap out of it!" yelled Fred, as he opened the backdoor and helped Maggie out so that she could get some fresh air, and then ordered Kat to do the same.

With Kat and Maggie still in a daze, Fred dragged the lifeless body back to his vehicle and hoisted him up into the front seat, started the vehicle, and lay him across the steering wheel. He then took a screwdriver from the glove compartment and proceeded to exchange the license plates.

"Kat and Maggie, I'm going to need your help," informed Fred, as he turned the wheels to the right in the direction of the gully. "I'll steer, but I need the two of you to push as I keep steering so that he goes over that embankment straight ahead and into that gully."

Kat and Maggie did as Fred ordered, and pushed the vehicle about twenty yards to the embankment, and watched, as the vehicle plunged into a gully and landed about thirty feet below the roadway.

As Fred sped away, he took a quick look at the two tear-stained faces of the two women that he grew to love and said, "I'm sorry that this had to happen, but this is only one incident of the many things that may happen to us before this nightmare is all over. It was necessary for me to kill him. It's important to me for you both to understand that," Fred implored.

Kat looked at Maggie and said, "We do understand, Fred. It's just that it was such a shock to both of us-the whole incident, I mean-but we'll be okay. Right, Maggie?" stammered Kat.

"Yes, Kat," answered Maggie, barely above a whisper.

Not a lot of conversation took place for the next hundred miles or so, because each was engrossed with their own thoughts as to the tragedy that just unfolded before their very eyes. *Fred was right, though*, surmised Kat, as did Maggie. *It was a necessity to take another human's life to protect theirs.*

As he continued driving, Fred went over and over in his mind a plan to get Kat and Maggie across the border unharmed, as he knew that there would be gunfire in their attempt to cross over with ramming the stiles with their vehicle. He didn't want to take that chance of the women being fired upon and possibly being hit by a stray bullet. With that in mind, Fred started whistling a tune to help lighten up the atmosphere a little and, in turn, to help Kat and Maggie to regain their perspective of the here and now. It worked. As they joined in with singing the words to the whistled tune, they reminisced about all that took place between the three of them from the time that they hired Fred to drive for them, which by now, seemed ages ago.

As they neared the crossover point within a mile or so of the border at Topsfield, Maine, Fred pulled over and stopped, turned off the dim lights, and took out his binoculars to check the border crossing. There were three guards standing outside by the upturned stile, smoking. Even with dawn at least three hours away, and this was a small town, he figured that there should be more guards, unless there were more in the small shanty station. He had to know for sure before they made their move to cross, so he turned to Kat and Maggie and ordered, "Stay here and wait for me to get back. Don't move out of this vehicle for any reason, understood?" ordered Fred.

Maggie was the first to respond with, "Right," while Kat nodded her head in agreement.

As the two sisters watched Fred lurk into the night and go out of sight, Maggie turned to Kat and asked, "Are you as scared as I am, Kat?"

"Yes, Maggie. I am. But we had better put fear behind us and get prepared for whatever is about to take place. Got your gun ready, Maggie?" asked Kat.

"Yeah, right here," answered Maggie, showing Kat the position of her pistol in her right hand and ready to be cocked at a moments notice.

"Good. And Maggie, I love you," interjected Kat.

Maggie caught on to the meaning of Kat's words with her own interpretation of, "if we don't make this, I just wanted to tell you," and in answer said, "I love you too, Kat."

Just then Kat saw movement off to the left, which startled her, but it was Fred returning. He opened the door and jumped into the front seat and informing them, "We came at the right time, ladies, with it being Saturday night, because there's five more guards in that shanty playing cards and drinking beer. Good ol' Musva would have them shot on sight if he knew," laughed Fred, then continued to tell Kat and Maggie of his plans. "I want the two of you to walk with your guns drawn at all times towards that shanty. Stay low and watch your step, because it's pitch black out there. I'll give you a forty minute head start so set your watches now; then I'm going to turn on my bright lights, rev the motor and speed right into the stile and crash through it. Hopefully all of them will jump into those three parked vehicles and chase after me, and that is when you make your move and run as fast as you can to the woods, and hide until you think it is safe to meet up with our contact.

"Any questions?" asked Fred as he held both women and kissed them on their foreheads. "I don't like this plan, Fred," responded Maggie.

"Me either. Why can't we all go together?" questioned Kat.

"Because it's too dangerous, and this way, they will be too intent on chasing me and give you the chance to get away," answered Fred. "Please, ladies, we don't have time to stand here and argue. I'll be alright, I promise."

With that said, Kat and Maggie had no choice but to follow Fred's instructions, and each in turn kissed him one more time before they left.

As Fred watched the two walk away into the night, he took time to contemplate his moves and to realize that his chances of escaping were pretty few, for they would certainly aim for his tires, or may get lucky, and shoot him, instead. But he had to do it this way and lead them away as far as he could. In the next breath, he said a prayer and said good-bye to two dear women, who became like sisters to him and the family that he never had. He then hit the bright lights, reved the motor, and headed toward the guards, hoping to hit all three in the process.

As Kat and Maggie approached the shanty, they could hear laughter coming from inside, and in the next instant, a crash, gunfire, and chaos taking place all around them. Fred made it through the two stiles among the gunfire, and gunned the motor with the three vehicles in hot pursuit, just as he figured would happen. As the two sisters watched, they took a deep breath and sigh of relief, as they stood from their crouched position behind the shanty and walked to the front. As Maggie lagged behind somewhat, because of a low hanging branch, Kat was the first one to reach the entrance. As she did, a figure appeared behind her with a gun pointed to her head and a voice rang out, "Freeze, and drop the gun."

Kat, in a startled state, complied. Before her gun hit the ground, a shot rang out and the guard lay dead on the ground behind her, because Maggie had no qualms in doing it, and thus shot him in the side of his head. The two beleaguered sisters took off running for the woods for cover and safety.

Fred was approaching ten miles according to his odometer and was far enough ahead of his trackers when he decided to turn around, cut his lights, and wait for them to catch up, which he hoped was soon, for they did get lucky and shot him in the right side of his chest. He was bleeding profusely, but he was able to stop it to some degree with the towel that was left lying on the front seat by either Kat or Maggie. This act on his part brought for a split second their images to his mind. With the headlights fast approaching him, he waited for another second before he turned on his bright lights, reved the motor, and with a sigh and a grin, plowed through the caravan, leaving nothing but pure carnage in his wake, and all four vehicles became engulfed in flames.

Kat and Maggie sat hidden amongst the dense forest and stayed there for over two hours and waited as Fred told them to, praying that he would show up at any minute. It was then that Kat retrieved her small flashlight from her coat pocket and flashed it into the cold, bleak sky at fifteen-minute intervals as a guide to their whereabouts for their contact.

Within an hour and a half, both sisters could hear a brushing noise, and the neighs of a horse getting closer. With trepidation, but also with hope that this was their rescuer, a voice rang out. "Katherine O'Brien, it's me, Bonnie Prince Charles."

The two exhaled a sigh of relief, as they recognized the right code used, signaling them that they were safe and saw them rescued in the clearing on horseback and reigning in two more horses behind him.

"My name is Charlie, ladies, and I will be guiding you to safety."

Kat and Maggie refused to leave as they planned to stay for as long as it took Fred to find them. This prompted Charlie to tell them that he came upon a fiery crash about ten miles away, and that no one could have survived it. Kat and Maggie were devastated by the news. They grew to love Fred, and the three had been through so much together and were so close to escaping. They wanted Fred to join them in the safety of the garrison, but that no longer was going to be the case.

The three fled on horseback weaving in and out among the trees until they reached some hills and headed for the other side when they heard a helicopter off in the distance but moving away from them. Charlie knew the Antichrist would suspect that all three fugitives died in the fiery crash that he came upon in his search for the two women, but caution was still needed to be observed, until they were finally behind the giant steel doors of the garrison, for it was only a matter of time that the carnage would be discovered, and also, that there was only one fugitive body to be found. With dawn already approaching and the three riding at a fast pace for what seemed an eternity but only a little over a half-hour, Charlie raised his hand and slowed to a stop. "We're almost to McAdam, so we can now slow down and give the horses a rest. I have an old friend there named,

Burly, and we can stay at his cabin for as long as needed and then take my land rover to my place in Sussex."

With the sun shining over Burly's cabin, which was located about nine miles on the other side of McAdam, it was a glorious sight to Kat and Maggie, as they were exhausted and chilled to the bone.

The three sat at a homemade solid oak table placed in front of the fireplace, and Charlie offered them a cup of freshly brewed coffee and each a blanket to cover themselves until the heat took the chill from their bodies.

"Where are we, Charlie?" asked Maggie.

"McAdam, Ma'am."

"No, I mean, are we still in the United States or Canada?" asked Maggie, which was a very reasonable question, because they really didn't know for sure when they left the shanty and told which way to go by Fred, that it really was the right direction that they fled to in the midst of all the confusion.

"You're safe for now in New Brunswick, Canada, Ma'am," answered Charlie.

"This man named, Burly, who is so very kind to let us use his cabin, where is he now?" questioned Kat.

"Probably been out hunting since first light, Ma'am. Ol' Burly lives off the land just like his father did and his father before him, and that includes hunting for his own food. I suspect he'll be coming in anytime soon now, ma'am," informed Charlie.

Kat and Maggie got their second wind after warming up, but mostly because they both had three cups of coffee by now, and sat discussing with Charlie the route that they would take from here to Sussex, New Brunswick, where Charlie lived in a cabin on the other side of the Caledonia Hills.

It was going on two hours since they arrived when they heard the door open and in walked a man, which they both assumed was Burly, and who fit his name to a tee, as he had to be all of six feet eight inches tall and built like Paul Bunyan. They expected Babe, his blue ox, to walk in behind his master at any minute. The all-imposing man now walking through the doorway turned out to be a real pussy cat in Kat and Maggie's eyes, as he handed each of them a bouquet of beautiful wildflowers that he picked just for them. He couldn't do enough for them while they stayed the three days enjoying every minute of his kind demeanor and listening to him tell tall tales of his Scottish ancestry.

When the time came for the three to leave for Charlie's cabin, Kat asked Burly one more time to join them and stay with them at the safety of the garrison.

"Thank you kindly, Lass, but I no' leave my homeland. These is my roots and I die here if must be, but I no' leave because of him. But God speed to you both nice lassies and Burly will never forget ye."

Kat and Maggie hugged and said their good-byes to a gentle giant, whom they would never see again, but would never forget.

Charlie, like Burly, knew the entire New Brunswick province and surrounding Canadian provinces like the back of his hand. He and his ancestors before him settled in this same area more than two hundred and fifty years ago.

According to Charlie, their journey would take them another two-hour drive to his cabin outside of Sussex with the Caledonia Hills as his backyard. His description of the beauty came nowhere near the true breathtaking scene that they encountered when they pulled into Charlie's long driveway to his cabin in the woods. As he opened the door, an envelope that was shoved under it, appeared on the floor before them. Kat and Maggie learned it was from Charlie's contact, and that the Calypso was waylaid at St. Johns, New Foundland, seeking refuge from a tropical storm out in the Atlantic Ocean. The delay would take them at least another day and a half to reach Tor Bay. With this news of a delay, Charlie estimated with the five-hour trip to Tor Bay in his land rover, they should

leave his place by no later than at 5:00 P.M. on Thursday and rendezvous with the Calypso between at 10:00 P.M. and 11:00 P.M. on Thursday night in a little known inlet between Thor Bay and Canso, Nova Scotia.

Charlie was a no-nonsense-man with a heart of gold and a real stickler for details and had Kat and Maggie parked and waiting for the Calypso to moor.

Maggie could barely wait another second in anticipation of seeing her youngest son, Chad, who she had not seen in over three years, and was the skipper of the large Schooner. Her wait only lasted another fifteen minutes when the Calypso came into view and moored fifteen yards from where they were standing. Chad ran down the lowered plank into his mother's waiting arms and lifted her up and twirled her around, as Maggie let the frustration, anger, fear and of the pent-up emotions of these harrowing tragedies flow in the form of tears. He cradled his loving mother in his arms and when her sobs began to wane and she finally looked up, her son had a look on his face that made all the earlier dangers just drift away. He then hugged his aunt Kat, and kissed her on the cheek and shook hands with Charlie. He offered him money, which Charlie refused, saying, "I did it all for two brave ladies, and for the love of my God and country. God bless all of you, for you will certainly need him with what lies ahead for all of you."

After saying their good-byes to Charlie and thanking him for his kindness, the two sisters bordered the Calypso. Maggie would be fine, but Kat, who hated water and would probably be sick the rest of their journey, didn't care, as she and her sister were now safe and on their way to a new life in a foreign land. But they would be with their loved ones continuing their work for God at the garrison, the reason why all of this was happening.

Main Command Post

Somewhere in the Highlands of Scotland

Late Fall, 2027

General David was in his office, which consisted of one of many bunkers that were built below a mountain range somewhere in northern Scotland. He and five of his top commanders were studying a large map that was hanging from one wall that pinpointed the strategic locations where his divided army would set up command posts throughout Europe.

Each commander had a total of ten thousand men deployed under his command, and was then divided into battalions with a fighting force of five hundred men, leaving the total number of battalions of each commander at twenty.

David called this meeting to discuss his temporary plan to divide one of the battalions again into a company with a force of 250 men per camp. One hundred and twenty-five of the men would form into a separate company and go on a raid against one of the Antichrist's outposts, return to their camp, and then the second company of one hundred and twenty-five men would move out to destroy another enemy outpost in the same region. This plan would mean less men and more hit-and-run raids—which was David's line of defense—with an officer who was highly trained in every aspect of combat techniques leading each company.

"It's not going to work, General," said Commander Scott Chase, commander of ten thousand infantry.

"I agree with Scott," inserted Commander Charles Rawson. "We're spreading ourselves too thin."

"Look, Gentlemen," retaliated David, "Our goal in fighting this bastard has to be divide and conquer, hit hard and withdraw. We have to catch his forces off-guard, and we can only do that with more raids and with fewer men. A battalion of five hundred men coming over a hill wouldn't be real difficult to detect. We want to catch them by surprise, like I said, not give them notification that we're on our way and giving them time to prepare a counter attack."

"I agree with the General" said Commander Joseph Owen. "Keep the enemy busy trying to figure out where and when we will strike again."

"What about you, John? Where do you stand on this?" inquired David.

"I'm all for the hit hard and withdraw," answered Commander John Connor.

"And you, Simon?"

"I also agree, but what I want to know is how long each company of two hundred and fifty men should set up camp before moving out permanently so as not to be detected?" inquired Commander Simon Chandler.

"Any ideas, Gentlemen?" asked David. After a lull, he said, "I want input from each one of you on every detail even if you think it is only a minute one. It's important that we agree on everything."

"A month?" asked Commander Owen.

"Too long," replied Commander Chase.

"Then what would you consider an appropriate amount of time?" questioned David of Scott.

"Three weeks, tops."

"C'mon, Scott. Three weeks? Won't work. Some of those passes that will be taken are in heavy duty, treacherous, and sometimes snow-covered terrains. You can't expect a force of one hundred and twenty-five men to travel those conditions, hit the enemy, turn around and return to camp, and move out again, all in a matter of three weeks. Especially, if it takes a week of travel there and a week back to camp or maybe even longer," argued Commander Owen.

"Scott, I agree with Joe. The two companies of one hundred and twenty-five men are at their appointed camps. One company moves out and returns, and then, and only then, will the second company move out. One company will be in camp at all times," agreed John.

"Hell, that won't give any of them time to take a crap let alone break camp and move out again on horseback if they have to travel any distance under those conditions," rebuked Commander Chandler.

"Gentlemen!" yelled David over the chaos. "We all need to calm down. I will not have any dissention among my Commanders in this army." David went on to explain, "Now, each company will have two scouts to check the distance of each target, the terrain, hiding places for our men, if need be, and any other pertinent details and report back to the commanding officer. From now on," continued David, "we will travel within twenty-five miles of the enemy outposts per raid one way."

"Twenty-five? For God's sake, General. We might as well be camped down the block at that distance," snorted Commander Rawson.

"Stow the reject remarks, Chuck, and give the General a chance to explain further," rebuked Commander Connor.

"Thank you, John," answered David. "I did a background check on each of you and know for a fact that all of you are experts in your field of combat. That's why I tracked you down and made you my Commanders. If you did your job and trained your officers with all the knowledge that each of you have, and they in turn trained the troops under their command, we have a fighting force that is highly skilled. We have informers in every major city from here to Istanbul, and that is how we learned of the locations of each enemy outpost."

"Can they be trusted to give us the correct information that we need?" asked Commander Chase.

"Yes, completely," answered David.

"How do you know for sure?" inquired Commander Owen.

"Trust me, Gentlemen, I know for sure. And I want each of you to memorize this map showing the location of each of your officer's region. The blue pins are the locations of their camps and the red pins are the locations of the enemy outposts. Each of your company of one hundred

and twenty-five men will set up camp at those specified locations and break camp within a week and a half after each raid and then move on. Each company will be out in the combat field for a period of three months and shall then return to your base camps. It will be at your discretion, gentlemen, when to send your troops back into combat at another predetermined location after you return here for further orders at the end of the three-month time period. All orders to your officers will be verbal; no written orders or any form of written communication, whatsoever. We can not leave any kind of paper trail that could get into the enemy's hands."

"What?" questioned Commander Chandler. "How are we going to keep in contact with our officers without written orders?"

"Pony express."

You could hear a pin drop with the silence that permeated around the room after that answer from David.

"Come again? You are kidding us, right, General?" questioned Commander Rawson.

"No, Chuck. I'm not. As a matter of fact, I'm dead serious. The Antichrist has an intricate system of detection devices set up within twenty miles of each outpost, and all forms of communication that we know of would emit signals as to our location if used. We have a large network of pony express riders, just like the ones that they used in the old west. These men are highly skilled horseback riders and will receive all their orders verbally."

"Again, David, can they be trusted?" inquired Commander Chase.

"Yes, they can. I chose each one personally. We are fighting a diabolical tyrant, gentlemen, who has the upper hand with the two things we lack: a larger fighting force and the use of communication technology. We have to be smarter and try and stay one step ahead of him and watch each other's backs. We are not cut off from the rest of the world. Far from it. We have our European underground railroad, access to cargo planes and

small ships, and close to five thousand people, who are in the background but definitely part of our team."

"In answer to your questions in full, Scott, as to who can be trusted, everyone under my command were checked by me, my mother or aunt Maggie, or officers trained by them. They have checked every person, whether military or civilian, just as the five of you were in the beginning for the unusual shape and color of the mole at the base of the index finger on the right hand for men and left hand for women. As soon as we accept them, because they want to be part of God's army, the mole appears. If not, there will be no mole, and what we have told them will be wiped from their memory by God. Those two women located this sight and started this entire operation from the very beginning and are very knowledgeable at recruiting and scrutinizing each new member who wants to join this army.

"Even though we have nearly fifty thousand highly trained and skilled soldiers, you must instruct your officers to withdraw if the odds of fighting are against them and to disperse and reconnect at a predetermined location. Each officer will dispense two cyanide capsules to each of his men, and instruct them to carry them on their person at all times, and to use one rather than to be captured by the enemy. All of the men under your command must be told of incidents of what has happened to civilians that the Antichrist believes are his enemy. A fighting soldier, who is captured will be tortured beyond belief, because he delights in inflicting unbelievable pain and suffering on enemy soldiers until they are almost dead and then beheads those who refuse to accept him as their god. He has pitted family members against each other, friends against friends, and neighbors against neighbors, because of fear for their own lives, or because they believe that he is the real savior. He has no soul and thus no conscience, and he is terrorizing our world with his evil ways, and I for one will fight the bastard, until I draw my last breath, because he leaves nothing but a path of death and destruction in his wake. That is why I can't stress this point enough: inform your officers again and again to tell their men to use the cyanide if they are wounded in one of the raids and have no means of escape, or instruct each man to end the life of a fellow soldier, who is unable to prevent being captured. For you see,

gentlemen, the enemy also amuses themselves with mutilating our men in any grotesque manner that they so choose while they are still alive, and if they get bored with beheading, they find other means to end our soldiers' lives."

David saw events in his dreams of the brutality assailed upon the civilians too, but did not share this knowledge with his Commanders.

General David called a special meeting with his five Commanders—Commander Joe Owen, Commander Scott Chase, Commander Charles Rawson, Commander Simon Chandler, and Commander John Connor—to discuss the raids on the Antichrist's outposts.

"I called Commander Chase in sooner than the rest of you to tell him of the death of one of his officers and a newly placed private. Do you want to tell them of the circumstances or should I, Scott?" asked David.

"If you don't mind, General, I'd prefer to tell them in my own way."

"Yes, of course, Scott. Go ahead."

"Captain Daniel Lewis was from my hometown, and when all of this madness started, he joined the army shortly after graduation. He excelled in the army and became my youngest captain to date. He died just a few months short of his twenty-fourth birthday. He was one hell of a soldier and will be sorely missed."

"I make it a habit of knowing all my recruits, and Private James Kane was only twenty years old. He too, joined my outfit right out of high school," informed Commander Chase, with moisture in his eyes and a heavy heart, for the loss of two good young men under his command.

David saw the look on Scott's face and asked, "Would you like me to tell the rest of it, Scott?"

"Yes, please."

"A verbal report came through to Captain Lewis from one of our sources that a new enemy outpost was being constructed at this point."

David pointed to a circle marked with red ink on the large map. "He and his battalion were stationed at his sub-camp, located here." David again pointed to a circle marked with blue ink. "Captain Lewis sent out a reconnaissance consisting of two scouts to survey the enemy outpost. When the two scouts did not return in what Captain Lewis thought to be enough time, and instead of sending out two more scouts per my orders, he took it upon himself to check out the situation with a troop of thirty men. The two scouts were found impaled on two stakes. Captain Lewis ordered eight of his men to remove the bodies from the stakes. Before they were able to dismount, the enemy came out of nowhere and charged his troops. Among the chaos, Captain Lewis saw that Private Kane was shot and fell from his horse. He went to him amid the gunfire but was shot down himself. Seventeen men were wounded to some degree, twelve seriously, but all managed to stay on their horses and escaped, except Captain Lewis and Private Kane. Those twelve men died before reaching camp. The others are recovering from their wounds."

"Two more scouts were dispatched from Captain Lewis's battalion and were told to scout the area where Captain Lewis and his men were headed. The directions were found on Captain Lewis' desk. They found the two previous scouts still impaled on the stakes probably left there to rot along the side of the road, as a warning to all that saw them of what could happen to anyone if they sided with us."

"What about Lewis and Kane. Are they dead?" questioned Commander Chandler.

"Yes, both men are dead. The two scouts found two bodies buried in the ground with only their heads above ground about three miles from the two dead scouts," informed David. "They were murdered by an old and popular means since wars began. Their heads were trampled over and over by the enemy's horses until they were unrecognizable. They were identified by their uniforms and some personal mementos found on their person."

David gave pause to let his Commanders deal with the horrible news that he just told them, and then slammed his hands down on the

conference table with such force that it nearly toppled it, because of the anger that continued to build within him.

"Damn it all to hell, how many fuckin' times do I have to tell all of you that you have to warn your men just what the enemy is capable of doing. The populace is at the bastard's mercy, but I'll be damned if we will continue to be. Those people don't have the means to protect themselves from him, but damn it, we do. That's what we have been trained to do: fight. And from now on, we will do just that. No more jackin' off in this army, Gentlemen or heads will roll. I can promise you that."

Just then, a lieutenant knocked on the door and entered and whispered something to David. He told his commanders, "I'll be right back," and stormed out of the room.

"I would say that he's really pissed off at all of us," said Commander Rawson.

"He's right in being damn angry with us. We can't tolerate any more of our men being mutilated by these bastards," responded Commander Chase, with difficulty contemplating just how much his men must have suffered before they died.

"I've known, David, for a long time and have never seen him this angry, and under the circumstances, I don't blame him one bit," intervened Commander Connor. "We have only ourselves to blame in letting our officers relay the message of the probable results, if any of our men are captured alive, and I'm sure David will let us know just that when he returns."

When David reentered the conference room and with the silence that engulfed throughout the room, they could literally hear a pin drop. David sat down at the head of the table and with a calmer voice said, "I know in his heart that Captain Lewis thought that he was doing the right thing by trying to save one of his men. A lot of times it is just a normal reaction—trying to save another human being without thinking twice of your own wellbeing-but because of his heroics, sixteen men from Commander

Chase's battalion are now dead and four of them, counting the two scouts, by unfathomable brutality at the hands of our worst enemy: the Antichrist. I have never felt such anger, sorrow or frustration in my life. As a matter of fact, I would like to walk over to that wall this minute and put my fist right through it."

This last statement from General David made his Commanders relax for a moment but knowing only too well that he was not through with them yet. Far from it.

"Corporal Adams informed me that the company of 125 men from your battalion, Scott, was sent out by orders from me to track down the enemy responsible for those atrocities and to leave no survivors. Two scouts located the enemy platoon of forty men at a camp twelve miles from where the bodies of Captain Lewis and Private Kane were found. They rode back to where your captain and his men were waiting and informed them of the enemy's location. Your company surrounded them and a small skirmish entailed leaving thirty of the enemy dead and ten on their hands and knees begging for mercy. How ironic! When the tables are turned, the real cowards emerge. They were all shot in the back of the head, execution style, and they didn't suffer needlessly. We may have retribution here in some eyes, but not for me, because the memories of four of our men will haunt me for a long time to come."

"Do we have any other business that you wish to discuss with me at this time?" questioned David.

"I would just like to know if this incident was a chance encounter or do we have a leak in our midst somewhere?" questioned Commander Chase.

"That is being looked into as we speak. For now, it is considered a chance encounter until I hear differently. Anything else?"

The five Commanders looked at one another and shook their heads in the negative.

"Good. Then I suggest all five of you shag your asses out of here and inform every man in your battalion, yourselves, all that transpired at this meeting. Don't, and I mean don't, leave anything out. Tell all of the entire fuckin', gruesome details. Got it?" ordered David.

"Yes, Sir," replied all five in unison before they filed out of David's office.

"Cindy, for goodness sake, you've let this sickness that you've been complaining about go on far too long. It's been two weeks, right?"

"Yes, but I'll be all right in a few days or so."

"That's what you said two days ago and you're still sick."

"Look Helen, you're my best friend, not my mother, and I wish you would stop nagging me. I've probably got a good case of the flu. I'll be fine in a day or two so just drop it, okay?" yelled Cindy.

Helen couldn't believe how Cindy had just talked to her. Her mood swings were happening more often, but she associated it with whatever she was sick with at the moment. She just nodded her head in the affirmative, and asked Cindy to excuse her, because she had to leave.

Good, thought Cindy. *I don't know how I became friends with that woman. All she does is nag the hell out of me every time we get together.*

Two days later when Helen invited Cindy to meet her for breakfast, because she was not about to give up on her yet, Cindy was nice as could be.

"I'm sorry, Helen for the way that I acted toward you the other day. I hope you can forgive me."

"Nothing to forgive, Cindy. I was just concerned about you."

"I know, and I'm grateful to you for that."

"You look better. Are you feeling any better?"

"For God's sake, Helen!" roared Cindy. "Didn't you get my drift the last time we were together? I'm fine. Oh to hell with it, I'm out of here," uttered Cindy. With an awful mean look on her face, she got up from her chair and left the mess hall in a hurry with everyone looking at them both and wondering what the ruckus was all about.

Helen was more than mortified at this outburst from Cindy. She just didn't know where to turn for help, or maybe she should just write her off after the way that she has been treating her the past month.

On her way back to the database area, she ran into Maggie in the hallway.

"Well, Hi, Helen. I haven't seen you in quite some time. How are you doing? You look great."

"Thank you, Mrs. Ryan, for the greeting and the compliment."

She's Cindy's mother-in-law. Maybe I could confide in her. I've had it with Cindy, and I don't care how angry she gets. I've got to tell someone about her behavior, thought Helen.

"Helen, are you all right?" questioned Maggie. "You seem upset about something. Can I be of any help?"

"Yes, Mrs. Ryan. You sure can."

"Let's go into the lounge and talk," suggested Maggie.

Maggie didn't seem to be too shocked after Helen related her story and worries that she had about Cindy.

"I'm sorry you had to take the brunt of Cindy's outbursts. I have noticed her behavior of late, and I will insist that she get a thorough checkup with Dr. Madison."

"Thank you, Mrs. Ryan. Your suggestion to her will ease my mind, completely."

"No, Helen. I'm the one who should be doing the thanking here. I hope Cindy will wake up and see what a good friend that she has in you. I'll keep you informed of what Dr. Madison finds out."

"Thank you, Mrs. Ryan. Please do."

"And Helen, this conversation doesn't have to be told to Cindy. Let's keep it between you and me until we find out what's going on with her," suggested Maggie, with a smile of gratitude on her face.

After Cindy's shift was over, Maggie gave her time to get back to her quarters before she knocked on her door.

"Who is it?" questioned Cindy.

"It's me, Maggie."

It is seeming to take her forever to open her door, thought Maggie, *or am I just being overly paranoid?*

"Hi, Maggie. It's been awhile since I saw you last."

"I know, dear. Kat and I have been swamped with paper work for the last two weeks, but there is an end in sight, thank goodness," chuckled Maggie.

Either my comment went over her head or she wasn't listening to me, thought Maggie, after seeing the look on Cindy's face.

"Am I interrupting anything?" Maggie asked, noticing how agitated Cindy seemed with her.

"No, nothing. I'm just a little tired, that's all. What's up, Maggie?"

"That paperwork that I just mentioned is in regard to health records. Yours show that you missed your yearly check up and it's way overdue, so I made an appointment with Dr. Madison to see you on Friday afternoon."

"I am a big girl now, Maggie. And I think I am very capable of making my own appointments whenever I want to keep them," retaliated Cindy, with a smidgeon of sarcasm to her voice.

"That may be so dear, But David, Kat and I are the bosses around here and what we say, goes."

"Fine," said Cindy, right before she slammed the door on Maggie, unexpectedly leaving her standing in the hallway with her mouth wide open in disbelief.

"Kat, have you noticed a change in Cindy's behavior lately?" asked Maggie, after finding her in the medical complex sorting through files.

"Now that you mention it, yes. She seems out-of-sorts and agitated lately."

"That's putting it mildly. She just slammed the door in my face."

"And what did you do?"

"What could I do? I was left standing in the hallway with a closed door between us. I don't know what's come over that girl of late. What would you have done, Kat?"

"I would've knocked on that door until she opened it, and I wouldn't have left until she gave me a mighty big apology, right before I punched her lights out." Kat waited a few seconds, then said, "Just kidding about the last part."

"Yeah, I guess you're right."

Kat looked at Maggie and just nodded her head in disbelief.

Cindy kept that appointment with Dr. Madison mostly, because she had no other choice, which aggravated the hell out of her. "Why is everyone picking on me lately?" she asked herself.

Her tests and blood work came back on Tuesday, and Dr. Madison requested that Maggie meet with him in his office.

"Maggie, it's nice to see you again. It's been way too long."

"I know, Henry. We've been busy going through medical files."

"That has to be a big undertaking, considering the amount of people who live and work here."

"Yes, it is."

"I'll get right to the point, Maggie. Cindy is in excellent condition, and she told me that she takes advantage of the exercise facility at least three times a week. I was happy to hear that, because all new mothers-to-be should not neglect that aspect of their pregnancy."

"You mean she's pregnant and expecting a baby?" gasped Maggie, with a smile of happiness and total disbelief with the wonderful news.

"Yes, Maggie. That's what usually happens when you are pregnant: you have a baby," laughed Henry.

"Oh, how silly of me to put it that way, but my family and I were all under the impression that Cindy couldn't have a baby," informed Maggie.

"I don't know why not. She certainly is healthy enough."

"When is the baby due?"

"She's about six weeks along. That puts her due date around February14. Possibly Valentine's Day, if she carries the baby full term."

"I asked you in here first, Maggie, to talk to you about a concern that I have about Cindy. It says here in her records that she was institutionalized, but gives no details as to the problem, or if she sought help. Can you fill me in on some of the details?"

"Yes. Cindy was institutionalized for a short time about two and a half years after she married my son. She had three miscarriages and lost both her grandparents, all in a short period of time. She went through so much and she needed temporary help to deal with all of those tragedies. If I can recall, she spent three months in a facility in Colorado Springs where my son Chris was stationed at the Air Force base there, training to be a pilot."

"I see."

"Why do you ask, Henry?"

"I wanted to find out just how much of a history of mental illness that Cindy has, because it could be detrimental to the baby, if she continues on with these mood swings that she has."

"Could it be that she's been acting like this because she's pregnant?"

"All women react differently to a pregnancy, and I'm not qualified to give you an honest answer, because I'm not a psychiatrist. But I do suggest that you have her make an appointment with Dr. Shaw. He's a good man and a fine psychiatrist."

"Yes, I've met him and his wife Muriel. Henry, would it be all right if I tell Cindy the good news?"

"Well technically, I should have told her the good news first, but I wanted to clear the air with her records. We're not living in a world of reality like it used to be. Yes, Maggie. I see no reason why you can't tell your daughter-in-law the good news, and I want you to make sure that she keeps all of her future appointments with me. Prenatal care is so important, and because of Cindy's age, it's more important that she do so."

"Alright, Henry. I understand, and will make sure that she sees you on a regular basis."

"Congratulations, Maggie. You're going to be a grandma," laughed Henry.

"Yes, Henry. This will be my first grandchild. Thank you."

"You're very welcome, Maggie."

After Maggie left Dr. Madison, she became aware of the fact that Marshall would not be here with her to meet his first grandchild and share in the wonderful occasion. This brought tears to her eyes and then

sobs of grief that she couldn't control. She found the lady's room, where she could be alone to cry until she had no more tears left. *I have to get my act together and tell Cindy of the wonderful news, and I can't do that with red eyes*, she berated herself.

Again she waited for Cindy to arrive at her quarters and mother-to-be and grandmother-to-be hugged and cried and hugged and cried again over the wonderful news: a baby.

Chris was notified of Cindy's condition, and he was at the garrison as fast as he could get there.

Within days, almost all of the family knew. Chad was easy to track down, but Tim was another story. He found out two weeks later.

Chris made a point of spending more time with Cindy, and her attitude and mood swings dissipated, completely, so Maggie did not push the issue of seeing Dr. Shaw, but she made sure that she kept her appointments with Dr. Madison.

The first thing Kat and Maggie did upon their arrival at the garrison was to place a plaque on the cornerstone of the Garrison Hospital Complex in loving memory, and dedicated to their beloved friend Fred, who gave of his life so willingly, so that they could go on living.

After a very long labor of eight hours and twenty-five minutes, little Linda Margaret Ryan made her first appearance to the world, weighing in at seven pounds and ten ounces and twenty inches long.

"She's beautiful, Cindy. Just like her mother," cried Chris with tears of joy.

"Oh, Chris. We finally have a baby of our own. Isn't it wonderful?" asked Cindy, with tears streaming down her face.

"Don't cry, Honey. Because it is wonderful, and we have to be happy and thankful to God for our beautiful little daughter."

Everyone in the family took turns holding Linda while Chris and Cindy looked on. Tears of joy and then laughter took over within the family circle.

Chad and Tim made sure that they were going to be with their brother for this wonderful event, and Chad arrived at the garrison one day before the baby was born. Tim arrived a few minutes before Cindy went into labor. Toward evening, Maggie found her three sons and David in the atrium smoking cigars in honor of the new father and sharing stories of their present lives since they all saw each other last. Her heart almost burst with happiness at seeing Chris, Tim, Chad, and David together again at last. Little did she know that this would be the last time the four of them would be together.

General David just finished a meeting with his five Commanders and was about to leave to do an inspection of the garrison when Kat walked in unannounced, because Corporal Adams was not at his desk.

"Mother, what are you doing here?"

"David, I told you three days ago that I would be bringing in a woman to replace the lead RN, Genevieve Harrison until she can get back on her feet again after the minor heart attack that she had."

"Ah, how is she doing, Mother?"

"You forgot, didn't you?"

"Yes, Mother. I'm sorry, but I did forget."

"You've got enough to worry about with running this place. No harm done. Corrine, this is my son, General O'Brien. David, this is Corrine Thomas," announced Kat, and hurriedly left her son's office, which surprised David to no end.

David extended his hand to Ms. Thomas and said, "Glad to meet you, Ms. Thomas."

"Thank you, General O'Brien. The pleasure is all mine." She put her hand into David's.

The chemistry between the two of them was felt immediately, and David held on to her hand beyond a reasonable time, because he was mesmerized by her beautiful haunting green eyes.

"I'm very sorry, Ms. Thomas. I did not mean to stare," gasped David, with a blush on his face, as he quickly let go of her hand. "Please, have a seat next to my desk," requested David, as he pulled the chair out for her, and then proceeded to go around his desk to his own chair.

"Thank you, General O'Brien."

"Please, Ms. Thomas. I prefer that all of the civilians, call me, David. There is no need for formalities with the usage of my last name."

"Alright, General David. If you wish," hesitated Corrine.

David had to grin to himself, because what he meant was for her to call him just David, not General David. She evidently couldn't bring herself to address him by his first name only. *God, is she beautiful,* thought David, and he caught himself staring at her again.

"Umm, how about you give me a little history of yourself," stammered David, which left him wondering what he had just said.

"Well, like you know already, my name is Corrine Thomas and I'm from Norfolk, England.

"Beautiful country, England," uttered David.

"Oh, you have been to England then, General David?"

"Yes, I was stationed over there for a short period of time during one of my specialized training courses with the army branch of the Green Berets."

"I see," answered Corrine, with about as much finesse as David, and continued with, "I graduated from the Brighton School of Nursing and Midwifery, third in my class of ninety women in 2023. The war was still going on at the time after my three years of schooling, and I wanted to

get involved and do my share, so joined a MASH unit similar to what you have in the States and started my post-op training. During that one year and four months, I cared for untold numbers of men and women that were near death, because of the atrocities placed upon them by their fellow man. I've had plenty of on-hand experience in such a short time with that terrible war. To this day, I still have nightmares in which I relive the inability to save everyone who came into my unit."

David was awe struck with the sincere emotions displayed by this caring and beautiful woman.

"On the lighter side, my father is an English professor, and my mother is an elementary school teacher. I have two older brothers named, Samuel and James, and a younger sister by two years, whose name is, Denise."

"How did you learn about us?" asked David.

"From a wounded soldier who came through my unit. He said that his brother is one of your officers."

"My mother passed your resume to me before she made a bee-line out of here, and on it, she says that you passed the mole test and have already been sworn in. May I see your left hand, Ms. Thomas?" questioned David.

"Why certainly, General David."

"Your resume is very impressive and coupled with the passing of your mole test, I have only one thing left to say to you, Ms. Thomas, and that is... Welcome aboard. As of now, you are officially a member of this army. Congratulations."

"Thank you, General O'Brien, I mean General David. I hope I live up to your expectations of me."

"I'm sure you will, Ms. Thomas," answered, David, as she rose from her chair and was about to leave. "Ms. Thomas, have you had lunch yet?"

"No, I haven't. Before I came in for the interview with you, your mother showed me this very large and impressive complex."

"Well, I was just about to go before you came in," lied David. "Would you care to join me?"

"That would be very nice, General David. Thank you for asking."

"My pleasure, Ms. Thomas."

As the two walked into the Mess Hall, all heads turned and stared at them both, as General David always ate in his office, never here. All of the soldiers stood at attention.

"Gentlemen, this is a Mess Hall, so sit and finish your meals," ordered, David, with a grin, as he knew what they were thinking by the expressions on their faces.

The conversation between David and Corrine during their lunch break went far better than the introduction. They both started to relax and enjoy each other's company, immensely. David wished his mother wasn't so well organized and on top of everything, because he really wanted to spend some more time with Ms. Thomas by showing her around the garrison.

"I never thought my son would ever date, let alone marry anyone," chuckled Kat.

"Why not?" questioned Maggie.

"His whole life has been working for God, and preparing to invoke his wishes of him with regard to building an army and fighting the Antichrist. I never thought that he'd take the time, let alone make room for a woman in his life. I'm certainly glad he finally did though, as Corrine's been a real asset to him, and they certainly love each other. And I have come to love her as a daughter," informed Kat.

"I know, Kat. Corrine is the best thing that ever happened to David, for he is less stressed-out, more relaxed, and has almost a continual smile on his face," remarked Maggie.

"He certainly never had that facial feature before she walked into his life," chuckled Kat.

"Now, Kat. You're exaggerating," quipped Maggie.

"Yeah, maybe just a little, but not by much," said Kat.

After a short but very meaningful interval with dating, David and Corrine exchanged vows in the garrison chapel on August 24, 2030 in a small ceremony with relatives and close friends in attendance.

Nine months and eleven days later on June 4, 2031, little Alexis Katherine O'Brien showed her face to the world. She was a beauty in her parents' and grandmother's eyes and the love of their lives.

Kat, in a million years, never even considered that David would possibly marry one day and have children, or that she would be a grandmother at some point in her life, but the beautiful bundle of joy cradled in her arms was what the joys of life were all about: children.

On September 19, 2031, a conversation was about to take place in David's office.

"General?

"Yes, Corporal Adams."

"There's a woman here by the name of Helen Armstrong who wishes a word with you."

"Helen Armstrong? Of course, Cindy's best friend and Lieutenant Armstrong's wife," recalled David. "Send her in."

"Yes, General."

"Helen, it's good to see you," announced David.

Before he could finish his sentence, a distraught Helen nervously informed David, "I can't find, Cindy, and I think she may have gone with the troops that left this morning," cried Helen in near hysteria.

"Helen, calm down and start over," prompted David. "I can barely understand a word you're saying."

"Cindy told me a few weeks ago that she hasn't seen Chris in over five months and only heard from him once in that amount of time. She was frantic with worry and missed him so much, and told me that she was going to sneak away with one of the troops when they went out on a reconnaissance and try and find him somehow. She would start at the last location that he called her from. I told her that that would be dangerous and utterly foolish. Besides, where would she even begin to look for him? It doesn't mean that he's still in the same place that she heard from him last. I thought that she would see the error in her actions, if I would continue to try and deter her. We talked it over some more, and I was sure that she had come to her senses. I guess I was terribly wrong."

"Why didn't you come to me right away, Helen?"

"She seemed, at the time, to agree with me that it would be a bad mistake, and that she not only would put herself in danger, but also her daughter, Linda. I assumed that the matter was finished. I'll never forgive myself, if something happened to her and Linda, never."

"Are you sure that she isn't somewhere in camp?"

"We were supposed to meet this morning for breakfast at 10:00 A.M. I waited until at 10:20 A.M. and when she didn't show up, I went looking for her. I can't find her anywhere, and no one has seen her."

"Corporal Adams!" yelled David.

"Yes, Sir."

"I want two scouts sent out immediately to track the troops that left on a reconnaissance run this morning at dawn. Then immediately go into lock-down. No one is allowed to leave until further notice from me. Have the entire garrison searched from top to bottom for Cindy Ryan," commanded David.

"Right away, Sir."

"Helen, I want you to continue looking for Cindy. Maybe she's visiting someone in sickbay or forgot to meet you," revealed David, knowing deep down that he was grasping at straws. He knew Cindy was one strong-willed woman and probably did exactly as she told Helen what she wanted to do: stow away with the troops that left at dawn. *God forbid, I hope I'm wrong,* thought David.

Two hours later...

"Sir."

"Yes, Corporal?"

"The garrison has been searched thoroughly, and there is no sign of Mrs. Ryan."

"Have twenty men ready to move out in ten minutes."

"Yes, Sir."

Just then Kat walked into David's office. "What's this that I hear about Cindy missing, and that she took little Linda with her?"

"I don't have time to discuss this with you now, Mother. Talk to Helen Armstrong. She'll fill you in on the details."

"But—"

"Later, Mother," said, David, again, as he rushed out of his office.

David led his men in the direction that his troops headed earlier.

Three hours later...

"Sir," said First Sergeant Evans.

"Yes?" replied, David, as he was reviewing a map with one of his other officers.

"Two men are approaching on horseback about three hundred yards beyond that ridge straight ahead. I can't make out who they are."

"Dismount and take cover," ordered David.

The two riders slowed, as they approached a row of trees below the ridge and came riding into the clearing with caution.

David stood and motioned them forward as soon as he recognized, Ol' John, as the men called him. He was the oldest and most capable of David's many scouts and a partner with Clarence, who was riding beside him, for who knows how many years.

"Still wearing that old hat with the feather, I see," jostled David.

"Yes, General. And now it has a few more bullet holes, and the feather is half the size that it used to be. Won't give it up. It's kind of like a security blanket would be to a kid," grinned Ol' John, showing a few teeth missing, before he spit out a wad of chewed tobacco to the ground. "They're all over on the other side of the ridge that we just came from."

"Any survivors?" questioned David after shaking hands with Clarence.

"None, General. All of them butchered like a herd of cattle at market. Never seen anything like it in all my years, and I hope to God that I never will again. Those bastards are merciless and they really enjoy killing, 'cause the carnage back there has mockery written all over it."

"You sure, John? No survivors?" questioned David again, with a dreadful feeling in the pit of his stomach.

"None, and not a horse to be found."

"General, may I have a word with you in private?" requested O'l John as he alit his horse and started walking toward David. "We found a woman laying beside the supply wagon. She was completely naked with her throat slit from ear to ear. I covered her with my blanket from my bedroll so as none of the men should see her. What in God's name was she

doing there?" questioned Ol' John before he removed his hat as a gesture of remorse.

"What about her little girl?" asked David.

"Lordy! You mean she had a babe with her too? We didn't find any little one. Heaven forbid! You think those bastards took her?"

"I don't know," answered David, as he removed his hat and hit it hard against his leg, before he ran his other hand through his hair. "I don't know. Mount up men!" commanded David, before they galloped full speed toward the ridge, knowing too well what they would find on the other side.

David was the first one on the scene and spotted Cindy's covered body by the supply wagon just where Ol' John said she was. He slowly dismounted and walked over to where Cindy lay. He pulled the blanket back just far enough to expose her head and shoulders. She laid face down in the dirt. David stood there motionless and light-headed at the sight of the woman he loved from childhood. As he was about to cover her, he caught sight of something out of the corner of his eye. *Oh my God, please no.* Two little toes were sticking out ever so slightly from beneath Cindy's body. He dropped to his knees and with trembling hands, he carefully rolled Cindy over and saw that her throat had been cut, and what he dreaded to be true: little Linda was laying face up with her long blonde curls embedded into the dried blood circling her neck. He quickly took off his coat and wrapped her lifeless body and lifted her into his arms. He walked over to the wagon and leaned against it for support. He was totally void of any emotion until he bowed his head and said a prayer in silence for the woman, who was such a meaningful part of his life, and the little girl that she adored. As he uncovered her face, for one last look at his precious cousin, he vowed then and there that he would spend more time with Corrine and his own beautiful little girl, Alexis. For this was a hard but true awakening of how the lives of his loved ones really is so very precious to him.

Ol' John was the first one to walk over. As he approached, David and saw the bundle in his arms, he wailed, "Not the little babe," and removed his hat and bowed his head to hide the tears that filled his eyes.

"Clarence!" shouted David.

"Yes, General," answered, Clarence, as he walked over to where David and Ol' John stood. In the twenty odd years that the two of them rode together, Clarence never saw Ol' John react to any situation like this before, and they had witnessed a lot of horror in those years.

"Ride back to the garrison and bring back plenty of blankets to wrap these men in and enough wagons to transport their bodies back."

"Yes, Sir," replied Clarence, as he took one more look at his partner and mounted his horse and rode off at full speed.

"Lieutenant Schultz!" roared David.

"Yes, General."

"Gather anything you can—brush, twigs, whatever—and cover every one of these men but fast," ordered David.

"Yes, Sir," he answered before ordering his men to do as the General commanded.

"You want me to take the babe, General?" asked Ol' John.

"No. She stays with me," replied David, softly. He walked to the other side of the wagon and looked out over the clearing, and vowed to himself that he would no longer be a general behind a desk, but one leading his men on every raid from now on.

Three days later at the garrison, David was in his office before the funeral service, worrying about his mother and aunt Maggie, and how they would cope, as they both loved Cindy like a daughter and shared so many precious moments with her. Aunt Maggie had so loved her granddaughter, Linda. He wondered about his cousin, Chris. Every

attempt to locate him had failed. He knew his cousin was still alive but where was he?

It was a bleak overcast day with a light mist starting to form as hundreds of men in dress uniforms surrounded forty-one flag-draped caskets, and one small one situated next to her mother. The mood that filtered the air was one of intense mourning for the poor souls, who lie waiting to be buried on a beautiful hillside overlooking a lush, green, flowered glen. The cemetery, in David's estimation, bore too many bodies of the brave men, who died in the line of duty. This would stop!

With his mother standing next to him on one side and with Maggie next to her, and his wife Corrine on the other side and all weeping silently, it is then that David had flashbacks of the beloved woman now lying in a cold pine box before his eyes. He was so very young when Cindy first came into his life but not too young to remember that day. She was like a big sister to him all through these years and would never forget the special moments in his life that took place because of her. She was gone now but would never be forgotten, because she was and always will be a special part of his life. Time would never erase the love that he felt for her.

The next day, David sent word for his Commanders to meet with him at the garrison in three days. His agenda: to pick one of them to fill his position as general-in-charge, so that he would be free to lead his men assigned to the garrison into every raid from now on against the Antichrist. He thought about all five of them and their qualifications and decided ahead of time on Commander Owen. Joe was the logical choice, not only because of his experience in years with the army, but because he was levelheaded and not prone to jumping the gun on important decisions. He would think them through and make the right choice. Joe it was, decided David.

That night while in his apartment going over a large stack of papers lying in front of him on his desk, David had a hard time focusing his attention on the mound of paperwork, because his mind kept wandering back to Chris. He recalled the wonderful times he shared with his favorite cousin who saved his life. But he could not shake the overwhelming guilt

that he was feeling right now, because in his mind, he did not, in effect, do everything in his power to save the lives of Cindy and Linda.

Kat went to bed early that night after checking with Maggie, which drained her emotionally. Her sister was the Rock of Gibraltar whenever she needed her, and now Kat found it hard to console Maggie when she herself was so bereaved over the loss of Cindy and Linda. She lay down on her bed and closed her eyes, but she soon discovered that it was a waste of time, because all she did was toss and turn. She got out of bed and put her robe and slippers on and decided to go up to the atrium for some fresh air. She took the elevator to the third floor and walked in the direction of the atrium. She sensed that she wasn't alone so inquired, "Michael, are you here with me?"

"Yes, Mistress Kat. It is I."

As Kat sat in one of the chairs, she was thankful when she noticed that the dome was closed, as the weather was chilly outside. She sat quietly for a moment, wondering why God let this terrible tragedy happen to Cindy and Linda, when Michael said, "Do not blame the Almighty One, for the tragedies that mankind has bestowed upon themselves, Mistress Kat. Remember our talk at the lake when I told you that mankind has brought on all that is happening in the world then and now, because of the negative energy that they have emitted for so many years?"

"Yes, I remember," answered Kat, wondering how he knew what she was thinking.

"And I also told you that the Almighty One will not interfere one way or another with the future tragedies the world will cause itself?"

"Yes."

"You were about to ask me why the Almighty One let this happen to your loved ones?"

"Yes, I was. But you answered me before I had a chance to ask. So, you're telling me that Cindy and Linda were a tragic part of what is happening and what will happen to all of us in time?"

"The Almighty One will not do anything to mankind, until the final three and a half years of Armageddon, nor will he help mankind to survive."

"I assume then that they must do it on their own—survive, I mean—to see Judgment Day?"

"Correct, Mistress Kat. There will be a great multitude of survivors, but in comparison with the number of people who have lived on this planet Earth, since 'The End Time' started, then the numbers are not so many. You and your family have the divine protection from the Almighty One, but that too will end some day."

"But, Michael, Cindy and Linda were part of my family and they were not protected. Why?"

"Because, Mistress Kat, Mistress Cindy stopped believing the moment she walked away and left the divine protection that was given to you and your family members and also to those, who chose to believe in what you were doing for the Almighty One and stayed with you, were saved. She was on her own the moment that she took that first step out of the door."

"If only I had known what she had planned, then Maggie and I could have talked her out of it."

"No, Mistress Kat. Her friend tried to reason with her and got nowhere. You and Mistress Maggie would not have been successful either. She was determined to go, and nothing or no one would have stopped her. She chose her own destiny."

"Michael, I haven't talked to you in weeks. Let's not let it go that long again, okay?"

"Whatever you say, Mistress Kat. But remember, you must summon me."

"Do you talk a lot with David?"

"Oh yes, Mistress Kat. We talk every day."

"Good, Michael. He needs someone to confide in besides Corrine, and I'm happy that it's you." Kat looked at her watch and was stunned that it was close to midnight.

"I'm going to call it a night. Good night, Michael."

"Good night, Mistress Kat."

Kat returned to the elevator and pushed two. As she came upon David's door, she saw the light shining from below it. *He's still awake*, thought Kat, as she knocked, softly.

"Who's there?" questioned David in a low voice so as not to awaken Corrine and Alexis and shocked that someone was knocking on his door this late.

"It's me, Mother."

"Mother, for goodness sake, what are you doing up this late and wandering the halls? Come in."

"I might ask you the same question, minus the part about the halls," chuckled Kat. "I went to bed early but couldn't sleep, so I went up to the atrium and had a long talk with Michael. He told me that you and he talk every day."

"Yes, we do. As a matter of fact, sometimes more than once a day. I don't know what I'd do without Michael to confide in."

"You could come to your mother once in awhile. That's what mothers are for."

"I know, Mother. But you and Aunt Maggie have enough on your minds overseeing the civilians here."

"I will always take time to talk with you, David."

"I know, Mother and thank you!"

"Is there any word on the whereabouts of Chris, yet?"

"No, none. But I have the word out to all of our sources that if anyone knows where he is, to have him get back here as of yesterday," chided David. "I'm really worried about him, mother. Losing Cindy and Linda could tear him completely apart. His family comes first, but Chris is reckless and loves danger, and that stolen stealth fighter that he pilots comes in a close second with his feelings."

"Well, just maybe, if Chris would have paid more attention to his family's needs and had more consideration for their feelings, maybe this whole thing could have been avoided," said Kat, in anger, but not really believing a thing that she just said. "And what do you mean by stolen plane?"

"Mother, the whole world is a war zone, and we have the enemy lurking everywhere. Our first priority is to kill the bastards before they get us, and we need every single person willing to do it. Stealth fighter, Mother, not a plane," chuckled David. "Yes. Chris stole it from his unit in the Air Force before the Antichrist laid claim to and confiscated everything from the Army, Marines, Navy, and any fighting force throughout the States first, then the rest of the world."

"What I don't understand is why you can't locate him. Doesn't he have to file a flight plan with you like the airlines had to do?"

"He did. But now he has taken it upon himself to strike when and wherever he wants to. He's always done and continues to do one hell of a job of blowing up the enemy's military installations. He's put one hell of a dent into their planes, tanks, transports, ships, aircraft carriers, weaponry, supplies, and more all over Europe. We need him, Mother, and I sure the hell don't know what we will do, if he can't continue to go on."

"I'm not worried about Chris anymore. He'll mourn his loved ones and then he will eventually get right back into that plane and do what he does best. David, I'm worried about you. You don't get enough sleep for one thing. It's past midnight, and you're in that office of yours promptly at 6:00 A.M."

"That's at 600 hours, Mom," laughed David."

"I never could figure out that military timing, and I'm not about to try now," laughed Kat, in return.

"It's a good thing that we can laugh about some things, Mother."

"David, I'm not kidding when I say that I am worried about you. What's going on?"

"You could always read me couldn't you, Mother?"

"Like a book!"

"I don't sleep well at night, so I guess I try and avoid it as long as I can stay awake."

"Why don't you sleep well?"

"I have psychic nightmares, which is what I call them, about the chaos, madness, and killings that go on every day in this so-called world that we are now living in."

"What do you mean by psychic nightmares?"

"Mother, I dream of other people's lives. I asked Michael why I didn't dream of Cindy, so that I could have saved her. He told me that my mind is too cluttered with details in regard to this place and the people I know. It doesn't really make a hell of a lot of sense to me, but that was his only explanation. I keep asking myself, why did she do it? She was strong-willed and not prone to making mistakes of any kind in her life, so why did she go and do something so utterly stupid that cost her life and Linda's?"

"She and Chris were very much in love and they have been since the day that the two laid eyes on each other. When a special love like that comes along, people don't rationalize their actions but think with their hearts. Cindy wanted to be with Chris so bad that she never even took into consideration what might happen to her and Linda. If she would have, she wouldn't have gone. David, Michael told me that no one could

have saved Cindy, absolutely no one, and that includes you. Since she chose to leave the divine protection that we all share, she was on her own as soon as she walked out that door. If this tragedy hadn't occurred when it did and she survived, she would have been living on a tightrope, until the inevitable happened to her, which in reality, could have been a week, a month, a year—who knows with the dangers that await anyone outside these walls? None of us can blame ourselves for what happened to Cindy and Linda. It sounds heartless, but the real world is not always so kind, and the ones who remain must go on."

"I know that you are right when you put it that way, Mother, but—"

"No more buts, David. From now on, we have to get back to the business at hand. You and I both have work to do for God. That's what we are here for, remember?"

"Yes, Mother. I remember, and thank you!"

"You're welcome. And when you go to bed tonight, ask God, if He could see to it that you could get more sleep at night. You'd be surprised at the wishes he does grant to those who are sincere. And by the way, why don't you steal some more of those planes back from that bastard, Musva? Good night, David."

"Good night, Mother."

As Kat slipped into bed and turned out the light, she asked Cindy's forgiveness, if she sounded so harsh. "It was the only way I could get David to snap out of his guilt, Cindy. I love you, sweetheart, and miss you and Linda terribly," whispered Kat, as she closed her eyes and fell asleep.

The five Commanders filed into David's office one by one and found him sitting at a long table with stacks of documents lying in front of him.

"Gentlemen, welcome, and have a seat," requested David. "I'll get right to the point. In light of the tragic event that took place less than a week ago, I have decided to—no, vowed to—get out from behind my desk and lead my own men into battle from now on."

The murmurs started immediately and the objections followed shortly thereafter.

"You can't be serious, General," stated Commander Connor.

"As a matter of fact, John, I've never been so serious in all my life."

"But, sir," interjected Commander Owen. "You run this army with diligence and expertise. No one can fill your shoes."

"I beg to differ with you, Joe. As a matter of fact, you are here by ordered to stay behind when the other Commanders leave, because I have chosen you to take my place."

"Umm…me? There's no way that I can replace you. I mean, this is a lot of responsibility you're throwing at me. I don't think I can do—"

"The job?" inquired David. "I carefully scrutinized all of you through your records and from what I know of you personally. Even though all of you would be qualified, I decided on Commander Owen as the best choice in my estimation."

"Wow! General, you sure hit us with a bombshell here," informed Commander Rawson.

"I know, Chuck. My decision was made after a lot of soul searching, and I do know now that it is the right decision."

David was overwhelmed as his Commanders rose from their chairs and gave him a standing ovation.

"I thank you all wholeheartedly, Gentlemen for your support. It means a lot to me, more than you'll ever know," added David.

"Who will take over for Joe's command?" asked Commander Chase.

"Good question, Scott. I had three choices in mind, but I decided on Sergeant Major Larsen Erickson, whom I've known since the first grade. He's a good man and one hell of an asset to this army."

“Corporal Adams,” called David through the intercom system.

“Yes, Sir.”

“Has Sergeant Major Erickson arrived yet?”

“No, Sir.”

“When he does, send him right in.”

“Yes, Sir.”

“Now for the other business at hand. After this latest tragic incident and others before it, I have decided I will be out in the field from now on and leading all raids personally. That means we will have to regroup with where and when the men under your command will be stationed. I have drawn up a plan, which you can see on the wall behind me. After discussing the details, I want each and every one of you to give me your opinions, even if you agree or disagree with me, because this is your mans’ army also. From now on, we will increase the number of raids and broaden our horizons. The enemy is building more outposts at an alarming rate, and our objective from now on is to eliminate them as fast as they appear. We will attack and destroy so quickly and methodically that they won’t know what hit them.”

“Do you think this last incident was a coincidence?” questioned Commander Rawson.

“No, Chuck. In my estimation, there is no such thing as coincidence. Not as many times as this has happened to us with supposedly running into the enemy by accident while our troops were on a reconnaissance run. This time they were too close to home to suit me. We have a leak in our army, Gentlemen, and you can rest assured that I will find out who it is,” claimed David.

“Have any suspicions as to who it might be?” asked Commander Chandler.

"No, Simon. Not as yet, but I have a gut feeling that I'm missing some important point that has been nagging at me, and I have yet to figure out what it is."

"You'll figure it out, Sir. Of that I'm sure," stated Commander Rawson.

"Thanks, for the vote of confidence, Chuck. And I hope you're right and the sooner the better, because too much is at stake: the lives of our men, because of a traitor in our midst. We have been too slack with dealing with the enemy, and as a result, they have regained some of the outposts that we attacked before. From now on, we attack, leave no survivors, and burn the outposts to the ground."

"No survivors?" Commander Owen, questioned.

"You heard me right, Joe. No survivors! I don't want any more prisoners taken alive. If any survive the attack, they are to be shot on the spot, execution-style like the platoon did after catching up with the ones that killed Lewis and Kane. I don't want one enemy soldier left alive to fight us again, understand? Are you all in agreement? Say so now one way or another," demanded David.

All of the five Commanders nodded their heads in agreement.

"Alright, now as far as assigning all of you new territories," started David.

"Sir, Sergeant Major Erickson has just arrived," announced Corporal Adams over the intercom,

"Thank you, Corporal. Send him in," answered David. He arose from his chair and walked away from the table to greet Lars with a handshake and a bear hug as he walked in.

"God, it's good to see you, Lars. How long has it been since we saw each other last?"

"About two years, I'd say. How are you, David?"

"You'll find out after I introduce my five Commanders to you."

After the introductions were out of the way and David told Lars to take a seat, he repeated to Lars what was said from the beginning of the meeting.

"Sounds like you have one hell of a problem with a traitor in your organization, General, and I would suggest—" Before Lars could finish his statement, a loud ruckus was heard from Corporal Adam's office. Before David could rise from his chair to see what it was all about, his cousin Chris took two large steps and was on David like a flash and was tackled by him before he had a chance to defend himself. The chair went flying and Chris was on top of David and trying to choke him while yelling uncontrollably, "You fuckin' son of a bitch! You let them kill Cindy and Linda. I'll kill you, you bastard!"

Even though Chris and David were the same height, and Chris was older but heavier, he had the advantage over David, because he had him pinned down and was stronger. David refused to fight back. Lars was the first one on Chris and with the help of Commanders Chandler and Connor, they pulled him off David. David rolled over and was gasping for breath, and he heard Chris yell as the three struggled to get him under control.

"I've been out there busting my ass and putting my life on the line, while you sit here on your ass, playing the big shot general, who couldn't even keep my wife and daughter safe as a favor to me. I wish to fuck that I would have left you at the bottom of that damn lake!" yelled Chris.

As David was being helped to his feet, he could still hear Chris' voice from the outer office as the three struggled to take him away. "I hate you, David O'Brien and I curse the day that you were born. You better hope I never set eyes on you again, because I swear to God, I'll kill you! Get your fuckin' hands off of me, I know my way out!" yelled Chris, as he was shoved halfway to the entrance and let go by Lars and Commanders Chandler and Connor.

For some reason, Lars wasn't going to let it end like this with David's cousin walking away. He was taller than Chris by three inches and a hell of a lot stockier. He caught up with Chris just as he exited the entrance to the garrison, grabbed him by the back of his collar, spun him around, pushed him up against the stoned wall, and said, "Look, you asshole, I should break every damn bone in your body, for what you just pulled in there. That man, that you claim to hate so much is my best friend and one hell of a general. He runs this operation as smooth as a baby's behind even though he has more damn headaches that he has to deal with to keep it going."

At that point, Chris tried in vain to break away from Lars's hold, as his nostrils flared with uncontrollable pent up anger over Cindy and Linda.

"I'm not done talking yet," said Lars, and he shoved Chris back up against the wall. Lars continued with, "I'm truly sorry to hear what happened to your wife and daughter. We've all lost loved ones. Think, man! It's not his fault what happened. We have a traitor in our operation whose been snitching our positions to the enemy. And besides, it isn't David's job to babysit every civilian person in this outfit, personally."

Lars saw the defeated look on Chris' face and let go of him and watched as he walked away with shoulders hunched and his head bowed low.

Lars returned to David's office and waited while David and his five Commanders were just finishing with picking up the rest of the papers off of the floor that were scattered all over the room.

"Lars, did my Cousin Chris leave the premises?"

"Yes, he was escorted to the road, got into an army jeep and drove away."

"He actually got into a jeep?" questioned David.

"Yes. He must have some connections to get gas. The Antichrist hoards it like it's gold, and we have to get it through the black market and have it smuggled in, unless of course, we have the beasts' number chipped somewhere on our person," informed Lars.

"I'm sure my Cousin knows of a dependable buyer, because he needs fuel to fly that Stealth fighter of his. Gentlemen, I apologize for the scene that you just witnessed. That was my Cousin Chris, and as you know from his conversation with me, that was his wife and child found at the scene of the latest massacre. Let's take a break, Gentlemen, and I'll see you all back here at 1300 hours, informed David, as he glanced at the clock on the wall. "Lars and Commander Owen, would you please remain?" requested, David.

The other four Commanders left and David, Commander Owen, and Lars were conversing when Corporal Adams announced to David that his mother and aunt wished to speak with him.

"Send them in," commanded David.

"Yes, Sir."

"David, is it true what we heard about Chris?" questioned Kat.

"News travels fast around here, I see," replied David. "Yes, Mother. Chris was here."

"And he didn't bother to come and see me?" asked Maggie.

"I'm sorry, Aunt Maggie, to learn that he didn't come to see you first, but he evidently was too intent with getting his hands on me."

"Why?" asked Maggie.

"He blames me for the loss of Cindy and Linda."

"That's ridiculous. What's the matter with my son?" asked Maggie, and then answered her own question with, "David, I know Chris is hurting deeply, but that is no excuse for what he did here. It wasn't your fault that Cindy took it upon herself to leave the safety of this garrison. I'm so sorry."

"Don't be, Aunt Maggie. If the tables were turned, I may have reacted the same way."

During the entire conversation between David and Maggie, Kat glimpsed over from time to time at the Gentleman seated across from David. She knew that she had met this person before, but she couldn't pinpoint exactly where.

David noticed Kat's attention to Lars and stated, "I'm sorry. Where are my manners? Mother, Aunt Maggie, do you remember Lars Erickson?"

"Of course, Lars. My goodness, how are you?" questioned Kat, while Lars rose to his feet and she gave him a big hug.

"Maggie, you remember Lars?" asked Kat.

"Yes, I do. Hello, Lars," said Maggie as she held out her hand in greeting.

"How long has it been, Lars?" inquired Kat.

"David and I ran into each other about two years ago, but as far as you and Mrs. Ryan, it was my graduation from high school that we saw each other last."

"Yes, I think you're right. I came to your graduation with David and Maggie. Are you here on business, or is this a social call to see my son?"

"He's here because I summoned him, Mother," informed David, before Lars had a chance to answer her question. "Lars is going to replace Commander Owen."

"And where is Joe going?" asked Kat.

"Here. He's going to replace me. From now on, I will be in the field with my troops."

"David, for God's sake, you're not serious are you?"

"Yes, Mother. I am."

"But does Corrine know?"

"Mother, please. We'll discuss this later."

Kat knew by David's tone of voice that he meant what he said, so she dropped the subject for now, but would definitely discuss this later with him after talking with Corrine.

"Mother, was there something else that you wished to discuss with me, or was it strictly to find out about Chris being here?"

"Yes. We not only wanted to hear about Chris, but I wanted to inform you that Maggie and I have found someone to take over Cindy's duties in regard to the database, but it can wait until later if you're too busy right now," informed Kat.

"I don't have a meeting with my Commanders, until at 1300 hours this afternoon, and Lars and I were reminiscing about the past, and Commander Owen is going over some records with Corporal Adams. So as long as you and aunt Maggie are here, you might as well stay and tell me what you came to tell me in the first place."

"If you don't mind, Kat, I would like to leave. I think I will go and lie down for awhile," stated Maggie.

"Are you alright, Maggie?" asked Kat, with a tinge of alarm.

"Yes, just a little tired. I'll talk to you later. David, I'll see you later. Lars, it was nice meeting you again, and I hope that I see more of you."

"Thank you, Mrs. Ryan. The pleasure was all mine."

"I'm worried about Maggie, David. It's bad enough coping with the loss of Cindy and Linda for her, but now this incident with Chris, because he didn't take the time to visit with his own mother. I just don't know."

"Aunt Maggie is strong-willed. I'm sure she'll make it through this."

"I hope you're right," answered Kat.

As Maggie was leaving, Commander Owen passed her in the doorway and said, "I'm so sorry about your terrible loss, Mrs. Ryan. You have my sincere condolences."

"Thank you, Commander Owen. How kind of you."

"Corporal Adams just went to lunch, so I figured I'd come back here and wait for him to return, so that we can go over more details together," explained Commander Owen.

"Of course, Joe. Have a seat," requested David.

"Joe," said Kat, "I just wanted you to know how happy I am that David has chosen you to replace him, and I think that you are the best choice, because you and David go back a long ways together."

"Thank you, Kat. I just hope I can fill your son's shoes."

"Now, you were saying something about replacing Cindy, Mother?"

"Yes. Maggie and I interviewed a woman this morning to take over Cindy's duties, like I said before. She's originally from the States—Denver, to be exact—and she is young, but she has all the qualifications and then some. Her name is Christine Johnson."

"Does she check out, Mother?" asked David, while not caring about how old this woman is or how smart she is.

"Yes. I had her repeat the oath of allegiance and checked her left hand right afterward. You know David, it never ceases to amaze me after checking thousands and thousands of people, how that mole never changes its size, shape or color. It still appears almost transparent, because of the light amber color and the little emerald green dot positioned exactly in the middle of it with the shape resembling a tiny Star of David," explained Kat.

"That's it! Oh my God, Mother. You've just told me who our spy is. Damn! Why did it take me so long to figure it out?" questioned David,

mainly to himself, before grabbing Kat and hugging her and kissing her right cheek and then he hastened out of the room.

"Corporal Adams!"

"Yes, Sir."

"I want you to check everything we have on John Paul Withers. He's a non-com who lives in Budapest. And Corporal Adams, make it fast and bring it into my office right away."

"Yes, Sir."

Kat looked at Lars with astonishment while David was gone and stated, "I was glad to be of help even though I don't know how I was of help."

"I'm sure that David will explain it to us as soon as he gets back here," answered Lars.

"I told Corporal Adams to cancel my meeting with my Commanders until at 800 hours tomorrow morning. This is too important!"

"David, please tell us what this is all about," implored Kat.

"I also told Corporal Adams to dig up everything we have on John Paul Withers."

"Are you talking about little Johnny, your childhood friend from kindergarten?" inquired Kat.

"One and the same, Mother."

"What's he got to do with all of this?" asked Kat.

"If the records prove me right, he's our spy."

Kat was stunned beyond words, until she calmed herself down enough to inquire, "Why do you suspect him?"

David went on to explain to Commander Owen, Kat, and Lars, "I was in Budapest two years ago. Actually, Lars, it was a couple of months after I

ran into you in Amsterdam. Anyways, I was there to meet with one of our intelligence agents to see, who he thought that was capable of replacing his partner, who, was careless, and thus, we suspect he was found out, and he was killed trying to escape Budapest. I stopped at a bar-restaurant to have something to eat, before I returned to my hotel and leave the next morning to return here. I just sat down at the bar and ordered a drink and asked for a menu. The bartender hadn't finished making my drink yet when a man sat down right next to me. I thought at the time that it was unusual, considering there were only two other people at the bar besides me, and there were plenty of empty barstools available." David recalled the entire conversation between him and John Withers and relayed it as such. "John started the conversation with, 'Aren't you going to buy an old friend a drink?'"

"I told him I certainly would, if I had an old friend here. He laughed and asked me, 'You don't recognize me, do you?' I looked at him and I didn't have the foggiest notion who he was and told him so, and informed him that he must have me mistaken with someone else."

"'No, I don't, David,' he said. 'Enough of the games. Who are you? How do you know my name? And most importantly, what do you want?' I asked him. 'It's me, David, John Withers,' was his response."

"'Thee John Withers from kindergarten?' I couldn't believe it. 'One and the same,' he replied."

"'I'll be damn, little Johnny Withers. Small world isn't it?' I said. 'Got that right,' quipped John."

"I asked if he was there on business. 'No. Actually, I live and work here, and I followed you in here,' he said."

"'Followed me? What do you mean?' He explained, 'I just finished work and was coming out of my building when I spotted you coming out of a building two doors away.'"

"I said, 'John, I didn't recognize you, so how were you so sure it was me?' and he told me, 'David, you haven't changed one bit in looks except

that you're a man now and not that little kid I knew. I stopped dead in my tracks when I first spotted you and felt—I don't know what you would call it—gut instinct, intuition, whatever, but I just knew it was you, so I followed you in here to make sure that I was right.'"

"'And if you wouldn't have been?' I asked. 'Then I would've had to apologize and walked away with egg on my face,' laughed John."

"Even as a kid, John was a smooth talker and a charmer, but most of all, a manipulator," interrupted Kat.

"I was too young to see those traits in him. To me, he was just my best friend for awhile," answered David. He went on with his story. "I asked him what company he worked for and he told me it was a conglomerate and they manufactured engine parts. I asked him what kind of engines and he told me every kind that you can think of."

"'What brought you to Budapest in the first place, John?' I asked. He told me, 'My mother's relatives are from here, and I decided one day that I wanted to meet them, so I looked them up. I liked this city so well that I decided to stay for awhile.'"

"'How long have you been here?' 'Going on five years now. If I was going to stay, I needed a job, and my uncle works where I do, and he got me in the front door so to speak. I worked my way up to manager of my division and the rest is history,' explained John."

"I asked, 'Do you like the work that you're doing?' 'Let's just say it's a job. It helps to keep a roof over my head, food on my table and some money left over in my wallet every two weeks. What about you, David? What are you up to these days?' he asked."

"I told him, 'I work for a telecommunications outfit out of Scotland.' He asked me, 'Any wife and kids?'"

"I told him no. 'You might say I'm married to my job, because I do a lot of traveling and just never found the time to date. What about you, John? Ever marry?'"

"He said, 'No way. I don't need a woman in my life. Can't trust them to stay faithful.'"

"We ate a meal together, small talked for about another two hours, said our goodbyes and promised to keep in touch with each other. I never laid eyes on him again," informed David.

"Then what makes you think he's our traitor?" questioned Commander Owen.

"I'm getting to that. Like I said before, I don't believe in coincidences. He knew exactly who I was, and probably followed me from the time that I arrived in Budapest."

"So you're basing your theory that he is our spy, because you don't believe in coincidences?" asked Commander Owen.

"That, and the fact that John is left handed. He absolutely could not do anything with that right hand of his. Before we parted, he held out his left hand to shake. I thought it unusual, but later on, after thinking through the whole incident with him, I had him checked to see if he was listed in our database as an enemy agent. He wasn't. Even though he was cleared, I still had a strong intuition that something wasn't right with him, so I had our agents keep close tabs on him for three months and nothing was reported to make us think that he was working for the enemy."

"That just about puts you back to square one then, David," noted Kat.

"Not quite yet. We knew that the leaks were coming out of Budapest, and that the agent that was murdered must have found out whom our spy was. You just gave me the answer, Mother. All women who are sworn in have our trademark appear on their left hand and men on their right hand. John ate his meal and drank his drinks with his left hand. Thinking back now, I don't recall seeing his right hand at all. He had it either in his lap, underneath his coat, or when we shook hands, he had it in his right pocket. It all makes sense now. He couldn't expose his right hand to me, because he had the mark of the beast implanted on top like everyone else who were loyal to Musva."

Corporal Adams informed David that there were no files on a John Paul Withers, and that he was not listed in the database either.

"There has to be some mistake, Corporal Adams. I saw the original file on him when we first had the database check him out. Go and check again, Corporal Adams."

"Yes, Sir." He came back a few moments later. "Nothing, Sir. We have nothing listed for a John Paul Withers."

"Could you have misfiled his folder? Forget that question, Corporal Adams. You're too good at your job for that to happen. You're dismissed."

"Yes, Sir."

"Interesting," informed David.

"What do you mean by that?" questioned Kat.

"The database is fed information every three weeks to keep the files up-to-date," said David.

"So if anything more was found out about your friend Johnny, the database would have registered that information?" inquired Kat.

"Correct," David answered.

"If it is listed in there that he was a known spy, why weren't we alerted of that fact on the database?" Commander Owen asked.

"The database is programmed to pick up any covert action taking place against us, but evidently, all the information found about John had to be all circumstantial," stated David.

"So if there was only circumstantial evidence in the database about him, why is it missing?" Lars asked.

"My personal opinion is that we are dealing with a highly organized spy ring and John is only small peanuts. He doesn't have the ability to run such an operation," responded David.

"So why destroy his files?" inquired Kat.

"Precautionary action, I suspect. No loose ends," informed David. "Since Joe is here now to take my place and to see that everything runs smoothly, I think, Lars, that you and I will take a trip to Budapest to do some snooping on our own. I want to tie up some loose ends here with Joe and my other Commanders and send for a cargo plane to take us there. Can you be ready in three days?" David inquired of Lars.

"Of course."

"Good. We'll leave then."

Two days later…

"Sir," came Corporal Adams voice over the intercom system.

"Yes, Corporal."

"There's a Rear Admiral Chad Ryan here to see you," announced Corporal Adams.

"Chad? Oh my God! Send him in, Corporal."

"Right away, Sir,"

David was halfway across his office when Chad entered and met him there. The two embraced before David said, "I don't believe it's you, Chad. You look great. It looks like the Mediterranean air has been good to you. Have you seen aunt Maggie yet?"

"No. I thought I'd stop in and see you first."

"Come on in and sit down. I assume the reason that you're here is, because you heard about Cindy and Linda?"

"Yes. But I didn't hear about it until three days ago. I had to make an ammunitions run with the *Calypso* to Belfast, Ireland. Since I was in the vicinity, I had to stop and see how mom's doing, because it's been a year or so since I saw her last."

"Vicinity, huh?" chuckled David. "The last time that you, Chris, Tim and I all were together was about two and a half years ago when you all showed up to celebrate the birth of Linda," reminisced David, with tears forming in his eyes.

"Right. And the four of us headed to that bar in the village and got shit-faced from drinking shots. Who started that anyways?" questioned Chad.

"It was Tim."

"Figures. I can hold my liquor with the best of them, but when I went to bed that night, my bed was spinning faster than an out-of-control top. I had a real doozy of a hangover for three days," laughed Chad.

"Rumor has it that the owner fired the bartender who served us," informed David.

"For what?"

"We emptied out half of his best stock of liquor,“ chuckled David.

"Rumor also has it that there's a spy in our organization, true?" questioned Chad.

"Yes, it's true."

"Know who?"

"I have a good suspicion, but I need more than gut instinct to go on," answered David. "Do you know a guy by the name of John Withers?"

"The mole? You think it's him? Yeah, I know him, and the guy is a real loser and likes to push his weight around and play the 'big shot' role. He's always dressed to a 'tee' because he wears $900 suits and only lies with the high class hookers and drives a red Ferrari. With a lifestyle like that, he has to be rolling in dough."

"And I know where he gets his cash flow from," informed David.

"Who?"

"The Antichrist. John's my traitor, and I think he's a double agent. To cut a long story short, I ran into him, or better yet, I think he followed me into a bar in Budapest where he lives and told me that he works in a factory that makes engine parts. In light of what you just told me, I think my gut feelings are true."

"Well, if he works in a factory like he told you, he must go in the front door and right out the back door, because I've seen him plenty of times on the street day and night. He owns and operates The Establishment, a bar-restaurant and hotel, which is a front for his high-priced call girls. He's been known to beat some of them up pretty bad. Mainly the ones with black hair, so he must have a thing with black-haired women."

"His mother had black hair and left his dad, Johnny, a younger brother, and sister, and ran away with his dad's best friend."

"Well, that explains it," commented Chad. "If I could take a wild guess, I'd say he uses his call girls to get information for him. For you to call him a double agent, he'd have to work for us then also. How do you figure that? Wasn't he checked out?"

"Yes, thoroughly, I thought. I think John is way down on the bottom of the totem pole, and this is a highly organized spy ring, and I want the top man."

"Someone from our organization?" asked Chad.

"Yes. And he's high-ranking."

"What makes you think that?" Chad inquired.

"The database automatically registers new information on someone every three weeks. It's been two years since I had John put under surveillance for three months, and we couldn't find anything proving that he was a spy. He's very cunning and never makes a false move, so he checked out, and he was clean. But now he is wiped completely from our

database, and his files are missing also. The only people who have access to the database are civilians who operate them and high-ranking officers."

"Wow, David! You have your work cut out for you. That must involve at least five hundred people."

"Try one thousand."

"How do you figure that you're going to find the leak with that many people involved?"

"I think I can safely rule out any civilians. The top man I'm looking for, in my estimation, is military."

"Vendetta against you? Money-hungry like Withers?"

"Possibly, but my guess is he is forced into it," answered David.

"What do you mean?"

"Everyone in this army has been checked out and cleared. He has a legitimate mole and can move freely, because of his rank and he can obtain inside information, easily. As you know yourself, Chad, military people are deeply dedicated to their branch of the service, and the man that I'm looking for could have loved ones in the hands of the Antichrist, and that is Musva's ace-in-the-hole: to get this man to do his dirty work for him."

"You've always been right with your gut instinct, David, and you may be right on this one too. Withers, the scum, would do it for money and money alone, but a military man, I don't think so. Besides, how could he spend a lot of silver or gold without anyone noticing? The Antichrist doles it out pretty freely, from what I hear," informed Chad.

"Could be in a number of Swiss bank accounts," declared David.

"You must know by now, David, that Musva moved his headquarters to Damascus after depleting the United States of all it's resources, and he left the country looking like a dumping ground with his massive amount of used and broken military toys laying all over the place?" questioned Chad.

"Yes, I knew from my informants that he is in Damascus, but I didn't know about the rest. God, I hate that bastard, for what he's done to this world. Have you seen or heard from Chris?" asked David.

"Yes, David. I have. He got in touch with me and asked me to meet him in Buenos Aires. He told me that his camp is somewhere in Brazil, but he didn't tell me exactly where. He usually stays in one place no longer than a couple of weeks for fear that he will be located."

"How is he?"

"Drunker than a skunk already when I met him at 1300 hours at some bar. Can't remember the name of it. When he sobered up, I had a long talk with him, but I know he didn't listen to a word that I told him."

"Mother thinks he will grieve the loss of Cindy and Linda and will eventually come around. What do you think, Chad?"

"No, I don't think so. He loved Cindy to the extreme, and after the three miscarriages that she had, and that they thought that they would never be able to have children, along comes Linda. She was his pride and joy. He's on a downhill spiral and no one can help him but himself. I love my brother, and it hurts me to no end seeing the shape that he's in."

"Oh, Chad, the whole thing is all my fault. Even though I didn't know what Cindy had planned, I should have had stronger rules in force as far as leaving the garrison."

"David! Don't let your conscience take you down with this. Listen to me, it wasn't your fault. It was just a terrible twist of fate, nothing else. So stop brow-beating yourself to death over this."

"Will I get to see you again before you leave, Chad?"

"I'm afraid not, David. I plan to spend the day with Mom and then head out. I don't like to leave the *Calypso* mooring for too long, even though my men are very capable of watching over her," laughed Chad. "So we had better say our good-byes now."

David and Chad hugged each other, and as Chad came to the entrance of David's office, he turned and asked of David, "Are you going after Withers?"

"Damn right I am."

"Watch your back. It's a dangerous world out there. And David, remember what I said about Cindy. Catch you later."

"Bye for now, Chad. And thanks."

David and Lars left early the next morning as planned on a cargo plane bound for Budapest.

They were back at the garrison within three days, and David called a special meeting, which consisted of his five Commanders, Lars, Kat and Maggie.

He filled his other four Commanders in on the details that he shared with Kat, Maggie, Lars and Commander Owen earlier in the week, and brought them up to date with all the facts. He said, "Our one and only intelligence agent met us at a predetermined location in Budapest. His friend and partner had a daughter, who was one of John's expensive call girls. John made the mistake of beating on her so as payback, she gave her father all the information that she received from her clients instead of going through John. We suspect that John had our agent killed, and his daughter disappeared the same time and was never seen again. We figured that he killed her too, but then again, no proof."

"When the agent told us that John's body was discovered in his apartment two days ago and was said to be killed, because of a so called burglary attempt, Lars and I were back to square one as we were two years ago. That's how long we have been after Withers, but had no proof that he was a double agent—nothing solid anyway. John wasn't stupid when it came to protecting his property. He had a state-of-the-art burglar system placed throughout the entire building and especially his living quarters, but yet his murder was classified as a burglary gone wrong. The news going around was that he must have known the person or people who killed him and let them in."

"Lars and I waited until night fall and picked the lock to his apartment, which was ransacked, thoroughly. Someone was looking for something. Lars found that something: John's ledger, hidden in a spring action floor board beneath his desk that became loose after Lars's foot accidentally touched it when he sat down looking for a false compartment in the desk. Seems that John would sift through all the feedback from his girls and make a decision as to how important each one was. Each entry was dated and the information entered in full detail. This would determine how much he was paid in gold and silver, and it was plenty. This ledger proved that he was a double agent, but it didn't prove to us why he was murdered. it could be that he became too greedy and wanted more money from both sides or was blackmailing someone high-ranking in our organization who could be the head of the spy ring."

"Why do you think it is someone of high rank who is behind the ring?" asked Commander Chandler.

"All the civilians that work with the database system have to have clearance from either a Commander, or one of your first or second lieutenants assigned to them, which could have between one or a thousand civilians, depending on their positions under his command," explained David.

"That, General, would be like looking for a needle in a haystack," noted Commander Chase.

"You're right, Scott. It was, but we never found the connection. We talked to all of John's girls to see if something out of the ordinary was said or done with their messages to the Antichrist or to us. One of them told us something very unusual: he owned a lot of suits that he could have worn each day and not the same one for a whole month straight. He wore one suit in particular every Monday, Wednesday, and Friday. It seemed peculiar and worth looking into, so Lars and I again snuck into his apartment. We looked through each suit pocket once and found nothing. The second time around, Lars found something white sticking out of a slit in one of his vests under the normal pocket, but this pocket was vertical. It was a small piece of paper folded to fit the pocket and

had some kind of letters and symbols, which had to be a code of some sort. We had another talk with our agent, and he said that that was the oldest trick in the book as far as the suits were concerned. The same suit that was worn on Monday, Wednesday, and Friday, told his contact that he had messages. If a different suit was worn on those days, it meant no messages," stated David.

"So now you had all these little clues that didn't add up to anything. Am I right, David?" inquired Kat.

"Right, Mother," stated David and continued with, "Halfway through our investigation, Lars and I went through the data on all the raids against us, and Lars came up with something very interesting. With every reconnaissance run, the horses to the supply wagon were taken, but the wagon was always left behind. Lars, would you tell everyone what you found?" requested David.

"Why bother unhitching the team when they could steal the wagons too? That was the question that needed to be answered. A team of five men went over our twenty-five wagons with a fine-toothed comb and found nothing out of the ordinary. Another dead end. About a month ago, George, who is head of the stables and everything that they entail, had one of the wagons hitched and was going to drive it out of the corral. He put his hand over the break release, which then accidentally slipped downward, and he ended up with a large sliver in his thumb. After checking it out, he discovered a vertical slit cut out to the underside of the break release. The slit was three inches long with a three-inch depth, which left enough room for a slip of paper with a coded message to be stored. The opening of the vertical slit was undetected to the naked eye, because it matched the color of the grain in the wood. After searching the rest of the twenty-five wagons, the same slit in the same location was carved. This is how they got their messages to the enemy and return messages from the enemy: the supply wagons. That was why they were left behind and no one was the wiser."

"Unbelievable," stated Commander Chandler.

"Yes, it is almost unbelievable," agreed Kat. "So now you have the means of how they got the coded messages to the enemy, but you still don't know who?" questioned Kat.

"Not quite, Mother. For six months, Lars and I suspected one of you five Commanders, but we had to figure out which one."

"Joe, do you want to fill in the gaps that I may have missed?" asked David.

"You certainly don't think I'm the one? Really, David, this is all quite ludicrous."

"Is it, Joe? You have the base camp closest to the garrison. According to the records for sign in, you were here on an average of three times a week."

"That certainly doesn't make me the head of a spy ring."

"No, you're right, Joe. You're number two in command. Cindy was the ring leader!" stated David, emphatically.

"David!" yelled, Kat, as she sprang from her seat and caused her chair to topple. "For God's sake, what are you saying? I refuse to believe such rubbish," stated Kat, who became emotionally drained upon hearing her son's words.

"Mother, please listen to all the facts that Lars and I gathered and then base your opinion," requested David.

"Who better than a woman. She would be above suspicion. Cindy was never checked for the mole, because she was already married to Chris and a part of the family. She was a double agent. Toward the end, she would get word to Chris via his connection, and give him the locations of the Antichrist's major installations throughout Europe. This probably eased her mind that she wasn't betraying Chris, but she was playing a dangerous game with both sides," explained David.

"Joe, you gave yourself away. You've always had the habit of doodling with paper and pencil during our meetings, and one meeting in particular

was no exception. Cindy was the one who devised that elaborate code system, and parts of it were on the piece of paper found in John's vest pocket. After going to the board during that monthly meeting, I happened to look over your shoulder before I sat back down and saw what I believed to be scribbling. I didn't think twice about it at the time, but later, I copied it from memory onto another piece of paper and stuck it into my wallet. After Lars and I finished our meal in Budapest, the waitress handed me our itemized bill. On the receipt were a bunch of numbers and some letters of the alphabet. That's when it hit me. I retrieved the copy of your scribbling that I had written from my wallet and compared it to Cindy's coded message. All five of your symbols matched perfectly to the one's found in John's vest pocket. How would you know parts of the code, if you weren't involved somehow? I started giving false time periods and locations when and where our troops would go out on reconnaissance runs again. It did the trick, because two scouts were sent out to one of the locations and found a troop of the Antichrist's henchmen waiting to ambush our men. That location sent to the enemy had to come from here and here alone."

"You really don't have anything on me. This is all circumstantial evidence that wouldn't stand up in a military court of law."

"I'm not done yet, Joe. That scene with my mother supposedly giving me the answer to whom our spy was, was a hoax for your benefit. I had Corporal Adams remove John Withers's file and replace it with a bogus file. If you had taken the time to look into his folder, you would have found blank pages, but you didn't have time, because my aunt Maggie left unexpectedly and would have caught you in the act, so you slipped it in between some papers that you were carrying in your hands."

"You were the one who ordered the killing of John Withers. John had a loose tongue when he had too many under his belt, so you knew about the ledger that he kept and that it also had Cindy, your name, and the names of seven other people, who made up the list of those involved in the operation. Under your name were entries of monies received every month to John. He was blackmailing you, Joe, wasn't he? He wanted more money from you, and when you knew that Lars and I were going

after him, you panicked, because you thought the entire operation might be exposed. You had two good reasons in your mind to get rid of John Withers. He let his own killer in, because he thought it was your man with the money."

"Yeah, it's all true. The guy was a real scumbag, and the world will be a better place without him," said, Joe as he slammed his hand down on the table. You could hear a pin drop, because the room was totally silent after Joe made that statement. Actually, everyone was stunned beyond belief.

"David, please tell me that everything you said about Cindy is some kind of a mix-up and not really true," begged Maggie.

"Sorry, Aunt Maggie. I wish I could, but I can't, because it's all true."

David looked over at his mother and saw the awful expression of mixed emotions showing on her face.

"Maggie, do you want to leave, because this is too much for you? We'll understand if you do," said Kat.

"Hell no! I've sat through this much and I want to hear the rest of it."

"We would never have suspected, Cindy, in a million years, but because her name was in John's ledger, the pieces of the puzzle were finally coming together. Cindy knew that if she and Linda hid in that supply wagon that they would be safe, because it wasn't supposed to be attacked," stated David.

"Then why was it?" questioned Kat.

"I assume that there was a mix-up in the orders given to the other side. Someone interpreted them wrong, and they were ambushed, instead. Cindy basically signed her own death warrant."

"Why didn't they know who she really was?" inquired Maggie.

"They were only soldiers, Aunt Maggie, not any of the hierarchy. They would not have known about Cindy or believed her if she tried to explain who she was. To them, she was just another traitor to their beloved leader."

"So, she left here knowing that she would be safe and would eventually find Chris?" inquired Kat.

"Yes. In her mind, she had nothing to worry about. She knew where Chris was located, and that is why she left on that certain day, because he was near and would be there for only a couple of days," stated David.

"What I don't understand is how she could get a message to the other side telling them to let her through, when she was in one of the wagons where the messages were exchanged only after the enemy massacred everyone?" questioned Commander Chase.

"There was to be no message hidden in the wagon. One of the younger pony express riders delivered the message explaining her plans to her contact, who would see to it that she arrived safely by Chris, after sneaking out of the wagon when the time was right. It's too bad that Cindy got him involved, because he's only a kid of seventeen, who was probably totally smitten with her and did her bidding every time she asked him to," explained David.

"Does Chris know any of this about, Cindy?" Kat asked.

"No. If he did, he wouldn't have been so upset with me."

"Joe, you might as well tell us the rest of the story. We know that Cindy had something on you to get you involved, but we don't know what it was," suggested David.

With a long pause and a look of total defeat, Joe started his story. "I am Cindy's real father. I married Cindy's mother, Evelyn, at a very young age. I was twenty and still wet behind the ears and she was only eighteen. Things were going smoothly, until Evelyn became pregnant and into her seventh month. The happy, about-to-be mother, completely changed and definitely not for the better. She became moody, withdrawn for days on end, and complained about everything. She was driving me crazy! I even got her mother and father involved hoping that they could do something to help her. Right before the birth of Cindy, she seemed better and after delivering her, she settled down, and was a good mother. This lasted less

than two years. My wife was a beautiful woman. She knew it, and just about every man in town knew it, because she practically slept with all of them. I didn't see the signs, because I worked one job and a part-time job so I was not home a lot. Some of this could have been my fault, because I should have paid more attention to her, but I needed to work two jobs to put a roof over our heads and food on the table. I told her that it would be temporary, until we could get ahead a little bit more."

"I came home sick from my regular job one day and found Evelyn, Cindy and her car gone. Her parents bought her that car, so that she would be free to use it to go grocery shopping or whatever. She used it mostly for the 'whatever.' It seems that she had been leaving Cindy with them everyday for that entire time, and she told them that she had taken a part time job to help out, and they were not to tell me, because I wouldn't stand for it and make her quit. She dropped Cindy off and picked her up at the same time every day of the week just like clockwork. They were overjoyed having Cindy stay with them, so believed their daughter's story and never complained or questioned her. Evelyn really used both of them and showed no remorse when I caught up with her after searching for her everywhere. I found her outside one of the bars out of town with her current man friend. We got into a real good screaming match in the parking lot and she told me that she hated her life and especially me. The only person she loved was Cindy, and she wanted out of the marriage and the sooner the better. I slapped her face with the back of my hand, and she took off running to her car with her man friend already inside waiting for her and she sped off. I never saw my wife again."

"Being angry, consuming too much alcohol and speeding, caused Evelyn to die in her car, which missed the curve, went over a large embankment, rolled over several times, and when it hit the tree at the bottom, the car burst into flames and killing both of them and charring their bodies beyond recognition. They knew one of the bodies was Evelyn by the charm bracelet that fell off her wrist and was found somewhere near the scene. Her father had given it to her mother, and she in turn gave it to Evelyn. Evidently everyone thought that the other body was me, so I figured that the man she was with was a drifter, because no one claimed

him missing. I didn't stay around long enough to find out for sure. I hit the road with my few meager belongings and took on a complete new identity. I told myself that Cindy was better off with her grandparents. Besides, how could I care for a soon-to-be two-year-old and work to make a living? I took the easy way out and never looked back."

"I settled in Denver and found a talented man to forge my birth certificate and driver's license and I had my fingerprints put into the National Database Center. It cost me enough, but the end results were good, and I became Joseph Edward Owen of Tupelo, Mississippi. I started working for a logging company outside of Denver for a couple of years, and with all the overtime hours, I had saved a pretty good sized nest egg."

"I heard about a company in Chicago that needed die casters, and I knew everything there was to know about die casting, because that is what I did for a living while married to Evelyn. I drove to Chicago and was hired on the spot. After a couple of years, I was promoted to foreman. The money was good and I was able to save enough for a down payment on a house. I met my wife, Theresa at a co-worker's barbeque. We married and had three kids: two boys and a girl. I enlisted in the Army with the intention of making a career of it and fifteen years later, I was serving with the Special Forces too when I met you, David, for the first time during WWIII, and the rest is history."

"So somehow Cindy found out your true identity and tracked you down?" questioned David.

"Yes. She told me that her grandparents adopted her and told her at about age ten that her parents died in a car accident. After her grandmother died and Cindy was left the house, she came across her grandmother's diary stating that they moved from the small town in Wisconsin that we all lived in, because of the shame that their daughter brought upon them and settled in Milwaukee. The only picture her grandmother kept was our wedding picture."

"Cindy told me that fate has a way of correcting the wrongs to rights in the game of life, when she spotted me going into the Arts and Science

Building in Chicago. She followed me to make sure that it was me, and of course it was.

"Within a few months, she knew everything about me, and I mean everything. She approached me one day while I was shopping for a present for my wife's birthday and told me who she was and what she wanted from me. She also told me that her grandparents had both Evelyn and I on a false pedestal all those years. But in reality, her father was a damn deserting coward, and her mother was the town whore, and that she hated both of us with a passion. She also told me that she could ruin my life with the snap of her fingers because of her connections. Not knowing my daughter all these years and being a complete stranger to me, I still sensed that she was unbalanced to some degree. How much, I didn't know for sure until I got to know her better."

"Cindy was not the Cindy that we all thought she was, was she David?" asked Maggie, with tears forming in her eyes.

"Yes and no, Aunt Maggie. In the beginning, when we all first met her, she was. And the side of Cindy that we all knew: a wife and mother, who was kind and considerate and loved her husband and daughter. The flip side of Cindy was the side that Joe saw: someone, who was devious, cunning and hateful. She was not the same person in the end, and we'll never know the real reason that drove Cindy to do all that she did to all of us, because it went to the grave with her. But I, for one, will still have fond memories of that sweet girl, who came into and enriched our lives for so many years," added David.

"I think it's time for all of us to take a break," said David, as he motioned to the two MPs standing at the entrance to his office and looked directly at Commander Owen and told them, "If the bastard moves, shoot him."

All of them were completely drained of emotions and were walking as in a mythical state of being as they continued to file out of David's office and headed for some fresh air. Maggie was the first to speak and inquired of David, "What will happen to him?"

"He will be tried by members of his peers and if found guilty, shot as a spy and traitor."

After everyone returned to David's office, Commander Owen continued with his story. "Cindy had me in her clutches and threatened to expose me. With taking on a new identity all those years back, I would have been dishonorably discharged from the Army and everything that I worked for to create a good life for my family would have been futile, let alone the disgrace to my family and the probability of facing criminal charges besides. I couldn't take the chance of all of that happening, so I went along with everything my daughter demanded of me. I was the one who betrayed you, David, and gave the information to the enemy on all the reconnaissance runs."

"My God, man, you betrayed all of us, because you didn't want to lose your status and the comfortable life that you were leading?" growled Commander Chase, as he arose from his chair and went after Commander Owen, with hatred in his eyes and ready to do bodily harm.

David and Lars intervened just before he got to Joe and wrestled him back to his chair.

"I'll have no more outbursts like the one that we just witnessed. Is that understood, Gentlemen?" demanded David. "Alright, Joe, go on with your story," David implored.

"I didn't do it for my sake but my family's. It was only two days later after Cindy told me that she would expose me if I didn't go along with her, and that our children would be taken from our residence in the dead of night. They were her ace-in-the-hole to keep me in line."

"How long has it been since they were abducted, Joe?" questioned David.

"Two and a half years next month have passed since I saw my kids last. Cindy told me that if I didn't cooperate, I'd never see them again."

"You can't trust the enemy, Joe. So what makes you think your children are still alive? Have you heard anything from them or about them since they were taken?" asked David.

"No, I haven't heard a word from them, but I found out six months ago that they were being held in an enemy camp near Singapore, and now they have been moved again to some other prison camp, and maybe another. I don't know anymore."

"Why in God's name didn't you come to me and tell me all of this, Joe?" asked David. "We could have figured out some way to get your kids back."

"I couldn't take that chance, can't you see? What if all our attempts would have failed? Then what? My children were alive six months ago, and I planned to keep it that way no matter what was happening to me. I'd do it all over the same way to keep my kids alive. My wife has prayed to God every night for the past two and a half years that she will some day see our children again, and she has cried herself to sleep every night. I'm still dealing with the shame of my actions, but can't you all see that I had to do it?" Joe pleaded for reassurance from his peers. No one answered him.

"So you have no loyalty to the Antichrist then?" asked Lars.

"None whatsoever. I did what I had to do to keep my kids alive and safe, and I'd do it all over again for the same reasons."

"Take him away," demanded David of the two MPs still stationed in his office. "And keep him guarded, until you have him under lock and key."

"My God, what that poor man has been through," Kat stated.

"No, Mother. Don't feel sorry for him. Joe made the wrong choices all along and because of him, too many of our brave soldiers lie on that hill over there. He didn't take into consideration what would happen to others with his betrayal of all of us."

In less than a year, on June 16, 2032, Chad married a girl named Louise, who he met years earlier while stationed in Maryland at the Naval Academy. They had a private ceremony at the garrison with only the immediate family in attendance. Chad had wanted his older brother, Chris to be his best man, but no one knew for sure where he was, or even, if he was still alive even after David exhausted all his resources in trying to locate him. If you don't want to be found, usually no one will be able to find you, Chad had told David in regard to his brother, Chris' whereabouts. Since Tim could not be located either, Chad asked that David be his best man. Louise gave birth to a baby boy nine months later on March 12, 2033, and they named him Anthony Marshall.

David never saw his cousin, Chris again. If it was hatred for David on his part or shame that kept him away because of Cindy, no one knew for sure. It was verified that Chris destroyed the second largest supply depot and headquarters of the Antichrist, but in so doing, intentionally crashed his Stealth fighter. David was devastated when he heard the news about the death of his favorite cousin, Chris. He made a point of tracking down Tim, so that he could be there for his brother's funeral service, and he put out feelers with all of his informants with the underground railroad network. It took nearly two weeks before one of them had heard that he was possibly in the Middle East near the city of Fallujah. As it turned out, the informant was correct, and Tim was found and told of the death of his brother Chris. Tim made the necessary arrangements, but informed David that he would not be able to get to the garrison any earlier than another two weeks, as traveling throughout the world wasn't like before when you planned an itinerary and booked a flight. Tim had to make arrangements through his operatives to get him home without danger.

Maggie could hardly contain the overwhelming excitement that she felt in anticipation of Tim's return to the garrison. It had been four years since anyone saw him, and with her grief for her first born still lingering so terribly in her thoughts and heart, she needed the comfort of Tim, also at this time to help put Chris to rest, as he died the exact same day that Cindy and Linda did but two years later.

On the day that Tim was to arrive, family members started to wait outside the garrison at different time intervals. Maggie was there the entire time when one hour, two hours, going on two and a half hours had passed, when an army jeep was spotted in the distance. All eyes turned toward the direction the jeep was approaching, as some in the family began to cry, some began to pace, but all had grins on their faces, because the long wait was about to come to a close.

"Here he is. It's really Tim," cried Maggie, as she was the first one to hug him as he alit the jeep, before it slowly came to a complete stop with Corporal Adams behind the wheel. Mother and son continued the embrace and hung on to each other for dear life, as tears of joy and sorrow flowed from both.

"Mother, you look wonderful," whispered Tim, as he was the first one to break the embrace and silence but was still in a very emotional state.

"Oh, Tim, you don't know how much all of us have been waiting for this moment to arrive. It's been so terribly long since we all saw you last," cried Maggie.

"Only four years, Mother," answered Tim, as he grabbed Maggie's hand and put his arm around her waist to steady her movements and to help calm her down, until a smile appeared on her face.

Chad gave his mother and brother a few more moments but then couldn't wait any longer, and as both brothers' eyes met, the two embraced.

"It's good to see you, Bro. How the hell did you get taller than me when I'm older?" Tim questioned with laughter.

"Because I ate all the oatmeal that Mother made us eat, while you fed your portion to all the dogs that we owned when Mother wasn't looking," chided Chad.

"Oh yeah, I remember that now," laughed Tim.

A solemn service unfolded as another funeral was held for the second time for this close-knit family, and in such a short time span since they put Cindy and Linda to rest, and now it was for Chris.

Kat was in awe as she watched her sister Maggie and witnessed her strong fortitude throughout the entire service, especially when David presented her with the neatly folded, ceremonial American flag and the purple heart awarded to Chris posthumously, because of his bravery and actions in the line of duty. She didn't think that she could do as well, if the tables were turned, but knew that Maggie would wait and mourn her son, Chris alone in her own privacy, as she had done every night since his passing.

Before, there were four. Now, the number was three, as the cousins met at the atrium after the funeral services. It's hard to feel what others are feeling at the same time and under the same circumstances, when a solemn occasion like this takes place, not like the jovial get together a little over four years ago when Cindy gave birth to Linda and Chris was present.

"If I would have taken the time to realize how precious a life is, especially one of our own, and with the state the world we're now living is in, I would have made sure no matter what that I could have somehow got home more often. I missed out on seeing my brothers and the rest of my family and now there's no turning back. I'll be damned if I'll let it happen again, and that's why I want to come home and join your army, David, if it's all right with you," explained a distraught Tim. He continued with, "I'm so very tired of the cat and mouse games that I have to endure daily with my chosen field with Special Forces with the remaining haphazard, rag-tag, worn-out army that was once the greatest fighting force in the world. Our numbers are few and dwindling on a daily basis."

David had to take a moment to grasp all that Tim just revealed to Chad and himself, as it was a shock to him to see the emotional state that Tim, the devil-may-care one of the family was in while telling his story.

"You don't need my permission to join, Tim. This is God's earthly army, not mine, and I would be honored to have you with us," informed David.

"I must say, brother, you have certainly knocked my socks off with your revelation," laughed Chad. "I thought you liked the adventurous carefree life that you've been leading?"

"I thought so too, but as I watched you and David being happily married and having children, I realized just how much I missed out on: a wife and family of my own. To me, that is the true meaning of life: family, as we don't know just how much time that we may have left on this earth. Even a day of what the two of you have is by far greater than what I have known. I see on a daily basis what the war and catastrophic events has done to this world, and I'm tired of the killing and dying. Do you see what I'm getting at?" asked Tim.

David and Chad looked at each other, and David was the first to speak with, "Believe it or not, yes, I do understand what you are saying, Tim, as I lived the same way: too busy and wrapped up with this place and the world outside of this garrison to realize what I needed in my life to fulfill it. I have a duty to my God to fight against the Antichrist, but I needed something else. I didn't come to this realization until Corrine came into my life and then Lexie. Looking back, I was just existing before. We live from day to day in this world, and I have learned to appreciate each precious moment now that I have both of them. And even if I can't be with them on a daily basis, family is what keeps me going," explained an emotional David.

"I had the *Calypso*. She was my whole life, I thought, with the wind at my back, the open sea, and the sky as my constant companion. I had a longing for a life of adventure, just like you, Tim. But the only difference between us, is that I realized that I needed something more in life a little earlier than you did. One day, about a year from the last time I saw her, and out of the clear blue sky, I found myself in port near Annapolis where Louise is from. I looked her up, found she wasn't married, wined and dined her, and asked her to marry me that same night. I couldn't believe I actually proposed to her. But what was more surprising to me, was when she agreed to accept my proposal and said, 'Yeah, why not. I've got nothing better to do.' She then told me that she loved me all those years and wondered how long it was going to take me to realize that I loved her." Chad laughed and continued on with, "Smart woman I have here and I love her dearly as I do my son, Anthony."

Just then Kat and Maggie walked into the atrium. All three arose from their seats in anticipation of Kat and Maggie wanting to sit.

"No, please remain sitting," said Maggie. "We don't plan to stay, and just wanted to tell you that we will be serving a brunch in about a half hour in the cafeteria. We sectioned off a portion of it, for just the family and close friends so that we will have our privacy."

"Alright, Mother. We'll be right behind you," informed Tim.

"David, Corrine is looking for you," said Kat as she put Lexie down and she ran to David and he picked her up and sat her on his lap.

Tim returned to the garrison less than two months later, and became a very big part of David's life because of his military experience, as did Lars, for the three fought side by side and were inseparable.

David and Corrine's living quarters…

"Corrine, please. We have discussed this so many times, and I thought you understood my reasoning and desire to get out from behind my desk and lead my soldiers into battle?" questioned David, after the two finished making love and David was holding her in his arms.

"I thought I did, David. But the closer the time, for each departure draws near, the more I change my mind. I don't want anything to happen to you. I don't know what Lexie and I would do without you," cried Corrine.

"Corrine, look at me," requested David, as he raised her head and exposed the beautiful green eyes that he so adored from the moment that he laid eyes on her.

"You knew from the start that I was born and raised with the intention of serving God by fighting the Antichrist in the End Time. I am living my destiny, Corrine, and I truly believe what Michael tells me that I will be safe for as long as I serve God in that capacity, because of his divine protection that he bestowed upon all of us."

"Yes, I know and understand all of that, David, but my mind always seems to linger back to the question that I ask myself: what if David doesn't come back to me?"

"You must have more faith in God, Corrine, and besides, remember who is watching over me: Michael the Archangel. You can't get more protection than that," laughed David.

"I know, David. I'm just being silly, I guess."

"Not silly, my darling. A loving, caring wife is what you are being," informed David, meaning every word he just said to this beautiful woman whom he loved beyond words.

Within days, David continued to keep that promise that he vowed to himself, and with his army, he continued to fight the Antichrist throughout Europe. He had chosen a young ambitious and very capable Major Cranston to take over the command of the garrison, with his mother and aunt Maggie to keep an eye on him. That left the garrison in very good hands.

David and each of his four Commanders had a cavalry army of nearly ten thousand men under their command, and each commander had a different country assigned to him once again, with the objective to move forward and destroy the Antichrist's outposts using guerilla-style combat and scorched earth techniques, which left nothing for the enemy or any alive to fight them again. They all were highly trained in combat techniques along with the martial arts styles of self-defense. They were a mighty force to be reckoned with and had to be, because the armies of Musva, even though they were getting lazy, out of shape, and less trained in military combat—were still a mighty offense against, David, because of the grandiose size of his military and seemingly growing rapidly every day. According to Michael, Lucifer was God's favorite Archangel, but he was not a warrior angel, and that was David's ace-in-the-hole and another one of the advantages over Musva, as he had no knowledge of fighting tactics and had to rely on his top generals for their advise. David knew about every last one of them—know your enemy—and knew also that there was but a handful with an exceptional knowledge of war strategy. He had served under three of them at one time or another and completely knew their fighting strategy and was able to take that knowledge and use it against them.

David's immediate army of nearly ten thousand men were divided into five units and covered northern, southern, eastern, western, and central Scotland, while his Commanders' armies followed suit with the same division of units and fought the Antichrist's armies in England, Poland, Ireland, and France. On and on his army trekked across Europe, with the same divisional strategy while invading Belgium, the Netherlands, Germany, Switzerland, and Austria. They fought each battle with ferocious tenacity destroying everything that belonged to the Antichrist with hit-hard-and-run tactics and leaving nothing but burnt ground in their wake.

The Antichrist grew so very tired of the cat-and-mouse games between his army and this man who dared to defy him for so long that he posted a ten million dollar reward, for the head of one David O'Brien, number one enemy of the State, in hopes that someone would betray him for that amount of money.

David left the decision to his trusted Commanders, when they felt that their men needed to rest and for how long and where, as battles not only entail fighting but also mind games against the enemy, with either strategy taking a great toll on an army unless used at advantageous times. With this theory in mind, David and his immediate army of two thousand, but now totaling 1,600 men, were on their way back to the garrison for a much needed respite, not only for the wounded to heal but the weary worn soldiers' spirit to heal. David needed the time to let his leg get stronger again, after nearly two years of battle in a war torn Europe.

Late Summer 2035

"Maggie, come quickly, they're back," shouted, Kat, as she hugged her sister, and the two ran to the front of the garrison and crashed through the solid steel doors into the outer courtyard to help with the wounded.

"Maggie, do you see, David, yet?" questioned Kat as she made her second trip out.

"No, Kat, do you?"

"No," was all Kat said in reply to Maggie.

While both sisters were working inside the garrison with helping to set up a make-shift hospital outside of the hospital complex, which was filled to capacity, because of the large influx of wounded, Kat looked up to see David holding Alexis and hugging Corrine tightly in his other arm. *Oh my God*! thought Kat, *he looks so very weary and tired but no matter, for he's alive.* Kat paused, lowered her head, and said a prayer of thanks for the safe return of her son. Hand in hand, they walked over to Kat and the four hugged each other, and tears of joy flowed among them as Maggie ran over and joined in.

David followed Corrine and carried Alexis to their living quarters, only after he made sure that every one of his wounded were being treated, and the rest of his men also were being cared for. With a quiet interlude between the three of them, he noticed, for the first time, how much his little girl had grown. She was only two and a half when he left and had a vocabulary of three word sentences with 'no' as her favorite word, but she was now talking a lot more and clearer. She called him Papa, which was the favorite form of greeting by Corrine, for her father when she was a little girl, and in turn, she taught her to use it with David. It brought a large grin and tears of joy to a very proud father.

Festivities were in abundance for the next month in honor of the return of David's entire army, which would start to return at intervals. They were reunited with their loved ones and that was all that mattered for now, because they knew at some point in time, that they would have to leave the safety of the garrison and go back out into a world gone completely mad.

"Mother, you look tired," said David as he looked up from a stack of papers and saw who was entering his office.

"Just a little," declared Kat.

She was about to take a seat in the chair near David's desk when a little voice said,

"Grandma." Little Lexie ran to sit on her grandma's lap, followed close behind by Corrine.

"We're on our way to the park. Anyone care to join us?" questioned Corrine.

"I would love to, but I have a meeting with two of my Commanders and Tim and Lars in about fifteen minutes," responded David as he lifted his daughter up onto his lap, and she started to reach for a pencil and she was about to scribble on some of the papers in front of her.

"No, Alexis," said Corrine, as she lifted her daughter onto the floor and headed for the door.

"What about you, Kat?" asked Corrine.

"I'd love to."

David looked at the three who meant so very much to him walking out of his office and waved good-bye to his precious little girl.

One month later

As David's four Commanders and one major were seated at the long desk waiting for his return, David, accompanied by Tim and Lars, entered the office and all five stood at attention.

"Gentlemen, please be seated," requested David. As he sat at the head of the table with Lars situated to his right, he began with, "On the lighter side, because of your loyalty and diligence of fighting in the service of God for the past two years, I commend all of you for a job well done. We have destroyed every known outpost from here to the start of the Russian Federation. The festivities that have been going on since our return will continue for one more day, and then we will honor the fallen with ceremonies lasting another two weeks thereafter."

It was then that David came across the dreaded part of his notes: a list of the names of those killed in the line of duty. A plaque with each soldier's name and rank, date of birth, and date of death, along with their dog tags, was attached to the walls in the inner rotunda in honor of their memory. From an original total of nearly fifty thousand men that

composed David's entire army, a total of eight hundred and forty enlisted men and one hundred and twelve non-coms made up the list of the fallen martyrs of God's Earthly Army to date.

"It has come to my attention that the armies of the Antichrist are building outposts at an alarming rate throughout the Russian Federation. Even though time is of the essence, we need an army that is reinforced and strong again, and therefore, we will move out from the garrison at two week intervals, after the two weeks of ceremonies honoring our fallen. That is only two weeks away, gentlemen, so I suggest that you start preparing your men now, if you haven't done so, already."

David then arose and went to the board showing a large map of the Russian Federation and explained, "As you can see, Gentlemen, by the red-colored tip of the stick pins denoting the locations of the enemies' outposts, there are hundreds and even more being built as we speak. Our objective is to destroy each and every one of those outposts, before we can even begin to think about moving on to the Middle East in our final quest to do battle with the Antichrist's army."

Just then, Corporal Adams walked into David's office and handed him a memo. After glancing over the information, David said, "Let's take a break for now, gentlemen, so that I can review some information that I just received from our intelligence. You're dismissed, and we will all meet back here at 1300 hours." As the group arose and started leaving, David asked Tim and Lars to remain behind, so that he could discuss with them the information that he was just handed by Corporal Adams.

"I just received word that Musva upped the ante on my head. Seems the price is now twenty-five million. Boy, it feels good to be wanted by someone," laughed David. "I would love to see the look on that bastards face after we finish with clearing his outposts from Russia, as it would be worth all and then some of that total bounty he has on my head."

"That's an awful lot of money, but anyone with half a brain shouldn't really believe that the bastard would deplete that much of his treasury and actually give that kind of money to anyone. More like he'd say, 'Thank

you very much. You've done a good deed for your god,' and no one would see or hear from the 'snitch' again. Musva would figure, if he's so quick to betray you, what's to prevent him from going against him for money also," analyzed Lars with a deep belly laugh that he was so well known for.

"I know," agreed David, "but that's a lot of money." He would discuss this later with Michael.

"Our informant also told me that they are building a new supply depot here at Bratsk," informed David as he showed Tim and Lars on the map. "This will alter my plans of attack somewhat, and I want to run through this with you two and get your opinions."

After explaining his ideas with attacking the Russian Federation, the three enjoyed a brief interlude of reminiscing, accompanied by a glass of David's best brandy, until his Commanders were due back in his office for his continued briefing.

"Gentlemen, please be seated," announced David. "Before we parted ways earlier, Corporal Adams gave me a memo, which in part stated that I have a bounty on my head now of twenty-five million. Seems I have grown in popularity with our greatest adversary," mused David.

"That could be a real problem for you, General," insinuated Commander Chandler.

"I really don't think so, Simon, but I will watch my back more carefully from now on," explained David. "Now for the business at hand, I also have been made aware of the fact through our informants that Musva is constructing a large supply depot here at Bratsk to handle all the supply needs of his army throughout Russia, and it will be the heart of their ammunition's vast storage. If my cousin, Chris were still here, we would have no worry, for he would destroy it before it's finished with his Stealth fighter, but we no longer have his courageous services at our disposal. So, gentlemen, it will be up to us to search and destroy."

As David rose and walked over to the board with the large map of the Russian Federation already denoting the locations of the known outposts,

he went on to explain further with, "Half of my immediate army, along with Tim, Lars, and myself, will be the first wave to move out and clear a straight path all the way to Bratsk, which is located here. This is almost the center of the Russian Federation, and will serve as our headquarters with the building of a main compound by my second wave of men. While we, the first wave, continues east destroying and holding that area until your army, Simon will meet up with my second wave, and they in turn will move out and rendezvous with me; split three ways, heading to the lower northern, upper southern, and the central third of that vast eastern section; and destroying all enemy outposts and taking control of the region."

"In reality, Gentlemen, this is what our finished objective of taking over the Russian Federation will look like," informed, David, as he pulled another map down over the existing map. "My immediate army will clear out all enemy outposts in this entire one-third eastern section moving north this far and south this far using the scorched land tactics. For however long it takes, we will remain in this one-third section, until we have it completely under our control. Simon, as you can see, your army will do the same as far as splitting up into three sections, north, south and central of the middle half of the country; destroying all outposts and remaining there until it is completely under your control. John, you're army will move into the entire upper one-third area of the country extending from here to here," pointed David at the map. "You will search and destroy all outposts in that area and maintain it under your control. Chuck, your army will move into all of the southern one-third of the country and destroy and control this area from here to over here," pointed David with emphasis. "Finally, Scott, you will be the last to lead your men into the remaining western section of the country and split up three ways, north, south, and central, also destroying and then taking control."

"With looking at our strategy on the map, it doesn't look like it will be all that hard to fulfill, but believe me, gentlemen, this will be our hardest objective so far to accomplish with our fight against the armies of the Antichrist: taking control of the entire Russian Federation. Let's take a short break and meet back here at 1600 hours to discuss any and all concerns that you may have, and I will answer all questions put to me."

"We've got a long road ahead of us, David," replied Tim as he, Lars, and David were the only one's remaining in his office.

"I know, Tim, but with his guidance, I truly believe we can continue with our diligent objective to fight the Antichrist with all the resources that we have at our disposal. We can't give up as there are too many out there that are counting on us to prevent Musva from taking over the entire world and implementing his diabolical plans to control then conquer all of the souls of mankind."

"I hope you're right, David. You do have more faith than I do, and hopefully the more I'm around you, some of it will rub off on me," noted Tim.

"It will, Tim. It will," assured David.

As his Commanders filed back into his office and took a seat, David could tell by the perplexed looks showing on their faces that they were not quite in agreement with his plans and stated, "Alright, Gentlemen, I can tell by the expressions on your faces that you must not agree entirely or not at all with my plans to overtake the Russian Federation. I would like to hear your objections," informed David.

Commander Connor was the first to speak with, "David, with all due respect to your leadership, I don't understand why I should take my men numbering nearly ten-thousand and move into the entire upper one-third of the country, where there are less enemy outposts to destroy compared to the rest of the country. Wouldn't it be better for me to split up my army with only one section in the north and leave the remaining two divisions in the central area to aide Scott with his one-third structural division, where the outposts are more numerous?" questioned Commander Connor.

"Thank you for the compliment, John," chuckled David, and then responded with, "Your question is a good one, and I presume that is on the minds of all of you, so I will answer it to the best of my ability as to why I figure that this is the best action to take. Our objective all along, as you know, gentlemen, is to fight Musva with hit-hard-and-run tactics.

This has been our best defense so far in beating him. That is why, John, we must use only one-third of our immediate men in each division to accomplish this feat. Ten thousand would be way too many and less effective. Actually, we would end up stepping on one another's toes, most likely. With your entire army controlling and guarding the upper one-third and Chuck's controlling and guarding the lower one-third, we will have the entire Russian Federation surrounded and should guarantee us the needed protection and security that we will need while the assigned combat armies will do their job with fighting and forcing the Antichrist's army completely out of the Russian Federation."

"I can realize your initial fears, Gentlemen, of possibly leaving some of our fighting forces spread out too thin, but trust me, like I said before, with our most successful tactics working, we should, in my estimation, leave it as is until something else might occur which would warrant change. Even though most of the population of Russia is in the western sections here, enemy outposts are strategically located more abundantly in the lower north western, central, and upper western sections of the southern area located here," informed David, pointing to all three sections once again for emphasis. "I have yet to figure out why Musva chose to build as many outposts in the highly unpopulated areas among some of the most hazardous terrain and harshest weather conditions, which, by the way, was one of the underlying reasons for my final decision. What I'm trying to say, Gentlemen, is that the best-laid plans may not be the best, but no one will know that for sure until they are acted upon. Now, is there any more that needs to be discussed at this time? Anyone?" David asked, as he looked around the room to ascertain any kind of gesture from his Commanders one way or the other. "Alright then, the hour is getting late, and we will have another briefing at the end of the week," assured David as he double-checked his schedule. "You're dismissed, Gentlemen."

David and Corrine's Living Quarters

"I'm sorry, honey," replied David as he entered their apartment and Corrine met him in the hallway. "I so wanted to spend a quiet evening with you and Lexie, but under the circumstances with the subject of the briefing, I just couldn't help the late hour."

"I understand, David. Lexie stayed awake as long as she could and then I carried her into her bed. I kept supper warm. Are you hungry?" questioned Corrine of her weary-worn husband.

"Starved."

"Good, because I made your favorite: beef pot roast, mashed potatoes with brown gravy, and asparagus spears. I cheated though and bought the apple pie at the bakery."

"This looks wonderful, Corrine, and I don't know how you do it. I don't mean just the cooking," corrected David after realizing what he said. I mean everything that you do. Even though Lexie is in daycare during the day while you are working long hours, you still find time to spend with her, cook, clean and please your husband in more ways than one and who, by the way, loves you very much," reminded David as he grabbed her, and kissed her diligently before he made short order of the meal in front of him.

"Ah yes, I have discovered the means to a man's heart: via his stomach," whispered Corrine as she watched her sleeping husband and finally kissed him goodnight and turned over.

Three days later

"Mother, you can't be serious. Please tell me that you won't even consider doing what you just told me you wanted to do. Your broadcasting over the radio twice a week reaches all of Europe, Asia, Africa, and beyond."

"I know, David, that that is what we have been told through our Radio-Free-Europe counterparts, but I miss mingling with the people like I did before we had to leave the States."

"Mother, the world, since you left the States has become a cesspool, literally. It's far from ideal out there with not one major city throughout having been left unscathed either because of the war or because of your catastrophic predictions that have been coming true, and leaving all landscapes far from the picturesque postcards of days gone by. The post-

war carnage continues even now: chaos prevails everywhere, because of starvation, drastically less available drinking water, diseases, plagues, ravaging storms, not to mention Musva's 'goon-squad-butchers' hunting down and killing anyone and everyone who doesn't want him for their god," warned David. "So please, Mother. Promise me that you will not do anything so utterly foolish as leaving the safety of the garrison while I'm gone."

"Now that you have explained it to me how it really is beyond these walls, I'm sorry David that I brought it up, and I promise that I will never leave the safety of the garrison," lamented Kat.

David, Tim, Lars, and his immediate army of less than five thousand troops left as planned at day break on a misty, dreary, overcast, day heading into an unknown future existence in a vast foreboding country. The loved ones that they just left behind experienced sentiments equaled in substance to the weather outside. Even though everyone's daily routine continued, thoughts were with those loved ones who had to leave them once again with not knowing for sure for how long this time.

Spring 2036

Even though Kat and her family had God's divine protection, as time went on and circumstances changed, this no longer rang true, as one of Chad's supposedly faithful crewmembers betrayed him for gold.

"Kat, my God, what's the matter. You're as white as a ghost," analyzed Corrine.

"Corrine, I need your help, dear. Something terrible has happened and we need to find, Maggie," panted Kat as she entered Corrine's office at the clinic.

"What do you mean?" questioned Corrine, in a near state of panic herself.

"It's about Chad," cried Kat as Corrine led her to a chair for fear she might collapse from the frenzied state that she was in, and quickly poured her a glass of water.

"Here, drink this slowly, Kat. Now, what's this about Chad? What's happened to him?" wailed Corrine.

"It just came over the news wire. The *Calypso* was intercepted by a submarine somewhere near Tahiti in the South Pacific Ocean. They tried to make a run for it and were torpedoed with no survivors. My God, Corrine, how am I going to tell Maggie that she has now lost another son?" wailed Kat.

"Kat, are they sure that there were no survivors?"

"Yes. Eye witnesses said it was blown right out of the water and was nothing but a ball of fire within seconds. No one could survive with what they did to it," relayed Kat as she was about to get up from her chair.

"No Kat, wait. You've got to sit a minute and get yourself calmed down. It will just make things harder for Maggie, if you are in an agitated state yourself while trying to tell her about Chad."

"You're right, Corrine," sobbed Kat as she tried to restrain her sobs of grief for her beloved nephew. "Maggie has been through so much grief, Corrine. I'm in fear as to how she is going to take this about Chad. Oh my God, Corrine, what about Louise? Whose going to tell her that her husband is gone?" wailed Kat in a now-hysterical state.

"Kat," cried Corrine, after retrieving a needle and a vile of liquid from her bag. "I'm going to give you a shot to calm you down."

"No please, Corrine. I can't go to sleep now."

"It won't put you to sleep but help you to relax. Take a few deep breaths now and it should start working within a few minutes," informed Corrine.

As the shot started taking affect in such a short period of time, Kat turned to Corrine and with a tear-stained face stated, "I'm feeling much better now, Corrine."

"Good. As a precaution, I called for Dr. Madison to meet us in Maggie's office. Major Cranston has been notified and is locating Louise and will escort her to Maggie's office so that the two can be told of Chad at the same time. I think this would be better for both of them, if they are together when they hear the news," informed Corrine.

"You're right, dear. I think that will be better."

Both Maggie and Louise had to be sedated after learning about Chad from Kat. Louise fainted and Dr. Stevens was worried about Maggie, for she went into such a comatose-like state for almost three hours before she came out of it.

A Week Later

Another flag-draped pine box sat in front of twelve semi-circling white chairs set inside a makeshift tent with a canopy top waiting for the family of Chad to arrive. He will be buried on the cemetery hill next to his brother, Chris. Even though the casket has no body, the dozen individual roses placed on the casket, attested to the love of and loving memory of those twelve individuals for Rear Admiral Chad Ryan, USN.

Russian Federation

David and Tim received word of Chad's death nearly a month after it happened. Kat penned a letter to him and never really expected it to get to him, but it did. He wrote his mother a long letter in part, informing her of Tim and his grief for the loss of a brother and cousin. They wished that they could have been with all the members of the family, at such a grievous time in their lives, but even if they would have known on time, it would have been impossible for them to return home for his funeral at that time.

Tim sends his love and asks that you keep an eye on aunt Maggie for him, as she has been through so much grief. Please tell aunt Maggie and Louise how very sorry we are mother for their loss. Please don't worry about Tim and I, for we have each other and we will get through this news about Chad together with the help of God. Give my love to Corrine and Lexie and a kiss for both of them.

Your loving son, David

Kat invited Maggie, Louise, Anthony, Corrine, and Lexie to her apartment for dinner that night and let them each read the long letter from Tim and David. Tears were shed and prayers were said for everyone involved.

One Month Later

"Hi, Maggie. Come on in and sit down. I'm glad you could come," said Kat, as she retrieved a chair from a table in her office for Maggie.

"Hi, Sis. Please tell me that there's no more bad news for me."

"Oh, Maggie, I'm so sorry that I had to be the one to tell you about Chad," realized Kat, after Maggie's statement and seeing the look on her face.

"No, Kat. I'm the one who is sorry. I have no business saying what I just did to you. I guess I have been on one hell of a 'pity-pot' since the news of Chad. I see Louise every day, and it tears me to pieces to see the drastic change in a once vibrant, bubbly, loving, and caring woman to one individual who now only goes through the motions of existing. Thank goodness that Anthony has Lexie as a playmate."

"Yeah, you're right. Even though Anthony is laid-back and Lexie is 'miss bossy,' they do get along really well with each other," laughed Kat.

"She does take after her father," chuckled Maggie. "I wish there was something that we could do to get Louise out of this awful emotional state that she's in."

"Maggie, you could talk until you're blue in the face to Louise about how things will get better—blah, blah, blah. But I really think that that old saying that 'time heals everything' is what helps the most. Only thing is, no one knows for sure just how much time it will take, or if it will ever really help like I just said, and evidently don't know what the hell I'm talking about in the first place, because I really don't feel what I just said

either," relayed Kat after a sigh and a deep breath, because she basically said all of that in one huge breath..

"Kat, have you been nipping?" questioned Maggie with a giggle.

"No. But you just gave me a good idea, though. Let's go back to my place and drink. What do you say?" mused Kat.

"About time something constructive starts coming out of that mouth of yours." Maggie added, "Meet you there in fifteen minutes."

After two stiff drinks apiece…

"Remember all the silly things we used to do and say to each other?" asked Maggie.

"Yeah, I sure do. We had a lot of them after I told you about General David for the first time," Kat recalled.

"I can still remember as if it were only yesterday when you invited me out to dinner and told me about David for the first time. You said, 'Maggie, I'm living with four angels,' and when you told David to say something to verify that what you were saying to be true and he didn't—"

"I remember, Maggie, how angry you made me feel later on after David finally opened his mouth and you told the both of us that we were in love. Did you really feel that way?" questioned Kat.

"Yeah, I did. After listening to the two of you talk about each other and to each other, that is what came to me, but you sure denied it vehemently," remembered Maggie.

"I know. But at the time, I never could have admitted it, because I didn't want to, I guess."

"That's because the two of you weren't communicating with how you felt about each other," analyzed Maggie.

"How could we communicate anything when all we did was fight with each other?" asked Kat, with a laugh.

"You still love him and miss him to this day, don't you, Kat?"

"Never stopped, Maggie. He has never been far from my thoughts all this time."

"Do you still think that you will find him some day and save him?"

"I don't know. Michael said I would, and I have no reason to doubt him."

With that said, Maggie suggested that they go over all the funny little sayings that they used to say to each other since they were kids, which they did after another drink each and a long medley of old songs ensued until the wee hours of the morning, so Maggie stayed overnight. The silly little sisterly talk did more for the two of them in the long run than they'd ever thought possible, for the light-hearted attitude showing through the two of them, which continued for a long time afterward, slowly started to rub off somewhat on Louise.

Garrison, Holy Cross Cemetery, September, 2038

The first wave of David's army was home nearly a month after successfully clearing the Antichrist's outposts from the Russian Federation. Success can come with an awful toll, and all the battles fought over there were no exception, as David lost two of his Commanders, Connor and Chandler, and almost half of his total army. In his estimation, there were more of his buried soldiers in some of the desolate unpopulated areas of the Russian Federation than the actual number of people living in those same areas. Even though his original objectives were met—destroying the Antichrist's major supply depot and ridding the country of all his outposts—the sweet smell of success never fully materialized in David's mind, because he left behind too many brave men now buried in the cold ground of a foreign country. As he recalled one of the many conversations that he had with Tim and Lars, one in particular now stood out in his mind, as he stood in silence in front of the two graves of his deceased cousins, Chris and Chad.

David, Tim and Lars were sitting around a campfire one chilly night in mid-September somewhere in the central eastern section of the Russian

Federation, before a timely battle was to ensue between David's army and one of the larger outposts of the Antichrist in less than six hours away.

"David," called Tim to get his cousin's attention. "You seem miles away. Thinking about tomorrow?"

"I was earlier, yes. But I was just thinking about Corrine and Alexis and how much I miss the two of them and everyone at the garrison. In my mind, they are all members of my family, probably because we've all been through so much together."

"Why are we really here, David?" questioned Tim, which left David astonished by such a question especially, coming from a career soldier such as Tim.

"We're God's army and following His wishes to fight Musva, and to keep him from conquering all the souls of his creation: mankind."

"I believe in God even though I'm not a religious man, and I get all of what you're saying. But thousands of people are dying all over this world every day and not all of them lost their souls to Musva, and we didn't fight to save them, so what's the difference?" Tim questioned, with a perplexed look on his face.

"We have no control over who will either join forces with Musva for whatever reason or fight him to save their souls. All we're doing is giving the ones who fight against him the choice of worshipping God and a chance to stay alive, if you want to call what we're going through—living that is," explained David.

"I look at it in two different scenarios," interjected Lars. "Like you said, David, all of mankind should have the God given right to worship and stay true to him in their lifetime without interference from a bastard like Musva. But since that isn't the case and we all have to die, fear of death by his many atrocious ways takes over, then most will succumb to his will. On the other hand, the ones that stay true to God will have to die, either by natural causes, which is highly unlikely, rather most likely instead by a disaster."

"What are you getting at then, Lars?" asked David.

"Basically, we all have to die. There's no getting around that. It boils down to what you want after death: non-existence, because you chose the mark of the beast, or eternity with God, because you refused to accept the mark of the beast. Choice is the key word here, and that, my friends, is up to each individual no matter what. We're giving the one's, who want to be with their Maker, a little more time possibly, even though we don't really know for sure how much more time they have left. Only God knows that timetable for each of us."

"How did you get so smart?" David questioned.

"Probably my Viking heritage," laughed Lars.

"David, are you alright?" questioned Corrine as she came to stand by her husband while the rest of the family slowly disbursed, and she left the solemn ceremony held for Chris and Chad just moments ago.

"Yes, sure I'm all right," stated David, hesitantly, because his mind was still back at that campfire with Tim and Lars.

"You seemed miles away," stated Corrine. "Are you sure you're alright?" questioned Corrine again.

"Yes, Honey, I'm fine," assured David, as husband and wife left the cemetery hand in hand.

Once again Kat and Maggie arranged for a section of the mess hall to be enclosed for the family to gather in private. Kat, Maggie, David, Corrine, Tim, Louise, Alexis, Anthony, and of course Lars and Michael were all that was left of the Ryan-O'Brien clan. They all were seated at a large circular table with David being the first one to speak, giving a short but meaningful eulogy honoring Chad. He also spoke of Chris, Cindy, and Linda, and afterward encouraged the rest of the family members to take turns with telling stories of real life incidents, with regard to the four now-deceased family members. He felt that this may be good therapy, not only for himself, but for all present.

In the beginning, somber moments were entwined with the eating of the meal, but as time went on, it became more bearable for all to recall their own stories, which eventually became more lighthearted because of their contents. When all was said and done, and each family member went his or her own way, a sense of peace overtook each one with a renewed feeling that with time, the healing process will definitely begin.

May 2039

"Michael, maybe you can talk some sense into her. Heaven knows I have been trying my best and nothing seems to work."

"No, David. It is not up to me to convince, Mistress Kat what she knows to be the truth."

"David, all I'm asking for is another week or two to stay here at the garrison," stated Kat.

"Mother, that's impossible and you know it. This is not a time for sentimental foolishness. I know it's hard for you to leave after what you and aunt Maggie went through to build this place and all that we have endured in the last twelve years, but please, Mother, it's too dangerous. They know of our location now and it's just a matter of time before they come for us. We're almost finished with destroying the database and have cleared out what we can carry in the wagons and then will torch the entire place so nothing is left for the enemy to use. In two days, you and your group must leave with three of the wagons and we'll rendezvous at Jericho as planned. Ol' John and Clarence conferred with Lars and the three mapped out what they think will be the safest route for you to take. You all will be safe with them guiding you, because the two have been my most trusted scouts. And I am more than confident that they will get you to Jericho unharmed. You will meet and stay with our many contacts along the route, who in turn will provide you shelter and keep you safe until you move on. So you see, Mother, you will be in good hands.

"As you know, Mother, all of the civilians will be sent back to their countries of birth, or if they wish, may join God's Army to continue fighting. We all will be nomads from now on. We will sleep under the

stars, eat out in the open, and will fight the enemy until we die. In God's name, this army will travel on horseback across the rest of Europe and into the Holy Land, destroying every outpost that Lucifer has ever built."

"I know, David, that you're right. I've known for a long time that this day would come and I have to accept it, because it's God's will. I've done his bidding thus far, and I will continue to do it until the end. I will be seventy soon and I'm still wondering why God has put up with me this long," laughed Kat.

"I can only speak for myself, Mistress Kat, but I truly believe that, because you are a woman doing a man's job that possibly the Almighty One did overlook some of your faults," informed, Michael, with a grin on his face.

"Thank you for the compliment, Michael, and I hope you are right," answered Kat. "I just thought of something: will you be going with us, Michael or staying with David?" questioned Kat.

"Now that the end is near, I will continue to guide, David," answered Michael.

"What do you mean by the end is near, Michael?" questioned David.

"He just means that the end is near for all of us with the battle of Armageddon, dear," interrupted Kat, before Michael had a chance to explain. She knew exactly what Michael was talking about. God told her from the very beginning, even before all of this madness started, but she still anguished over telling David what was truly in store for her and her little group once they left the garrison. She was only trying to stall, until she had the courage to tell him, as he had a right to know all that there was to know of the future for everybody concerned, and she knew it was time to tell him. Yes, the time was now...

"David, do you remember when you were celebrating your seventh birthday, and I told you about your father and showed you his portrait that I had painted from memory?"

"Yes, Mother, even though I was young, of course I still remember. But what does that have to do with this?"

"I'm getting to that," hesitated Kat, trying to think of what to say next. "Your father has been a major role in this whole scenario, and it is because of him, indirectly, that we are standing here now, and—"

"Mother, I feel you are stalling," interrupted David. "What you have to tell me can't be any worse than what we have had to endure so far."

Kat, with a dreadful look on her face, blurted out, "We will not make it to Jericho no matter whose guarding us."

"What are you talking about, Mother? Of course you will make it."

"David, please listen to me. I have known all along when, where, and how I will die. Not everyone will have that privilege, if that is what you want to call it. But that is what I consider it: a privilege from God, Himself. Our little group will be captured by the Antichrist on our way to Jericho."

David started to say again, "No, Mother, you have to be mistaken," he anguished, but did not finish his statement, as he exited his office and the garrison and headed for the cemetery. He stood in front of Chris and Chad's headstone for only a second before he dropped to his knees in deep despair and cried until there were no more tears to shed.

"I've got to go after him," cried Kat.

"No, Mistress Kat. He must deal with this himself, as no amount of words from you will lessen the agony that he is now feeling. Only time will help ease the pain."

As David arose to his feet, he saw Michael standing at the head of Chris' headstone and said, "I refuse to let this happen to my family, Michael. I will not sit back and let it happen, never," anguished David. "I have done what he asked of me all these years, but I can't and won't let him take my family from me. Not now, Michael, when I need them the most."

"You have no choice, David. It's the Almighty One's will that you will continue to fight against the Antichrist. This world and mankind will not go on forever. Your mother has given you insight into some of your future and her gift of prophecy will transfer to you after she is gone. She and the rest of your family will join the Almighty One in his kingdom, just like you will some day and those that follow you, because they believe in what you are doing in his name."

"I know, Michael, what I have to do, but I can't do this," stated David, unable to finish his sentence, because of the tears forming in his eyes again and the emotional turmoil that he was facing.

Kat couldn't sleep that night before their departure so put on her robe and slippers and headed for the atrium. She wanted to talk with Michael for what she knew would be the very last time. As she sat in a chair and stared at the beautiful night sky, Michael greeted her with, "Good evening, Mistress Kat. You wish to speak with me?"

As Kat turned her head in the direction of his voice, she gasped. There, in all his glory, stood Michael the Archangel, who has been such an important part of her life for close to forty years.

"Michael, I can see you. Why after all these years can I finally see you now?"

"This will be the last time that we will be together and can converse, and the Almighty One thought it would be very special for both of us if you could actually see me."

"I'll say! My goodness! You are very impressive. I just didn't picture you looking like this. That portrait that my son has of you doesn't quite do you justice. You are quite magnificent. Michael, are you blushing?" chuckled Kat.

"Yes, Mistress Kat. I guess I am," laughed Michael.

"I'm going to miss you terribly, Michael. We've been together for so many years and have gone through a lot together, yet it seems like just yesterday when we first met. Do you remember?"

"Yes, Mistress Kat. I certainly do remember," responded, Michael, with a wide grin on his face. "I came through the wall and tried to subdue you to calm you down as the General ordered. You had knocked him out cold with an uppercut, as you Earthlings call it, to his chin. That is when we both spoke to each other for the very first time. I will never forget it, Mistress Kat. You were quite a handful for the General."

"More like a real pain you know where for the General," laughed Kat.

"Well, that too," agreed Michael, "but he loved you dearly as you have loved him dearly all these years."

"Yes, Michael. I have. I never stopped loving him or thinking about him on a daily basis all this time. He gave me our son, which helped me to cope with his leaving, but the void in my heart for David was always there, even now, Michael. Was it all do to the fact that he broke that Cardinal Rule and gave me our son that really kept us apart in my lifetime, or was the time that the two of us spent here not the right time for us to be together?"

"You are correct with both assumptions, Mistress Kat. It wasn't one over the other but the combination of both. Yes, General David stepped over the line with breaking the Cardinal Rule, but you had to finish the Almighty One's bidding for him. So you see, it really wasn't the right time for the two of you to be together."

"Michael, you once told me that someday I would learn the secret, which would allow David and I to be together once I pass over and become a spirit."

"Yes, Mistress Kat. I did."

"Is this the right time that you can tell me?"

"Yes, Mistress Kat. The time has come to tell you as you have earned that knowledge and now have a right to know the truth. You see, when the General broke the Cardinal Rule by becoming emotionally involved with his assignment even though his motives were good ones, because he

learned to love you, the fact remains that he was wrong and therefore was called back by the Council, stripped of his rank and duties as a general, and demoted to a private in God's Army of Warrior Angels. But he also lost the divine protection from the Almighty One because of his actions. You see, Mistress Kat, the Almighty One's Army of Warrior Angels do battle with other Life Forms on other planets and stars far beyond your galaxy. They are known as the Peace Keepers of the entire universe. If at anytime anyone of the Warrior Angels does something to displease the Almighty One, they too lose his divine protection because of wrong doing."

"So what does that actually mean, Michael?"

"They could be killed in battle and cease to exist."

"Michael, are you telling me that David may no longer exist? Please, Michael, tell me that that isn't so and that he still exists on the other side," begged Kat.

"He still exists, Mistress Kat. Of this I know for sure."

"But, without God's divine protection, he could be killed during any battle that he continues to fight in?"

"Correct, Mistress Kat. That is the truth."

"So there is nothing that can be done to help him?"

"Yes, there is only one way."

"Please tell me, Michael."

"The one whose life he saved must save his life in battle."

"You mean me?"

"Yes, Mistress Kat. Only you. When it comes to pass, you, as a spirit, must save his life."

"I'm not quite following you, Michael. This is so overwhelming for me."

"As a spirit, you must locate the General and save him as he fights in a battle."

"But how do I find him and how will I know which battle?"

"You will find him and you will know when the time is right which battle."

"So if I find him and somehow save him, then that will make everything right in God's eyes and then David will become a general again, and we can be together in Eternity?"

"Only if the Almighty One so chooses to make him a general again."

"Michael, we seem to be talking in circles here, and I have a feeling that you're not telling me the whole story of what I must do. Will God grant us permission to be together for Eternity or not, Michael?"

After what seemed a lifetime of silence before Michael answered her question, Kat became despondent with a foreboding feeling that she wasn't going to like Michael's answer.

"Mistress Kat, when I use the word *killed*, I only do it, because that is what mankind believes: that they must die first in order to pass over to the other side."

"Yes, Michael, that's true. We believe that we must die and then our souls leave our bodies. I know all of that but—"

"In the General's case, The Almighty One is granting you the chance to save him and restore that divine protection, but in the process, if you succeed, you will cease to exist. Now am I making myself clear as to what will take place, Mistress Kat?" questioned Michael, with a look of sadness on his face and a terrible pain in his heart for the woman that he truly loves.

With Michael's final explanation, it left Kat totally void of any feeling, whatsoever. All these years she kept going, not only because of God's work that she had to do for him, but also with the belief that she and her beloved David would be together for Eternity. Now she finally knows the truth: her eternity was only temporary.

She had one final question to ask of Michael, then she would say her good-byes. "Michael, will David and our son be together throughout eternity?"

"Yes, Mistress Kat. Father and son will be the leaders of the Peace Keepers throughout eternity."

"Thank you for everything that you have done for us while on this Earth. I have one more favor to ask of you, Michael. Please watch over my son and keep him safe. Will you do that for me, Michael?"

"Yes, Mistress Kat. I will do that for you, until it is his time for him to join the Almighty One."

"Thank you! I will always love you, Michael the Archangel," stated Kat as she hugged him and took one last look at the magnificent being before her eyes that has been such a wonderful part of her life from the first minute that she met him, so very long, long ago. She turned and slowly walked away.

Early the next morning, twenty-five people mounted their horses and headed out of the garrison in single file with three supply wagons following behind. It was an emotional tearful departure for all, as hugs, kisses, and handshakes were plentiful. Kat, Maggie, Corrine, Alexis, Louise, Anthony, and nineteen others, including Ol' John and Clarence, who were so very close to Kat and Maggie and considered family by both of them, made up the small group. Kat turned around in her saddle and took one more look at her beloved son with tears flowing down her face. She threw him a kiss and waved good-bye before they were out of sight. She knew what challenges awaited them within the next month and prayed for guidance that she could follow through with stamina and courage for all that God had planned for her little group of nomads.

Two Months Later

Ol' John and Clarence were truly the driving force that kept Kat's group going, not only in spirit but also with stamina. Some terrains were more dangerous than others because of their location, but their biggest adversary was actually the weather. One of Kat's biggest concerns was a young woman named Theresa, who was by now into her seventh month of pregnancy. She was so tiny in stature and build that Kat was becoming more fearful for her and her unborn baby's welfare. Kat was the only one in the group who knew what was to take place in the future for all of them. She knew at some point in time that she would have to tell her family, and again she agonized, as she did with David, as far as when the right time would be.

Somewhere In Bulgaria

David, along with Tim, Lars, and his army numbering less than twenty-five thousand continued to trek across Europe destroying the Antichrist's Outposts in Slovakia, Hungary, Romania, and now Bulgaria.

David and Tim were but a skeletal version of themselves in spirit since ascertaining the knowledge of their family's demise. As he recalled the final conversation between mother and son before her departure, Kat refused to tell David exactly how they would die, but did tell him when. Are there really any proper words to say to express one's feelings with the knowledge that you will never see that loved one again? Hardly. And that was the way both Kat and David felt, so very little conversation was carried on between the two, but the looks on each of their faces and the love that shined in each other's eyes, told the whole story.

David hid the truth from Corrine, because he couldn't bring himself to tell her. He wanted to remember his loving wife and daughter as they appeared then, as this was the only way, in his mind, to keep him from the brink of madness.

Three weeks later

Kat knew that time was running out for her and her family and must tell them what awaited them a few short weeks away. Late one evening

as all the family members, minus the children, sat in a circle around the campfire, Kat told them just what was going to happen to all of them. She also described what the other side was like according to Michael. She was amazed at their reaction: mutual acceptance. She understood their feelings, for at this point, she had had enough of this life, for the sorrow was getting to be unbearable even for the bravest of heart.

Two weeks later

One early evening, Ol' John and Clarence were standing by one of the supply wagons when Kat approached them, and as she felt a drop of rain, she said, "We have to get out of the open and try and find some shelter before the rain starts, because Theresa is in labor."

"Oh my," replied Clarence, with a worried look on his face. As the little troupe made haste with following Ol' John's instructions to pack everything up and get moving, their destination was a cave about three miles away discovered by Clarence earlier in the day during one of his scouting maneuvers.

Within sight of the cave, the three wagons were hidden within a clump of trees and the troupe gathered sticks and anything else needed to build a fire, then followed Ol' John as he ascended the winding path to the entrance of the cave with Theresa enfolded within his arms. Clarence proceeded to build a campfire from the large pile of sticks and Kat and Maggie laid down several large comforters and pillows on the floor of the cave, before Ol' John laid Theresa down gently onto the makeshift bed.

As the torrential rain pummeled the roof and the water fell like a waterfall over the entrance of the cave and down onto the surrounding terrain, all twenty-five members made themselves as comfortable as they could. Kat, Maggie, Corrine, and Louise all nestled around Theresa, while a distance away Lexie and Anthony sat huddled with the other children around one of three campfires built by Clarence.

Minutes turned into hours and Corrine knew that this was not a normal pregnancy that Theresa was experiencing, as she was not in a lot of pain but was sweating profusely and became more delirious as time passed.

As dawn approached, Clarence stood watching the beautiful sunrise off into the distance. Just then, a shot rang out and he pummeled down the cliff to a gully below. Ol' John scrambled for his rifle and headed to the entrance of the cave where he volleyed gunfire with six members of Musva's army. He too succumbed to a similar death, as did Clarence. Theresa was the third victim as she died shortly before the soldiers rushed the cave. Her baby was never born.

Late Fall 2039

As was customary for prisoners of war, the Antichrist had all captives thrown into a stockade to wait for their demise after captivity on the Sabbath, to be exact, the day that God rested. Boys seven and older would eventually be trained to be soldiers in the Antichrist's army, while the girls twelve and under would become slaves, eventually. All prisoners were held in a wooden stockade adjacent to the huge wooden platform stage built, for the sole purpose of massacring all enemies against the State while being televised for the rest of the world to see. It was a magnificent setting for all of Lucifer's followers to see: the massive lights extending the length of the stage and all sorts of colorful banners attesting to the fact that the Antichrist was their true god. For five days and nights, they were allowed no food and only a ladle of water to drink once a day while waiting in the cramped enclosure with temperatures well into the 100-degree heat. All survived but a few. Their heads had been shaved and they were stripped of all their clothing and replaced with knee-length gunny-sack type robes before being paraded around the stage with ropes around their necks and being pulled along in humiliation by Lucifer's guards. They were each lead to a separate pole and bound by their hands facing the loathing and laughing crowd. Thousands upon thousands of the Antichrist's true followers gathered each Sunday to watch the festive activities. But this was more than the usual Sunday of mayhem. These people must be more important was the thought of most of the crowd, which started to grow in numbers and became restless in anticipation of their beloved god to make an appearance.

"For God's sake, David, think! After all that we have gone through, you just can't throw it all away on a hopeless act of retaliation," begged Tim as

he and Lars reigned in David's stallion and was accompanied by twenty-five members of his army. "Even with our company of 250 men, we're still outnumbered ten to one. Aunt Kat told you that this was going to happen and to stay out of it, because there was nothing that we could do to save them without getting ourselves killed. She told you that you must survive to fight against the Antichrist another day.

"She's right, David. She has accepted her destiny with dignity and you must now honor her wishes no matter how hard it is to see your mother and all of your loved ones down on that stage awaiting their fate at the hands of that bastard," yelled, Lars, as he continued to help Tim hold David to the ground.

David knew in his heart of hearts that what Tim and Lars was telling him was the truth. He and his men needed to live to fight another day. *But how can I live with myself while my wife, daughter, mother, and the rest of my family are going to be slaughtered, and I stay here and do nothing about it?* anguished David.

Kat endured everything the others did and more. A rope around her neck was given to Lucifer, who was waiting in the wings for her. He tugged hard on the rope around Kat's neck, which made her fall three times, before they reached the center of the stage once more. There he stood in all his glory with a floor-length gold undergarment and a purple robe, which was the sign of royalty, over it, which extended to the floor and tied with a golden rope that also touched the floor. He wore a gold crown on his head with multiple valuable stones encased in the front and highly polished Hessian black boots that were only visible when he again proceeded to pull a half-dead Kat around the stage by her roped neck, until he became bored then stopped again at center stage. He turned his back to the crowd and positioned Kat in front of him, so that only she could hear what he had to say. "It seems your loving God has deserted you, Katherine Frances O'Brien. Where is he now when you need him the most?"

"Standing next to me where he has always been," rasped, Kat, with a voice that was almost inaudible.

"You could have been my queen instead of my greatest adversary for twelve years."

"I would rather have died," sneered Kat right before he took his right fist and slammed it into her face. Kat reeled backward from the powerful blow but was still conscious as he jerked the rope close to his face.

"Your wish will be granted, but first you must enjoy the drama, which I have planned for you and is about to unfold. Take her and tie her back on her pole," ordered Lucifer as he pushed her away from him with great anger and disgust.

"Let the festivities begin my faithful followers," shouted the Antichrist to the crowd, who had now worked themselves into a frenzy.

The first of seventeen of Kat's remaining family was shot in the head exactly seven minutes after Kat was retied to her post. She watched in horror as the assassin stepped in front of the next victim and shot that person in the head exactly seven minutes later and on down the line he went. The Antichrist planned it that way and wanted Kat to agonize over each and everyone being killed in front of her, so he had her head bound with the rope from around her neck wrapped several times around her forehead and tied to the post, so that she could not look away. As tears poured down her face, she had to watch in horror as six men, four women, four boys, and three girls from her family were slaughtered at the hands of the Antichrist. Her heart began to pound so hard that it blocked out the noise of the crowd as the assassin approached Chad's wife Louise and shot her in the head and then moved onto her son, Anthony.

"No, no. Not my grandson," cried Maggie.

As the assassin stood in front of her daughter-in-law Corrine, whose daughter and David's only child Lexie was taken away before they were caged, and was now about to be shot, Kat fainted. A bucket of cold water was thrown at her face, which brought her back to consciousness, and within minutes she heard the shot ring out and saw her being shot in the head just like the rest. Her beloved sister, Maggie was the only one left.

Kat looked straight at her and whispered, "I love you," and lowered her eyelids twice as a sign that Maggie understood, for they talked about the end many times. As the final shot rang out, Kat's body began to shake uncontrollably as she watched Maggie's body slump forward.

The Antichrist took her rope in his hands and again began to parade her around the stage. The sneers and laughter from the crowd was almost deafening while they threw stones or anything that they could get their hands on at Kat while the Antichrist left her alone in the middle of the stage with ropes tied around her waist to poles that stretched out from both of her sides and held by two guards to hold her up from a distance. He knew that she was near death so quieted the crowd so that he could make a speech.

"This woman has eluded me for twelve years, because she was protected by a sorcerer who is now dead, just like she will be seven minutes after I finish talking to you, my faithful followers."

The crowd cheered for what seemed an eternity to Kat, and at that point the Antichrist pushed her to her knees.

"See? She has bowed down and worships me in the end, proving her love for me just as all of you have time and time again. But unfortunately she has done it too late. This is what will happen in the end to all who elude me and betray me in the future. Look upon this woman with scorn and disgust and all like her who are still out there. All I ask of you is to prove your love for me once more by turning those traitors over to me. With your help, we will rid this world of trash like her and finally be able to live in peace with me as your beloved god."

Kat was led to an artificial tree stump, which was placed behind the Antichrist, and she was held up by the same two guards. She could hear the drum rolls, faintly behind her. She looked straight ahead and off in the distance and could see, as if he were right in front of her, Michael, in all of his glory, atop a magnificent white stallion. As the stallion reared up, Michael gestured with his arm and Kat knew instinctively that this was his way of saying good-bye. At that moment, a male voice roared to

the crowd, which could be heard for miles around and an eerie silence prevailed. "Fools, all of you. You have sold your souls to him, a false god, and for that you will never see my face, your true God in eternity."

The crowd became fearful and continued the silence until the Antichrist yelled, "Fear not, my faithful followers, for that was the voice of a traitor just like her." He then ordered his guards, "Find the blasphemer and bring him to me."

Kat looked over to the right of her beyond the crowd and saw a beautiful light standing on a hill with what looked like people huddled around it. The light became brighter and larger and she could see a figure with hands extended to her, and she whispered, "My Heavenly Father, it is truly you. I have done your bidding. You have my family with you. Please take me home." As the drum rolls began again, she was pushed to her knees and her head forced across the tree stump. The last thing that Kat heard was the swooshing noise of a sword.

"This is what happens to the ones who betray me," Musva jeered to the crowd while strutting around the stage like a peacock in full bloom, holding Kat's head with both hands high above his head as the cheers and dancing ran rampage from the mob and continued into the night.

David, once again, had to be restrained not only by Tim and Lars, but several of his men, because of the daunting hatred and revenge that he wanted to bestow upon the Antichrist for what he had just done to his beloved wife, mother, aunt Maggie, and the rest of his family. He vowed to himself then and there that he would kill the enemy with cold-blooded determination and without mercy from now until the day that he died. His mother was the Antichrist's greatest adversary with words, but he would continue to be his greatest adversary with the sword, for a man with a hardened heart, will make an enemy most feared.

A few days later, Kat, as a spirit appeared to David while he, Tim, Lars, and a few of his men were sitting around a campfire one night before another morning raid, experiencing an overwhelming grief that they all shared, completely stifling their senses, which left them deeply encased in

a morbid bondage of despair.

"We are all happy and together again with our beloved Father now, David. Our work here on earth is finished and our journey has ended. Go, my son, and do his bidding in my place by telling the world of the true God who waits for them and tell them what they must do to save their souls. Fear not, for Michael will always be with you to help guide you until the end."

David, upon hearing those words from his mother, began to weep. It gave him an overwhelming sense of comfort as he felt her enfold him with her undying love that she had shared with him his whole life, and which renewed his willingness to go on with life by just hearing her voice, and knowing that his beloved family were all together again on the other side and waiting for all of them to join them one day. He knew he could now conquer his grief and continue on with God's bidding, just as his mother did all those years past…

Middle East 2042

David, Tim, Lars, and his army continued to fight the Antichrist's army throughout the Middle East. One night in a dream, David, just like his mother, saw exactly when and how he was going to die. But for now, the door to death and peace of mind was still closed for General David Michael Gabrielle Thomas O'Brien…